MAKE THE PLAY

A KINGS OF HEART NOVEL
BOOK 2

LUCKY HART

Make the Play

A Kings of Heart Novel

Cover Art by BootyFeathers

Cover Design: Lucky Hart

Editor: Kailey Gillotti

Proof readers: Ken Baldwin, Vix

Sensitivity Reader: Mel Cerna

Created with Vellum

For my fellow neurodivergents and the people who love them, this one's for you.

AUTHOR'S NOTE

I want to start by saying this book features both a mixed-race main character and an autistic main character. Neither of these things are the plot of the book, but they are a part of each character's identity, and they cannot be ignored or erased.

As someone in an interracial marriage raising mixed-race children, Jason being Mexican-American is close to my heart. That said, no matter how much of certain experiences might be based on conversations with my own spouse or my own experiences raising our children, I cannot speak for those who have lived experience. If you read *Cross the Line,* you'll see that Jason's experience isn't the same as Alec's because even within one family each person can have a different perspective. This is why I'm eternally grateful for my spouse and sensitivity reader who helped me. I did my best to authentically represent a nuanced portrayal of being Mexican-American, but Jason's experience will not be representative of everyone.

As an autistic author, writing an autistic main character was deeply personal to me. I was honestly a little terrified to write this book because while Emerson is not me, many of his feelings and experiences are ones I and other autistic people face, and that is a vulnerable thing for me to share. Despite the nervousness I feel, it is a privilege to be able to bring neurodiversity to the queer romances I write.

All of this being said, there are a few things I'd like to remind the reader. Autism is a *spectrum.* You cannot be more or less autistic, but you can have more or less support needs. At times Emerson's on screen support needs will vary. When they are lower, this does not make him less autistic.

All autistics, including high-support needs autistics, deserve to be loved without needing to mask. In that vein, please understand that all autistic people are going to have different feelings, lived experiences, and social and emotional needs. Emerson is not going to remind you of a little boy you know with autism because he's not a child. Autistic children grow up into autistic adults, and while they do not become less autistic, many of them, if given the right tools and support, will develop regulating and coping strategies.

While there is no on-screen ableism, Emerson's upbringing was one that was devoid of the support and acceptance he needed and deserved. Being raised in a family rife with internalized bias deeply impacted his self-esteem and led to high masking, which impacts him well into adulthood. If that will be triggering to you, please protect your mental health.

Above all, I wanted this to be a story about finding yourself and finding love. This book is incredibly soft because being autistic in a world that isn't meant for you is hard, and writing autistic joy and love is healing. I hope you love Jason and Emerson as much as I do. Thank you for reading.

CONTENT WARNING

I am a firm believer in being able to go into a story fully informed. If you don't want or need content warnings, feel free to skip these. If you do, then these are for you.

Though this story is meant to be a happy one full of love and joy, Emerson's past was not easy and falling in love does not magically erase traumatic memories or coping mechanisms. This story contains:

- Death of a parent (past, off screen)
- Bullying by classmates and a family member (past, but affects MC character now)
- Family neglect and ableism (past, but MC deals with emotional repercussions)
- Autistic MC going temporarily nonverbal
- On screen accommodations (including but not limited to texting while nonverbal, ear defenders for noise sensitivity, safe foods, etc.)

1 JASON

RADIO BLARING and windows down to let in the warm summer breeze, Jason speeds down the freeway, feeling good.

As they are most years, football tryouts have been grueling, but they're over now, leaving Jason free to enjoy his last weekend of freedom before he goes back to work full time next Friday.

The new school year might not start until the week after, and he might not have as much prep work as some of the teachers, but there's a lot more to get ready as the PE teacher than most people realize, especially with his second job as head football coach at the high school. Hell, he's spent all summer working on his playbook, watching old game tapes, and looking for ways to help his players achieve excellence. Losing several members of his starting lineup to graduation left a gaping hole in the team, but Jason is looking forward to the challenge. Though, perhaps not as much as he's looking forward to this afternoon.

Taking the next exit onto Carrillo Street, he turns up his music until he can't hear himself think, feeling his fatigue fade with every mile he drives closer to his brother's house. When Charlie, one of his older brothers, originally threw him a barbecue to celebrate Jason's last weekend of freedom during his first year of teaching six years ago, none of them realized it would become a tradition.

Jason has the route to Charlie's house on the top of the hill memorized, and it only takes a few side streets and turns before he feels worlds away from the freeway. Cruising down the palm tree lined street in the cozy suburban neighborhood Charlie calls home, Jason can't help but smile. Most of the houses in this area were bought by developers and rebuilt in the last few years, but Charlie's little bungalow sits nestled at the end of the street in all its aged glory.

The house might be small and unassuming compared to its neighbors, but the property in the back is massive because of its location on the corner, which affords picturesque views of Santa Leon and its coastline. According to Charlie, the views and privacy are exactly why he bought it. Jason also privately thinks it's because Charlie was the first of them to get his own home and wanted a backyard big enough for them to get together. Granted, they have their parents' house, which they all still frequent, but there's something special about hanging out with your brothers watching the sun set behind the glittering coastal views.

By the time Jason parks in the driveway and makes his way down the side yard, he can hear Charlie's atrocious taste in music blaring over bluetooth speakers. Despite the volume, his music isn't loud enough to drown out the sounds of Charlie and Andrew bickering. Jason pushes open the side gate to find his twin brothers facing each other, identical looks of exasperation marring their faces.

If it weren't for the fact that Charlie looks like he got dressed in the dark in his neon green shirt, paint-stained jeans and cow print crocs while Andrew looks like he just came out of a board meeting in pressed khakis and a button-down, Jason isn't sure he could tell them apart, especially not since they got the exact same haircut. The jury is still out on whether they did it on purpose. Neither of them will answer him when he asks, so he assumes it's another one of their weird twin things.

"The patio furniture is fine," Charlie tells Andrew, brandishing a pair of bright yellow tongs at him like a weapon. "Chill out and sit down."

"I'm always chill," Andrew protests. "But if I weren't, it would be because you don't take anything seriously."

"I take anything seriously that warrants it." Charlie shrugs.

"Do you two ever stop bickering?" Jason interjects, pretty sure neither of them noticed him come in.

"Oh, Jason's here," Andrew says, validating his theory. "Hi."

"We don't bicker," Charlie says. "I tell him he's wrong and he denies it. It's a very friendly conversation between two adults."

In a clear ploy to annoy Andrew, and in sharp contrast to actual adult behavior, Charlie sets down his tongs on the edge of his barbecue before inching backwards to move one of the potted plants behind him. Despite Andrew's growing frown, he pushes it into the center of the patio, something even someone like Jason, who doesn't have strong opinions about how other people organize their yards or homes, thinks looks strange.

"You're absolutely insufferable," Andrew sighs, wasting no time moving the plant back to where it was before. "I'm trying to give your yard a semblance of order."

"Who said I wanted order?" Charlie counters at the same time Oreo, one of Charlie's outdoor cats, streaks by so fast Jason only gets a brief glimpse of her black fur before she disappears into the bushes behind Agnes, Charlie's mostly blind cat who is asleep in the shade. There's no sign of his other cat or the dog.

"I need a beer to handle you two," Jason groans, desperate for something cold to drink. While he wasn't the one running drills at tryouts, spending all week kicking his kids into shape after most of them spent the summer eating junk and not exercising was enough to give him a raging headache.

"Beer and Coke is in the cooler," Andrew helpfully supplies. "With ice, because I brought some over."

"Yeah, well, who bought the beer?" Charlie asks.

"Me," Andrew smirks. "You know because I put it in your fridge last week when I brought you groceries because you were living on takeout."

Charlie opens his mouth then closes it again, clearly realizing he can't argue. Jason laughs, shaking his head before walking to the large red cooler situated on the edge of the deck. He flips the lid open, grabbing a beer and popping the can. He chugs half of it before he realizes Andrew and Charlie are staring at him.

"What?" he asks, wiping his mouth with the back of his hand.

"Where's Theo?" Charlie asks.

"Uh, at home I'm assuming. Why?"

"Why?" They echo, abandoning arguing in favor of doing that freaky twin thing they do where they can speak in complete unison without even trying. "You two always come together."

"I mean I called him on the way over but he didn't answer," Jason says, refusing to tell them about the time he'd used his spare key a few weeks ago and got an eyeful of something no brother ever wants to see. He realized then it's smarter not to use his spare key unless it is an actual emergency anymore. "I did talk to him last night, though, and he said he'd be here with Alec."

"Huh," they both say, heads cocked to the left at the exact same angle. With their hair now cut in exactly the same style, Jason is reminded of when they used to dress more alike growing up and no one, not even their parents, could tell them apart.

"Stop that," Jason grumbles.

"Stop what?" They ask in such succinct unison it weirds Jason out. They turn to look at each other as if having a telepathic conversation that makes Jason feel left out.

With a heavy sigh, Jason takes another chug of his beer and wishes Theo were here. Or Alec. He loves his older brothers, really he does, but they're a lot easier to handle one on one or with someone else as a buffer. It's probably a good thing neither of them really date because he can't imagine where a significant other might fit with that bond. Anyone partnering with either of them would need nerves of steel, that's for sure.

"I'm going to go inside and check on the food," Andrew announces.

"What's there to check on?" Charlie asks, already trailing after him like a lost puppy.

Once they're inside the house, Jason takes advantage of the silence to relax, letting his stress and worries fade into the background while he sips his beer and stares at the horizon. His own house doesn't have views like this, but he's only a ten minute drive from the beach which he prefers, especially since his dogs love it. Still, he's going to appreciate the view while he can.

Unfortunately, his peace is short-lived because ten minutes later, Andrew comes out of the house carrying a tray of vegetables for the grill. Behind him, Charlie follows along, yammering about some art show he has coming up next week and whether Andrew is coming with a plus one.

"Why would I bring anyone?" Andrew frowns. "I'm perfectly happy single."

"Are you though?" Charlie asks, looking unexpectedly concerned. "I wonder sometimes if—" but the rest of his words are cut off by the familiar high pitch of his youngest brother Alec's voice.

"The party has arrived, fuckers." Seconds later Alec appears, coming down the side of the house with his usual shit-eating grin in place. One step behind him is Jason's childhood best friend Theo, whose eyes track the backyard in search of Jason. The second he sees him, he holds his hands up while he mouths an apology.

"You're late," Andrew says.

"Thirty minutes, big deal." Alec shrugs. "Besides, we all know that no party truly starts until I arrive."

"Sometimes I don't think your ego can get any bigger, and then I'm proven wrong," Charlie says, looking like he's trying very hard not to smile.

Alec merely smirks. "Tell me I'm wrong."

"You're wrong," Andrew deadpans, earning him a middle finger from Alec. The gesture is immediately followed by a hug. With his arms wrapped around Andrew, Alec rises onto tiptoes to whisper something that has

Andrew exhaling a heavy breath as he smiles. Some of Jason's earlier tension melts away.

For all Alec's brashness, the truth is that he's got a way with people, particularly those with the highest walls like Theo and Andrew. After another whispered interlude that has Andrew laughing, Alec moves on to Charlie, who he engulfs in a hug.

Taking the opportunity to steal his best friend, Jason nods in the direction of the patio furniture, hoping his meaning is clear. Without waiting to see if Theo is coming, because he knows him well enough to know that he will definitely follow him, he bends down to snag another beer for Theo from the cooler. When he turns his head to glance behind him, he's gratified to see that Theo is indeed right there. He offers Jason an easy smile and a thanks as he accepts the beer.

"I really am sorry for being late," Theo tells him, waiting until Jason's occupied one half of the couch before settling himself in one of the armchairs opposite him. "Alec was—"

"I do not want to know," Jason interrupts, holding up his hand. "We talked about this when you two started dating, remember? Details are so not necessary. Ever."

"We're not late because we were fucking," Theo laughs, but his cheeks flush.

"Aw, it's adorable that you can blush about that," Jason teases, not sure he will ever get tired of seeing Theo lovesick. After a lifetime of watching him run away from anyone who even mentioned feelings, it seems fitting that someone as stubborn as his baby brother is the only one to break through his walls. "You know you can talk to me about anything, right? Except sex with my brother."

"I have no desire to talk about fucking Alec with you."

"Sometimes I fuck Theo," Alec yells from across the yard, the nosy fucker.

"No one needs to know that," Jason reminds him, shooting Alec the middle finger.

Alec's laughter rings out loudly, fading away as he gets caught up in conversation with the twins. Jason returns his attention to Theo, surprised to find him intently staring.

"What?" Jason asks.

"You know that goes both ways right?" Theo pops open his beer, taking a slow sip while fixing his blue eyes firmly on Jason.

"What does?"

"That you can talk about anything with me," Theo clarifies.

"Uh-huh," Jason hums. "Of course I know that."

"Good." Theo taps his fingers against the can, turning towards Alec and the twins when Alec laughs loudly again. His attention isn't diverted long, but the lovestruck expression on his face as he stares at Alec has something uncomfortable churning in Jason's gut. He gulps down his beer, hoping to push the feelings away.

"So how were tryouts?" Theo asks when he's finished making heart eyes at Alec.

Jason brightens, both at Theo's attention returning to him and the welcome change of conversation. "They were good. I've got a handful of returning players so we're gonna have a solid start. We lost a couple amazing seniors, though, so it's gonna be tough to fill in all the gaps on my starting line."

"Think you guys will take it all the way to state?" Theo asks.

"Hard to say with my starting cornerback and receiver off to UCLA this year."

Theo whistles and Jason nods. The difficulty of high school sports is how rapidly the lineup changes. No matter how good his starting line is, it's never forever.

"I'm sorry, Jason. That's rough."

"It's all good, you know I love a challenge. Besides, some of the kids who tried out were pretty good. Sanchez and Smith both tried out again, which is a no-brainer since they were on my reserve last year. They never made it off the bench, but they showed up to every practice and game without complaint. They're hungry for it this year."

"You're going to start them, aren't you?" Theo asks.

"Hell yeah." Jason smiles. "Aside from them, well, a few of the other players were in rough shape but that happens. You know as well as I do how easy it is to go soft after seven weeks of summer if you slack on training. We even had a couple freshmen who puked on day one. They didn't make it through to the last day, but some of the newbies really held their own. They're green as fuck, but I like their dedication."

"You always did love an underdog."

"I like an opportunity," Jason corrects. "Every player has something to offer."

"Spoken like the head coach of state champions."

"Cheers to that." Jason grins, still not over his team making it all the way last year. It'd been a bright spot amongst the stress of Alec's accident and recovery last year and the realization that his best friend was apparently dating his youngest brother.

It means a lot that Theo understands how much this team means to Jason. He's not just the coach. He teaches these kids and he loves it. Watching some of them live out their dreams feels damn good, as does having the privilege to help them do it.

"We should talk," Theo says.

With three little words, Jason's good mood evaporates.

"Oh no," Jason groans. "Please don't tell me something bad happened between you and Alec. If you two ever break up, I might die. Then you'd have my death on your hands. Do you really want that?"

"You and Alec are both so goddamn dramatic," Theo snorts. "We just got engaged, we're not breaking up. Besides, you know how I feel about him."

Jason exhales a heavy breath, nodding. When he reaches for his beer, he's surprised to find it empty. Before he can try and get another one, Theo is passing over his own half-full can.

"Thanks." Jason leans back and stretches his long legs out, resting his feet on the arm of Theo's chair. "So what's up then?"

"It's about you."

"Me?" Jason frowns. "What about me?"

"Are you happy?"

"What the hell are you on about? I'm always happy."

"Happy like I was happy?" Theo pushes and Jason wishes he could be mad at Theo for seeing through his bullshit.

"Look, I'm ninety-five percent happy, alright?"

Theo looks the opposite of happy, his face pinching up in a familiar expression. "Last month at Alec's birthday you said—"

"Whoa, whoa, whoa," Jason interrupts. "We do not need to bring that up. Consider that a momentary lapse in judgment."

"I'm serious, Jason. You've been there for me through all my bullshit. Let me do the same for you."

"Fuck you very much," Jason grumbles. Theo is the only

one who can pull that shit with him and have it work, something he damn well knows. He scrubs a hand over his face, the prickle of his three day beard rough and scratchy. He really does need to shave.

"Me and Alec were talking and—"

"You and Alec talk about me?"

"Of course we do," Theo answers as if he can't believe Jason is surprised. "You're my best friend, and for all the shit you and Alec give each other, you know he adores you."

Unwilling to examine why that makes him so happy, Jason focuses on the fizzle of carbonation in his beer. He sips it slowly.

"Fine, maybe I was a little bit jealous when we talked at Alec's birthday." Jason hates that he has to admit this, but he can't exactly demand emotional honesty from Theo and then be a dick and refuse to offer it in return. "We've always done everything together, and you're doing something without me."

Theo's face falls, which is exactly why Jason didn't want to say anything.

The last thing Jason wants is for Theo to feel guilty. He's so happy with Alec, and yeah, maybe Jason is a little, or a lot, jealous sometimes because things are changing in ways that have shifted his relationship with Theo, but that doesn't mean he wants to acknowledge it. Besides, it's not like Theo is neglecting him. They still spend plenty of time together, albeit often with Alec now too. Which, again, isn't even a problem. Jason loves his pain-in-the-ass little brother. He's so happy for both of them, and that is exactly why his weird feelings should remain a non-issue. He really shouldn't have said anything, but he's never been able to lie, especially not to Theo.

"Shit, Jason."

"Don't look at me like that," Jason sighs. "It's not like I'm wallowing or anything. It's just hard sometimes, you know? I think seeing you happy and ready to get married has me thinking about things."

"Things like?"

"Man, you go to therapy for a few months and suddenly you're my therapist? I think I liked it better when I was the one asking you questions."

Theo knocks Jason's feet off the chair. "Smart ass."

"Wow, Alec has been a really bad influence on you." At Theo's laugh, Jason finds himself relaxing. This is just Theo, the person who knows him best in the world. If he can't be honest with him, who can he be honest with? "Maybe I've been thinking a little bit about how I'm thirty now and how weird it is that my baby brother and my commitment-phobic best friend are both getting married before me. To *each other*, no less."

"You're not upset, are you?"

"Fuck no," Jason says, refusing to let Theo worry about that. Yes, it's still weird for him sometimes, and yes, maybe he occasionally feels like a third wheel, but he doesn't resent either of them. "I'm so damn happy for both of you. I promise. It's just a glaring reminder of how single I am, you know?"

Theo's expression softens. He leans forward, elbows on his knees as he lowers his voice, likely so they're not overheard by any of his nosy-ass brothers. "Do you want to start dating again?"

"Who said anything about dating?" Jason balks, horrified by the very prospect. Just because he's lonely doesn't mean he wants to date.

Theo holds his hands up in mock surrender. "I'm just saying, you haven't been on a real date since Nicole. I know things ended badly, but maybe it's time to get back out there. You know, if that's what you want. Which, judging by what you said, I feel like maybe you do, even if you don't want to admit it. You played wingman for me for a long time, so it's only fair I get a chance to return the favor."

"I appreciate the offer, but I'm not looking for anything right now," Jason assures him. "Besides, the start of a new school year is always busy. It's not like I'd have time to try and date even if I wanted to."

"Maybe you'll meet someone at school," Theo says.

"Dude, half the staff is over fifty or married already. Everyone else is either not my type or—wait, why are we still talking about this?"

"Because you want a relationship."

"How the hell did we go from me maybe going on a date to a relationship?"

"Because I know you," Theo answers. "You are the most monogamous man I've ever met."

Much as Jason wishes he could deny Theo's words, he can't. Unlike his best friend, Jason was never built for the casual one-and-done thing, which is why it'd been so easy to throw himself into work and playing wingman for Theo whenever his past relationships inevitably failed. He's always found it easier to focus on other people and what they need, but with Theo off the market and his own normally busy schedule in its summer lull, there's been way too much time to think about himself lately. He does not like it.

Staying busy is the way to go, which is why Jason can't wait until the new semester starts. Then he can pack his schedule full enough it won't matter if he sometimes misses Theo or gets lonely. Or both.

"It's okay to want something for you, you know?"

"Alright, therapy session is over," Jason grumbles. At Theo's earnest expression Jason sobers. "Fine, fine. I can want things for myself. Blah, blah, blah. I meant what I said before, though. Besides starting next week, I'll be too busy to think about dating, but if for some reason I change my mind and decide I want a girlfriend—which I won't by the way—then you'll be the first person I tell."

"Promise?"

"Yes, Daddy, I promise."

Theo flips him off, his smile familiar and safe.

"Excuse me," Alec interrupts, draping himself across Theo's lap with a self-satisfied grin. "The only person who gets to call Theo 'Daddy' is me."

"Gross," Jason groans, covering his ears. "Fuck off."

"I did earlier, thanks." Alec leans back, resting his head on Theo's shoulder and giving him a smug smile that Theo should be discouraging. Instead, all that happens is that Theo blushes while wrapping a possessive arm around Alec's waist to keep him in place. It's as sickening as it is sweet, and Jason is never going to get used to it.

"If it helps," Theo starts, directing his attention back to Jason, "Alec doesn't call me Daddy. He's just fucking with you."

It does not help because the seed has been planted, and Jason does not want a single mental image of his best friend and baby brother fucking. He doesn't say that though because he strongly suspects Theo might start filtering himself for fear of bothering Jason. He'd rather deal with unwanted mental images than lose another part of his relationship with Theo.

"So what were you two talking about?" Alec muses. "Let me guess, me?"

"I know this is hard to believe, but the world does not revolve around you," Jason points out.

"Excuse me, but if I'm not the center of my own fucking life, what is the point?" Alec says, reaching for Theo's hand. He links their fingers, pulling it up over his chest looking happier than Jason's ever seen him. The thought sets off another rush of unwanted emotions churning in Jason's gut. He does not want to be jealous of his baby brother or his best friend. They both deserve this.

"So, tell us more about this team of yours," Theo prompts, offering Jason a welcome distraction.

Relief floods Jason at the chance to focus on something besides himself, and he feels a smile pull at his features as he starts to talk. Charlie and Andrew join them a moment later, hanging on his every word like he's talking about the NFL and not a high school football team, but it feels good, a sense of stability settling in Jason's chest as thoughts of relationships and loneliness fade into the background. This right here, an evening surrounded by his favorite people, is all he needs.

2 JASON

JASON WAKES SLOWLY, body heavy with sleep and his mind fuzzy. The promise of more sleep is tempting, but the sunlight streaming through the open window is bright enough to have Jason frowning and covering his eyes, well aware it's time for him to wake. All it takes is a little movement from him to alert his four-legged companion that he's no longer sleeping before a warm, wet tongue drags across his jaw.

"Really, Freddie?" Jason groans. "I just woke up."

The bed shakes under Freddie's happy pitter patters and Jason can't even be mad. He was such a scared little shithead when Jason first got him, eating his shoes, yelping for hours and pissing on everything when he got nervous, which was multiple times a day.

It'd taken hard work and a lot of patience to get Freddie to trust him after Alec found him at the pound. Somehow he accidentally turned Freddie into the world's most spoiled dog, but considering his start in life, Jason thinks he deserves it. Freddie is the happiest dog alive now, even if he is still scared of most people and sometimes even his own shadow.

Freddie licks him again, a sure sign that if Jason doesn't get out of bed, he's going to be covered in dog drool soon. Removing his arm from over his eyes, he's met with Freddie's adorable, crooked smile. Jason returns the smile, and Freddie takes this as permission to lick his cheek.

"Buddy, no," Jason says, making sure to keep his tone happy so Freddie doesn't think he's in trouble. If there's one thing Freddie hates, it's raised voices.

Freddie barks, his tail wagging happily before he licks Jason's face again. Sprawled across the end of the bed, his other four-legged companion, Stella, copies him by barking for no other reason than because she can.

"Who needs an alarm clock with you two?" Jason grumbles, shaking his head before sitting up and throwing off his blankets.

He's barely pushed his feet into his slippers when his alarm goes off, not that he needs it. Between his internal alarm clock and his dogs, he's usually awake before it has a chance to sound. It's always better to be safe than sorry, though. Jason was late to orientation his first year teaching after he overslept, and ever since his body is determined to ensure he never makes the same mistake.

"Up and at 'em," Jason says, but Stella and Freddie don't move so he tries another tactic. "Time to eat."

That does the trick, sending both dogs racing out of the bedroom and down the hallway, the sound of their claws on the tile floor all too familiar. Jason spares a few seconds to relieve himself in the bathroom and splash some cold water on his face before heading to the kitchen. Though it took him less than a minute, by the time he walks through the archway into his kitchen Stella is, for reasons unknown to Jason, somehow on the goddamn kitchen island. Jason has a lot of questions about whoever owned Stella before him, most of them surrounding why a seventy-five pound husky mix thinks she's a cat.

Unlike Stella, who delights in climbing up to places she definitely doesn't belong, Freddie is safely on the ground. Not surprising since he's still too scared to even climb on the couch alone. While he might be waiting where he belongs, he isn't doing it quietly, howling at his empty food bowl like he hasn't been fed in a year.

"You know, I think Alec picked the noisiest, neediest strays he could find for me." Despite his occasional complaints, he wouldn't trade his loud babies for anything in the world. "Alright, alright, I'll feed you."

Ignoring the way his body is screaming at him for its morning coffee, he fills both of their bowls with kibble and fresh water first. Only once they're happily eating does he shuffle towards his coffee machine. Bleary-eyed and definitely not entirely awake yet, he jabs the power button before popping in a coffee pod from the drawer. He's not even sure which flavor he chose, nor does he care. All he wants is caffeine and food. While the coffee brews, he takes two breakfast sandwiches from the freezer, popping one of them in the microwave while he gets everything ready.

He all but inhales his first breakfast sandwich, too hungry to even care that the center is still a little frozen while gulping down his coffee. Come next week he's gonna have to be up at four-thirty if he wants to have time to walk his dogs before work, so he supposes getting up at seven today isn't so bad. He probably should've tried to adjust his morning routine sooner, but sleeping in over summer is so damn nice.

He makes a second cup of coffee and scrolls through his

email, making sure to keep an eye out on any pertinent work stuff. The only thing of importance is a staff memo about Mrs. Schumaker, the freshman English teacher, needing to leave already this year for personal reasons, meaning they're going to be bringing on a new teacher. Slowly sipping his coffee, he scrolls down for more information but finds none.

Well, today is definitely going to call for donuts if he wants to get any information. Technically, Jason always brings donuts for everyone on the Friday before school starts. He feels like it starts the year off right. Who doesn't like donuts? Still, today is extra important, and if Jason wants the 411 on this new teacher, he's gonna need to drive across town to get Mabel's favorite donut. The fact that her favorite is the same as his best friend's but they've got a forty year age gap never fails to amuse Jason, who takes his coffee as he moves to the front door.

He hasn't even reached the hook with the leashes near the front door before Freddie and Stella are following along. Jason grins. Today is going to be great.

"WELL, if it isn't my favorite lady. Aren't you a sight for sore eyes?"

"Starting early with the flattery this year, Mr. King?" Mabel grins, her too-dark rouge making it look like she's blushing.

"Never too early for you, Mabel." Jason shifts the stack of donut boxes under his left arm so he can grab the white paper bag off the top. "Got your favorite, didn't want anyone else taking it."

"Buttermilk knot?" she asks, peering inside the bag.

"You know it," Jason grins. "You and Theo single-handedly drive the demand."

"How is that boy? Such a nice man, that Theo. I remember when he used to come in here looking for you. He never got into trouble like you did."

"Are you calling me a troublemaker, Mabel?" Jason pretends to be shocked. He isn't really. He never did anything too horrible when he was a student, but he wasn't above shenanigans.

"You know, between the two of you, it was always you getting Theo in trouble. I'll never forget that senior prank with the goats and—"

"Now, now," Jason interrupts. "We don't need to relive senior year. I keep hoping maybe you'll forget about that."

"I might be seventy, but I'm sharp as a tack, young man."

Jason can't help but grin. Mabel's been in the front office as long as Jason can remember, working the desk when he and each of his brothers attended Santa Leon High. When he'd first started working here, seeing her in a more professional capacity had been a little odd, but once he stopped feeling like he was going to get into trouble for being in the office, he developed a rather wonderful friendship with Mabel. She's easily one of his favorite people on campus and he's probably going to sob like a baby whenever she retires.

"I know you are, and since you're so sharp, I bet you know all about the new teacher." He widens his smile.

"Oh, are we getting a new teacher?" Mabel pretends to look at her long, shimmering nails. They're hot pink and very glittery, matching her oversized glasses.

"Mabel, you can't hold out on me."

"I'm sure Mrs. Hernandez will send out a staff-wide email soon."

"You and I both know she did that this morning," Jason sighs. "It gave me nothing. I need details."

"You know, I always thought that Alexander was the nosiest King, but now I'm not so sure."

"I like to think of it as curious more than nosy. Besides, how can I welcome our new staff member if I don't know who I'm looking for? Come on, give me something, Mabel. You know everything at this school." She smiles and Jason knows he's got it in the bag, but he continues anyway because she really is the best. "You know we'd all be lost without you. You're the glue that holds us together. You're our shining star. You're—"

"Alright, alright," Mabel huffs. "Mr. Miller is here from—"

"Morning, Mr. King."

"Morning, Mrs. Hernandez." Jason straightens, offering his principal a wide smile. She's a little stern at times, and definitely doesn't share Jason's love of office gossip, but she's fair, decent, and a good administrator on the whole. "I got your favorite—blueberry."

Jason pops open the lid on the top box of donuts, withdrawing a napkin from his pocket and offering it to her.

"Thank you." She takes the donut in question, offering a polite nod to both him and Mabel before heading towards her office.

"Now, about Mr. Miller," Jason starts, turning his attention back to Mabel and frowning when he realizes she's on the phone. She holds up a hand, shaking her head, and Jason resigns himself to having to wait. Ten minutes later there's no end in sight to her phone call with the district to handle some kind of IT problem, and Jason decides to get his day started, aware he needs to open up his own office and get things in order.

Before heading across campus, he takes a detour to the staff room where he leaves the donuts, sneaking one himself. He picks one of the larger donuts, something covered in chocolate with chocolate chips in the layers inside, letting the carbs and sugar fuel his morning as he heads off, intending to figure out exactly who Mr. Miller is.

Since today is a staff development day, it's a prep day more than anything else. Some of the other teachers have classrooms to finish setting up or curriculum to finalize, but Jason's work is a little less tedious. As the physical education teacher and football coach, he doesn't have a classroom and his office is already set up, something he made sure to do when he stopped in last week to handle some paperwork from his preseason tryouts.

Technically speaking, Jason doesn't even need to be on campus today, but there's not a chance he'd miss it. The first week of school is always kind of chaotic and busy, so having a day to get himself back in the groove of things and catch up with his coworkers before the students arrive on campus is perfect. He also likes to make himself useful and a lot of the other teachers usually need help unloading boxes or moving furniture. That's how Jason ends up spending his morning after he finds Mrs. Montalvo, one of the science teachers, struggling to get an armload of boxes and a wagon of necessities into her classroom.

The following few hours are spent helping her bring up some miscellaneous supplies from the storeroom, along with helping her rearrange her lab desks and change a light bulb. It's nearly noon by the time he's finished helping her and his breakfast sandwich and donut feel ages ago. Making his way across campus he heads to the vending machine near the cafeteria, kicking himself for not taking the time to pack a lunch today. He's gonna need to get back into the habit unless he wants to starve to death or live on takeout. Neither of which he really wants to do since when football starts, he'll be living on that for dinners. Maybe if he sweet talks Alec, he might cook for him at least once a week.

Pausing in front of the vending machine, he eyes the selection, wondering if he can talk to the vendor about getting a different flavor of Pop-Tarts stocked. He can't figure out why it's always strawberry when brown sugar cinnamon is clearly the superior flavor. Lost in thoughts of Pop-Tart fillings, it takes him by surprise to notice someone unfamiliar walking past him. They look decidedly lost, muttering to themselves.

"You need help?" Jason asks, abandoning his snack mission to turn and face the stranger.

With a closed campus there aren't usually people Jason doesn't know around, but on staff development days it's not uncommon for some of the staff to have friends or family helping them set up. Though over the years, Jason's gotten to know most of them as well and this guy is entirely unfamiliar. He also looks too old to be a student but definitely too young to be the new teacher.

"I'm looking for a classroom," the guy answers, eyes never leaving the paper in his hands. His lips move as he silently reads whatever is on it.

"Luckily for you, you found an entire school." Jason crosses his arms and grins.

That grin falls when the guy doesn't laugh at his joke. He does however, look up from his paper, and piercing green eyes meet Jason's. The eye contact lasts only a second before the guy averts his gaze, giving Jason a moment to really take him in. He's shorter than Jason, though as the tallest person on campus at six-foot-five, that's not an uncommon occurrence. The man is not much shy of six feet but his build is lithe and compact, making him seem smaller than he actually is. Or at least smaller than Jason, but then again, who isn't?

Unlike Jason, who is dressed down in a pair of running shorts and a faded Santa Leon t-shirt, this guy has on a dark green, short-sleeved button-up without a single wrinkle and a pair of equally unwrinkled dark wash jeans. Even his sneakers are pristine, not a scuff in sight. Equally noticeable is the way the deep green of his shirt makes the light green of his eyes stand out. Then again, everything about him stands out, from his fair complexion to the vivid red of his hair. His eyelashes even match, letting Jason know it's definitely his natural color, though in the bright sunlight they look almost translucent and far lighter than the hair on his head.

Unable to stop staring, the only thought swirling through Jason's brain is that this guy looks like someone off one of the book covers of those fantasy romance novels Andrew likes. He blames this thought on his curiosity at the barbecue with his brothers last week when he'd caught sight of Andrew's Kindle on the patio and snuck a peek to see what his big brother was reading. Jason had only gotten through a few pages, just enough to realize whatever the book contained was something called bonds and a fated mate, before Andrew snatched it away, red-faced and embarrassed.

Looking at this guy now, Jason can't deny there's something ethereal about his appearance. It's not just because of his vivid hair and fair complexion, but also the shape of his face with the delicate curve of his jawline and full lips. He's pretty, Jason realizes. Incredibly so. Jason has no qualms about noticing or appreciating this. He has eyes after all, nothing wrong with using them, even if in the past he usually only paid attention to guys when Theo was around. He is the world's best wingman and knows his best friend's preferences, making it easy to spot someone Theo might like. Of course now that Theo's marrying his brother, it's been ages since Jason bothered paying attention to men. Then again, anyone with two eyes would look at this guy in front of him and notice how attractive he is.

"Do you know where it is?" the pretty guy asks.

"Huh?" Jason blinks, realizing he missed something with his wandering appreciation.

"I said—" he starts, breaking off with a heavy sigh. "Never mind, I'll find it myself."

"Sorry, I was...distracted," Jason says, frowning when he realizes the guy is walking away. Unable to resist someone in need of help and still curious about who he is, Jason takes several long strides to catch up to him.

"You're following me," he says without turning to look at him.

"I'm helping you," Jason counters.

"By walking next to me and distracting me?" He looks at Jason, eyes darting between the paper map in his hand and his feet.

"No, by showing you to, uh—" but Jason's words get stuck in his throat when the guy stops and turns to face Jason with a defiant set of his jaw. He isn't smiling, which is unusual because people always smile at Jason. "You know, uh, wherever you're going."

"What are you, the welcoming committee?"

"Not officially," Jason grins, undeterred by lack of a smile on the other's face. "Although I did bring donuts into the office today, and you're welcome to have one. Usually they're for staff, but I'd be happy to go into the front office and get you one if you wanted. Are you more of a maple glaze or sprinkle man?"

"I don't like donuts," he replies, walking away.

"Everyone likes donuts."

"Obviously everyone does not, in fact, like donuts." The guy continues walking but turns to look at Jason like he has two heads. "Statistically speaking, only an average of three percent of Americans dislike donuts. So while most everyone likes them, it's not *everyone*."

Jason's smile returns, inordinately charmed by his prickliness. "Is this your way of telling me you're special?"

The guy hums something noncommittal, turning to walk away again.

Undeterred by his refusal of donuts and propensity not to smile, Jason continues to follow him. "What do you like?"

"What?"

"If you don't like donuts, what do you like?"

The question seems to take the man completely off guard and he tilts his head, studying Jason while his pace slows. He's not running away, at least not completely. "Who are you?"

"Jason." He holds out a hand. "And you are?"

"Late," he answers, shaking his head.

"Late for what? There's nothing going on today but—"

"Setting up," he finishes. "So much to set up."

"Ah, you're helping someone. Is it the new teacher?"

"I'm not helping the new teacher," he replies, tone unexpectedly clipped given how innocuous the question seemed to Jason.

"Okay, maybe the—"

"Do you know where the English building is?" he interrupts, the sharpness in his tone overshadowed by the way he takes a measured breath.

Jason's seen enough frazzled students to recognize the signs of anxiety or stress and to be well versed in not taking that kind of thing personally.

"Sure, but you're on the wrong side of campus," Jason answers, softening his tone. He takes a step into the other's personal space so he can pluck the map from his hands and turn it around. "This building here is the front office, but you're going down here right now. See, this walking path here is where we are now. If you continue down this way, you're going to pass the gym and then reach the sports fields. Soccer is here, baseball is down there, and right past us another hundred feet down that hill and behind the gym is the football field."

"Ugh, that's definitely not where I want to go."

"Not a fan of football?" Jason asks, unsure why the guy's expression has him wanting to laugh rather than be offended. He looks so completely horrified at the idea.

"God no. Football, or sports in general—just no."

"No sports," Jason laughs. "Got it."

The guy sighs heavily, tracing his finger over the path Jason just drew, tapping the spot where they currently stand. "This campus is...spread out. I looked at this map online, too, but it's different in person. I swear I thought schools like this only existed in movies with everything outside and full of all this sunshine and palm trees, but no."

Jason can't help but be charmed by his rambling. "I take it this isn't what your own school looked like?"

"Not even close. My high school was all one building, and there definitely wasn't so much grass and trees and well —this," He opens his arms and gestures at the general scenery. "This place looks like a vacation destination, not a prison."

As far as Southern California schools go, it's not that atypical, but living this close to the beach combined with their more favorable tax bracket means Santa Leon is one of the nicer high schools in the area, especially for a public school. Between the landscaping and copious seating areas for lunch and breaks, it really is a beautiful campus.

"I mean, schools should never look like a prison," Jason says.

"Mine did."

"Well, that sounds depressing," Jason says with a frown. "Where did you go to school? It can't have been in SoCal. I don't think I've ever seen a high school like that around here."

"It was—no, it wasn't here." His expression shifts and he reaches for his left hand, spinning the gold ring on his pointer finger. There's some kind of engraving on it, but Jason can't tell what. "So can you tell me where the English building is, please?"

"Of course," Jason answers, feeling a prickle of guilt for being such a yapper when it's clear this guy isn't in the mood. "The English building is behind us, just to the left of that tall building there, which is our library and—" but he's cut off by someone calling for him.

"Coach!"

Jason turns to see one of his senior players running across campus. As a teacher and coach, Jason isn't supposed to have favorite students or players, but he definitely does, and Matty is one of them. Not that he gives any of them preferential treatment. Jason makes sure he's impartial and fair, but he'd be lying if he said he didn't go above and beyond for some of the kids, the ones who need more than the school can give. Kids like Matty. Despite his academic struggles, he works his ass off, never complains, and he's so damn polite. He's also doing everything on his own, working a part-time job to help his mom in the summer and on weekends with his rigorous football schedule.

"I thought I told you I didn't need to see you until classes start, huh?" Jason's smile gives away that he's teasing.

"I know, Coach, but I wanted to know if I could talk to you about something."

"Everything okay, Matty?"

"Yeah, it's just—" Matty fills his lungs with air, looking oddly small considering his bulking six foot two frame. He's radiating anxiety, the same kind he saw coming off the guy beside him, and a familiar urge to soothe hits Jason. He hates when people are upset.

"Why don't we head down to the field," he suggests, knowing Matty is always most relaxed there. "We can toss the ball around and talk."

Matty's exhale is palpable. "That'd be great, Coach."

"Just let me say bye to—" but Jason stops mid-sentence when he notices he and Matty are alone, his mystery companion now gone. He can't help but frown, turning around towards the library, but there's no sight of him.

Turning his attention back to Matty, he jerks his thumb over his shoulder towards the football field. "Come on, kid. Tell me about your summer."

Matty's chatter fills the silence, and Jason can only hope the stranger finds what he was looking for before he affords Matty his full attention.

3 EMERSON

EMERSON QUICKENS HIS STEPS, desperate to get far enough away to avoid further conversation. He passes a few other teachers, plastering on a mask of indifference and offering them a curt nod and what he can only hope passes for a polite smile. At the earliest opportunity, he slips into the shadows behind the tall building he now knows is the library, trying to hide from any potential social interactions.

It takes a solid minute for his heart rate to slow enough that he can catch his breath, but even then his heart continues to thrum erratically in his chest. With a heavy sigh, he closes his eyes, tipping his head back against the brick wall to try to calm his breathing. It doesn't work well, though considering the interaction he just had it's possible nothing could calm him down right now.

It's just Emerson's luck that when he finally gets himself to California and on campus to start his new job, the second person he meets and insults is the football coach. This is exactly why Emerson avoids small talk. He's terrible at it. So terrible, in fact, that he tried to avoid the guy to begin with, possessing just enough self-awareness to know his growing anxiety about everything being new and different was going to make him rude.

All Emerson wanted was to find his classroom and get things set up so he might feel a modicum of control, which might in turn help regulate his nervous system. It's currently screaming at him about all the changes he's endured in the last twenty-four hours. Emerson hates change.

Fate is not on Emerson's side today, or ever, judging by the unfortunate circumstances of most of his life. The damn man—Jason, he'd said his name was—had not been put off by Emerson's attitude or tone, and instead of leaving him alone like most people did when he made a bad first impression, he followed him. In response to this unexpected turn of events, Emerson snapped at him and offered an unsolicited statistic about donuts before insulting organized sports. All in all, things couldn't have been worse. Or so he thought. Then a student in a football jersey called Jason "Coach", giving enough contextual information for even Emerson to conclude who Jason must be. It was at that point he chose Jason's distraction to make his escape, leaving him where he is now, hiding behind a building, still unsure where his classroom is and afraid he's ruined his chances of fitting in here before the school year even starts.

There's an uncomfortable warmth in his cheeks, but whether from running or anxiety, he has no idea. His brain can't tell the difference between being overheated and his life being in danger. Either way, it's an unwanted sensation that leaves Emerson unsure if he wants to cry or lay face down on the ground. Probably the first since Emerson doesn't like the way grass feels on his bare skin, and the cement is too hot to touch.

If things had gone according to plan, Emerson would

have been in Santa Leon well over a week ago. He had a solid plan for this move. If he'd been here when he wanted to be, then he would've had enough time to settle into his new studio apartment. He would have had time to walk around and get to know the lay of the campus without the pressure of also getting his classroom ready. He would've been able to act normal when he met one of his fellow staff instead of running away from them and potentially ostracizing himself before the school year even begins.

Unfortunately, things had not gone according to Emerson's plans. Instead of being here when he wanted to a week ago, there'd been an issue with the moving company that required him to stay an extra day and make sure his belongings actually made it across the country. This small delay meant he missed his flight, leaving him unable to get another one that he could afford for almost another week. That second delay was the worst because it meant Emerson missed the new staff orientation meeting the principal set up for him, and as a result his chance to get to know anyone on campus before the school year started, leaving him lost and confused.

Unease mounts while Emerson taps his fingers against his palm, willing himself to relax. He can do this. He wants to do this. If only his brain would get the memo and stop jumping into fight or flight mode every time his routine gets messed up.

"Are you sure this won't be too much for you, Emerson? You know how bad you are with change. Maybe you should stay home and work here so you don't, well, you know. Your uncle can always get you a part-time job someplace where you won't have to be around too many people."

The words ring in his head, a harsh reminder of exactly why he needed to get away. His aunt wasn't trying to be cruel, but then again, she never was on purpose. Most people weren't. Only...Emerson didn't need to constantly be reminded he wasn't like other people, or that he wasn't good at the things most people were good at, like being a person. His aunt always seemed determined to remind him he'd fail before he even tried.

As far as Emerson is concerned, the only thing that matters is that he wants this, that he's wanted this for years. Even if it doesn't always make sense. High school had been a hellscape for Emerson, and he'd wanted to disappear nearly every day. It doesn't matter if no one else understands how Emerson can want to be a high school teacher when some of his worst memories were born during that time. It had also been where he'd finally gotten the words to understand himself. He'd been so tired of feeling like an alien, unsure why he couldn't just be like everyone else no matter how hard he tried. Then Mrs. Monroe, his sophomore English teacher, had come along, saw through all his masking and got him the resources he needed to get diagnosed. It had given him the foundation to accept the other things about himself, like being gay. Even if he hadn't bothered coming out to anyone until after high school, having that label for himself had made all the difference.

Now he's here, twenty-six-hundred miles away from everything and everyone he knows, with the chance to start over. He's not here to be someone new, or different, just to be the version of himself no one else ever seemed to want him to be.

"Are you alright, dear?"

Emerson blinks, opening his eyes and coming face to face with the older woman from the front office who gave him the map this morning. She'd been on the phone when he arrived at the office, and Emerson had been anxious to find his classroom and unsure exactly how long it was socially appropriate to hang around. So, he'd departed as quickly as possible, which had turned out to not be the wisest choice.

"I'm fine," Emerson tries, so used to lying about his own mental state he's not sure he would know how to be honest with anyone if he tried. He twists the fidget ring on his finger, spinning it as fast as he can while trying to keep the rest of his body still. "I didn't catch your name back at the office, my apologies."

"I'm Ms. Farwell, but you can just call me Mabel." She smiles, the wrinkles on her face exaggerated with the action. She reminds Emerson of someone's grandma, not that he'd known his own.

"Alright, Mabel."

"Come on then, Mr. Miller," Mabel says. "Let's get you settled. I think you're going to love Santa Leon High."

The tightness in Emerson's chest loosens when she reaches for his arm. Sure, he probably won't make a lot—or any—friends, but after years of dreaming of making it to California, here he is, finally in his mom's hometown. Not just here, but with an apartment of his own and an actual teaching job. All the things his family was certain he'd never manage. He can do this. He has to do this.

Emerson has waited too long and worked too hard to let his own brain fuck things up for him now.

WITH MABEL'S HELP, Emerson finally finds his classroom. While Mabel talks, he mentally rehearses what he might say if she asks why he couldn't find it, unsure how much he wants to reveal. During his zoom interviews the principal had seemed impressed by Emerson's attention to detail and passion for English. The truth was, his attention to detail was born out of a compulsive need to plan and be in control. Whereas his passion for English and desire to teach was influenced by reading, his lifelong hyperfocus. Being autistic offered him a specific skill set he knew could be an asset, but he'd still shied away from offering up his diagnosis, unsure how neuro-affirming Santa Leon High is.

The voice of his family, always reminding him how difficult and particular he is, seems to haunt him every time he thinks about getting to know new people. Would they see his quirks and personality as a positive, or view everything about him in a deficit model like his aunt and uncle do?

"Just this way, dear," Mabel says, her voice dragging Emerson back to the present.

"I'm going to get lost on Monday," Emerson sighs, hating himself for voicing that fear out loud. He twists his ring, rubbing his thumb over the engraving to try and ground himself.

"You'll get the hang of it in no time. Give it one day and you'll know this entire place like the back of your hand," Mabel assures him. Before Emerson can get a chance to point out how unlikely that is given his propensity to get lost anywhere and everywhere she laughs. "You know what? I have a wonderful idea! It'll be perfect. Just perfect."

Emerson remains silent, unsure if he's supposed to ask her what she's talking about or wait. Thankfully he's spared having to play the '*what is the socially acceptable response right now*' guessing game by Mabel speaking.

"I'll let you settle into your classroom. If you need anything, just call the office or come see me. We take care of our own here, Mr. Miller. We're all glad to have you here."

A lump forms in Emerson's throat at those words. The

last person to say something like that to him was his mom. She'd always been happy to have Emerson around, but she'd been gone a long time now. Long enough to forget what it was like to have people want you around.

"Thank you," Emerson whispers.

It's not until she's gone, leaving him standing outside the door to his classroom that he realizes he never did find out what her great idea was.

That unknown fades into the background as he settles on focusing all his attention on where he's going to spend the majority of his days from now on. It's a far cry from the drab brick buildings he's used to. The English building, like most on this campus, is a single story building. Each one is spread out across the sprawling campus and even has its own door to the outside. Emerson's room is the one right at the end, giving his room a full view of the grassy quad. Everywhere he looks is green grass and swaying palm trees with white buildings blending into the picturesque scenery.

It almost feels like a dream, and Emerson has to remind himself that this is real. It's not some elaborate scenario he conjured up in his room while unable to sleep, but his actual life. He's really here, living on his own and making things happen for himself. It might not have been easy, and yeah, Emerson's insides are churning uncomfortably with all the newness as everything in him tries to slot this new life into orderly boxes and predictable routines. But for all the discomfort, there's relief, too. After a lifetime of restrictions and rules of other people's making, he's finally on his own. It is as terrifying as it is exciting.

Entering his classroom for the first time does nothing to settle the excitement or apprehension. Both war within him in equal measure. Just as they'd promised, the classroom has everything he could need—rows of desks lined up in the center, bookshelves lining the walls ready to be filled, and a desk in the corner for Emerson. One of his own choosing. Not somewhere he's being put because the teachers wanted him close by to avoid distractions when other kids picked on him, but a desk he earned.

Walking to it, he skirts his fingers over the wooden edge. Like everything else at Santa Leon High, it looks nearly new, and it's not lost on Emerson how much nicer this place is than the school he went to, not just in topography but in resources. Then again, he supposes, that's what happens when you're a high school in an affluent beach town with a state championship football team. There's definitely no lack of financial resources here, and while Emerson might have no connection to the alumni, locals or sports teams, his little classroom will reap the benefits all the same.

Emerson makes his way to the windows next, opening the blinds further to let in more light. The wall of windows looks out into the open quad, an expanse of tables, grass and trees meeting his view. Emerson didn't even know this many palm trees in one place was possible but as he takes them all in he can't help but smile. He might've grown up with his nose in a book, but his imagination was filled with the kinds of trees that might have been found in the Shire, not a palm tree-dotted coastline. Yet he can't deny that the sight of so much earth and green has his chest loosening all the same. Emerson has always loved nature, though he's not sure even a tree-lined view will be enough to make this adjustment easy on him.

Despite this being his dream move and dream job, Emerson has an itch under his skin—overcome by the desire right now to run away and escape, not because he doesn't want it but because the task of settling in and figuring out new routines feels almost insurmountable. He hadn't been able to voice any of that to his family though. They'd never understand how he could struggle with things he wanted to do. Then again, they never understood him at all.

Reaching into his pocket, Emerson fidgets with the loose threads while he looks around and tries to picture where everything will go. The more he imagines, the lighter he feels inside. He mutters to himself as he paces the room and plots. Within the hour, he's got the entire thing laid out in his mind, the perfect picture of where it might all go. He spends the next hour rearranging the furniture so the bookshelves flank the window and the student's desks form a circle instead of a row. He finds a few spare cushions shoved into the closet which he tosses into the middle of the room for flexible seating before he sets about taking stock of the supplies left for him and what he might need. It turns out it is not nearly as much as he was assuming, all things considered. The hardest part is going to be figuring out how to get the rest of his books and plants from his apartment to his classroom without a car. The idea of taking them on the bus and having other people touch them has him shuddering in displeasure. He makes a mental note to check Uber prices before rising to stand.

It's not until he's walking out his classroom door, arms stretched out overhead to get rid of the stiffness from rearranging furniture all day, that it occurs to him how late he's stayed. He pulls out his phone to check the time, frowning when he realizes he missed his alarm for dinner. Despite the late hour the sun still sits high on the horizon line, the pale blue sky dotted with clouds. The sight momentarily renders Emerson speechless because he's pretty sure the sky doesn't look like this in Pennsylvania. His mom used to talk about the big skies in Southern California, about missing the smell of the salt in the air and the feeling of the sea breeze on her cheeks. She'd been born and raised here, moving away for college where she ended up pregnant with Emerson and dropped out. After that it'd just been the two of them and there'd never been enough money to move back. At least, that's what she used to tell him so he didn't feel bad. She's not here to remind him, though, and a pang of guilt hits him. Maybe if he'd handled change better they could've moved back here. Then his mom wouldn't have gotten into that accident, and he wouldn't have been forced to grow up with people who never wanted him.

Blowing out a heavy breath, Emerson rocks on his heels. There's still so much left he wants to do in his classroom, but he probably should try and get the bus back home before it gets dark. He can make a couple Eggo waffles and a long to-do list. Then tomorrow, he can get started.

TWENTY-SEVEN MINUTES. That's how late the bus is. He knows because he checked the bus schedule twice this morning, and it said right there on the website in bold print that the last bus from this specific stop would arrive at five after seven, which is exactly why Emerson all but raced across campus to the bus stop to ensure he wouldn't be late. He made it on time, but so far the bus hasn't.

With every car that passes by his unease rises. He hates when things don't stick to the schedule.

Sighing heavily, Emerson drops down onto the bench next to the bus stop sign, lowering his face into his hands. He needs to formulate a new plan, but he's tired and overstimulated. He should be at home right now getting into his nightly shower so he can put on his home clothes and decompress. He should not be sitting on a bench waiting for a bus that is definitely not coming.

Walking is out of the question, not because he's opposed to the act itself but because Emerson would absolutely get himself lost. Maybe in a few months when he knows the area better he could swing the four mile walk, but right now he has no doubt he'd take a wrong turn and end up somewhere other than his own apartment complex. Which means his only option is to get an Uber. Even knowing this is what he's going to do, he hesitates to pull out his phone and open the app. He hates getting in cars with strangers. Sometimes they have the radio on to music he doesn't like, the volume outside of his control. Then there's the fact that he can't predict whether he'll get a silent driver who just wants to do their job and get paid or one of the ones who makes small talk with Emerson. He hates small talk.

He's also still haunted by the Uber he had to take from the airport to his apartment this week where the car smelled like someone dumped a bottle of fabric softener in it. The smell had been so strong he'd nearly jumped out of the moving car. It'd only been his utter exhaustion from the long day of travel and his anxiety at the prospect of having to figure out a different driver that had kept him in the car.

Frustrated, Emerson pulls on his hair. The tinge of pain stops him, and he forces his hands into his lap, fidgeting with his ring instead.

This is exactly why he should get a car and drive. Except, Emerson doesn't drive. Technically he can, but only because his aunt and uncle had insisted on him getting his license when he turned twenty-one. He never could understand why other people were so bothered about whether he could drive or not. He knew how to take the bus. What did it matter if he could drive a car? It hadn't been worth the argument, though, so Emerson had allowed his aunt and uncle to bully him into driving lessons that had been absolutely horrible and made Emerson physically sick with anxiety. He passed his test, got the license and then promptly refused to use it, despite the fact his aunt and uncle both saw it as a failure. Then again, they saw most things about him as one.

When he got the teaching job here, he debated getting himself a car. He'd read it was more of necessity in Southern California than the area he was from because of city development and underfunded public transit, but he'd ultimately decided against it. The last thing he needed after upending his entire life was more unease. What he ended up doing was renting a small studio apartment that was located on a bus line. Something that is clearly not doing him any good since the bus isn't here.

He didn't budget having to take an Uber today. It's already going to be a tight squeeze with his savings since he won't get paid until the end of the week. Incidentally, that is also when the second and final payment for the movers is due if he doesn't want finance charges, which he absolutely doesn't. He spent a small fortune moving his stuff across the country, probably more than it was worth, but Emerson couldn't bear to part with or replace any of his favorite things regardless of cost, which is why he needs to stick to his budget now.

Resigned to the unfortunate truth that he actually has no options, he pulls out his phone and opens the Uber app. His hand hovers over the app when someone speaks.

"Hey, you."

Emerson's eyes shoot up from his phone to the street, met with the sight of a familiar smiling face. Parked at the curb directly in front of him is Jason, his smile relaxed and easy as he leans across the passenger seat towards the window he's put down. Unlike Emerson who feels like a ball of nothing but anxiety and stress, Jason looks utterly relaxed and happy. Maybe he's picking someone up. Emerson turns around to look behind him but there's no one there.

"Do you need some help?" Jason questions.

Emerson blinks. Okay, he's definitely talking to him, then. Though why, Emerson can't imagine.

"I'm waiting for the bus."

Jason whistles. "This route is pretty unpredictable. Especially in summer."

A sigh falls from Emerson's lips. The confirmation isn't unexpected but it is unwelcome. He'd been warned the bus lines might be less reliable in the suburbs, but the well organized online schedule had been so promising.

"Where are you going? I can give you a ride."

"Are you an Uber driver?"

"Me?" Jason shakes his head. "Definitely not."

"Then why are you offering me a ride?"

"Because you need one, obviously. Unless you'd rather get an Uber." Whatever face Emerson makes must answer the question because Jason actually laughs. "I'll take that as a 'no' then. Come on, get in and I'll give you a lift."

Despite the generosity of the offer, Emerson hesitates. This would solve his problem and save him money he doesn't have right now, but it will also put him in close proximity to the man he half-insulted earlier before running away. Not that Jason looks remotely bothered by their earlier exchange. That smile on his face is still there, unwavering and wide, like finding some random guy you don't know on the side of the road is a good thing. Or maybe it's one of those fake, polite smiles people paste on their faces when they're actually not in a good mood. So many people smile even when they don't mean it, making it frankly exhausting to try and parse through. Or maybe Jason has the opposite of a resting bitch face, and he has a resting happy face.

"Is there someone you want to call instead?" Jason asks. "If your phone is dead, you could borrow mine or—"

"There's no one," Emerson finishes.

The expression on Jason's face is impossible to make out, his smile shuttering for only a moment before reappearing, though not in full. Emerson can't imagine why he cares. "Why don't you let me give you a ride home. I'm sure you've had a long day."

"Do you use air freshener?" Emerson blurts.

"Air freshener," he repeats, glancing around the inside of his truck like he's not sure what he's looking for. "Uh, no, I don't."

Decision made, Emerson stalks towards the truck. If he's got to get in a car with a stranger, at least this one has been vetted by the school district and is unlikely to be dangerous, aside from being exactly the kind of guy Emerson would normally avoid under any circumstances, that is. Emotional discomfort is something Emerson is well-versed in handling at this point, and something he can deal with if it means he can get back to his apartment in one piece and without spending money.

Deciding to get into Jason's truck and doing it prove to be two different things. The damn truck is as large as the man driving it, with lifted wheels and a massive step that Emerson barely manages to get his shoe onto even with his long legs.

"Sorry, it's kind of big." Jason laughs. "You need help?"

"I'm good," Emerson mumbles, using his pitiful amount

of noodle arm strength to heft himself into the truck, which is far cleaner than Emerson expects. Not that he gave too much thought to the inside of Jason's vehicle, but if pressed, he would've assumed a football coach would have a car littered with trash and gear and smell like sweaty gym socks. Instead, the car is relatively clean, the cup holder containing a protein shake and a water bottle. His seats are smooth and cool, likely from the air conditioning currently blasting cold air at Emerson's flushed face.

After the uncomfortable metal bench and hours of rearranging furniture, the inside of Jason's truck is literally a balm to Emerson's nervous system. Unable to resist the comfort, he relaxes into the massive bench seat, his entire body slumping while he closes his eyes and lets out a heavy exhale of relief. He's never actually been in a truck before, but now that he has, he's not sure how he's supposed to sit in a regular car again knowing how superior the seating is in here.

"The seats are cooled," Jason explains when Emerson lets out a little happy sigh again. "Feels good, doesn't it?"

Emerson hums out a noncommittal reply, embarrassed by his unfiltered reaction. Normally he's a lot more composed around strangers and at least tries to put effort into pretending to be polite, but he's too done-in right now, more than he even realized before stepping into the truck. His body aches from moving furniture, his muscles unused to any kind of physical labor, and the last thirty minutes spent sitting in the sun waiting for a bus that never came tipped him over the deregulation limit.

"Not gonna lie, that was one reason I splurged on this truck," Jason continues, undeterred by Emerson's silence. "The heated seats didn't appeal too much, can't say we need those often with our tepid weather here, but cooled seats after hours of practice or a hot summer day? Sign me the fuck up. Seriously worth every penny."

His rambling is unexpectedly comforting, and Emerson finds himself smiling before he can stop himself, almost immediately trying to force the smile away out of habit. Jason isn't his cousin, but the idea of giving someone fodder to hold over him makes his stomach turn, ruining whatever flicker of good mood had tried to ignite at Jason's words. He reminds himself that for all Jason is being friendly, they have nothing in common besides working at the same high school. Once school starts next week, Jason likely won't interact with Emerson again because there's no chance they will ever run in the same social circles. Mainly because Emerson has no delusions of being included in anyone's social circle. Even during the long months of student teaching, he'd been unable to make any friends. It's a possibility that Emerson is as unlikeable as his cousin and high school bullies always told him he was. It's equally possible that his desire to avoid being rejected meant he used to hide in the bathroom during his breaks and lunch times, and when you do that, it's kind of impossible to make friends.

"So, I didn't get your name," Jason says, seemingly determined to try and get to know him. Whether this is from genuine curiosity or that he just has good manners and social skills remains unknown. What is clear is that if Jason did get to know him, he would realize how different they are and distance himself the way most people do, but while they're stuck in his truck together the least Emerson can do is attempt polite conversation.

"Emerson," he offers, fidgeting with the fabric inside his pocket. He tugs on the loose thread, twisting it between his fingers as dread fills him.

"Emerson, huh? I like it." Emerson likes it, too. It was

something his mom gave him that no one could ever take away from him, one of the few things he was proud of growing up. His name has always felt like him, even before he understood who that was. Unaware of what his off-handed and simple compliment could mean, Jason barrels on. "So Emerson, where are we heading?"

"I live on Paseo del Ocaso," Emerson says. "The, uh, the apartment building on the corner."

"No way! I live on Avenida de la Playa." At Emerson's silence, Jason explains. "It's just a few miles from your place. Once you pass your apartment complex you go another half a mile then make a left on State Street. Or if you were coming on the 101 going South, you'd take the Leon exit, then head West, taking you to Mariposa Way which is between both of us."

"I know you're speaking English, and yet everything you just said might as well have been in a foreign language," Emerson says.

Jason laughs softly and Emerson holds his breath, unsure if he's said something wrong.

"Guess I'm a directions guy like my dad. Sorry," Jason apologizes. "You're pretty new to the area, right?"

"That obvious?"

"A little," Jason laughs. Though he doesn't seem to be laughing at Emerson, the little knot of tension in his chest doesn't fade. He's never been able to relax around other people, not even his own family. The last person he felt comfortable enough around to just be himself was his mom and she's been gone so long he can hardly remember what it felt like not to hide. "So where are you from, Emerson?"

"Pennsylvania," Emerson answers, turning his eyes out the passenger window, a far safer thing to look at than the man sitting beside him with the mile-wide smile and chin dimple. It is deeply inconvenient to notice how big and handsome Jason is, while also having the urge to jump out of the moving car to avoid feeling awkward around him because he's a stranger. Not that Emerson thinks he'd be less awkward if he wasn't a stranger. There are people he's known for years he's still awkward around, but that's kind of just his default at this point. It's why Emerson doesn't have friends back home, and why he really never dates, ever. Most of the time he retreats into his books and avoids social interactions, not wanting to be perceived too deeply. It's easier to keep people at a distance, or avoid them entirely. Then he won't have to spend all his time exhausted by the effort of trying to fit in.

The other glaring issue in all of this is that Jason probably isn't gay or queer. The label wouldn't matter to Emerson, especially not since even if he was, there's no way he would be interested in Emerson anyway.

"Can't say I've ever been there," Jason continues. Emerson wonders if he always talks this much. "Actually, I don't know anything about Pennsylvania. What's it like there? Is there anything you miss? Did you like it?"

There are too many questions for him to answer them all, but they make Emerson think about how flat the landscape where he grew up compared to the mountains that border Santa Leon. He thinks about the city full of skyscrapers and cars and buses he was raised in, about the sweltering humidity and bugs. He thinks about his bedroom that shared a wall with his cousin Landon who was the same age as Emerson and spent his entire life resenting that Emerson came to live with them, and made sure Emerson knew it. About the lack of privacy and constant overstimulation from his music and his friends and his teasing. He thinks about the way his aunt and uncle's apartment had never felt like home. How nothing had felt like home since the day his mom died.

"No," Emerson answers quietly, not even sure which question he's answering. All of them, perhaps.

Just because Jason is making small talk on their drive, doesn't mean he's actually trying to get to know Emerson. He's probably just being polite. Emerson has to remind himself not to be too honest. People don't usually want that. Like when they ask how you are and you're supposed to say fine or good, even when it's not true.

"I'll make sure and scratch it off my travel list," Jason laughs, making a show of scratching something off an imaginary list midair. "Speaking of travel lists. You know where I wanted to go really bad as a kid?"

Emerson has no idea if this is a rhetorical question but he answers anyway just to be safe. "No."

"The Hershey chocolate factory. I guess that makes me a liar because it's in Pennsylvania, which means at some point I did want to go there. I was convinced it was like the chocolate factory in Willy Wonka, but like without the Oompa-loompas and stuff. Or that creepy tunnel during the boat ride." Jason shudders dramatically. "That tunnel gave me nightmares. I did like that room with edible flowers. I always wondered what it would taste like. Did you ever want to eat one of those?"

Unsure how they went from small talk about Emerson's place of origin to eating Willy Wonka flowers, Emerson can do nothing but turn and stare at Jason while trying to make sense of the giant, rambling man beside him. He knows he's not that great at understanding most people, but this is beyond that. He can't comprehend how someone who looks like Jason—so big and handsome, a quintessential jock—is also so nice to him for seemingly no reason. Well, there's got to be a reason. There's always a reason. It occurs to Emerson that maybe someone at the school put him up to it.

The silence stretches on, but Emerson finds himself unable to contribute to the conversation. He has no idea what to say and is very preoccupied by trying to figure out what Jason wants from him, so he continues to stare.

Seemingly unaffected by Emerson's intense eye contact and inability to uphold his side of the conversation, Jason continues to talk. "Oh come on, don't tell me you weren't also freaked out by that tunnel."

"I was not a fan of the movie," Emerson offers, surprised at his admission.

"Was it the tunnel? It was the tunnel, right?"

"No." Emerson how honest he should be. "I, uh—I don't like chocolate, so the idea of an entire factory full of it makes me gag."

Thinking about it at all makes Emerson shudder with a visceral revulsion. The only thing worse than solid chocolate is liquid chocolate. The smell and texture alone is such a sensory ick.

"Emerson, you're killing me," Jason groans. "First you don't like donuts and now you don't like chocolate? Are you even human?"

"They tell me I am," Emerson sighs, waiting for Jason to say something unkind in response. His cousin and the rest of his teammates on the football team never had a shortage of barbs about Emerson's preferences, his personality, or anything about him really. He'd learned early on not to let people know anything about him, trying to bury himself in his books to avoid being perceived and ridiculed. Not that it really helped much. Especially not when he had the tendency to hyperfocus on whatever books he was reading to the point he zoned out around other people or info-dumped on them, both of which made him an easier target. He'd hoped becoming an English teacher might offer a cover. If books became his job, it might be safer, more expected from others, for him to be so intense about them.

To Emerson's surprise, there's no unkind remark, only the echoing sound of Jason's laugh. It makes his cheeks burn and his chest ache. He should be used to being laughed at but if he's learned anything, it's that sometimes there's no getting used to a world that isn't designed for you. Maybe no matter how hard he tries, he's always going to stand out in all the wrong ways.

"You're funny, Emerson."

The words stop Emerson's train of thought. The warmth in his face doesn't fade but his heart slows a beat. Oh. Jason was laughing at him, but not *at* him. That's...new.

A lump forms in Emerson's throat, a rush of heat spreading through his body. He has no idea how to respond to Jason's words. Thankfully, he's spared from having to when someone behind lays on their horn, clearly unhappy with Jason not gunning it through the intersection.

"I'm going, I'm going," Jason mutters to himself. "Honestly, that's the one thing I hate about drivers here, impatient fuckers."

While Jason continues to talk about the local drivers, Emerson's attention wanders to their surroundings. Street names and cardinal directions might be impossible for him to follow, but he's pretty decent at memorizing random landmarks. Or he tries to be, anyway. It's a necessary skill when considering how often he's gotten lost, even in places he's been before. He doesn't want that to happen here, not when he doesn't even have anyone he could call to help him. At least back home his uncle would come get him, albeit with a lecture that always left Emerson feeling full of shame and embarrassment.

Doing his best to try and memorize the landmarks, he tracks them all trying to gauge how far away they might be from his apartment. So far he's been too anxious about things while on the bus to really focus on the surroundings, but with Jason now silent and the inside of the truck blissfully quiet and cool, he's able to focus his attention on things that might help him orient his location if he ever does go the wrong way.

Leaning his elbow on the door, he rests his chin on his upturned palm while his eyes track the surroundings. The problem for Emerson is that until he has some kind of frame of reference for something—visiting a location, making up a story about what might've gone on there, his brain refuses to hold on to the information. It'd gotten him in so much trouble at school and from his aunt and uncle who seemed determined to believe the worst of Emerson, that he just didn't pay attention. He tries to pay attention now, but all his brain keeps doing is focusing on the sound of Jason's breathing and wondering if he's going to speak again, and if so what might he ask Emerson? He tries to rehearse what he might say if Jason asks him a basic question about work or moving, so he'll be prepared just in case.

To his relief, Jason doesn't engage him in any more uncomfortable small talk. Rather, he offers the exact information that Emerson desires but hasn't yet mustered up the ability to verbalize.

"I'm not sure how used to the area you are yet, but it's just a couple miles further to your place," Jason says. Whether he can tell Emerson is antsy or this is just another example of his propensity to talk, Emerson has no idea, but it's appreciated either way. "Luckily the traffic isn't too bad this time of day. If it were even half an hour earlier, we'd be crawling right now. Which reminds me, I wanted to warn you. Don't ever leave between five-thirty and six, unless you just wanna be sitting on Via Princesa for forty minutes with all the people who commute inland trying to get back home. Don't even get me started on what the traffic does to the bus being on time. You're gonna wanna leave right on time or stay later past your classes, maybe do a little grading on campus so you don't have to take it home."

"How do you know I'll have grading?" Emerson asks, realizing he never did tell him that he was the new teacher. Then again, given how personable Jason is there's no shortage of people who could've told Jason all about him. He wonders what they said. He tried to tell them as little about himself as possible during his interviews. And the only people he's met besides the principal and vice principal is the nice older woman who works in the front office, though Emerson can't remember her name.

"Used my impressive powers of deduction after you disappeared to figure you out."

"Oh." Emerson wonders what he figured out, spinning his ring rapidly.

"Nah, I'm just shitting you, I don't have any powers of deduction." Jason laughs, as if he's said something very funny. "Between you and me, my observational skills are not always the best, but people like to talk. And when I had lunch with Mabel, she mentioned showing the new English teacher to his class, so it wasn't very hard to put two and two together. Not too many lost guys wandering campus before the semester starts."

"The campus is really big," Emerson retorts.

"It is," Jason agrees, taking Emerson's brusk tone in stride. "I mean, I went there so I already knew it like the back of my hand before I started teaching, but I can see how it might not be as easy to navigate if you didn't, especially based on what you said about your own high school. We're lucky to have such a beautiful campus, but some of the buildings are not close together. And it's really not laid out in a logical manner, which can be a nightmare for some of the students and staff. Thankfully a few years back, right before I started teaching, they repaved all the pathways and fixed the ramps for the older buildings, but it was definitely designed by people who didn't think about the implications for accessibility. And don't get me started on why freshman English is near the library but the senior English building is across the quad near the gym. Or why half the science classes are on the East side of campus, but for some reason the labs are down near the new auditorium. None of it makes any sense. Seriously, you wouldn't believe how many freshmen I've found near tears during the first week of school because they get lost and are too embarrassed or overwhelmed to tell anyone."

Emerson blinks, entirely surprised to hear such thoughtful observations.

"Here's your place," Jason continues, like he didn't just drop a mouthful of conscientious observations Emerson's way. "Did you want me to drop you off at the front gates on Saratoga or pull around the back? I'm not sure exactly where your apartment is or which would be easier for you."

Honestly Emerson has no idea which way is better. The first day he got here he'd navigated his way to his apartment from the back because that's where the Uber took him straight from the airport. Which means it's now the only way he's ever entered and exited the apartment building now that his brain has cemented it as the way in. Logically he knows he should explore the complex and check out the other entrance but Emerson is not really a fan of having multiple options for things. He likes to find one that works and stick with it.

"Back entrance," he answers, the feeling of being put on the spot making him sound sharper than Jason deserves.

"You got it," Jason says, flipping on his turn signal and merging into the left lane to enter the parking lot for Emerson's complex. Jason easily navigates his way to the gated entrance in the back, at which point Emerson has perfectly rehearsed what to say, but all of it goes out the window when Jason turns to him and smiles in a way that reveals dimples—one in each cheek—and a warm smile. "It was really nice meeting you, Emerson. I'll see you at school."

All his perfectly practiced dialogue is nowhere to be found, his brain nothing more than a highlight reel of Jason's dimpled smile and friendly face. Emerson might be very gay, but he's not sure he's ever been as attracted to anyone as he is to Jason. Has anyone else ever had such pretty brown eyes or a nicer smile? Emerson can't imagine they have. Or maybe it's just that Jason being nice to him is causing his brain to malfunction. Most of the people he's found attractive in the past lost their aesthetic appeal when he realized he didn't like them as a person. This entire situation would be so much easier if Jason was a jerk.

"Emerson?" Jason prompts, because of course he does. Emerson isn't saying anything, is just staring at Jason without getting out of the car or thanking him for the ride home. Both things he should do. Somehow what comes out of his mouth is not a thanks though.

"You'll see me Monday," Emerson blurts.

"I will," Jason agrees, his easy smile still firmly in place like he doesn't mind the idea. "No running away from me this time."

"I can't make any promises," Emerson replies honestly, surprised when Jason laughs.

"I like you, Emerson."

That weird feeling in his chest intensifies, and Emerson has no idea if it's unease, or hunger, or if the weird rushing in his ears is because he didn't drink enough water today. Emerson hasn't been sleeping well, not yet used to his new place, even if he did pay a small fortune to have his old pillow and mattress delivered across the country just so it would feel the same. Being tired always fucks with Emerson's ability to regulate his emotions. As does being hungry. Or being around people too long.

"I'm going to leave now," Emerson says.

Jason's smile doesn't falter. "Alright."

With an embarrassing grunt, Emerson flings the truck door open, half-falling out of it as he stumbles down the step. Jason's earnest 'are you okay?' echoes in his ears as he all but runs from him for the second time, not even turning around to wave. Emerson just needs to get to his apartment, put on his pajamas, tuck himself into his weighted blanket, and eat an Eggo waffle. Then maybe everything will make more sense.

4 JASON

A BLARING alarm startles Jason from a deep sleep, making him regret choosing his loudest sound when he set the alarm last night. Then again, considering it's early enough not even his own internal alarm clock or his dogs have had a chance to wake him, it was probably the right choice.

Though he knew the alarm would come extra early today, he can't stop the groan that leaves his lips as he rolls over and buries his face in his pillow. It's still pitch dark outside, far too early for any normal human to be awake. It's definitely going to take him a few weeks to get used to getting up before the sun again. He is never going to be a morning person naturally, but he is willing to do anything for his fur babies, including waking up at the ass crack of dawn to ensure they get a nice long walk before he has to leave them for the day. He feels guilty enough about how many hours they have to spend alone during the football season, the absolute least he can do is ensure they get their exercise in.

No matter how valid his reasoning is, his body still desperately wants a little more sleep, and he ends up hitting the snooze button on his alarm, pitching him back into beautiful silence. Jason's body takes the quiet as permission to go back to sleep, but that only lasts a few seconds before Freddie is whining and making the entire bed shake with the force of his butt wiggles, clearly desperate for Jason's attention. Despite the shaking of the bed, he keeps his eyes shut, eager for one more minute of rest. Jason abandons this desire when Stella jumps on top of him, giving him a face full of fur as she rolls over his head.

"You are not allowed on my face, Stella," he reminds her.

Stella barks while Freddie licks his ear. Jason takes that as his cue to let the morning begin. Stella and Freddie clearly aren't going to let him sleep any longer, which he shouldn't do anyway. Rolling out of bed, he scrubs a hand over his face while his eyes adjust to the dark and begins mentally psyching himself up for the day.

The morning passes in a blur of making coffee, taking the dogs on a quick three mile run then hurrying home to shower and have more coffee. While he chugs that down, waiting for his breakfast sandwich to reheat in the microwave, he packs his lunch, suddenly realizing he's going to need to stock up on more snacks he can throw in his bag if he doesn't want to starve to death. He ends up adding a protein shake and a green apple Gatorade to his cooler, unsure of what drinks he has in his office, along with his sandwich and fruit. Somehow he manages to get his ass out of the house shortly after seven, only five minutes past his original goal. All things considered, Jason is pretty damn proud of himself, especially since he knows the traffic around the school will be an absolute cluster fuck on the first day back.

Sure enough by the time he gets to campus the drop off line is backed up into the second lane with freshman parents trying to come in off the wrong street—almost as if they didn't read the two e-emails and the mailer the school sent out explaining which roads to use. The side lot for students is also three-quarters full, meaning anyone who tries to get to school with five minutes to spare will be screwed.

Between the chaos off the main road and normal morning traffic, it's a miracle Jason can even pull into the front lot and find his parking spot by seven-thirty. Shutting off the ignition, he grins while surveying the sight before him, teachers unloading their cars with extra supplies and students everywhere greeting friends after the summer break and waiting for a new year to begin.

There's little Jason loves more than the first day of school, ripe with reunions and new opportunities. Maybe it's because Jason absolutely loved high school, or maybe it's because he loves his job, or maybe it's just because he loves being around people, but the energy on the first day invigorates him more than his two cups of coffee.

He gets out of his truck, leaning over the back to grab his cooler when he hears shouting. Turning around, he's met with the wide-eyed face of Arlo Rosales, one of his freshman players. Arlo's a good kid, talented, but green as fuck and desperate to live up to his family's reputation. The Rosales boys are legendary, and Arlo's got no shortage of older brothers or cousins whose reputations and skills he'll constantly be compared to in the coming year. Neither of Jason's older brothers had played sports, but he'd still been unable to escape every teacher comparing him to Andrew's academic excellence or Charlie's outstanding art skills, so he can only imagine how hard it is for Arlo living in the shadow of so many family members who played before him.

"Hey, Arlo."

"Morning, Coach King," Arlo says, tapping his fingers on his backpack straps.

"You ready?" Jason asks.

Arlo tightens his grip on his straps, holding on so tightly his knuckles turn white. "Sure, Coach. I'm ready for anything."

"Are you nervous?"

"Why would I be nervous?" Arlo asks, looking like he might pass out.

"High school is a big change from middle school. My best friend had to hold my hand on the first day."

"You're lying," Arlo gapes.

"I never lie," Jason tells him seriously. "Between you and me, I don't even know why I was nervous. I'd been so excited for high school, talking it up all summer. Then we got here and I couldn't get out of the car. My older brothers drove us and they parked and I just froze. My best friend literally had to hold my hand and drag me out of the backseat."

"I don't have a best friend," Arlo says quietly.

"You will. The team is your family, Arlo. We've got your back, alright? You need anything, you tell me or one of the guys. In fact, hang on." Jason lifts his fingers and places two of them between his lips, whistling loudly. At least two dozen students turn their direction, but Jason only cares about one. He waves his arm, grinning when Matty sees him and takes off running towards them.

Beside him, Arlo remains quiet, gaze darting between Jason and Matty with unmasked shock. He can't blame him.

Matty's a senior and the star quarterback, probably even more of a legend than any of the Rosales boys. He's also poised to get scouted for a D I scholarship this year if he can keep his grades up, so it's no surprise Arlo is staring at him with wide eyes. He can't help but wonder if that's what he and Theo had been like when they both made the team freshman year.

Matty comes to a stop directly in front of them, smiling widely. "What's up, Coach?"

"Thought maybe you could make sure Arlo finds his way around campus today."

"I can find my way," Arlo protests.

"No way, man. This campus is like a maze. My freshman year I ended up in Mr. Murphy's sophomore science instead of my freshman lab," Matty laughs. "I didn't realize until class was half over."

Arlo doesn't say anything, but the hint of a smile on his face is enough.

"Come on, we'll figure out where your first class is. You can have lunch with me and the guys too." Matty throws an arm around Arlo's shoulders, pulling him towards the grassy area where a few other guys from the team are waiting for his return.

Jason watches Arlo approach the older players, relieved when he's welcomed into their fold with a few claps on the back before being pulled into their game of toss the football. Even though he suspected that's what would happen, it still feels good to see it, and Jason breathes a little easier knowing his guys will make sure that Arlo settles in. He meant what he said. The team is a family, and Jason has a zero tolerance policy for toxic behavior or bullying. He's not sure if it's that policy or he's just lucky, but his last few years of kids have been amazing. Sure, not all of them have been as close as others but there's never been an instance where anyone was left out, which is exactly what Jason wants.

With a renewed excitement for the semester ahead, Jason turns, fully prepared to head across campus to drop his lunch off in his office before his first class when he catches sight of a familiar head of red hair trudging up the steep sidewalk from the direction of the bus stop. Jason hadn't given too much thought to why Emerson was taking the bus the day before but he does now, wondering if it's by choice or not.

His musing on Emerson's choice of transportation shifts into a different kind of curiosity as he watches him drag a wheeled tote behind him while trying to balance a massive box of books, a travel tumbler and a tote bag that's slipped down to the crook of his elbow making the entire situation look mildly uncomfortable. Behind him, a student riding a skateboard stumbles over the crack in the sidewalk, slamming into Emerson's back. This sends him careening forward, his box crashing to the ground and splitting down the side causing his books to go flying in every direction while his tumbler rolls into the gutter.

Jason drops his cooler and runs, skidding to a stop beside Emerson, who looks like he's not sure if he wants to chuck his books into the gutter with his wayward drink or maybe himself.

"Sorry dude," the teenager says, picking up his skateboard then stepping over Emerson.

"Need some help?" Jason asks, squatting into a crouch.

"Why is it always you?" Emerson groans.

"Sorry," Jason apologizes, not entirely sure what he's apologizing for but sensing it might not be a good time to ask given the current circumstances.

"No, you—ugh," Emerson groans, mumbling to himself

as he starts stacking the books. "This is what I get for taking personal belongings on the bus, but my Uber had the smallest trunk ever on Saturday, so I thought, 'fine, just bring the last box on Monday on the bus. What's the worst that could happen?' The worst it turns out is that the bus was seven minutes late which might not sound like a lot, but I had a plan. A plan, Jason. Then a little kid with sticky hands touched the box and sneezed on it which is frankly disgusting. As if that wasn't bad enough, someone tried to sit on the box since it was next to me and smashed down the corner which is probably why it broke so easily."

He pauses to take a deep breath, leaving Jason to stare. That's the most words he's said since Jason met him, both times combined. He's not done either.

"I don't even know why anyone would sit next to me, especially on my box. There were plenty of available seats, and there's really nothing about me that screams come sit by me. Does my face look approachable to you?"

"Um," Jason hums. Truth be told Emerson kind of has a resting "don't talk to me" face so he has no idea how to explain why that makes Jason want to do the opposite.

Charlie always tells him he doesn't know when to quit and maybe he's right. Something about this reminds him of when Alec called him sobbing to adopt Freddie, and he'd shown up at the shelter to find out he was there to adopt a dog no one else wanted. They told him Freddie was antisocial and aggressive, clearly trying to warn him off, yet it made him want to take him home even more. In the end, Freddie turned out to be the least aggressive dog that Jason's met, but he sure as hell was terrified, and his bark had been far worse than his bite. All he'd needed was a gentle hand and a lot of love and stability. Not that Jason thinks

Emerson is a dog needing adoption, or saving. Though he could use a helping hand today.

"Ugh, forget I said that," Emerson huffs, rubbing a hand through his hair and sending it into further chaos, the thick red strands sticking out in almost every direction as if he's had his hands in it all morning. "Also this hill from the bus stop to campus is really steep, and this box was heavy, and now I'm going to be late. Late. I'm never late. I can't be late on my first day of teaching. Oh my god, what if I get fired?"

Jason blinks, both surprised and yet not, to see the spiraling. Growing up with Theo as a best friend, he's well versed in this level of anxiety. Though Theo's spiraling was usually internalized, not spoken aloud, it's easy to imagine the root feelings might be the same even if the presentation is different. He suspects Emerson might need a little reassurance and a steady hand which Jason can definitely offer.

"You won't be late," Jason promises. "Go to your class. I'll pack up all your books and bring them to you."

"I can't let you do that." Even as he protests he takes one step, eyes taking in the people around them moving towards the school. It's obvious some part of him wants to accept. Jason's eyes roam over the lines on Emerson's face, tracking the edge of anxiety that colors his features. Jason isn't sure how old he is, definitely younger than he is; he looks young enough that this might very well be his first teaching job. Jason recalls the nerves from his own first year all too well. They'd been damn near crippling that first week, and Jason isn't even an anxious person by nature.

"You can," Jason asserts. "You're part of the Santa Leon High family now. I've got you."

Emerson opens and closes his mouth several times as if unsure how to respond. Maybe Jason is a little too bossy.

His brothers have told him he can come on a little strong but he's never quite mastered the art of being less.

"Maybe." Emerson takes a deep breath, his anxiety palpable. The inexplicable urge to fix things hits Jason square in the chest. He knows he can't just take on everyone else's problems but he also can't stand seeing people suffer, especially Emerson. Something about the look in his eyes is deeply affecting.

"Go, Emerson," Jason urges.

"Then you'll be late," Emerson frowns.

"Don't worry about me," Jason says, fairly confident that he can get Emerson's books and supplies across campus without struggle and have plenty of time to spare to get to his first class. If not, then worst case scenario he's five minutes late, but he's pretty sure none of his seniors who have P.E. first thing are going to complain about an extra couple of minutes to talk to their friends while Jason sets up. "I'll leave everything outside your class so it's there when you're ready, I promise. You won't even know I came by."

"Thank you," Emerson says.

"No problem, and Emerson? The building next to the library, last door on the right," Jason reminds him.

With that last prompt, Emerson takes off in a hurry, walking up the sidewalk and towards the front of the school, leaving Jason behind with his forgotten rolling tote, tumbler and a mess of books. It really doesn't take too long for Jason to gather them all up, sparing only the briefest of glances at the novels in the box. They range from a worn copy of *The Hobbit* to a *Wrinkle In Time* and a dozen or so other novels that Jason's never heard of. He stacks them all in the box, careful of the split edge as he balances it under his arm, dragging the tote with him and retrieving his abandoned cooler bag on the way.

Most of the kids are already inside when Jason makes it to the front office just as the first bell rings.

"Not like you to be late, Jason," Mabel scoffs, sliding the teacher sign-in clipboard to the edge of the desk for him.

"Are you kidding me? I was late almost every day of senior year," Jason laughs. "Although I have rectified that since I started working here."

"Don't remind me," Mabel says with a shake of her head. "The number of tardy emails you made me write. It's amazing they hired you."

"What can I say, my winning personality was irresistible," Jason smirks, lowering the box of books onto the edge of the desk as he signs in.

Mabel peers inside the box, her keen eyes tracking the wheeled tote behind him. She doesn't get a chance to ask about it though because a parent comes in, tugging their freshman behind them which Jason takes as his cue to leave. Hurrying through the front door once more he takes a detour down the left path and rounds the corner just in time to see Emerson through the open window. He smiles to himself, glad to see he made it. He wheels the tote beside the door, carefully stacking the ripped box of books on top of it and leaving the tumbler on the ground beside it. He's only made it two steps before his own curiosity gets the best of him, and he peers inside the window, most of his form hidden behind the hanging vines of a plant.

"Welcome to freshman English 100, my name is Mr. Miller and—"

"You mean remedial English," a kid in the back snarks.

Emerson doesn't balk at the interruption, leaning back against his desk and crossing his arms. "I prefer to look at it as foundational skills. There's no shame in needing to go over things again to ensure that your understanding is as comprehensive as possible moving forward. The more you learn and understand here in my class the easier the next few years will be for you. We're going to be working on strengthening your literacy and comprehension skills while having some fun with books along the way."

Watching him now there's no signs of the anxiety that plagued him on the sidewalk not fifteen minutes ago. Physically he looks the same—wild red hair and captivating eyes —but there's something different about him when he's in front of his students. There's a confidence in him that wasn't there before, as if standing in front of a room of nearly thirty teenagers is where he's meant to be.

"Books aren't fun," someone groans.

Rather than look annoyed at the remark, Emerson actually smiles. The sight of it transforms his face, softening the sharp edges of his features into something quite striking.

"On the contrary, books are a lot of fun. Maybe you just haven't read the right ones. I'm sure you've had some teachers before who had some strict rules about what you were going to read, and while there will be assigned books this semester, we're going to branch out a bit too. I'll be filling my personal library over there with an array of books from manga and comics to fantasy and everything in between. I've also spoken to the librarian about hopefully expanding the audiobook selection for you guys and—" Emerson pauses when a hand goes up at the front of the classroom.

"Yes?"

"My grandma said audiobooks don't count as reading."

"Well, your grandma is wrong," Emerson replies. "All books are reading."

He says it in a way that leaves no room for argument, as if it's just a fact.

"If there are no more questions, we're going to go around the room and introduce ourselves. I'm pretty terrible with names, so I'm going to need you all to give me one unique fact about yourself to help me out. Think you can do that?"

There's a chorus of replies, but Jason is prevented from further eavesdropping by the two-minute warning bell ringing. It's a stark reminder of exactly where he is and what he's doing—spying on Emerson while his own students are waiting for him.

With quickened steps, he jogs across campus to get to his own class, sending thoughts of Emerson into the background.

CASE OF BEER in one hand and two pizzas poised under the other, Jason kicks at the front door with his sneaker. When there's no immediate answer, he does it again harder. He waits a minute or so before sighing, shifting the case of beer onto the top of the pizza boxes so he can knock on the front door with three firm, swift raps of his knuckle.

"You two better not be fucking," Jason yells. He waits a solid thirty seconds before another knock, at which point he raises his voice enough to be heard through the door. "If you don't answer the door in two more minutes, I'm using my key to get in. But fair warning, if I have to see anyone's pasty ass again, I'll fucking riot."

"My ass isn't pasty," Alec replies, opening the front door with a sly grin. Considering he's wearing nothing but his boxers and one of Theo's sweaters, Jason chooses not to analyze his expression. Then again, looking like the cat that ate the canary has become Alec's default look lately, and after his traumatic car accident last year, it's a sight for sore eyes, even if the reason for it is something he prefers not to think about. Those first few months after he got hurt were rough.

Along with the return of his smile as he healed was the return of his sass, something which seems to have magnified tenfold since Theo proposed. He's absolutely insufferable and Jason kind of loves it, willing to endure anything if it means his baby brother is safe and happy. Not that he will say that out loud. Alec's incorrigible enough as it is.

"Your ass on the other hand," Alec says with an insufferable tone. "Well, let's just say you got Mom's complexion. Your ass is so pale it makes the moon hide."

Alec isn't wrong. While Alec got their mom's freckles and curly hair, he'd taken after their dad and *abuela* in complexion like the twins had. Between the four of them, Jason's always been the one who was the most white-passing and in turn who took all the ribbing for how sunburned he'd get in the summer while his brothers simply turned a sun-kissed brown.

"You're just salty because I took all the height genes," Jason retorts, falling back on his favorite insult.

"Fuck off," Alec huffs, making a show of grumbling as he throws his arms around Jason in a hug.

"I love you too," Jason grins, unable to resist annoying Alec by messing up his curls.

"You fucking—" Alec starts, only to be interrupted by Theo stumbling out of the hallway wearing noticeably more clothing than Alec is. He smooths the front of his sweater down before offering Jason a bashful smile.

"Sorry, we were um, making the bed."

"Making the bed," Alec echoes. "That's a good one. I like that. I'm going to use that on Mom and Dad next time they come over for dinner and get here early like they did last month."

"Only if you want them to spontaneously combust," Jason snorts.

"Please," Alec scoffs. "Mom and Dad know me and Theo have fucked."

"We all know you and Theo fuck, that doesn't mean we need to be reminded so often." Jason arches an eyebrow, unsurprised when Alec's smile merely widens. At least Theo has the decency to appear abashed. "Now move your scrawny ass out of the way so we can get this pizza night started."

"Alright, cranky pants. We all know you get hangry," Alec says, moving out of the doorway before scooping up Rio who immediately lays herself across Alec's chest and purrs loudly. The only other cats Jason has been around for any length of time are Charlie's, which isn't much to go by since his outdoor cats are two of the most antisocial little fuckers he's ever met and his nearly blind senior cat doesnt like anyone but Alec or Charlie. He had no idea a cat could be as clingy and affectionate as Rio. Or at least, she is with Alec. She mostly just tolerates everyone else.

"I'm not hangry," Jason protests, but the grumble of his voice betrays the truth. He had lunch at eleven forty-five and then got so busy with classes and practice that he hasn't eaten since. Unless you count the bag of trail mix Jason got out of the vending machine at two, which he doesn't. That's a tasty little treat, not something to sustain a man who weighs two-hundred fifty pounds.

"Let the man sit down," Theo laughs, dropping a kiss to the top of Alec's head on his way to the sofa. He lowers himself into the corner while Jason sets the food and beer on the coffee table before plopping in the center of the couch. It's amazing to think this is the same house that used to be mostly barren aside from Theo's prized—and in Jason's opinion hideous—rug and his never ending stash of beverages in every room.

Gone is the bachelor pad vibe, now replaced with new signs of life, and of Alec, everywhere. Glancing around, he can't help but notice all the little ways it's changed over the last few months. Alec's extensive sneaker collection lines the shoe rack by the door, a half-drunk can of Coke sits on the coffee table along with a stack of his textbooks, and there are several pencils, all chewed up at the ends, on the edge of the TV console. Most noticeable of all, there are photos on the mantle and walls, not just of Alec and Theo but of the entire King family, Jason especially. One of him and Theo when they were in first grade, a few from high school and even a new one on the end table from Alec's birthday last month.

"That's new," Jason notes, pointing out the frame on the end table. Even after watching photo after photo appear once Alec moved in, Jason still isn't used to seeing them displayed. Theo never once put out a single photo before, almost as if acknowledging the Kings were his family might somehow make it too real—make it something he could lose.

"It was Alec's idea," Theo offers, because of course it was. Alec didn't just fill their house with photos of him and Theo, he filled it with all the people who love Theo. Hell, there are more photos of Jason and Theo together than with Alec, and knowing that Alec did that—made sure to remind Theo with tangible proof he'd never lose Jason—means more than he will ever be able to explain.

"Of course it was," Alec smirks, dropping into Theo's lap. "I'm a fucking genius. Should've gone into interior decorating but no, I had to decide to switch my major and go for a doctorate of physical therapy, and now I'm going to be in school until I die. Unless I expire from studying first, which is a definite possibility."

"If it's that bad, why did you pick that major again?" Jason asks, still not entirely sure he understands.

Alec shrugs. "I had some really good physical therapists after my accident, and I thought it might be nice to find a way to help other athletes remember they can have a life after an accident too, you know? That they're more than just their sport. It's easy when you push your body that hard to think that's all you are, and I just want to help. Instead, I'm going to die from studying too much."

"You won't die," Theo assures him.

"We don't know that yet, the semester only started this week. Speaking of the new semester," Alec sighs, lowering Rio to the ground before standing up. "I'm going to get started on some reading. I'll leave you two boys alone, don't get into too much trouble without me."

Theo's grin is wide when he seeks out Alec's face, that smile widening further when Alec gives him a quick kiss on the cheek before meandering into the kitchen. Jason feels a renewed appreciation for his brother. He loved him before, but seeing the way Alec treats Theo—how deeply happy he makes him—well it's impossible not to love him even more.

There's nothing in the world that makes Jason happier than when the people he loves are happy.

"So," Theo says, grabbing a paper plate off the top of the pizza box. "I was a little worried you might not make pizza night this week. I know once the semester starts it's harder."

"Don't remind me. Between classes and practice, this week has been grueling, but the first game isn't until next week, and I was feeling—" Jason pauses, trying to articulate it. He's never been great at parsing his own emotions. He can tell when his friends and family need something but when it comes to himself, it's more of a vague blob inside his chest most of the time. If he's not happy, which he usually is, it's kind of hard to make sense of it all. "I dunno."

"You know nothing will change now that me and Alec are getting married, right? If that's been on your mind." Theo piles a plate with several slices of pizza before passing it to Jason. "You're always going to be my best friend, and this is always going to be your second home."

Jason takes too big a bite of pizza, nodding with his mouth full. He does know that, so he's not sure what the unsettled feeling in his chest is, the one demanding he come visit Theo despite being exhausted after a full week of teaching and coaching. He'd stopped at his place to feed his dogs and take them for a walk but then came here immediately after.

"So," Theo continues, clearly picking up on Jason's disinterest in talking about himself. "How was the first week of classes?"

"Good," Jason answers, popping open the can of his beer and gulping down enough to parch his thirst. "I've got a mix of grades this year, so it'll be good to get a feel for all of them. A lot of the kids I've taught before, which is nice because then I know what they need, you know?"

"And the teachers? Caldwell still have a stick up his ass?"

"Fucking Caldwell," Jason grumbles, frowning at the name alone. He'd been Theo and Jason's senior English teacher and had made no secret of how much he disliked the football team when they were in school, a feeling which he apparently extends to football coaches. "He was a dick when we went there, and he's still a dick now. Sometimes I wonder why he still has a job. Part of me thought he'd be nicer once I started teaching, but I swear every year that passes gets worse. He hates me. No one hates me, Theo."

"To be fair, I think Caldwell hates everyone."

Jason hums, knowing Theo is right but disliking it all the same. Rather than linger on Caldwell, his mind supplies him thoughts of someone else entirely. "There is one new teacher though."

"He a dick too?" Theo asks.

"Nah," Jason shakes his head. "He's—interesting. Name's Mr. Miller."

Theo sits up straighter. "Interesting how?"

"I don't know. He's pretty for a guy." Jason shrugs, thinking about Emerson's distinctive hair and delicate features. He's the kind of guy Jason might have pointed out to Theo in a club if he were still single. He glances over his shoulder to see Alec leaning over the kitchen island with his head buried in a text book, his headphones on and his pencil tapping a mile a minute. He's pretty sure Alec can't hear him, but he's not willing to risk being murdered for voicing that thought out loud. "He was kind of a mess in an endearing way."

"Damn, first day and you've already found a stray."

"Emerson isn't a stray," Jason protests.

"Oh it's Emerson and not Mr. Miller?" Theo arches an eyebrow and Jason curses. This is the downside to having the same best friend for over two decades. They notice everything. Even when there's nothing to notice.

"Look, he was having a rough time, and I helped him out, and that's that. I think he's gonna be a good fit at the school," he says, thinking of the little bit he overheard from Emerson's first class. "We need more teachers like him. That's all. I just wanna make sure he finds his place here. For the school."

"For the school," Theo echoes, something unreadable in expression.

"Exactly," Jason grins, something in him settling. This was a good idea. Pizza, beer, and bestie time definitely cure all. His year is going to be great, and maybe he can make sure Emerson's will be too. For the students, and the school of course. Not for any other reason at all.

5 EMERSON

EMERSON'S DAY is not off to a good start.

For the sixth time in the last two weeks his bus is late. It wouldn't be such a big deal if Emerson were capable of handling being late to things but he's not, especially when he has no idea if the bus is going to be two minutes late or ten. Last Friday he tried taking the earlier bus to the school to avoid this happening, but it turned out that losing almost an hour of his morning to catch a different bus threw his entire routine off so badly that Emerson had wanted to cry. He hadn't because he doesn't cry every time he's out of sorts anymore like he did as a kid. Instead, he had gone through half a bag of Warheads to try and combat the rising deregulation, because he read a tip online once that sour candy helped with anxiety. Unfortunately all the Warheads did were make him mildly nauseous, which only increased his anxiety.

After that day, he realized he shouldn't take the earlier bus to campus since he can't handle a full day of teaching without having a little quiet time in the morning to wake up slowly. He likes to roll over and read his kindle in bed for twenty minutes before puttering to his kitchen and putting on the kettle. While he waits for the water to boil, he takes a very quick shower and by the time he's out the water is ready. While his tea brews, he makes two Eggo waffles, eating them one-handed while he packs his lunch. Always the same—a plain peanut butter sandwich on white bread, a container of Ranch Doritos—never a baggie because who wants broken chips—and a banana. This has been Emerson's morning since he started student teaching and deviating from it, while not impossible, is not preferred. It took him a long time to find a routine that helps him start his day regulated and calm.

Unfortunately, this morning he is not feeling remotely calm. He got to the bus stop at the time he was supposed to, yet ten minutes later the damn bus still isn't here. Emerson was raised in a big city, and while he much prefers the picturesque landscape of Santa Leon to his hometown, the one thing he sorely misses is more reliable public transport.

With a heavy sigh, Emerson looks at his watch. He set a stopwatch when it hit 7:15am, and it's been six minutes. So far there has been no rhyme or reason or discernable pattern to the days the bus is late or amount of time it deviates. Once it was one minute, another time was fourteen minutes. It makes Emerson's insides churn uncomfortably. He dislikes unpredictability.

Why are you always so difficult? Why can't you be more flexible? Why can't you relax like your cousin?

Emerson clears his throat, pushing his aunt and uncle's voices from his head. He'd hoped putting some physical distance between them might also put up a mental one, but so far that's not been the case. Growing up, they made no secret of how much they wished he was more like his cousin Landon. Even after his autism diagnosis in high school, they'd struggled to accept and accommodate the way his brain worked. They were of the mentality that everything could be overcome with hard work and a positive attitude. They were so sure he could be different if he just tried harder or wanted it more—so sure he could be like Landon, who was easygoing and successful. It didn't matter that he was also a massive asshole; he was charming and friendly enough when he wanted to be that everyone turned a blind eye, including his parents. Landon was their baby boy and the light of their life, and they stoutly refused to believe he could be a bully. Then again, they didn't see any problem with their own behavior either, so maybe it wasn't so surprising.

As a kid, he'd been told he should be grateful his aunt and uncle took him in when he had nowhere to go, but the older he's gotten the more aware he is that he shouldn't have had to mask everything just to have a home. Emerson was thirteen when he realized that's why his mom never lived close to her brother, why they only talked on holidays. They didn't understand Emerson, and they'd clearly never understood her, not in life or in death.

Thinking about his mom makes his eyes water, and Emerson breathes the salty scent of sea in the air through his nose, his throat tight. He thought coming here might bring peace but so far all it's done is make him feel like the inside of a snow globe someone won't stop shaking. When he was five, his kindergarten class had a field trip to the zoo. His mom handed him a ziploc bag with a small stack of crumpled one dollar bills from her waitressing job, whispered '*have fun and don't let them make you feel bad*' before she dropped him off in front of the school to go to work. He used the money to buy a plastic snow globe with little monkeys and tigers on it, shaking it up hard so all the glitter would float through the water. He cried so hard when it broke a few months later, glitter clinging to his small hands and his mom's lips pressed to the top of his head promising it would be okay. The next day there'd been a new snow globe on the table when he got home from school. If his mom wasn't hungry for dinner that week, he hadn't noticed because he'd been too happy with his gift.

Emerson sighs again, scrubbing his hands over his face before looking at his watch for what feels like the millionth time. If the bus doesn't get here in the next two minutes, he's going to end up being late for work, a possibility he doesn't want to think about.

"You need a ride?"

Emerson jerks his head up at the question, surprised to see a familiar face. Emerson has maybe, possibly, gone out of his way to avoid said face. Because it's very distracting to be thinking about how handsome someone is, and wondering why they're being nice to him while trying to focus on being a functioning adult. And also because he's unequivocally certain that if Jason got to know him, he would get annoyed with him the way Emerson's family always did. That's why it's easier to just stay away from people. Especially people like Jason who are handsome and friendly and well-liked by everyone.

"I'm just waiting for the bus," Emerson announces with more confidence than he feels.

Jason turns to look out the window before returning his gaze to Emerson. "I don't see the bus. This route can be kind of unreliable. We get a lot of kids marked tardy because of it. The principal has been emailing the city about it but—" he stops and shrugs. "Anyway, we're obviously going the same way, so you might as well let me give you a ride to school."

"Why are you smiling?" Emerson asks, unable to stop himself.

"Why not?" Jason counters with another easy smile.

Emerson can't imagine smiling so much for no discernible reason. He can't deny the smile looks good on Jason though, natural even. As natural as Emerson's resting frowny face. Growing up, he'd been chastised more times than he can count for looking mad or ungrateful, even though he hadn't even felt those things. He learned how to smile on command, but it takes a lot of effort. Somehow, Jason makes it look natural, the lines at the corners of his eyes and the deep dimple in his chin making it appear as if his smile is actually meant to be there. Between his rich brown eyes and striking black hair, he's handsome in the most devastating way. The kind of way that reminds Emerson he's never been on a date, or kissed someone and probably never will. It's impossible to do those things when you can't relax enough around someone to even be friends. He supposes some people kiss and date, or even have sex, without that component but it's not something Emerson is interested in. He spends enough time masking in his day-to-day life, he's never wanted to do it during more intimate moments too. Even when that means it robs him of opportunities.

"Emerson?" Jason prompts, his smile unwavering. "Can I give you a ride?"

Given his past experience with jocks, namely Landon, his first instinct is to say no, but Emerson bites the response back. Breathing in slowly and deeply, Emerson tries to approach the offer with logic. It seems impossible that Jason is as nice as he seems, especially being a football coach. Jocks aren't this nice. That's not even touching how attractive Jason is or the fact that in the two weeks since Emerson started teaching he's come to learn that he is, without question, the favorite teacher at Santa Leon High. Even if it wasn't verified by the award he won the last two years—displayed in the gym according to one of his students—it'd be easy to see from the way students and staff talk about him.

Even avoiding Jason's side of the school, there's been no escaping his presence. Something Emerson definitely tried, if only to take a moment to shield against making a fool of himself in front of the unequivocal star at his new school. He thought becoming a teacher might free him from the unfavorable social dynamics of his past. Yet there's no escaping the popularity chains and friendship groups he is not a part of. All that taken into consideration, there is literally no reason for Jason to be offering him a ride unless he feels sorry for Emerson. Which, well, sucks because Emerson hates when people pity him or assume he's not capable of things just because he needs different accommodations. There's no place for Emerson's wounded pride today unless he wants to be late, and the last thing he needs is to look unreliable at work.

"Alright," Emerson says, fighting his instincts screaming at him. "You can give me a ride."

There's no reason for Jason's smile to widen but it does, his large body tipping sideways so he can swing the door open. The only thing worse than developing a crush on someone popular and easy to like, is developing a crush on someone who is most likely straight. Pushing those thoughts aside, he walks to the truck and opens the door, surprised when Jason holds a hand out for his bag.

"I can do it myself," Emerson points out.

"Now what kind of gentleman would I be if I didn't help?" Jason asks with a wink, taking Emerson's bag and setting it in his backseat while Emerson hefts himself into the truck.

Emerson wants to point out that Jason doesn't need to keep helping him, but that seems ungrateful and also pointedly untrue given that he, in fact, needed his help on more than one occasion already. Sighing heavily, he reaches for his ring and realizes it's not there. He always puts it on before his shoes, but one of his neighbors had knocked on his door this morning looking for their lost cat, and he'd been so worried about being late after being unsure how to get out of the conversation, he'd hurried from his apartment apparently without his ring.

A knot forms in the pit of his stomach. He always wears it. Always.

"You alright?" Jason asks, waiting until Emerson buckles his seatbelt before merging into the busy morning traffic.

Emerson has enough experience with neurotypical conversations to be aware this is probably one of those times where someone is asking him a question they don't really want the answer to. The thing a lot of people fail to understand about Emerson is that he's perfectly capable of reading social situations, sometimes. He just doesn't understand the logic in the frequently arbitrary rules and therefore often can't bring himself to follow them.

"No," he answers. "I forgot my ring, and I always wear it, and now I won't have anything to fidget with, and it's going to throw off my entire day."

"Do you want me to turn around so you can go back and get it?" Jason asks, already tapping the brakes as if to slow down and make a u-turn at the next intersection.

"No," Emerson answers because the prospect of being late is worse than not having his ring.

"I'm afraid I don't have any rings, but—" Jason pauses, opening the center console. Inside is an array of brightly colored fidgets: a puzzle ball, a spinner, a little tub of thera-putty and a couple squish balls.

"Why do you have all this?" Emerson asks.

"Alec," Jason answers, resettling his eyes on the road. Whether that's because of the increased traffic in front of the school or to afford Emerson a moment to search the little treasure trove in his truck, he has no idea. Usually he prefers no one noticing him, but Jason's manner of picking up on something being wrong isn't to point it out in a cruel way or correct him, and that's kind of, well—nice.

"Who is Alec?" Emerson blurts. It's possible Jason was going to offer up that information next, but Emerson tends to lack impulse control when curious.

"My baby brother. Well, twenty-two last month, so he'd probably kick my ass for calling him a baby, which naturally means I gotta do it as often as possible." A solid laugh rumbles out of Jason's chest but it's fleeting. "He uh, had a pretty nasty car accident last year. Needed a lot of physical therapy and doctor's appointments. Me and the twins—"

"What twins?"

"My older brothers," Jason offers, seemingly unbothered by being interrupted yet again.

"How many do you have?" Emerson asks. He might've been raised with his cousin for half his life but he certainly never felt like Emerson's sibling. At least not one he wanted. He wonders if Jason is close to his siblings. From the way he talks, it seems like he must be, but then everyone probably likes Jason. Emerson doesn't have that kind of amiable personality, unfortunately.

"Three, well four, if you count Theo but that's kind of a grey area since he's marrying Alec."

"Your brother is marrying your brother?"

There's an awkward moment of silence during which Emerson worries that his tendency to interrupt people when he has a question, or his brusk mode of asking those questions, might have rubbed Jason the wrong way. Thankfully the moment passes when Jason's booming laughter fills the cab of the truck while he pulls into a parking spot then shuts off the engine.

"Holy fuck, no," Jason snorts. "But also, yes I guess, but also no."

"I'm so confused," Emerson mumbles, settling on one of the squishy stress balls. He wraps his fingers around it, focusing on the give of silicone beneath his fingers and the resistance each time he squeezes. It relaxes some of his tension, affording him something else to focus on while Jason tries to stop laughing.

"You know what, how about I explain over lunch?"

"Lunch," Emerson repeats.

"Sure. The whole twins slash Theo slash Alec story. It's a great one. Lots of drama and pining and intrigue. Hell, it could be a book."

"I—I like books," Emerson says, unsure what to make of the flutter in his chest when Jason directs his smile at Emerson.

"Good, then we'll have lunch together. Where do you usually eat anyway? I haven't seen you around the teacher's lounge or the cafeteria."

"Were you looking for me?" Emerson gapes.

"Well sure," Jason answers easily. "We hit it off so well that first day."

All Emerson can do is blink. They hit it off? That's certainly news to him. He'd liked Jason well enough, in the way you like a complete stranger seeing you at your worst when you don't really like anyone. He supposes he likes him more this morning than he did before. Probably not something he should voice out loud, though.

"Anyway," Jason continues, saving Emerson from having to figure out how to continue the conversation. "I usually have an open door lunch in my office for the kids on Fridays but the LGBTQIA+ club and the football team, which are the kids who usually come by, are busy. There's some kind of last minute meeting. I saw the notification in my group chat with Stevie who heads the club. Have you met Stevie? He's great; he teaches sophomore algebra. Anyway, my assistant coach is running some plays by my guys after lunch since we've got our first game tonight which means my office is all free."

Emerson sits up straighter. The head football coach and PE teacher at Santa Leon high hosts some of the LGBTQIA+ club in his office with the football players? Emerson has never heard of anything like it. At his old school there hadn't even been any kind of queer club, and the kids who were openly queer, like Emerson, were absolutely never allowed to associate with the jocks.

"That is, if you'd like to join me. We could have lunch in the cafeteria if you'd rather but—" Jason stops, his lips curling up at the corners. "I'll take it that's a no."

"Was my face answering before my mouth again?" Emerson asks with a sigh. No one was ever able to train him out of that. Turns out, he can't force the socially acceptable expressions onto his face when he is supposed to, or keep the unacceptable ones off his face either. His entire personality is like one of those giant orange traffic cones, no one can look away from but everyone avoids.

"It was," Jason laughs. "To be fair, the cafeteria is pretty fucking loud. I think I've got some Loops in the center console, which Andrew left, but you're welcome to borrow them if you want. Honestly it's not my favorite place to eat though. I usually make an appearance once a week because the kids like it. And my freshman players especially need the morale boost, but once the semester goes on, I'm usually free to eat in the teacher's lounge or in my office in peace."

"Except Fridays," Emerson notes.

"Except Fridays," Jason agrees.

"Why?" Emerson questions.

"Meet me in my office for lunch and I'll tell you," Jason says as if trying to entice him. As if he wants Emerson to be there. It makes absolutely no sense. Jason King makes no sense.

Normally, Emerson hates things that make no sense, but something about Jason feels less irrationally annoying and more like a puzzle he eagerly wants to piece together.

"I could do lunch," Emerson says.

"Great, I'll see you—"

"Coach," someone shouts, hitting the front of Jason's car with a football. Emerson jumps a foot, but Jason just laughs, high tailing it out of his truck and grabbing the ball, throwing it all the way across the quad and back to the group of players in the grassy area. One of them, the blond kid who'd interrupted them that first time, makes a perfect catch leading to a series of catcalls and hoots as the players cheer—whether for Jason or their own, Emerson has no idea. But he suddenly feels far less like he belongs here than he did when it was just him and Jason hidden away in the cab of his truck.

"Sorry about that." Jason runs a hand through his hair. "So lunch, you know where my office is? You know what never mind, of course you don't. I'll meet you at your classroom and walk you there. Don't leave without me, alright?"

Standing in a sea of students, people still calling Jason's name while the first bell rings in the background, all Emerson can do is nod.

"See you later," Jason grins, leaving Emerson alone with his confused thoughts and a strange warmth in his chest at the memory of two dimples and warm brown eyes.

AT EXACTLY TWELVE there's a knock on Emerson's door. It's open but Jason knocks anyway, giving Emerson that little bit of warning before filling the doorway with his bulk. Like this morning, there's an easy smile on his face as he leans against the door jamb, crossing his arms over his chest. He's wearing a Santa Leon High football shirt that stretches just this side of too tight across his chest and a pair of basketball shorts.

"You ready, Mr. Miller?"

"Oh no, you can't call me that," Emerson blurts with a firm shake of his head. He grabs his lunch bag off the floor under his desk, crossing the room. It's not until he's standing in front of Jason that he realizes how abrupt he was. "I mean, uh, please don't."

"No, Mr. Miller?" Jason asks, taking a step back from the doorway so Emerson can sneak through. His expression is hard to read, his eyes studying Emerson, though for what he can't fathom. "Just Emerson then?"

He nods, unsure how to explain that Mr. Miller is reserved for the students and class time. This is lunch time, and his brain delineates that very differently. If the principal or someone else from the district who was technically his boss called him Mr. Miller, he's not sure he'd care because that would make sense but Jason is, well, not his boss.

"I know it's weird," Emerson mumbles.

"Not weird," Jason shrugs. "Do all your friends just call you Emerson then?"

"Why?" Emerson asks, eyes darting between the line of Jason's jaw and the stray students running late to lunch. None of them seem to be paying nearly as much attention to him or Jason as he is to them so he tries to relax. In his classroom it's easy to fill his role, but once he steps into the hallways with all those teenagers, especially ones who aren't his students, the little safe lines his brain has drawn are less sturdy.

"Just want to make sure I call you what you like."

The thoughtfulness catches Emerson off guard, and he has no idea what to do with the rush of feelings swirling inside him. If Jason is like this with everyone, and he must be because Emerson is nothing special, then it's easy to see why he's so beloved.

"What, uh, what do your friends call you?" Emerson asks rather than answer that his own friends don't call him anything because he doesn't have any.

"Usually just Jason, but I had a handful of nicknames in high school which—we do not need to go into. Do me a favor and don't ever ask my brothers, especially Andrew. He's got a memory like a fucking hawk."

There isn't a single scenario Emerson can imagine where he might talk to one of Jason's brothers, but he keeps that thought to himself. There's something reassuring about the way Jason just offers up tidbits and future scenarios like he simply assumes he and Emerson are going to continue being friends, and this isn't some kind of strange forced social nicety between coworkers. Even if it is, even if Jason is this nice to all his coworkers, it's still the closest thing to a friend Emerson has had since, well, ever.

"Everyone just calls me Emerson, you know, back—" he pauses, unable to call it home. It was never home. There was no home after his mom died. Only family that didn't really want him and a place he never fit. "Where I'm from. I don't think I ever had a nickname."

"You never had a nickname?" Jason echoes, stopping in his tracks. He turns to face Emerson, genuine surprise written across his face.

"Um, no? Unless you count like mean ones but I don't think you meant that kind."

Jason's smile fades swiftly. "I fucking hate bullies."

"Yeah," Emerson mumbles, not sure why he said that out loud. He hadn't planned to. Jason probably didn't wanna know that, and more to the point, Emerson doesn't want to remember how unkind kids had been, how unkind his own cousin had been.

"This means we're starting at ground zero," Jason says. "Just so we're on the same page, how do you feel about nicknames?"

While Emerson's brain attempts to process the question, the rest of his body hones in on the warmth at his lower back. It takes Emerson a few seconds to realize that warmth is coming from Jason's large hand, placed there to make sure Emerson doesn't take the wrong path when the walkway ahead of them splits, something he's embarrassed to admit he was about to do. There was definitely a question he's supposed to be figuring out an answer to, but all Emerson's brain is capable of doing is focusing on the way he can feel that touch through the cotton of his shirt, on how unexpectedly safe it feels to know Jason isn't letting him get lost or berating him for almost going the wrong way, like a lot of people would have.

Without preamble or words, he's ensured Emerson takes the right path.

"Down this way," Jason announces, hand lingering.

Emerson can't remember the last time someone touched him. His aunt and uncle weren't affectionate, and his cousin only touched him to shove him out of the way or mess up his hair, the kind of touches meant to irritate Emerson, not soothe. Back in high school, Landon spread a rumor about Emerson that he had some kind of venereal disease, as if desperate to ensure that no one would ever go near Emerson. Not that he'd needed to, people have never flocked to be his friend, or date him.

When Jason removes his hand a few seconds later, Emerson feels the absence acutely. It's pathetic how desperate his body is for a bit of touch that's not demanding or forced.

"So nicknames?" Jason prompts. He doesn't look annoyed or frustrated about having to draw Emerson's attention back to the conversation and that too soothes something in Emerson, so used to feeling a step out of line with other people in conversations. So often he has to work extra hard at thinking ahead for how to answer, or practicing the right amount of eye contact, or getting distracted by other thoughts that he ends up losing the thread of conversation. Other times he gets too excited and dominates, forgetting to let the other person talk, though this is rare, since Emerson learned to tamp down his desire to info-dump and keeps most of his thoughts safely inside his own head.

Only, when Jason offers him an easy smile, Emerson

forgets why it's safer to keep his truths hidden and answers honestly. "I don't know how I feel about them to be honest."

"Guess we'll have to find out, eh, Red."

Emerson scrunches up his nose, earning him one of Jason's laughs. "Alright, not Red. First option knocked out. Came up with that one on the fly. Give me some time to think, and I'll come up with something better."

"You don't have to," Emerson points out.

"I know," Jason says, "but I want to. Unless you don't want me to."

He's so used to telling people what they want to hear, it's a little startling to realize that he doesn't feel that way with Jason. Somehow, despite barely knowing him, he doesn't feel like he needs to lie. Maybe it's the fact that Jason has already seen him at his worst more than once, or maybe it's that he offered him fidgets and seems to care what he wants to be called, or maybe it's that talking to Jason doesn't feel exhausting like it does with other people. Whatever the reason, something about Jason makes him want things he's never ever let himself want before. He knows he can't have them, not with Jason, but maybe if he tried, friendship might be on the table.

"You could, um, try," Emerson hedges. He twists his fingers, hoping he doesn't look quite as nervous as he feels. "If it makes you happy."

"You're a good sport, Emerson." Jason swings an arm around his shoulder, about to say something when he pulls back. "Shit, sorry. I'm kind of...a touchy guy. You might've noticed, but that doesn't mean it's okay to do it without permission. Maybe you hate being touched or something."

"I don't hate being touched," Emerson mumbles.

"No? Good." Jason reaches out again, and though he doesn't loop his arm all the way around Emerson's shoulder again, he does give it a squeeze. The touch is fleeting but firm. It's a deep pressure that has Emerson exhaling the ball of tension in his chest. "Here's me. My office is through the gym in the back corner."

"You can fit all the kids in there?"

"Nah, usually I just pull out a bunch of gym mats, and people eat there or sit on the bleachers. Sometimes it's only one or two kids, other times it's two dozen. That gets loud which I don't mind as much as when they steal my chips."

"I don't want anyone to steal my Doritos," Emerson snaps, tightening his grip on his lunch bag. Landon always stole his food, even though he would eat anything, because it gave him some kind of power trip to take the few safe foods Emerson had. He can recognize that he's maybe a little defensive about the prospect, but there's no taking that little outburst back now. Thankfully, Jason seems unfazed by it.

"Luckily there's no students in here today, but I promise if a time comes where someone tries to steal your Doritos—" Jason interrupts that thought with his next question. "What kind do you have anyway?"

"Ranch," Emerson answers softly, unable to take his eyes off Jason's expressive face. Maybe that's part of what makes him easy to be around. His expressions and moods are so exaggerated that Emerson finds him easy to read, a far cry from how he feels around most people.

"Solid fucking choice," Jason replies.

"Is there a choice you wouldn't like?" Emerson asks, sensing that Jason might be happy with anything and everything.

"Not really," Jason answers, confirming his suspicions with a smile so over the top that Emerson can't help but return it. It is perhaps the first genuine smile he's experienced since moving to Santa Leon. He's gotten so used to masking, to pretending to have everything together all the time so no one questions what he can handle, that he forgot what it felt like to be relaxed and happy.

"So, you wanna eat in my office or out in the gym?" Jason asks.

Emerson looks around, slightly overwhelmed by the massive room with its echoing acoustics and too many windows. Gym was kind of a nightmare for him in high school on so many levels, and while he's not a student any longer, he's still not sure he's up for this place yet. "Your office."

"Office it is," Jason says, taking a step forward. "Follow me."

Emerson does, trailing after Jason towards the corner of the gym where there's a door tucked just off to the side behind a metal cage filled with basketballs. Jason reaches for the door handle, drawing Emerson's attention to the rainbow sticker with the words *'you are safe here'* stuck there at eye level where no one can miss it.

Safe.

What an elusive yet desired promise. So few things in Emerson's life—places, people, food—are ever truly safe. To some people, it's probably nothing more than a sticker, but for Emerson it's so much more. He reads it again, the tightness he carries inside loosening imperceptibly.

Stepping inside Jason's office reveals a room, both in size and design, much like he might have expected. There's a desk with two chairs in front of it and the wall behind it adorned with Jason's degrees and various trophies and awards from coaching. That's where the expected ends. Opposite Jason's desk are more awards and trophies, but the surprising thing is what's above them, the upper half of the wall covered in pride flags. The kind Emerson never got to see growing up. The kind that would've made him feel so much safer if anyone at his old school had one. The kind that makes it clear the sticker on Jason's office door isn't there by accident or for show.

Everything about Jason is a dichotomy. His job as the physical education teacher and head coach along with his very visible jock aesthetic would indicate someone cocky and domineering, yet there's a gentleness in his demeanor that is entirely unexpected. Jason has an easy countenance that is at odds with everything Emerson has ever known about jocks and now this. Is he queer too? Or an ally? It shouldn't matter, but Emerson desperately wants to understand.

"That's a lot of flags," Emerson says, unsure how else to broach the conversation.

"I wanted to get one of each, but I ran out of wall space, you know? I got as many as I could though. My younger brother Alec helped me pick them out. That's him here," Jason says, stepping around Emerson and pointing to a photo of Jason with what he can only assume is his family. He taps his finger against the picture, pointing out the youngest person there, someone with a freckle faced smile and unruly curls. He couldn't look more different than Jason aside from their wide smiles. "Then these two handsome assholes are my older brothers—that's Charlie on the left and Andrew on the right. Twins, obviously. And then there are my parents between us and here next to Alec is Theo."

"Theo is the uh, the one dating your brother?" Emerson says, hoping he got it right.

"Yup," Jason confirms. "Weird as hell at first, partly because Alec is the baby of the family and had never actually dated anyone but also because Theo's been my best friend since we were seven, so just meshing those together took awhile for my brain to handle. But you know how it is."

Emerson does not in fact, have any idea how it is, but he stays quiet while Jason hums to himself, squatting down to open a small fridge next to the bookshelf. He pulls out a foil wrapped sandwich, a can of Coke and two containers of what appears to be butter spread. Confused, he watches Jason set them both down beside his sandwich along with the can of soda. Unable to bite his tongue at what he's seeing, Emerson leans forward, elbows on his knees.

"Are you eating butter for lunch?" he asks.

"Butter," Jason echoes, looking down at the desk before laughing. Jason peels back the plastic lid to reveal the contents inside, bright green grapes in one and chunks of cut up honeydew melon in the other. "No butter here. Just fruit."

"Oh," Emerson says, feeling a little silly and a lot embarrassed.

"My *abuela* and dad did it, so now me and my brothers all do it too. Even though it drives my mom nuts when she's looking for actual butter and all she finds is leftover rice or fruit. But it's a waste to throw away perfectly good containers, you know?"

"Sure," Emerson agrees, unable to stop thinking about Theo and Jason's brother. He's never had a brother or a best friend, but if he did, he's not sure he'd want them dating. It feels messy, and Emerson doesn't like messy things. "Does it bother you?"

"Does what bother me?" Jason asks, holding out the container of grapes to Emerson, who does not actually like grapes but isn't sure if it would be rude to say no. He accepts one, almost putting it in his mouth to be polite then feeling revulsion rise at the idea of the skin on the grapes in his mouth. He ends up passing it back and forth between his fingers.

"Your uh, your brother and your friend dating." At this point, Emerson isn't sure if it's rude to bring the conversation back up but he's curious, and also very bad at small talk. Turning it around on Jason is so much safer than having him ask Emerson questions about himself, questions that he probably wouldn't know how to answer without being too honest or lying, both of which are apparently socially unacceptable.

"It did at first. A little bit. Or a lot if I'm being honest." Jason drops down into one of the chairs, using his foot to not at all subtly turn the other chair towards Emerson before peeling back the foil on his sandwich. "Not so much now. They're both happy as hell now which is all that really matters. I love them, and if they're happier together then that's all that matters."

He shrugs, taking a massive bite of his sandwich and leaving Emerson reeling.

There's so much to unpack in just a few sentences. Jason's ease with saying he loves his best friend and family and the way he so clearly only wants the best for them. It makes Emerson's gut ache in the kind of way where he can't tell if it means he's emotional or hungry—a sort of pinging emptiness.

"You want some?" He asks, offering the container with honeydew melon now. "I always pack a bunch in these containers at the start of the week and end up hitting the vending machines instead. Then come Friday, I realize I didn't eat any fruits or vegetables all week," he says, half-laughing at himself like he's said something funny.

Never in his life has Emerson met anyone whose baseline temperament seems to just be happy. Jason's is, and it has the ache in his chest throbbing. What must it be like to be so relaxed and at ease with yourself? He can't even imagine.

Sometimes Emerson wishes he were like a character in a novel, the kind who knew his own feelings and what to do with them, and not someone who has a screenshot of an emotions wheel on his phone because indigestion and anxiety feel exactly the same. Whatever he's feeling now is confusing and overwhelming, and Emerson plops himself into the chair opposite Jason. He opens his lunch bag, hiding his uneaten grape in the bottom before unpacking his own food, desperate for the opportunity to focus on something more familiar.

6 JASON

LEANING BACK IN HIS CHAIR, Jason watches Emerson carefully unzip his lunch bag. There's something mesmerizing about the movement of his hands. As a coach and avid football fan, Jason spends a lot of time looking at other people's hands, particularly men's. He can tell from the shape of a guy's fingers and the breadth of his palm what his grip might be like or how much strength it might possess. Looking at Emerson, it's obvious his hands are anything but those belonging to an athlete. His fingers are long and delicate, with pale skin and not a callous in sight. He has really nice hands, Jason decides, taking another bite of his sandwich to avoid saying that out loud. Usually he doesn't filter himself too much, but he suspects Emerson might not be quite as comfortable with his unsolicited praise as Theo, and he's definitely not about to tease him the way he does his brothers or other friends.

He might not know him well yet, but he knows enough to be certain that Emerson requires something different. Probably because Emerson is different. Maybe it's the low hum of anxiety around him or his unexpected honesty. Or maybe it's the fact that Jason very strongly suspects he's neurodivergent and struggling, but everything about him calls to that part of Jason that needs to protect. Jason's taught and coached long enough to know a lost boy when he sees one, even if he's aware enough to know Emerson isn't a boy and isn't actually in need of rescuing. What it does seem like he could use is a friend, something Jason always likes more of. Especially because he likes Emerson and his no nonsense quirks.

"So what did you pack besides Ranch Doritos?" Jason asks, trying to make some casual conversation.

"It's kind of boring." Emerson answers in a monotone voice, carefully lining up his lunch on the edge of the desk beside him. There's a hunch to his shoulders, as if boring might not be his own thoughts on his lunch but someone else's. "I uh, I eat the same thing every day. Just a peanut butter sandwich, chips and, um, a banana."

"Listen, peanut butter is one of the best foods ever invented," Jason grins, hoping to put him at ease. "My favorite candy is *mazapán*. It's so fucking good. It's this little round disk of peanut butter perfection. Growing up it was harder to find, but I buy them by the box at the *panaderia*. Man, I could go for one of those right now. Have you ever had one?"

"I honestly have no idea what that even is," Emerson admits, popping the lid off his Tupperware and removing his sandwich, which as far as Jason can tell is nothing but peanut butter on plain white bread. Not even jelly. Jason loves jelly. Then again there's very little Jason doesn't love.

"It's a Mexican candy, my *abuela* loved them and got me and my brothers hooked when we were younger. Well, most of us. Charlie's a weirdo and hates peanut butter."

"*Abuela*?"

"Let me guess, I don't look Mexican," Jason says good-naturedly. "I get that a lot. My mom's white and my dad's mixed. His mom, my *abuela*, immigrated here when she was a teenager. Out of all my family, I definitely got my mom's complexion."

"I was actually going to ask what '*abuela*' means," Emerson says. "I don't speak Spanish."

It's not often Jason gets embarrassed, but his ears heat, and he scrubs a hand over his face. "Sorry. I guess I've got a little bit of a sore spot from growing up being told I don't look Mexican like them, but I shouldn't have assumed that's what you were going to do, that wasn't fair. I've gotten that kind of comment my entire life, especially since my brothers are darker than me. Although, Alec looks a lot more like our mom, and the twins look a lot like my dad."

"I have my mom's hair," Emerson says so quietly Jason barely hears him speak.

"Yeah?" Jason says, unsure why that little tidbit feels like a treasure. He gets the feeling Emerson doesn't share a lot about himself with people, so the fact that he is now makes Jason feel damn good. "Well for what it's worth, it's very nice hair."

Automatically, Emerson's hand flies up to touch his hair, untameable as always. When he catches Jason watching him, his cheeks flush pink. He drops his hand, grabbing his chips and shoving one in his mouth, averting his gaze. There's something handsome about the way his blush colors his pale cheeks and Jason can't help but stare.

"Thanks for telling me, Emerson."

Green eyes fly up to meet his gaze. The peanut butter sandwich is halfway to his mouth, but he doesn't take a bite, lowering his gaze. "You're welcome."

Jason decides here and now, he and Emerson are going to be great friends.

"Hey, you want a Coke?" Jason asks, suddenly realizing Emerson doesn't have a drink. Without giving him time to answer, because really, who doesn't need a drink with lunch, Jason moves to the corner to open his mini fridge. The sight inside reminds him he needs to go shopping because it is woefully understocked. Inside is nothing but two cans of Coke and a water bottle. He doesn't even have any green apple Gatorade or juice left. He's really gonna have to get better at grocery shopping. Especially if Emerson is going to be joining him for lunch again.

"You don't have to," Emerson tries.

"If I offered it, then it means I want you to have some, if you want it that is. I think if I ate a peanut butter sandwich without a drink I might die, just saying."

"That's improbable."

"But not impossible," Jason grins, waggling his eyebrows.

Emerson blinks, staring at Jason with a blank expression for several seconds before the corners of his lips turn up in a smile that transforms his face, brightening his features and making him look even younger.

"How old are you?" Jason asks. "Uh, sorry, was that rude? You just look kind of young."

A pinch forms between Emerson's pale eyebrows, lips turning down in a frown. "I'm twenty-six."

"I didn't mean it in a bad way," Jason hurries to clarify, worried he's said the wrong thing. Hopefully, a little honesty can smooth it over. "I turned thirty last year, and I possibly have a little bit of a complex about it."

"If it helps, you don't look old," Emerson offers, taking a

bite of his sandwich. He chews slowly before adding, "probably because you dress like a teenager."

Jason looks down at his slightly wrinkled Santa Leon High t-shirt and basketball shorts, barking out a laugh. "Guess I better not wear grown up clothes then, huh?"

There's no big smile from Emerson this time, but the corner of his mouth twitches like he wants to and isn't sure if he should. "You might end up looking thirty if you do."

"That's it," Jason whistles, cheeks hurting from the breadth of his smile. "I'm throwing out all my adult clothes right now."

"Is being thirty that bad?" Emerson asks. He criss crosses his legs in his chair, contorting himself into a position that Jason's much larger body cannot comprehend. His eyes are on Jason, the eye contact suddenly intense.

"I mean in general, no?" Jason answers, aware he makes it more of a question than a statement. "I think it's just like a combination of my baby brother getting engaged when I've been single forever and then, you know, being surrounded by teenagers all day. It's silly."

Jason reaches for the can of Coke and the water since Emerson never did answer, setting them on the desk beside him in a silent offering. "I never pegged myself as the kind of guy who would freak out at turning thirty but the last year was—weird."

"Bad weird?"

"Some of it," Jason admits, unsure why he can say that to Emerson but hasn't been able to admit it to Theo or his brothers. Probably because they were all too deeply entangled in Alec's recovery and the subsequent changing family dynamics with Alec and Theo's relationship. His best friend and his brother needed him to be okay, like always. If occasionally he wasn't, well it was easier for everyone, Jason included, to ignore that.

"Maybe I don't want to be thirty then," Emerson replies very seriously.

"It wasn't all bad though," Jason continues, as much for Emerson as himself. "But there were a lot of changes and I guess some of them got to me more than I want to admit. Getting back to teaching and coaching, back to my normal routine, has been good."

"I'm not part of your routine," Emerson points out.

"Not all change is bad," Jason points out. "Besides, who says this isn't going to be our new routine? Maybe you'll be back Monday because you realize how winning my personality is, and if not that, you might be desperate for a soda from the mini fridge."

"Pop."

"Huh?"

"It's called pop where I'm from."

"Pop," Jason echoes, emphasizing the *p*.

Emerson nods, reaching for the can of Coke. He cracks open the tab, waiting for the sizzle of carbonation to die down before he takes a sip. "Thanks. It's not Dr. Pepper, but it's good."

Dr. Pepper. Jason mentally adds that to his shopping list, determined to start keeping some in his fridge. Just in case Emerson really does come back to have lunch with him again. It would only be polite.

When he looks up from his musings, he finds Emerson shaking his plastic container of Doritos before lowering two of his long fingers in. He pulls out a large, unbroken chip, but instead of eating it, he holds it out to Jason. "Want one?"

"Sure," Jason grins, accepting the chip and popping it into his mouth.

Emerson taps his container of chips again but doesn't eat anymore, opening and closing his mouth a few times like he's not sure if he wants to say something. Jason's seen it before in some of his players, or his students. He knows from experience pushing won't make the question come out so he waits. Patience isn't usually his strongest suit, but time and practice have made him a better listener.

His silence is rewarded a minute later when Emerson softly clears his throat. "Can I ask you something?"

"Sure." Jason sets his Coke can on the edge of his desk then leans forward, positing himself in Emerson's direct line of sight. "What's up?"

"Why do the kids from the LGBTQIA+ club come here?"

He's not looking at Jason but rather at the flags on the wall making Jason's chest constrict. There's a reason he's so vocal about his support, and it's not just for his brothers and Theo, though that's part of it. It's for every person that has to look for a goddamn flag or a sticker because *safe* is not their default.

"You want the short or the long answer?" Jason asks.

"The honest one," Emerson replies.

"I was in high school when my older brothers both came out. Well, came out might be the wrong word. Charlie's never really come out because he doesn't like labels, but he brought a boyfriend home for Thanksgiving that first year he came home from college and then a girlfriend home for Christmas. When our parents asked what was going on he told everyone to stop focusing on who he dated. We found out a few months later that Andrew is ace and well, there's a story there but it's not mine to tell."

He glances up to find Emerson watching him with the same intense eye contact as before, the kind he never uses when speaking, almost as if every ounce of his being is focused on listening to Jason right now.

"Not long after that Theo came out to me as bisexual and then a few months later, my baby brother Alec came out as gay, very loudly and vocally in the fourth grade talent show." Jason takes a deep breath, offering Emerson a smile. "They were all so brave in their own ways, and it fucking killed me that they had to be. Over the course of a few years, I watched the people I love most have to keep coming out, or worse hiding because they didn't feel safe. It was so goddamn unfair that just because they didn't fit into someone else's box, they were more likely to get bullied or hurt. They needed me to be strong, so many people needed me, and I decided then and there to take all the heat you know? I was a jock, and I'm straight and stupid as it is, so people didn't say shit to me. Not like they did to them."

Scrubbing a hand over his jaw, Jason sighs. He is in dire need of a good shave. "When I started teaching here, they had a different coach, and he was—more traditional. He retired my second year of teaching, which is when I took on the head coaching position. At that point, my suspicions were confirmed, and I realized there was some toxic shit going on and I could change it. The stupidest thing about all of it is why the fuck people care what I think? I'm just the football coach. But I realized my opinion held sway and—I wanted that to matter."

"That's brave," Emerson says.

"I dunno, maybe." Jason shrugs, never comfortable with receiving accolades for this kind of thing. "I think it's basic human decency, you know?"

"You're not like the jocks I knew back home," Emerson says. "We didn't have a club like this but if we had, well, let's just say we wouldn't have been welcome with the football team. By we, I mean, um, that is, um—I'm gay. I didn't tell the principal when she hired me. I wasn't sure...I mean I think it's more liberal here than where I'm from, but I didn't know how that might impact my job prospect. That is—"

"I'm not going to out you to anyone, Emerson." Jason reaches out, laying a hand on his knee to still the way it bounces rapidly. Emerson's entire body shudders with the force of his exhale and he shakes his head from side to side.

"No it's—I don't want to be a secret anymore. I did that for...a long time. I just wasn't sure if it was safe."

"I wish I could say everyone here is accepting but the truth is there are a few teachers who, well, I wouldn't invite to my place for a pizza. Let's put it that way. But overall, it's a good school, and we'll have your back. I'll have your back. I promise. You don't have to be anyone but yourself, Emerson."

Emerson retrieves the stress ball he'd borrowed from Jason's truck out of his lunch bag, focusing on the compression while he speaks. "The other thing is uh, you know. I'm sure you've noticed, I'm not very good with people."

"You seem to be doing just fine, and your students love you. You've got one of my freshmen—Arlo. He says your class is great. Coming from Arlo, that is high praise because he hates school."

"Arlo...Rosales?" At Jason's nod, some of the tension bleeds out of Emerson. "He's a good kid."

"He is," Jason agrees.

"The thing is, um, there's something else that you might want to know about me. You know if we're going to be friends, which I thought we might be working towards."

Aside from Theo, most of Jason's friendships are more

casual, but he can tell that isn't going to be the case with Emerson. At least he hopes not. He's already trying to figure out a way to make sure they can have lunch together again, to find a way to finagle himself into Emerson's routine to get to know him better.

"No if about it, Emerson. We're already friends. You shared your Ranch Doritos with me, that's practically bestie shit right there."

"I'm autistic," Emerson says in a rush. "No one else knows that either, but it's not a secret. Or I guess it is. I wasn't sure about telling anyone here. I was a little nervous if I did, they might think I can't handle the job, which I can. I'm a good teacher, it's just sometimes people think if you need extra help or accommodations that you can't do anything and—I don't know. Sorry, I'm rambling. I've never had to tell anyone, not like this, but I thought if you were gonna be around me, you might want to know why I'm, you know, the way I am." He slowly trails off, looking more unsure than when he started talking.

"Emerson."

"Yeah?"

"Thank you for telling me." Emerson exhales a shuddering breath, the tightness in his features loosening as he directs those wide, doe eyes at Jason. "For what it's worth, I like you the way you are."

The corners of Emerson's lips turn up in a smile, and the breadth of it is a tangible thing that Jason feels right in the center of his chest. That smile right there, toothy and unmasked, makes Jason's heart beat faster. Everyone should look that happy, especially Emerson.

It isn't fair that the default even now is straight and neurotypical, to the point Emerson didn't know if he would be safe just being who he was born to be. It makes Jason want to throw something when he thinks about it too hard. He hates that people have to hide or feel unsafe.

For whatever reason, Emerson chose Jason as the one person in his new life to trust with the pieces of himself no one else knows about yet, and it triggers Jason's protective urges. He has to tamp down the impulse to tell Emerson he will literally fight anyone who hurts him, aware that's probably too much, too soon, but Jason's never pretended to be anything but what he is. He protects the people he cares about, and in a very short time it's becoming clear to Jason that Emerson is now one of those people. He will be damned if he lets anyone or anything make Emerson feel like he has to shrink back into a closet or hide his needs.

Jason takes a steady breath, trying to will his overeager nature into submission. The last time he felt this protective over someone he was seven. He'd taken one look at Theo with his knobby knees and lack of school lunch and known he was going to keep him. Jason has that same feeling now. Emerson might not be a kid but neither is Jason. Maybe making friends isn't the same as it was on the playground, but Jason wants to keep him all the same. The intensity with which his brain is screaming at him to take care of Emerson is too hard to ignore, so he doesn't.

"Hey, Emerson."

"Hmm?"

"Can I drive you to work?"

"You already did," Emerson points out.

Jason can't help but smile, charmed by how literal he is.

"That's true, but I meant again."

"Like if the bus is late?" Emerson asks, head cocked to the side. He's studying Jason intently like he's looking for something. Jason can only hope whatever it is, he finds.

"Not exactly," Jason says, leaning forward. "I was just thinking that I could pick you up on Monday."

"Why?"

"Well, I pass your place on the way to school anyway. It makes sense from a logical standpoint," he says, offering something concrete and easy to understand but unable to hold back from being equally honest. "But also because we're friends and I think it would be fun."

"Fun," Emerson echoes. "You want to pick me up because you like me?"

"Of course," Jason says, unsure what to make of Emerson's blank expression. It occurs to him that putting him on the spot might not have been the best option, but his eagerness to help had overruled everything else. Before he can say any of that the bell rings, signaling the end of lunch and causing Emerson's expression to shutter further.

"I have to get back to class," he says, carefully packing his trash and containers back into his lunch bag. "Thank you for um, everything."

"Anytime," Jason says, grabbing a Post-it note off the corner of his desk, scribbling down his phone number and offering it to Emerson, with what he hopes is a non-threatening smile. Jason knows he's huge, between his massive stature and bulky body it would be so easy for him to be intimidating. He learned early on a smile and a laugh went a long way to making others more comfortable. It helps that Jason is genuinely in a good mood most of the time, but even when he's not, he tries to pretend he is for other people's comfort. "Here's my number. The offer for a ride is always there, no pressure or time limit on the offer. Just let me know."

Emerson's delicate fingers brush over his own as he

takes the sticky note, curling his hand around it before shoving it into his pocket. "Thank you."

"You can call me anytime."

"That's not going to happen," Emerson deadpans.

"Oh, uh—"

"I don't like talking on the phone," Emerson explains. There's a pinch between his eyebrows like admitting as much is stressing him out. "I know it's stupid but—"

"Texting then." Jason offers, softening his smile. "I like texting too. You can text me about the ride if you want, or anything else, too."

Emerson opens his mouth, but whatever it is he means to say is silenced by the loud ringing of the warning bell causing Emerson's shoulders to hunch. He's tall, but the way he shrinks in on himself makes Jason wonder how often he tries to take up less space.

Given that Emerson is more used to his own building than the gym, Jason isn't confident that he can find his way back to his own classroom. He has his own class that will be coming through those gym doors soon, so he probably shouldn't leave. Unfortunately, his brain doesn't much care about logic where Emerson is concerned.

"You want me to walk you back to class?" Jason finds himself asking.

"No," Emerson says with a shake of his head. Absent-mindedly, he tugs on his hair, making it look like he just walked through a windstorm. It's endearing really, even if Jason wishes he could bring back the relaxed smile Emerson wore just a few minutes before. "I need to get back, and you have class too, but I'll see you around."

"Yeah, you—" but before Jason can even think about doing anything spontaneous like inviting Emerson to the football game tonight, he's gone, leaving behind his half finished can of Coke on the edge of Jason's desk and a whole lot of unfamiliar emotions.

"HOW ARE YOU FEELING, JASON?" Eddie walks over, clapping Jason on the back. Eddie's been his assistant coach for two years, and in that time he's rapidly become one of Jason's favorite people. He's dedicated, damn good at wrangling the team and, best of all, he loves football as much as Jason does.

"Feeling good, Eddie. Feeling really good." Jason stands all that much taller, breathing in the familiar scent of freshly mowed grass and ocean air. There's few things Jason loves more than the combination of a fresh field and a sea breeze. It settles something in Jason as he closes his eyes and lets the wind ruffle his hair.

"I'm feeling good too," Eddie replies, rubbing his hands together gleefully. "The twins are with their grandparents tonight for a sleepover and Amy is having a girls' night. I've been looking forward to this game all summer. You think we're ready?"

"The boys are ready," Jason nods, as they head down to the field together, unable to stop smiling. There's something so damn exciting about the first game of the season.

Right now, the stands and field are empty aside from Jason and Eddie, but soon they'll be full. In less than an hour and a half, everything around them will change—teachers and students will flood the stands, packing them tight and filling the night with the low hum of excited bystanders. And sure, a lot of the staff and students don't care about football, but they show up for the school, for the team, and that energy fuels on his boys to play harder.

It's not just the people in the stands either, it's everyone else who plays a part in game nights. From the band to the cheerleaders to the student council volunteers running the snack bar. Games nights remind Jason of what working as a team and most importantly, working hard can get you. There's nothing quite like the energy of a home game. And while sometimes lackluster in terms of playing intensity, the season opener's energy can't be beat. Jason can't fucking wait.

Sure, a summer spent relaxing and hanging out with his brothers, Theo and his dogs was great, but the truth is he's happier during the school year. He loves being busy, watching his kids succeed and feeling a part of something.

"Matty's already in the locker room," Eddie offers, nudging Jason in the side harder than is strictly necessary. In turn, Jason messes up his hair. Somehow the longer they work together, the more like siblings they behave, and though Eddie is a decade older than Jason, he definitely acts like his little brother sometimes.

"He doing his pregaming?" Jason asks, by now used to Matty's pregame routine after coaching him the last few years.

"If by pregaming, you mean sitting in the corner with his headphones on blaring music while not moving, then yes." Eddie scrubs a hand over his beard. "I remembered what you said last season, so I didn't bother him."

"Good man," Jason says. Not all of his players have pregame rituals but Matty does, and messing with it will just fuck him up. He's had the same routine since he was a freshman, long before he became starting quarterback. Somewhere along the lines, it became less of a routine and more of a superstition no one dares to interrupt. Not unless they want the game to be a total shit show because when Matty is off, the entire team is off.

The game isn't for another hour, but Jason's got a pregame ritual too. It's the same one he had back when he played on this very field in high school. He used to come out to the field when it was empty just like he is now, staring at the wide open stands and freshly lined field, and soaking it all in. He's always thought of it a bit like the calm before the storm, letting that peace settle over him and guide him when things get hectic. Back when they played together, Theo used to tease him, telling him the grass was going to look the same at game time as it did before, but something about seeing it all empty has always settled Jason. It reminds him that whatever happens come game time, there's always another chance. Nothing is forever. There's always another chance.

"Ah, shit."

"What's wrong?" Jason asks.

"I forgot the playbook in your office. I know you specifically asked me to swing by and get it before I came down to the field. I'm sorry."

"Don't worry about it, I'll go. I need my water anyway. Why don't you stay here in case any of the newer guys show up early. Make sure they're hydrated and stretched. They probably won't see game time today, but they're part of the team, and they need to learn how to be ready now, so that next year when they're on that field starting they've already got good habits. Then there's Arlo. He's gonna show up any minute trying to use the weight room before the game. Don't let him try to work out, he pushes himself too hard."

All of that is probably unnecessary since Eddie knows what to do without being told, but sometimes it makes Jason feel better to repeat the obvious. Almost as if saying it out loud, fortifying a plan, can manifest it into happening exactly the way it needs to.

Eddie crosses his arms, eyes on the field. "You got it."

"I'll head over to my office and get that playbook then meet you back here."

"Sounds good, Coach."

Satisfied that everything is in good hands, Jason strides across the field, smiling to himself as he watches his sneakers leave their mark in the grass. It's been over a decade since he and Theo played on this field, but the memory has never completely faded. His brothers have teased him about being a teacher and coach, saying he peaked in high school and would never leave. Maybe they're not too far off. Jason loved high school, loved playing on a team with his best friend, loved everything about it which is why his decision to become a teacher while the rest of his family chose loftier, better paying careers had been easy. Sure Jason is never going to make the big money like Andrew or his parents do, and yeah he won't ever become well-known like Charlie is in the art world, but he's damn happy here. As far as Jason is concerned, watching his kids grow up, being a part of them finding their footing before they venture off into the real world, is the most satisfying job on the planet. It doesn't hurt that he gets to play football or run around doing obstacle courses and have fun most of the time. Honestly, Jason has the best fucking job.

Lost in thought, he doesn't notice someone approaching until they're standing directly in front of him and it's far too late to change course without being rude which, despite his internal desire to do so, Jason won't indulge.

"Hello, Mr. Caldwell. Fancy seeing you here on a Friday evening. Are you coming to the game?"

"Of course I'm not," Mr. Caldwell snaps, like the notion

itself offends him. To Jason's knowledge, he's never been to a game. Not when Jason was a student and certainly not since he started working here. He's never met anyone who seems to dislike high school sports, or high schoolers, as much as Mr. Caldwell. Why he is a teacher at all is something Jason has never been able to figure out. "I was looking for you."

"Me? Why?"

Mr. Caldwell sighs. "I thought it pertinent to remind you that if any of your players fail they can't play."

"Yeah," Jason says, "I know the academic policy."

"Then you might want to encourage your players to actually study rather than spending all their time worrying about a meaningless sport that won't get them anywhere."

It's on the tip of Jason's tongue to point out that football is a four billion dollar industry, and more importantly as far as Jason is concerned, that his kids happiness is worth more than money. There are invaluable skills taught through sports, but even if they weren't applicable to a career, his players love the game, which is more than enough. He bites the words back though, not in the mood to argue with Mr. Caldwell. Not today.

Nothing, not even the world's most cantankerous, unlikeable teacher, is going to ruin his mood. He refuses to give him the power.

"All my boys work hard, Mr. Caldwell. They're also aware of the policy." Jason smiles, though it's forced to say the least. He absolutely hates this fucker. "They're good kids, which you'd know if you gave them a fair chance."

"Every student in my class gets the same chance. If they choose to squander that opportunity for success, it's not my problem," Mr. Caldwell snaps, straightening his tie. "Keep your players in check or there will be consequences."

Not for the first time is Jason tempted to tell Mr. Caldwell exactly what he thinks of him. He doesn't, not because he cares about the consequences for himself directly, but because if he did there's a chance it would impact his ability to coach or teach, and he won't do that to his kids.

"You have a great evening, Mr. Caldwell," Jason tells him, widening his smile, knowing it'll piss Mr. Caldwell off. "You live off Seaward, right? I'm sure you'll hear us cheering when we win, and you can celebrate the Santa Leon Wildcats from home."

The death glare Mr. Caldwell sends him makes Jason's smile split his face in earnest. He watches Mr. Caldwell depart, ignoring his grumbled, under his breath complaint about noise levels and sporting events needing to be banned. Jason wouldn't care so much about him hating football, some of the other staff do too, if he didn't seem determined to make it his life's mission to take that out on his players in the classroom.

He does a mental check of his players' schedules as he walks towards his classroom. He knows Matty and Ricardo both have Mr. Caldwell, but he's got to double check on his other senior players, wanting to be aware of which of them might need a little extra support this semester. Mr. Caldwell's class is no joke, and his desire to see football players fail is something Jason won't tolerate, especially not when that could jeopardize any of his players' futures. For all Mr. Caldwell thinks football is a joke, more than one of his senior players is on track to be scouted for college. Both Matty and Ricardo are looking at getting into D I schools with full rides. Jason knows that neither of their families can afford to send them to college if they don't get those scholarships—something they can't do if Mr. Caldwell fails them.

Jason makes a mental note to go over his starting players' course loads over the weekend to make sure he knows exactly what they might need. Especially Matty. Last year was rough for him academically, and while Jason did what he could, his hands were tied because Matty didn't—still doesn't—have an official diagnosis to get him the kind of support Jason strongly suspects he needs. Limited by stupid bureaucracy, the most Jason had been able to do for Matty last year was get him to attend a few extra tutoring lessons. Now that he thinks about it, he should make sure to remind all his players of this so none of them feel singled out.

Pausing in the middle of the walkway, he opens his notes apps to make an actual note to himself, well aware he will absolutely forget this thought by tomorrow if he doesn't write it down. He's about to click out of his notes app when Emerson's face filters into his thoughts, and he finds himself making a new folder simply titled Emerson. There he types out the few things he's learned about the other man, including his dislike of donuts and affinity for Ranch Doritos, peanut butter and Dr. Pepper. At the last second, he adds on 'dislikes being late' as well. It's not much but it's a start. He's never made a folder like this for any of his other coworkers or friends but Emerson is different, his likes and dislikes more than simple preference. If Jason can remember things that might make him feel more at ease, regulated and happy, he wants to.

No sooner has he closed the app then a text message from an unfamiliar phone number pops up on his screen. Jason opens it, unable to stop the ridiculous smile that spreads across his face.

Arlo told me you guys have a game tonight. Every Friday he said. He was quite horrified I didn't know this. Social etiquette makes me think I should wish you luck. Or am I supposed to tell you to break a leg? I can't imagine you'd want that in football though.

Jason quickly adds Emerson's name to his contact list before shooting him a reply, a pep in his step as he pockets his phone.

7 EMERSON

WITH TREMBLING HANDS, Emerson stares at the phone in his hand, hardly able to believe he actually texted Jason. Sure Jason gave him his number and said he could text him anytime, but that was an incredibly vague offer that Emerson had not intended to take him up on. Not because he didn't want to text Jason, rather because the parameters of the offer were too vague for him to be sure how to go about.

He'd all but twisted himself up in knots inside when Arlo mentioned the game. In hindsight, half of the student body wearing spirit wear should've been a tip off, but it wasn't until Arlo's comment at the end of class that he put two and two together. He spent the next few hours winding himself up over whether it was a good idea. In the end, the memory of Jason's dimpled smile and their time spent together at lunch was enough for Emerson to overcome his nerves and click send.

That momentary bravery is rewarded when his own phone, rarely used with only five contacts—three of which are work-related—buzzes beside him on the couch.

Jason
definitely no broken anything in football

but good luck is always appreciated

Emerson grips his phone tightly, embarrassed at his own smile and finds his reply coming with a swiftness that negates his ability to overthink.

Emerson
I don't understand football enough to know how much is luck and how much is skill, but on the off chance you need both I'll wish you both.

but good luck to you — today and every day

Looking up at his television he watches Gandalf stride across the screen. He's seen this movie so many times he knows every scene by heart, the familiarity of it comforting in the deepest way. He watches it for a minute, subtitles on as always, when a thought occurs to him. Maybe Jason isn't a Lord of the Rings fan. Maybe he won't understand the reference.

Worried about the reception of his last message, he sends another text just to make sure.

Emerson
That's a reference from Lord of The Rings. In case you didn't catch it.

The Fellowship of the Rings to be exact.

Jason
afraid I did not catch that

but I haven't seen the movies since they
came out

A frown mars Emerson's features as he stares at his phone and starts rapidly tapping out a reply.

Emerson
Please tell me you've read the book?

Jason
if I say no will this end our new friendship?

Emerson
Well, it won't end the friendship but I will be shocked. The book is amazing. I mean the movies are also amazing. The cinematography alone is a masterpiece. I'm watching it right now. But the book is better! The book is always better, Jason.

If you've only seen the movies then you don't even know that when Frodo, Sam and Pippin are fleeing the Black Riders they run into the wandering company of Gildor, a Nildorian elf who keeps the hobbits safe! The elves even send the message along about them being pursued by the nine which is integral to the one ring making it all the way to Rivendell. I don't know how the filmmakers thought something this crucial could be cut.

As soon as he hits send, he's hit with a staggering wave of regret. His family always said he was too intense. Back home he used to watch the movies on his laptop in his bedroom rather than the family tv, because when he watched it in the living room they'd ask why he didn't watch something different for once. That, or Landon would take the remote and fast forward through the good parts while telling Emerson he'd seen it enough times.

Over the years, he learned to pretend he liked things less than he did in order to avoid being judged and ridiculed for his hyperfixations. Yet here he is, finally making an actual friend for the first time in his adult life, and he's gone and infodumped a mountain of text at Jason, about elves no less! Maybe this is why he doesn't have friends. Maybe Landon was right. Maybe—

Jason
which book is that in?

Emerson blinks at his phone, mouth agape. Jason isn't making fun of him, or changing the subject. He's asking a question. A question about something Emerson likes.

It's probably pathetic. It's definitely embarrassing, but something painfully tight unfurls in Emerson's chest. He pulls his knees up to his chest, resting his chin on them as he tries to decide how to reply. He could give the short answer. He *should* give the short answer. But Jason did ask, which means he must be at least a little bit interested.

Emerson
It's in Fellowship of the Ring, which is the first book. But you should really read The Hobbit first. Not that you're offering to read the books now. Just in general. I know a lot of people think it's just a little prequel that you can skip but it sets up the world perfectly. Besides, who wouldn't want more of the Shire?

Jason
ive seen the hobbit it was good

but let me guess, not as good as the book?

Emerson bites the inside of his cheek so hard it almost bleeds, grateful there's no one around to see the ridiculous smile on his face. It's just a few texts, only it's not *just* anything. Not to Emerson.

Emerson
Exactly. The book is so much better, Jason.
But also the movies are masterpieces.

To Emerson's intense relief, Jason is a quick texter, and his response is almost immediate.

Jason
ive never been much of a reader but your enthusiasm has me curious maybe ill check it out

also I wont be able to check my phone during the game in case you send more messages

but ill read them when I get home tonight

The text is simple enough, yet Emerson's response is anything but. In one single message, Jason managed to show more consideration for Emerson than his family did his entire life. Not only letting Emerson know he isn't being ignored, but that he won't be bothering Jason if he sends more messages.

With a flustered huff, Emerson pulls on his hoodie and tugs the strings closed, feeling the inexplicable need to hide even in his own home. How is it that Jason could see his needs so clearly when no one else ever could? Is he like this with everyone? Even as Emerson thinks the question, he knows the answer. Of course he is. This is clearly why everyone he's met at the school adores Jason. He's thoughtful and kind and makes people feel safe.

Jason is a stupidly handsome, stupidly considerate human being, and it's probably a good thing he's straight, or Emerson might do something equally stupid and accidently fall in love with him. Given that he's entirely off limits, Emerson doesn't have the double-edged worry of being rejected romantically and platonically, which somehow makes the prospect of Jason's friendship just a little bit less scary.

This is totally fine. Emerson can absolutely handle making a new friend, even with the most popular man at Santa Leon High. The thought makes Emerson laugh to himself as he smashes his body into the corner of the couch and cocoons into his weighted blanket.

Maybe this isn't such a horrible idea after all. Maybe somewhere in Santa Leon there's a future for Emerson after all. A happy one. The kind his mom would've wanted him to have.

Maybe, just maybe, he can be happy here.

EMERSON IS NOT HAPPY.

The bus is late. Again. At this point, it would be more accurate to say the bus being on time is a fluke. He's not sure why he didn't take Jason up on his offer. They texted on and off all weekend, mostly about Lord of the Rings, to Emerson's surprise. Given that Jason hasn't read the books, he had an awful lot of questions, each of which Emerson answered in explicit detail.

Rather than be put off by the long texts, Jason would reply—sometimes quickly, sometimes not—with a question or a thought that made it clear he not only read the messages but was interested. More than once, Emerson thought about sneaking in a quick text taking Jason up on the offer for a ride. Except they weren't talking about rides, they were talking about movies and books and at one point, though Emerson isn't sure why, tacos.

Unsure how to segue the conversation, and worried he might come off as too clingy, he'd let their conversation come to a conclusion Sunday afternoon when Jason was taking his dogs on a walk. That was another thing Emerson learned. Jason has dogs. Two of them. Emerson very much wanted to meet them the second Jason mentioned them, but he didn't voice the thought, unsure if that was in the realm of their friendship.

More than once growing up, he made those kinds of assumptions, and it usually ended up with him being ridiculed or losing friends who weren't comfortable with Emerson's intensity.

Turns out, having a friend is complicated. Or maybe, given how easy things are with Jason, the only one complicating things is Emerson's brain.

Either way, he did not allow himself to ask Jason for a ride. Which is why instead of being seated in Jason's comfortable truck with his handsome smile to start Emerson's day, he is stuck at the bus stop next to a small child with a snotty nose, waiting on a late bus. The bus does in fact show up eventually, six minutes later than it's supposed to be. Thankfully, that's not horrible, all things considered, and not late enough to negatively affect his morning. At least that's what he thinks until he gets to school and sees Jason's truck already parked. The depth of irritation that Emerson feels about this is enough to have him aggressively spinning his fidget ring as he walks across campus.

Around him, students greet their friends, and various staff slowly stroll through the parking lot making morning small talk with other teachers. Emerson doesn't linger. Aside from Jason, he's yet to make any friends, possibly his own fault. He hasn't even made it to lunch in the staff room or the cafeteria, preferring to hide away in his classroom. Nor has he attempted anything beyond a polite greeting with most of his coworkers. All of his mental energy has been directed towards settling into his new place and new job.

Sometimes he wonders what it's like to approach new things with anticipation rather than anxiety. It seems impossible that anyone can do that, but Emerson knows some people can. It makes him kind of resent the fact that his own brain is hardwired to dread even the most mundane things, to the point he even avoids things he likes solely because transitions and potential unknowns often require more spoons than he has. Learning about the spoon theory after his autism diagnosis—something most often used by those with chronic illness and disabilities to discuss their limited energy—has greatly helped Emerson come to terms with the fact that many daily tasks take more out of him than his neurotypical peers.

Deep in thought, he makes his way to the front office. When he steps inside, Mabel isn't at her desk and aside from a teacher whose name he forgets leaving the office after him, it's otherwise empty. Breathing a sigh of relief that he won't have to deal with any unwanted small talk this morning, he pulls his favorite pen from his pocket, the tip barely touching the sign in sheet when he hears a familiar voice filtering out from the small room just off Mabel's desk. He knows it houses the office printers and fax machines along with a wall of cupboards filled with extra supplies.

Mabel explained all this when she caught Emerson peeking in there last week.

"I'm not joking, Mabel, I wish I was."

The sound of Jason's deep voice has Emerson breathing deeper. He really does have a nice voice, the pitch of it unfairly soothing as is the cadence of his speech. He's exaggerated and excited, which makes it easy to judge his moods and track the flow of conversation.

"You get yourself into so much trouble, Mr. King."

"You say the sweetest things," Jason laughs.

"Only you think trouble is sweet," Mabel chastises. "Now get me that box there from the top, and tell me what happened next."

"Are you sure you want to know? It's pretty scandalous, Mabel. I don't want to offend your delicate sensibilities."

"Delicate sensibilities, my ass," Mabel snorts. "You tell me the rest of the story before the bell rings, or I'll add your name to the top of the volunteer yard duty rotation list."

"Mabel Farwell, I am shocked."

The sound of Mabel's laughter fills the otherwise empty office. He shouldn't be standing here listening to their conversation. He has no excuse aside from enjoying the sound of Jason's voice, which is possibly *not* a thing most friends do, but then it's not like Emerson has a lot of experience to compare it to. Jason says something too quiet for Emerson to make out, but it makes Mabel cackle and reminds Emerson that he is not special. While Jason's friendship might mean more to Emerson than he wants to admit, even to himself, he knows it is probably just one in a million to someone like Jason, who is friends with everyone.

Wanting to get away before he's caught, he hurries to scribble his name across the sign in sheet, adding the time when Jason steps out of the side office and Emerson forgets to disappear in favor of staring. Jason's got on a short sleeve Santa Leon High t-shirt today, the dark hair on his forearms and muscles in his biceps on full display as he grips the large box Mabel must've wanted him to get. He's freshly shaved, making the dimple in his chin more prominent when he smiles.

No matter how much Emerson might want to pretend he doesn't have a tiny crush on his new—and only—straight friend, he most definitely does.

"After that debacle I ended up on the front porch locked out and Stella, the absolute menace that she is, yanked my towel off and ran," Jason says with a shake of his head, stopping dead in his tracks when he catches sight of Emerson. "Hi Emerson."

Jason says *"Hi Emerson"* with that relaxed grin of his, so clearly unbothered about being caught talking about his sexual escapades. Not that he should be ashamed. He's an adult and can do whatever he wants. Emerson certainly has no room to judge. If he didn't want to hear about something like this, he shouldn't have eavesdropped. It's none of Emerson's business who Jason is involved with. Yet he can't help but wonder who Stella is. Did Jason go on a date this weekend in between texting with Emerson?

Something uncomfortable churns in Emerson's gut, and he doesn't like it, not one bit.

"Good morning, Mr. Miller." Mabel straightens the bright pink scarf tied around her neck, her smile firmly in place. "Can I help you with anything this morning?"

Emerson shakes his head, tapping his pen against the edge of the desk. He stops when he catches himself, clicking the pen shut before pocketing it. "I was just signing in."

"You let me know if you need anything," Mabel says,

more of a statement than a question as she settles herself at her desk.

In the two weeks since Emerson started, she's told him that at least a dozen times. Emerson has yet to take her up on it despite the fact that he has a laundry list of things he could use help with in his classroom. He's pretty sure she's just being polite and the majority of his issues aren't anything the school is going to help with anyway.

"Put that box there on the floor so I can go through it later," Mabel tells Jason, patting his arm. "Good man. What would I do without you?"

"Find someone else who can reach the top shelf probably."

Mabel swats Jason's arm, shaking her head. "You get out of here and stop causing me trouble so I can work."

"You love me," Jason grins, grabbing his cooler and backpack off the floor before nodding towards the front door. "Come on, Emerson."

Relieved by the explicit direction, Emerson trails after Jason who reaches for the door and holds it open, allowing Emerson to easily slip under his outstretched arm. Given his height, it shouldn't be so easy to do so, but Jason's got nearly five inches on Emerson, making him feel small in a way he's unused to. He was taller than his aunt and uncle, even taller than Landon who hated it. He's used to being the tallest one in the room, to folding in on himself to avoid being noticed. Something about the way Jason's body and personality take up space so he doesn't have to is something Emerson doesn't know how to make sense of. All he knows is he likes it, gravitating into Jason's orbit as his earlier tension slowly bleeds away.

"You ready for another Monday?" Jason asks, falling into step beside Emerson.

"As ready as I can be," Emerson answers. He must not do as good a job of hiding his own mess of emotions because Jason stops him with a hand to the shoulder. The touch is light enough Emerson could brush it off; he doesn't. Because it's Jason and it feels good, and Emerson is tired. Not from lack of sleep, tired in the way it's hard to explain. Tired in the way he gets sometimes when his brain takes in too much, and all his energy is used to keep himself at the same base level other people seem to just exist at without trying.

Some days, he manages just fine, and other days, well other days the effort is herculean.

Jason gives his shoulder a gentle squeeze. "Was there a problem with the bus?"

"It was six minutes late," Emerson says, frowning. He should stop. He knows he should stop. Were it anyone else, he wouldn't have even answered, but this isn't anyone else, it's Jason. Who's got those damn big brown eyes trained on Emerson like he's the only person on this campus. He's looking at Emerson like he cares what the answer is, and all of it just comes spilling out. "And there was a kid who kept crying, and she got snot on my pants, and I wanted to tell you good morning, but you were already gone because the bus was late and—" Emerson cuts himself off just before he adds the part about what he overheard about the woman who took Jason's towel. He already sounds neurotic; he doesn't need to sound jealous too. Even if he is, just a little bit.

It's not even that Emerson has a crush on Jason. Though, standing here staring at him basked in early morning sunlight, watching the way it glints off his pitch black hair, it's impossible to deny. Physically, this man is exactly what Emerson would like: big, soft, kind. And painfully off limits. That's fine. Emerson doesn't even care about dating. He'd much rather have Jason's friendship anyway. It's just that his friendship isn't a certain thing yet, not in the way Emerson's brain needs it to be.

He knows Jason is his friend. It's impossible not to because Jason makes sure he knows. What he doesn't know is how deep the friendship is allowed to go. He's never had many friends, and the few he's had over the years always became strained when Emerson was too, well, Emerson. He's always been too *something* for people. Too quiet. Too talkative. Too excited. Too stoic. Too intense. Too boring. Too rigid.

The last one has always been the biggest one. How many times growing up did he hear it? From teachers, from his cousin, from his aunt and uncle. The critique on his facial expressions, either too expressive or not expressive enough, or the commentary on his emotions when he felt things too strongly or somehow didn't feel them at all.

Emerson, there's no reason for you to be so upset, no one else is. Emerson, you need to calm down, people are staring. Emerson, you need to learn how to let things go, you're taking this too seriously. Emerson, why can't you like things a normal amount, you make things stressful for other people. Emerson, why can't you just be different.

It took Emerson a very long time to realize maybe he wasn't the problem. Maybe his family wanted him to fit into a box when he was a circle, not a square. Regardless, the damage was done and he hears their voices now, reminding him he needs to not overwhelm Jason. Except he doesn't know how to be less, he never has. Which is exactly why it's easier to avoid people entirely rather than try to mask. Emerson doesn't do casual, in anything. Not in the books he loves or the movies he watches and certainly not in the people he enjoys. Not that there's ever been very many. But when there is something he likes, something he loves, his hyperfocus takes over because Emerson has always been all or nothing, and right now he wants to be all with the giant of a man staring at him, like how he feels matters.

He wants to be all in with Jason, at least in regards to their friendship. He's a lot of things, but delusional is not one of them. He reminds himself of this while tracking the way Jason's school t-shirt clings to his body. He's got muscles, that's clear, but there's a bit of softness at his belly and hips that Emerson suspects would feel very nice in a hug. A platonic hug.

This would all be so much easier if Jason weren't so painfully, devastatingly handsome. He looks like someone out of a magazine, or a museum. Or maybe a movie star. He's just so big that even at five-foot-eleven, Emerson has to tilt his head up to look him in the eye. Which is apparently a thing that makes Emerson's pulse race. There's also a steady countenance about him, a quiet strength in the way he carries himself. He looks like he could take on an Orc with his bare hands and win. He—*oh no*. No, no, *no*.

Under no circumstances is he going to go there. The last thing he needs to think about is how sexy Jason would look in an Aragorn costume.

Even now he can feel it, feel that compulsion in his brain where something he likes starts to change from a casual interest into a hyperfocus. Once that happens, Emerson is done for. There is no going back. No casual anything. In the past, this part of his brain has always been directed at things he could control, things he could hide, like books. Like his obsession with Lord of the Rings.

In all of his twenty-six years, he's never felt his brain try to latch on to a person. But it is now, and if he isn't careful, he's going to scare Jason off with his intensity. He knows he is.

"Earth to Sunshine."

"Sunshine?" Emerson murmurs.

"That got your attention," Jason chuckles, "though judging by that cute little pinchy thing going on between your eyebrows, I'm going to go out on a limb and say it's definitely one for the no column."

As far as Emerson is concerned, he's less like sunshine and more like the nimbostratus cloud that blocks the sunshine. Thankfully, Jason begins to talk again, sparing Emerson from having to figure out how to say that without upsetting Jason. It might not have been a nickname he'd stick with, but he likes that Jason is trying to find one and is loath to inadvertently stop Jason's attempts by running his mouth.

"No worries, Emerson. I've got plenty more where that came from. We are going to figure out the perfect nickname for you if it kills me."

"I prefer you alive."

"Thanks." Jason's eyes crinkle at the corner. "I'm quite partial to this life of mine. I think—"

"Watch out," someone yells.

Emerson's head swivels around just in time to see a football headed directly towards his face. He should duck, or move, but his body chooses this moment to freeze in panic. Emerson can do nothing but hope his face doesn't break when Jason's massive hand flies out to catch the ball one handed.

Various students whistle and scream, earning them one of Jason's famous smiles. He pulls his arm back, launching the football across the quad in an impressive throw directly towards Matty who catches it, setting off a fresh round of cheering. When Jason returns his attention to Emerson, his expression softens.

"That was a close one." He lifts his hand, the same one that stopped a football from hitting him in the face, and smooths back Emerson's hair. Jason's hands are so unlike his own, so much larger with a wide palm and thick fingers. It's all Emerson can do not to shudder, an ache deep in his chest as he imagines how it might feel if his hand kept going, if it cupped the back of Emerson's head.

Jason tips his chin down to study Emerson's face. Usually he balks at this level of attention, but somehow coming from Jason it doesn't trigger his nervous system's fight or flight mode. Jason's gaze doesn't make him feel judged or unsafe—the opposite really—and with every second he keeps his attention focused solely on Emerson, some of his earlier tension fades.

"You good, Emerson?"

"Mhmm," Emerson hums, unsure if his body is capable of speech when all his brain is thinking about is how big Jason's hands are. "You—how?"

"Played in high school. Wide receiver," Jason answers with a shrug. Emerson is certain that's some kind of football position, but which one he has no idea. "Come on, I'll walk you to class."

Emerson doesn't hesitate to follow, body thrumming with adrenaline from the near miss. Beneath that, something else simmers, but Emerson doesn't have time to try and figure out what it means.

8 JASON

TAPPING his pen against his desk, Jason sighs heavily. He's got a handful of game tapes he wants to go over before Friday's game, but he's feeling a little too restless to do that right now. Normally, the hour gap between the end of classes and the start of practice is when Jason finishes up work for his own classes or coaching stuff, but for some reason he can't seem to focus today. He leans back in his office chair, staring at the ceiling when it occurs to him he hasn't had an afternoon snack yet.

Vending machine calling his name, Jason rises from his desk and grabs his phone off the corner, jingling the quarters in his pocket as he makes his way towards the cafeteria. There's a vending machine near the gym that's a little closer, but he knows from personal experience that by Wednesday that one is in desperate need of restocking. That won't happen until tomorrow, so he makes the longer trek across campus, hoping for a very specific snack. Specifically one that is flat and shaped like a Pop-Tart.

Fifteen minutes later, Jason rips open his Pop-Tart and eats the first one in three bites before he slows down on the second. When he finishes, his stomach feels better, but he's still a little restless. He makes his way to the front office to see if Mabel needs help with anything, but stops when he spots Mr. Caldwell inside already talking to her.

Change of plans then. Turning, he walks back the way he came, plopping himself on one of the benches and withdrawing his phone. He swipes up, unlocking the home screen before opening his contact list. Theo is at work and never answers his phone while there, and Charlie never answers his phone period. Alec usually answers, but Jason's pretty sure Wednesdays are his long day on campus, which leaves Andrew. Perfect.

Tapping his brother's name he waits, listening to the rings. On the fifth, he's sure he's going to be sent to voicemail when the phone stops and a familiar voice drifts over the line.

"Jason? What's wrong?"

"Why would you assume something is wrong?"

"You never call me."

"What are you talking about? I talk to you all the time."

Andrew pauses. "Yeah, in the group chat or when we hang out with everyone else. You almost never call me."

"Sure I do." Jason protests. He leans forward, frowning. "Wait, never?"

"Is something wrong, or was everyone else busy?" Andrew asks, avoiding the question.

"I can just wanna call my big brother," Jason says, a little stab of guilt in his gut at Andrew's assumptions.

"Oh." Andrew sounds surprised, which only makes Jason feel even worse.

"You're not busy, are you?" Jason asks, realizing he doesn't know Andrew's schedule as well as the rest of his brothers.

"Nothing that can't wait. I was just running some numbers." He listens to the sound of Andrew rapidly typing. "There, I saved my data, just in case. What's up?"

"I just wanted to talk," Jason tells him. "How are things with you?"

"Same as always. Well, except for Charlie being weird as shit."

"Charlie's always weird," Jason points out.

"Yeah, but like weirder. He's cranky as fuck."

"Is he still upset about Theo and Alec getting engaged?"

"I don't think so. You know it took him a long time to get over things right after the accident, but he and Theo are in a decent place now. It's definitely something else, but he's not telling me."

"That is weird," Jason concedes, unsure he can recall the twins ever keeping anything from each other.

"I'll figure it out, don't worry. I can handle it."

"I wasn't—"

"How are things with you?" Andrew interrupts, before Jason can get a full sentence out.

"I'm good."

"Cut the bullshit. What's wrong?"

"How the fuck do you do that? Do you have, like, mind powers?"

"I don't need mind powers to know my baby brother. Something is on your mind. I can tell. Come on, spill."

"There's this guy," Jason says, surprised at how easily that comes out. He's not sure he even realized what was bothering him. Leave it to Andrew to parse it out in less than five minutes.

"I'm going to need more than that, Jason. Friend? Coworker?"

"Both," Jason tells him. "He's the new English teacher.

He's—great. He's kind of quiet until he gets to know you then he talks a lot. Especially about things he likes, like Lord of the Rings. He's sweet too, and he makes me laugh."

The line goes so quiet that Jason thinks the call dropped. He turns his phone to look but the call is still connected.

"Andrew?"

"This guy," Andrew prompts, "are you spending a lot of time together?"

"Well sure, we're coworkers. He takes the bus in the mornings, so I wait for him in the parking lot, you know, just to make sure he gets there alright and see how he is. Oh, and we've started having lunch together a few days a week in my office. I'd do it every day, but sometimes I can't make it because of coaching stuff. You know how busy the beginning of a new season can be. When that happens, I make sure and swing by his class at the end of the day to see how his day went. You know, normal coworker stuff."

"Right."

"Why did you say 'right' like that?" Jason frowns.

"I didn't say it like anything."

"You did. You had a tone."

"I didn't have a tone."

Andrew definitely had a tone, but Jason doesn't bother arguing. No one wins an argument with Andrew King. Not even Charlie. If any of the King boys could've been a lawyer like their parents, it's Andrew, but he's always been a numbers man.

"Anyway, there's just one little problem," Jason sighs, only realizing now that he's talking about it, how much it's been bothering him.

"Which is?"

"Well you know how unreliable the buses can be here.

Sometimes, a lot of times, they're late, which obviously bothers Emerson." When Andrew doesn't immediately seem outraged Jason continues. "He likes when things are on time and predictable. He's, well—"

"I get it," Andrew says, and Jason's entire body relaxes. Of all his brothers, Andrew would be the one to understand.

"Then you see the big problem."

"Not exactly."

"The bus is late. I offered to give Emerson a ride to work every day so he won't have to deal with that, and he hasn't taken me up on it. Maybe I need to just offer again."

"Or maybe he likes the bus."

"He doesn't like the bus," Jason argues. "It's crowded and loud."

"Well then maybe he has another reason for not taking you up on the offer." Andrew's tone shifts into that big brother one where he's going to tell Jason something he doesn't want to hear. "You know you can't fix everyone's problems. Maybe—"

"Oh wow I have to go," Jason blurts. "One of my players is waving me over."

"Jason."

"I'll talk to you later, Andrew."

"Alright but—you know I love you no matter what, right? That nothing could change that?"

It's a weird thing to say right now, but Andrew has always been like that with Jason and Alec. Protective. Demonstrative. Making sure they're okay.

"Sure, of course. I love you too," Jason tells him, realizing maybe he doesn't say it enough to Andrew. "I really do gotta go. He's coming over right now. Bye!"

Taking the chicken shit way out, Jason hangs up to

avoid any other brotherly advice, pocketing his phone before heading back to his office. At least his conversation with Andrew made one thing clear: there is a problem, and Jason is determined to fix it somehow.

Emerson is his friend, and friends take care of each other. Jason is just being a good friend, nothing less and nothing more.

THE CONVERSATION with Andrew lingers in the back of Jason's mind. As much as he wants to barrel into the situation like he might with Theo or one of his brothers, he knows that approach won't work with Emerson. He needs a gentler hand, a more patient approach. Jason doesn't want to overstep either, hesitant to make Emerson uncomfortable, which is the only thing that holds him back.

Casually as he can, Jason drops hints about picking up Emerson on Thursday when the bus is late again. Emerson doesn't pick up on it, so he tries again on Friday, but that too fails. By the following week when not even his hints over text on the weekend work, he realizes that direct communication is the only way to go with Emerson. Yet even knowing this, Jason hesitates, not wanting to put Emerson on the spot in case there is some reason he doesn't want to ride with Jason.

Not that Jason can think of a good reason. He knows now without a doubt that Emerson doesn't like the bus. He also knows Emerson enjoys his company because he's taken to smiling when he sees Jason waiting by his truck in the mornings, which makes Jason very happy. That first smile from Emerson in the morning is enough to fuel him through the long day of teaching and practice.

Something about knowing he's the only one on campus who gets Emerson's unmasked smile, that he's the one who Emerson shares lunch with and laughter with, makes Jason feel ten feet tall. He can't quite understand why everyone else isn't clamoring to hang out with Emerson when he's so obviously the smartest, most interesting person on campus, but it's their loss. Besides, Emerson has made it clear the only person he's interested in spending prolonged periods of time with outside of his teaching is Jason, another thing that floods him with pride.

He might have plenty of friends at work, but none of those friendships come close to being as satisfying as the one he shares with Emerson. Somehow, over early morning conversations and shared lunches, Emerson has become someone Jason can't imagine going a single day without talking to. Luckily for him, he doesn't have to since they've easily fallen into a routine of texting at night when Jason gets home from practice and on the weekends when they don't get to see each other at work.

It's strange because it's so unlike his friendship with Theo, not stronger or better just—different. Comparing his friendship with Emerson to the one with Theo is a train of thought Jason doesn't want to go down. Mostly because it's kind of confusing and he'd rather focus on things that are more tangible, like figuring out how to get Emerson to take him up on his offer to drive him to work.

Incidentally, this is exactly how Jason finds himself driving to work ten minutes after he would normally already be at work.

Nearing Emerson's apartment building he taps his break, slowing his truck down enough that the person behind him lays on their horn within a nanosecond. They haul ass around him at which point Jason offers them a smile, only to receive a middle finger in return.

He slows down further, not wanting to pass the bus stop without being sure Emerson made it to work on time. Judging by the cluster of people milling around, he hasn't. Flipping his blinker on, he pulls up to the curb a few car lengths back wanting to be positive. It only takes him a few seconds to spot the familiar head of red hair. Emerson's hunched forward, leg bouncing as he taps on it. Jason slowly inches his truck forward to get a better look, catching sight of Emerson's ear defenders pushing his hair off his face and highlighting the sharpness of his high cheekbones.

The sight of him makes Jason smile, though this is quickly followed by a wave of guilt. If Emerson is still here, then his bus is late. While it's not going to make him late for work, it's enough to mess with his schedule. This will be the fourth time this week it's happened. Jason knows, even without Emerson complaining, because he waits for his arrival every morning.

Some of the people around him turn to stare, likely because Jason is now pulled halfway into the loading zone, but since the bus still isn't here, he doesn't care much. He waits a few seconds and is rewarded when Emerson lifts his head, meeting Jason's gaze head on. There's a flicker of surprise, then his lips turn up in the corner that way they do when he's genuinely pleased and yeah, Jason feels ten fucking feet tall. This was definitely the right choice. He's so glad he didn't listen to Andrew.

Emerson rises from the bench, shouldering his bag and walking towards Jason.

"What a coincidence running into you here."

The space between Emerson's pale eyebrows furrows.

"How is it a coincidence? Don't you drive this way every day?"

"I do," Jason confirms. Where he might tease Theo or his brothers, something infinitely softer comes out when he's around Emerson. "Bus is late again."

"It is," Emerson sighs, turning to look down the street. There's no sign of the bus.

"Let me give you a ride to work," Jason offers, already leaning sideways to grab the handle. "Hop in."

"Are you sure?" Emerson asks.

"I wouldn't say it if I wasn't sure," Jason tells him. "Get in the truck, Emerson."

This is clearly the right thing to say because Emerson hurries into the truck, tossing his bag on the seat for Jason to move before hefting himself inside. He stretches out his long legs, pushing his ear defenders off and around his neck before running a hand through his hair. It's in absolute chaos this morning. It's honestly kind of adorable.

"I swear I brushed it," Emerson mumbles, patting it down.

"Your hair is too powerful, Pumpkin."

Emerson splutters, opening and shutting his mouth several times.

"That another no?" Jason laughs, unsure why the sight of a faint blush on Emerson's cheeks makes him want to come up with a million more nicknames. Much as he wants to settle on the right one, there's something fun about his reactions to the ones Emerson dislikes. Especially now.

"I do not enjoy squash."

"No squash, got it," Jason says, trying and failing to keep a straight face.

"You're laughing at me."

"I mean, yes," Jason admits, "but only because you're kind of adorable."

"What?"

"Adorable," Jason repeats. "Surely people have told you that before?"

"I—*no*," Emerson hisses, buckling his seatbelt while Jason merges back into the flow of traffic. "That's just...no."

"Huh, they should. Or maybe pretty. That's true too."

The response to this comment is complete and utter silence, which has Jason stealing a glance at Emerson to find that the faint pink on his cheeks has darkened into a deep red that stains his cheeks and now trails down the line of his neck.

"Guys must've called you pretty before," Jason continues, unable to comprehend anything but this being the truth. Hell, Jason is straight, and he can see plain as day that Emerson is gorgeous. Everything from his pale eyelashes and high cheekbones to the fullness of his lips, it all screams beautiful. Surely people have told him before. "Ex-boyfriends at the very least?"

Emerson mumbles something unintelligible.

"What?"

"No," Emerson practically shouts. He looks embarrassed, fidgeting with his ring before adding, "I don't—that is, *ugh*."

When he groans loudly, Jason can't help but worry that he's fucked up. He's never seen a problem complimenting people regardless of gender. Anyone who says men can't offer compliments is full of shit as far as Jason is concerned. Except maybe Emerson doesn't like to be complimented? Maybe he's like Theo and is shy about it.

"Would you rather I didn't say that again?" Jason asks.

"I mean you are pretty, but if you don't like compliments, you can just tell me to shut the fuck up."

Emerson merely groans again. "I thought you were straight."

"I am but, I have eyes, Emerson." He grins, hoping to ease whatever it is that's got Emerson sitting stiff as a board. "You deserve to be complimented. Unless you don't like it, and then I'll shut my big mouth. I might not know when to be quiet, but I'm definitely good at doing what I'm told."

There's half a beat of silence before Emerson says, "That's not what Mabel told me."

"Emerson Miller, how dare you and Mabel conspire against me."

"I wasn't," Emerson says seriously.

"I know," Jason says, reaching over to give his knee a squeeze. "I'm just teasing. And also, Mabel is correct. I was a bit of a shit in school, but not like a mean shit just—you know I had two older brothers I was constantly compared to at school, and I was kind of desperate for people to like me? Playing football, making people laugh and joking around got me the attention I was craving. It was nice to be seen outside of my brothers or my last name. Sometimes I maybe took it a little too far, but I was an idiot teenager."

"I think teenagers by nature are kind of idiots."

"Somehow I don't think you were. I bet you didn't get in any trouble, did you?"

"You'd be surprised," Emerson says. "Turns out asking clarifying questions in class can be seen as argumentative."

"If you can't handle kids asking questions, you probably shouldn't be a teacher," Jason gripes, slowing his truck to turn into the school parking lot.

"I wish more people agreed with you," Emerson sighs. "You'd be surprised how many people, including teachers, thought I was being disrespectful or argumentative because I asked questions for things that, apparently, I should've known the answer to."

Emerson's expression takes on an unfamiliar edge, his body language radiating discomfort in a way that makes Jason want to have a strong word with every person responsible for making Emerson feel this way.

"Seriously, fuck people who make kids feel bad," Jason says, glad his windows are up so the students hovering nearby in the parking lot can't hear him. He's not in the mood to mince words right now. "The absolute biggest 'fuck you' to them."

"It's okay, Jason."

"It's not though." Jason shakes his head, pulling into one of the teacher parking spots. He flips off the ignition but makes no move to get out. "My brother Alec was one of those kids that was a lot to handle, too fidgety and loud, always got in trouble for talking back. He was a good fucking kid, but he wasn't built to sit in a square in kindergarten, or to have calm hands or a quiet mouth or whatever other ableist bullshit they spewed that made him feel so bad about himself. It pisses me the fuck off." Jason takes a deep breath, not wanting to upset Emerson with his tirade but also unable to stop himself. "Adults should be there to support kids, not tear them down. So fuck anyone who made you think the way you processed information or what you needed was wrong."

"Jason."

"Fuck them, Emerson."

"Okay," Emerson whispers, staring at Jason with wide eyes and an unreadable expression.

"I'm sorry," Jason says with every ounce of conviction he can muster. "It just makes me so mad. I think most people, most teachers are really fucking great, but there are always some who aren't and—and they don't matter. They're not your people."

"I'm not sure I have people," Emerson says in a tone that sounds matter of fact, yet manages to threaten to break Jason's heart into tiny little pieces. He wants to protect Emerson with a ferocity that takes him by surprise, the same kind of intense need he'd felt when he met Theo on the playground. Friendship isn't as simple as it was back when he was a kid, and yet Jason can't help but wonder why it can't be. Emerson is great—sweet, smart and easy to be around. If he wants them to be friends, then he should make it happen.

"Come to my place on Saturday," Jason blurts, an idea taking shape.

"Why?"

"Pizza," Jason answers. "You like pizza right?"

"I like cheese pizza," Emerson offers, the slightest tilt to his head, like Jason is something he doesn't understand. Truth be told, Jason hardly understands himself right now. All he knows is that Emerson deserves people, and Jason has good people, the kind who would like Emerson just as much as Jason does if they got to know him, he's sure of it.

"Good, then I'll order cheese pizza, and you'll come to my house. You can meet my dogs."

"I like dogs." Emerson sits just a little bit taller.

"You can meet Alec and Theo too."

"Wait, what?" Emerson blinks.

"Theo and me have a weekly pizza night. Usually we do Friday nights, but during football season it gets moved to Saturdays. And now that Theo and Alec are together, Alec usually comes. Sometimes he's hanging out with his friends or too busy studying, but I'm pretty sure he's coming this weekend. We switch off weeks, and last weekend was at Theo's place, which means this week is at my house, so it's perfect."

"Perfect," Emerson utters like the word is entirely foreign to him. "You want me to meet your brother and your best friend? Are you sure? I don't want to intrude or anything. I'm not...fun."

"I think you're fun," Jason tells him.

"I dunno," Emerson mumbles.

"You don't have to," Jason hurries, wanting to give him a choice. Yet once those words are out, they don't sit quite right. He can't explain why this is so important, only knows it is and while he doesn't want Emerson to feel pressured, he really wants him there. "But it would make me really happy if you came."

"You want me there?" Emerson asks as if there is actually a question.

The bell rings, but for once neither of them move, not even Emerson, though Jason knows he's heard it.

"I really want you there," Jason confirms. Then he waits.

Outside the truck, students are laughing and yelling as they hurry to class, but Jason is frozen, watching the slow rise and fall of Emerson's chest before he nods. "Alright, I'll come."

JASON ADJUSTS the couch pillows for the fourth time in the last fifteen minutes, giving Stella what he hopes is a very serious expression.

"You leave them alone this time now."

Stella barks, leaping onto the couch and knocking the

pillows to the floor. Jason sighs, giving up and gathering them up. He hasn't been able to use couch pillows since he got Stella who, for reasons unknown to Jason, hates them. When it's just Theo or his brothers, he doesn't bother, but since Emerson is coming, he'd wanted the place to look nice.

He moves to the fireplace, stacking them in the corner when the knock at the front door comes. Surprised, he turns to look at the clock. It's not even six yet, way too early for Alec and Theo. Maybe Emerson is early. That would give them some extra time together which would be nice. Between Friday night's game and Saturday morning practice he's barely gotten to talk to Emerson in the last twenty-four hours. In fact, the only text he got today was a short reply letting him know Emerson is still coming.

Hurrying to the door, he yanks it open, ignoring Stella and Freddie's excited barks. His wide grin turns to a frown. "What the fuck are you doing here?"

"You invited us," Alec answers, shouldering his way in past Jason. "Unless you're getting senile in your old age and forgot. So where is this mystery person? Are they here yet? That was a shitty welcome by the way. Maybe you need etiquette lessons. You want to practice before your company gets here?"

A knot of tension forms between Jason's shoulders. Alec and Theo are always late. He expected them to be here a good twenty or thirty minutes after he told them. It was supposed to give him time to make sure Emerson is comfortable and give him a little tour.

"I didn't forget. You're just early." Jason peers out the front door watching Theo walk up. He lifts his hands in silent question and Theo returns the gesture with a shrug. "Since when are you two early?"

"Since you invited someone to pizza. I want to meet

them. Honestly though, I'm just glad you're over what's-her-face."

"Why are we talking about Nicole?" Theo asks, stepping into the house and closing the front door behind him.

"We are not talking about what's-her-face, because we don't mention her name." Alec glares at Theo. Even though Jason isn't still upset about his ex-girlfriend, it's clear Alec still is.

"Now let's get back to the situation at hand. Jason invited a date over. He's never invited anyone, this is huge."

"It's not a date," Jason protests. "Besides I've invited someone over before."

"No, you haven't," Theo replies, pulling Jason into a bear hug. "You're lucky I managed to put Alec off as long as I did. He's been trying to come over for the last two hours."

"I have not," Alec protests, squatting down so Freddie can climb into his lap. After Jason, Alec is definitely Freddie's favorite person, and his tail whacks the hardwood floor as he licks Alec's face. "Who's the best boy in the whole world? Yes, you are."

"Did you want to come to see me or the dogs?" Jason laughs.

"The dogs obviously," Alec says, flipping Jason off before laying on the floor. Stella barks excitedly, jumping all over Alec.

"You guys better not jump on Emerson when he gets here, or I'm putting you in the garage," Jason grumbles.

Alec's head snaps up. "Who's Emerson?"

"The guy coming. I told you."

"No, you told Theo you invited someone. You didn't say it was a guy."

"Emerson," Theo pipes up. "The new English teacher?"

"Yeah, he—"

"Why do you know who Emerson is and I don't?" Alec demands.

"Best friend privileges," Theo answers, turning his attention to Jason. "I didn't realize you two were so close."

"We're friends," Jason answers. "I'm not replacing you."

"I didn't think you were. It's just, well, I know I've been...busy with stuff." Stuff. Code for Alec.

"I told you, it's fine," Jason says. They've had this conversation before and if it were up to Jason, they'd never have it again, but Theo's guilt complex is apparently in full swing again. It's exactly why Jason didn't elaborate when he mentioned this to Theo. Well that, and he knew Theo would tell Alec, and he wasn't ready for that conversation.

"Because you have Emerson," Theo says.

"What the fuck is going on?" Alec asks, eyes darting between Jason and Theo.

"I'll tell you later," Theo answers.

"No, I wanna know now," Alec counters, rising from the floor. "Who's Emerson? What am I missing? What—"

Theo swiftly moves into Alec's personal space, crowding him back till his legs hit the sofa and wrapping a hand around the back of his neck. Alec lets out a sound that Jason absolutely never needs to hear any of his brothers making before Theo silences him with a kiss.

Averting his gaze, Jason watches the clock until he hears Theo clear his throat signaling it's safe to look. When Jason turns around, it's all he can do not to laugh at the dazed look on Alec's face.

"Whipped," Jason whistles.

"Fuck you," Alec says with decidedly less bite than usual. He adjusts his sweats, turning away from them both. "I need a Coke. I'll be right back."

"Check the fridge," Jason says, realizing he forgot to buy any Coke for Alec but not wanting to admit that.

"Obviously," Alec retorts, nearly in the kitchen when he yells, "Just wait until you get a partner, I'm gonna give you so much shit."

"I'm not dating," Jason turns to yell, startled when he turns back around to find Theo staring at him. "What?"

"Emerson."

"Yes."

"When is he coming?" Theo asks.

"Uh, I told him six, and he's usually on time. Unless the bus is late then—"

"Why the fuck is the fridge full of Dr. Pepper?" Alec bellows from the kitchen. "Who drinks fucking Dr. Pepper?"

Before Jason gets a chance to answer, Alec reappears in the living room looking decidedly disgruntled. He's holding a can of Dr. Pepper in one hand, but he hasn't opened it, instead staring at it like it's personally offended him.

"What the fuck, Jason?"

"It's soda."

"Soda is not Coke," Alec retorts. "This is a flavor abomination. It tastes fruity. Who wants fruity soda?"

The question is clearly rhetorical, yet Jason finds himself answering anyway. "Emerson."

"Emerson," Alec repeats, sounding out each consonant in the name like he's never heard it before. "Are you telling me the fridge is full of Dr. Pepper for your new friend? Oh my god, is this—"

"Alexander," Theo interrupts, curling his fingers around Alec's hip.

"What?" Alec asks, tone softening exponentially as his attention immediately shifts from Jason to Theo.

"I'll take you to Sonic to get a Coke."

"At least someone cares about what I like." Alec directs this at Jason, like having the wrong soda is a mortal offense.

Theo pulls Alec towards the front door, but his attention is on Jason. "We'll be back in thirty minutes."

"Why are we gonna be back in thirty—*oh*." Alec grins. "Yeah, we'll be back in thirty minutes."

Not at all wanting to think about why it's going to take them thirty minutes to get Alec his goddamn Coke but also grateful that Theo is giving Jason a reprieve from the twenty questions, he shuts the door behind them before turning his attention to his fur babies.

"You two need to behave better than Alec, or I'm putting all three of you in the other room when Emerson gets here."

9 EMERSON

STANDING in front of Jason's front door, hand curled into a fist and poised to knock, Emerson has a rush of doubt. What the hell is he doing? Emerson doesn't go to people's houses to hang out. Not with a handsome, popular football coach. Not with anyone. The last time he'd gone to someone's house for pizza, he was fifteen, and that had ended with Emerson spending most of the time in the bathroom hiding.

The social unknowns for this kind of situation have always caused more stress than they're worth, especially once Emerson realized people liked the masked version of him better. He is more than capable of getting along in social settings, of pretending he doesn't have to overthink every part of a conversation or plan eye contact. He knows how to avoid infodumping at people, even though the urge sometimes claws at him. Being high-masking is exactly why it took him so long to get diagnosed in the first place. *You're lucky you have lower support needs,* someone told him once, but all Emerson heard was, *your autism doesn't affect us, so we don't see it.*

Anxiety rises the longer Emerson stands at the front door hesitating to knock. He knows what to expect tonight in abject terms, but he would feel better knowing exactly what he's walking into. That's not possible since he's never met Theo or Alec.

"You can do this," Emerson mumbles, lifting his hand with every intention of knocking. Before he can, the door is yanked open to reveal Jason, his bulk blocking the inside of the house.

"You came," Jason grins as if Emerson standing awkwardly on his front porch is the best thing that happened to him all day. It's actually ridiculous how nice Jason is. Sometimes Emerson swears it must be fake, then he remembers that Jason is the least fake person he's ever met, and something in him settles.

"You did invite me," Emerson replies.

"I did." Jason's smile widens. "I'm really glad you're here."

Behind him a dog barks loudly, nearly knocking Jason over when it tries to shove its way between Jason's legs.

"Calm down, Stella."

"Stella," Emerson croaks, experiencing a visceral flashback to the conversation he overheard between Jason and Mabel earlier this week. The woman who took Jason's towel hadn't been a woman at all, it'd been his dog. While Emerson has no grounds for feeling relieved, he is. He's also incredibly embarrassed. Maybe this is his karma for crushing on his straight friend.

"Uh-huh. This attention seeking pain in the ass right here is Stella," Jason says, widening his legs so she can sneak through. Despite her speed, Jason is quick to grab on to her collar to stop her from charging at Emerson, for which he is very grateful. "She's a sweetheart. A menace, but also a sweetheart. She doesn't get to meet new people often, so you'll have to excuse her piss poor manners. If it's too much, just say the word, and I'll put her in the garage."

"You don't need to do that," Emerson mumbles. "This is her house."

"If she makes you uncomfortable, I do. Besides, it's not like she's being punished if she goes out there. I installed an AC unit so it never gets too hot, and she has a bed and a lot of toys. She's spoiled. Her and Freddie both."

"Where's Freddie?" Emerson asks, trying to peer around Jason.

"Probably hiding behind the couch. He's scared of everything."

"That's relatable," Emerson remarks. "I would also hide behind the couch if it was socially acceptable."

"Well, I'll do my best to not do anything that makes you want to hide. Unfortunately, I can't make promises for Stella or Freddie." Jason's smile is easy, kind, like Emerson admitting he would rather hide than be here isn't grounds for ending the friendship here and now. "You can come in, you know. How did you get here by the way? When you told me you didn't need a ride, I didn't ask."

"Uber," Emerson answers.

"There's a bus stop on the corner."

"I know." Emerson does not want to admit that he looked up directions, then decided the possibility of getting lost was too high and ended up calling an Uber to bring him directly to Jason's front door. He's not even sure why he turned down Jason's offer for a ride. Well, yes he is. Because until the second he stepped out of the Uber, his brain was desperately looking for a way out of this situation, even though he wanted to do it. Sometimes his brain is a jerk like that, trying to get out of things that he wants to do just because they are new and make him uncomfortable.

"Next time you should just let me pick you up," Jason says, bracketing Stella with his legs and moving them both out of the doorway so Emerson can step inside.

"You should probably wait until the night ends to issue a second invitation."

"Why would I do that?" Jason questions, like he genuinely can't imagine.

"I—" Emerson starts, cutting himself off. *He's not your cousin, or your family*, he reminds himself. Jason's not going to get annoyed with Emerson because he's overwhelmed or different. He's spent most lunch breaks with Emerson the last two weeks and isn't sick of him yet.

Yet.

"Would you like to meet Stella?" Jason offers, almost as if sensing Emerson's need for a distraction. "I'm going to let go of her collar, she's probably going to lick you but she doesn't bite. If you need her to stop, let me know."

Emerson nods, relieved to have something else to focus on. Jason kicks the front door shut before loosening his hold on Stella's collar. Sure enough, she barrels towards Emerson, who is prepared this time, laughing at the armful of dog he gets. She does lick his hands and his cheek, trying to climb into his lap and knocking him on his ass. Emerson can't help but grin, charmed by her exuberance. She's kind of like Jason really, over eager and easy to understand. And he realizes, heart thumping against his ribs, happy to see him.

"Stella, don't scare him away, we want him to come back."

"I'm not scared," Emerson assures him, smoothing his hands over Stella's fur. It's thick, not as soft as he expected but soothing to touch. The more he pets her the more she calms until she's sprawled in Emerson's lap panting happily. "I think she likes me."

When Jason doesn't reply he looks up, unprepared for the way Jason is looking at him.

"What?" Emerson asks, suddenly worried he did something wrong.

"How did you do that?"

"Do what?"

"Calm her down," Jason gapes.

"Uh, she likes her tummy rubbed." To prove his point, he strokes Stella's tummy, delighting in how easy dogs are to read. She's happy and lets Emerson know it. No platitudes or fake niceties. Maybe one day if he's lucky, he can have his own dog.

"I know, just—she's not like this. I mean with me, yeah. But no one else. Not even Alec." Jason squats down, staring at Stella. He reaches out, smoothing his palm over her side in time with Emerson's strokes. They continue like that for long seconds, each of them petting Stella, separate but together. It's nice in the kind of way Emerson never would've expected.

"I like your dog," he says after what feels like a very long amount of silence.

The smile that spreads across Jason's face is familiar, comforting, and it startles Emerson to realize how used to it being aimed his way he's getting. He has no right craving that soft affection directed towards him, yet he does, and there is no one to blame but himself. Well, except maybe Jason and his damn big smile.

"Clearly the feeling is mutual," Jason says, lowering himself to the floor. Unlike Emerson who's sitting cross-legged, Jason stretches out his long limbs so they're bracketing Emerson and Stella. The material of his gray sweats pulls obscenely tight over his thick thighs.

"Don't move."

Emerson freezes, fingers curled in Stella's thick fur as his heart immediately lodges itself in his throat.

"Don't panic either," Jason says in a soothing tone. "I just see Freddie peeking around the back of the couch. He's watching you."

"What do I do?" Emerson asks.

"Just wait for him to come," Jason says. "Pet Stella again. I think he's jealous. When he realizes you'll pet him too, he's gonna come out."

"Alright," Emerson whispers, afraid to even breathe too loudly and risk scaring Freddie off.

Despite Jason's instructions, he doesn't move his hand. He's supposed to, he knows, but he's frozen, afraid of messing up and scaring off Freddie.

"Breathe," Jason reminds him. Emerson takes a steadying breath but still doesn't move. Not until Jason lowers his hand over Emerson's, guiding both of them in a soothing motion over Stella's back. "This okay?"

Okay. What a vague word. So easy to lie, so impossible to judge. Emerson has been okay for most of his life but what does that even mean? He was okay when his mom died, okay when he moved into a home where he was unwanted, okay when he was bullied, okay when he was diagnosed. Emerson has always been okay.

So no, he's not okay right now. He's something else. Something he doesn't understand. Here on the floor of Jason's house, Emerson feels more welcome than he ever did in his own home.

"Emmy?"

Emerson's heart gets stuck in his throat. Every time Jason suggested a nickname before, his instant reaction was no. They'd felt wrong, like the too itchy shirts his aunt used to buy him. This nickname is like soft cotton, no tags, perfect fit. It feels like him in a way that makes his jaw wobble.

"Guess that's another fail," Jason says with soft laughter, misreading Emerson's silence.

If Emerson could talk, he might scream. It's not a no. He wants to hear it again. Needs to hear it again. If only his brain didn't paralyze him sometimes, rendering him unable to talk even as his brain works overtime. Going nonverbal is the strangest feeling. Because he knows he's capable of speaking, yet the words simply won't come out, no matter how hard he tries.

"Emerson?"

He opens his mouth but a reply won't come. It's embarrassing how much that makes him want to cry, makes him feel like a child again ready to be chastised for being antisocial or too shy even though he'd tried explaining he didn't stop talking on purpose.

Jason's gaze isn't full of exasperation or annoyance, making the words somehow lodge themselves so firmly in Emerson's throat he might as well be choking on them. If he doesn't get it out now, he knows he won't ever get the nerve to do it later, but the plea is stuck on the tip of his tongue. *Please*, he wants to beg. *Please*.

Slowly Jason scoots closer, his thighs bracketing Emerson's knees while Stella chuffs for attention.

"You with me?" Jason asks.

The smallest of nods is the most Emerson can manage, but it earns him one of Jason's smiles, loosening the knot of tension around his chest. He's not mad, or calling Emerson rude or weird. He's just smiling at him like, well—like Emerson is okay just how he is.

"Was the nickname that bad?"

Tell him. Tell him.

The words won't come. Being able to contextualize his thoughts but not being able to give voice to them is like being trapped, and the spiral of frustration and shame only makes those words slip through his fingertips like grains of sand. He knows exactly what he should say, what he wants to say, but he simply can't.

The air in his lungs doesn't seem to register, and every lub-dub of his heart is grating and overstimulating. It's not fair. He's not even unhappy and—someone is texting him. No one texts him. No one but Jason. Startled, Emerson's attention is drawn to Jason who is holding his own phone between his large hands. He taps out a message, and Emerson's phone buzzes again.

Emerson breathes in deep. Once, twice. All the while Jason's eyes stay on his phone, waiting. Waiting for Emerson to take his phone out of his pocket. Somehow, despite knowing whose name will be on the screen, he's not prepared when he swipes it open and reads the messages.

Jason
hey

I thought maybe this might be easier.
talking without talking ;)

Being hyperverbal means Emerson is rarely lost for words, but the few times this has happened to him in the past, he was met with misunderstanding and confusion. Yet here is Jason meeting him where he is, without demand or judgment. Suddenly the words trapped in his mind have a place to go, and his fingers fly across the screen.

Emerson
How did you know?

Jason
you're not the first person I've seen go nonverbal before. Matty before a game, my brother when he was younger

Emerson
I'm sorry.

Jason
dont ever apologize for how your brain works

but if it was something I did or said tell me so I dont do it again

please

Emerson hesitates, glancing from his phone to Jason who he catches staring. Jason's face has that same easy smile he always gives Emerson on it, which makes what he types next just that little bit easier.

Emerson
The nickname.

Jason
shit that bad?

Emerson
No. Not bad.

He looks up, watching the crease lines that form between Jason's eyebrows as he reads the message. He can't blame him for being confused when Emerson hardly understands himself. Does he like it? Maybe. He's not sure. He's so rarely sure about his feelings.

> **Emerson**
> When I was a kid my mom got me these feelings blocks. I used to get so frustrated that I didn't know which one I was feeling that I'd knock the tower down.

It's an innocuous enough confession, but it's the closest Emerson has ever come to sharing anything about his mom with anyone since she died, about his life before. Chewing on his bottom lip, he looks up and watches Jason. There are no typing bubbles, but he's doing something, and Emerson is content to wait, resuming his petting of Stella's back while watching Jason tap and swipe at his phone.

Eventually his phone buzzes and Emerson drops his gaze, lips tugging up in the corner when he sees that Jason has sent him a feelings chart. Except he's modified it and Emerson has to tap it to zoom in, curious what he's written. There at the bottom, instead of the word confused, the little emoji face has been crossed out and replaced with the blocky, messy handwriting he now knows belongs to Jason along with the words "needs to pet a dog."

Laughter bubbles up out of Emerson, startling Stella and Jason judging by the way his eyes dart up. His smile is hesitant but pleased. A second later a new text comes.

> **Jason**
> pretty sure petting a dog cures all

Emerson fights off a smile, typing his own return message.

Emerson
Are you volunteering yours?

Jason
consider Freddie and Stella yours, and I your humble servant

The smile breaks free, even as his words still won't, but that's alright. Jason doesn't seem to mind.

Emerson
You should probably be more careful making such generous offers. You never know what someone else's motivations might be. What if I text you at two in the morning demanding cuddles?

Jason's reply is swift.

Jason
from me or the dogs?

Emerson reads the message four times, sure he's misreading it. Jason can't be flirting, can he? No one has ever flirted with him before. Well, there was one guy in college who constantly tried to get Emerson to wear his jacket, but he always smelled like Spam. This can't be flirting because Jason is straight. Maybe friends cuddle. Emerson has never had a friend he was close enough with to know, but Jason is a touchy feely guy. That's probably all it is.

Before Emerson can formulate an appropriate reply, loud voices at the front door draw his attention away, startling him enough he drops his phone on Stella who barks before racing to the door with a wagging tail.

"I'm about to become the replacement human," Jason laughs.

"Are you gonna let us in or what?" someone yells. "Why is the door even locked?"

Steeling himself for the inevitable awkwardness, Emerson is unprepared for his phone to buzz again.

Jason
you still okay with this? we can do it another night or if you want you can hang out in my room for a bit until youre ready to meet them

The last thing he feels sure about is meeting new people, especially right now. But something about Jason's easy offer to accommodate his needs without questioning him, or trying to get out of hanging out makes Emerson feel unexpectedly brave.

Emerson
I think I'm alright, if you're okay with things being incredibly awkward. I don't think, well, I don't know if I'll be much of a conversationalist.

Holding his breath, he waits for the inevitable. For Jason to politely reschedule. It'll be better than avoiding him.

Jason
thats okay Alec talks enough for everyone

he means well but he's kind of like Stella

Emerson
Are you comparing your little brother to a dog?

Jason
definitely

When he looks up it's to find Jason with a smug grin. Before he knows what's happening Jason is yelling, "Hey Alec, did you know you're like Stella?"

"Open the door and say that to my face, dick face."

This is followed by a deeper, calmer voice. "Should we come back, Jason?"

Jason turns his attention to Emerson who shakes his phone, sending one last text.

Emerson
You can let them in, but thank you. For everything. No one has ever done something like this for me.

Jason's expression as he reads the message is unreadable, but he turns it into the all too familiar smile quickly. He rises to stand with an impressive amount of grace for someone so large, holding a hand out to Emerson who readily accepts the help. His own fingers curl around the width of Jason's broad palm, squeezing tightly before Jason gives a tug and hefts him up. He blinks, startled to come face to face with Jason. Or as close to face to face as you can with someone who is six-foot-five.

"We got this, Emerson, and if you need a swift escape I'm just a text away." He pats his pocket, shooting Emerson a wink before moving around him to unlock the front door.

Two men step inside, and Emerson quickly recognizes each of them from Jason's photos in his office. Theo is tall, though not as tall as Jason, with broad shoulders and the bluest eyes half-hidden behind his thick glasses. Despite his size, his presence doesn't command attention the way Jason's does, easily falling into step behind Jason's younger brother who, despite his much smaller stature, demands more attention than anyone in the room.

"Fucking finally. Thought you were gonna leave us out there all night," Alec grumbles. He sucks on the straw in his large drink before shooting Jason the middle finger.

"I was busy," is all Jason says, unruffled by Alec's attitude. "Alec, Theo. This is Emerson. Be nice."

"I am the nicest," Alec retorts, shooting Emerson a charming smile. While they don't look alike on the surface, when Alec smiles he looks so much like Jason, the shape of their happiness much the same. "Everyone loves me. Obviously Emerson will too. Right, Emerson?"

Emerson stiffens at the unexpected question. As if sensing his unease, Jason moves into his personal space and before Emerson knows what's happening that big, warm hand of his settles at the back of his neck giving a gentle squeeze. He's grateful for the contact, especially when Alec's eyes dart between Emerson and his brother. Before Alec can say anything else Theo wraps an arm around Alec's waist, lowering his chin to the top of Alec's head and offering him a friendly smile. "Nice to meet you, Emerson. Sorry we're late. This Coke addict needed a hit."

"Yeah because someone," he pauses, directing his glare at Jason, "filled the fridge with Dr. Pepper."

Pleasure and discomfort rise in equal measure. Jason has kept Emerson's favorite kind of pop in his mini fridge during lunch recently, but Emerson assumed he liked it too, even if Jason usually picks the green apple Gatorade and not the soda. The idea that he's been buying it just for

Emerson makes him feel warm in the cheeks, but the pleasure is short-lived because Alec looks decidedly annoyed by the prospect.

He opens his mouth, but the apology won't come, and he bites his lip with a sigh. He's off to a horrible start. Jason's brother and best friend are going to hate him.

"You know you could bring your own Coke next time," Jason points out.

"Fuck off," Alec grumbles, chewing on the end of his straw. He meanders forward, setting his soda on the coffee table before throwing himself on the couch. Stella jumps up on top of him, licking his face and barking. "I know, your daddy is so annoying, isn't he? Bet you're so glad your favorite person is here, aren't you?"

"Ignore Alec," Jason tells Emerson in a mock whisper.

"I can literally hear you, asshole."

Theo and Jason laugh at the same time, each of them grinning at Emerson like something is funny though he has no idea what.

"You want something to drink?" Jason asks Theo.

"You got any of that craft beer left?"

"I think I've got a can or two in the back of the fridge," he tells Theo before turning his gaze on Emerson. "Are you thirsty?"

Emerson has no idea if he's thirsty. He drank water a few hours ago. Usually he doesn't notice he's thirsty until a headache comes on. Either way, he nods because he could probably use a drink, and it affords him some way to participate in what's happening.

"Why don't you come with me to get the drinks," Jason says in a way that manages to sound like a gentle command and not a question. It's too easy to let Jason's hand move from his neck to his shoulder, guiding him towards the kitchen. The warmth and weight of his hand on Emerson's shoulder soothes away some of his deregulation, while making him ponder what it might feel like if Jason's hand inched lower to his waist. His hand is huge, and with it touching him now, it's all too easy to imagine what it would feel like to have that solid warmth somewhere else.

No one touches Emerson, and yeah maybe he's a little touch starved—or a lot—but Jason is also handsome and kind, and Emerson is probably a horrible person for thinking about Jason touching him like that while Jason is just being a good friend.

It's not until they're alone in the kitchen, the sound of Theo and Alec's voices fading into a low hum in the background that Emerson manages to find his voice. He holds the words in, watching Jason rummage around in the fridge pulling out a cold water bottle and a can of Dr. Pepper, which he passes to Emerson.

"Take both," he says, not making Emerson choose.

He's got his back turned to Emerson, chattering away about the beer he's looking for that he picked up at some craft brewery last week when Emerson manages to speak.

"I'm sorry."

Jason jerks, slamming his head on the shelf in his refrigerator. He curses softly under his breath turning to fix his frown on Emerson.

"Why?"

Breathing deeply through his nose, Emerson weighs the options. He could try and force more words out, but they feel heavy in a way he's never been able to explain. Or, he could text. Jason didn't seem to mind talking to him like that before. Decision made, he sets his drinks on the kitchen island so he can grab his phone, typing out a succinct message.

Emerson
About the Dr. Pepper. I don't want your brother to be mad. You don't need to keep anything special around for just me.

The lines on Jason's forehead creep together in a way that's unnatural on his otherwise jovial face. No one should ever make Jason King frown.

"Emmy."

Emerson inhales sharply, causing Jason to curse again.

"Sorry, fuck. You said no, and I just—"

Taking the one and only opportunity he might ever get, Emerson's fingers fly across his phone, grammar be damned.

Emerson
please

say it again

The lines on Jason's forehead deepen.

"You don't hate it?" he asks.

He's used to Jason's voice: loud, excited, booming, confident. He's not sure he's ever heard it sound so uncertain. He wants to remedy that. Quickly.

Emerson
It was nice. More than nice. I...I loved it.

The slow spread of joy across Jason's face is a wonder. So much of Emerson's life has been wasted trying to understand the people around him, unsure how they felt about a given social situation or even about Emerson. He doesn't have to do that with Jason. His face is so easy to read, his friendship so freely given.

Jason King is a gift, and Emerson has no idea what he did to deserve him.

"Yeah?" Emerson nods, and that clear happiness on Jason's face makes Emerson's insides squirm. He's not sure anyone has ever looked at him like this, and Emerson is entirely unprepared for the feelings it invokes.

Lowering his eyes to his phone, Jason types out a message that does nothing to curb the storm of emotions warring inside of Emerson.

Jason
I really want to hug you

would that be ok?

As a kid, Emerson used to imagine himself in one of his books. He'd be brave like the protagonist or popular. Sometimes he pretended he had enough coordination to dance or that everyone wanted to be his friend. After his mom died, they changed. He imagined he was a beloved hero or part of a daring trio. Occasionally, he imagined being swept off his feet by Prince Charming, one who didn't wear too much cologne or like loud parties. Mostly though, he dreamed about belonging, about what it might be like to be the leading kind of character, the kind that other people wanted around.

For reasons he doesn't begin to understand, Jason makes him feel like that.

"Emmy?" Jason whispers.

The words are as fragile as the broken snow globe from his childhood, his head a mess of water and glitter that's going to stick to everything when it breaks. Jason's got him shaken up and turned around, Emerson hardly knows which way is up. What he does know is that Jason is right here, his friendship the kind of safety net Emerson has never had before making what he says next just that little bit easier.

"Yes."

There's no hesitation from Jason as he closes the distance between them before Emerson is being hugged, really hugged, for the first time since his mom never came home. The embrace is barely there, almost as if Jason is afraid to hold on too tightly, and that makes something inside of him fracture. All the closed off needs and wants splinter into an infinite number of new cracks.

"Tighter," he chokes.

Jason doesn't ask if he's sure, trusting Emerson to know what he wants and needs. Slowly, Jason's arms tighten around him in the sweetest pressure, affording the permission Emerson needs to return the hug, relishing in the feeling of Jason pressed so tightly to him. To his relief, Jason doesn't pepper him with questions or release the hold too soon, seemingly content to let Emerson's fingers dig into the back of his cotton shirt and bury his face in Jason's shoulder.

There's undeniable strength in the arms that hold him but softness too, from the swell of his tummy to the slow cadence of his gentle breathing.

Has Emerson ever felt this good? This safe? Pleasure buzzes in his brain at the full-body contact, his entire nervous system sighing in pleasure the same way his body relaxes beneath the comfort of his favorite weighted blanket. Except hugging Jason is ten times better than his blanket, the curve of his muscles and softness surrounding Emerson in his strength and scent. While Emerson might be woefully inexperienced in this particular thing, he's certain there's no better hugger in the world than Jason.

Settling into the embrace, he focuses on the rise and fall

of Jason's chest, the faint ba-bump of his steady heart, and the hand that strokes up and down his back. Every bit of tension and unease bleeds from him in the most cathartic release he's ever experienced.

A loud knock at the door has Jason pulling back and though Emerson is disappointed to end the hug, it's hard to focus on anything besides the thrum of contentment pulsing through him.

"That's the pizza," Jason says, taking a small step back. "I should get it."

"Alright," Emerson nods.

"Are you okay?" Jason asks.

"I'm good," Emerson answers, surprised at how truthful the words are. "Really good."

The corners of Jason's mouth turn up in a smile, somehow smaller and softer than his usual, yet more affecting than any of them have ever been because this one is because of Emerson, *for* Emerson.

Someone clears their throat, and Emerson spins to find Theo in the archway, an unreadable expression on his face as he stares at Jason. "Pizza's here."

"Shit, yeah. I'll get that."

Jason moves past Emerson, pausing to give his arm another squeeze before he's gone, heading to the front door and leaving Emerson alone with Jason's best friend. He's heard enough stories about Theo to know how important he is to Jason—his favorite person in the world, Jason had called him once.

"So," Theo starts, moving towards the fridge. "You and Jason."

It's not exactly a question which is probably for the best since Emerson has no idea how to respond. Is Theo unhappy he crashed their pizza night? Jason insisted he and

Alec wouldn't mind, but maybe Jason was wrong. Doubt knots itself around his heart, the tension doubling when Theo doesn't say anything for long seconds, opening the fridge and pulling out a beer. He closes the fridge with his hip, blue eyes piercing in their intensity as he stares at Emerson.

"I don't know if you know this," Theo starts, popping the tab on the beer can, "but Jason has never invited anyone to our pizza nights before."

Emerson has no idea how he would know that.

"You're different," Theo continues, something in his tone gentling. Despite his size, he's got the same nonthreatening aura as Jason, and it's hard to continue being stressed out when he looks at Theo's smile or remembers all the nice things Jason has said about him. Maybe he's just a little jealous? If that's the case, he can reassure him.

"Jason is just being nice," Emerson tries, entirely out of his depth to navigate this situation.

"Jason is nice," Theo agrees. "He's the nicest guy I've ever known. He would do anything for the people he cares about. *Anything*."

He's not saying things that Emerson doesn't already know, though why he's saying them Emerson has no idea. Are they just talking about how wonderful Jason is? Because if so, that's easy.

"He's the best," Emerson agrees, thinking about the shape of his smile and the feeling of his arms. Best hardly begins to cover what Jason is. "I've never met anyone like him. He's funny and kind and helpful. He's...incredible."

Theo's smile grows. "You like him."

"I think anyone who meets Jason would like him," Emerson points out.

"Lots of people like Jason." Theo's smile dims. "Not everyone deserves him."

That makes Emerson frown. Have people been mean to Jason? He can't imagine that when Jason is so easy to like. But then, people are kind of terrible, so nothing would surprise him. Emerson almost asks, the question just on the tip of his tongue, when Jason reappears in the kitchen.

Jason's eyes dart between Theo and Emerson. "I'm not interrupting something, am I?"

"Not at all," Theo answers. "Emerson and I were just bonding."

"That right?" Jason grins, expression brightening. "Over what? Let me guess, you two were singing the praises of my dazzling charm and good looks?"

"Here I thought Alec had the market cornered on being conceited." Theo turns his gaze on Emerson. "One thing you'll quickly learn is there is no one who loves a King man more than, well—a King man."

Jason barks out a laugh, swinging his arm around Theo's shoulder. "Yeah, yeah. Says the man who loves two King men."

"Look what it's got me," Theo says with a grin.

"I'm gonna eat all the pizza if you guys don't hurry up," Alec yells from the other room, interrupting whatever it is that's happening between Theo and Jason. "Well maybe not all of it, this one has pineapple. Disgusting."

"Pineapple on pizza is the best," Jason yells back. He turns to Emerson and Theo with expectant eyes. "Right?"

"No," Theo and Emerson answer at the same time.

"I see how it is, my two favorite people teaming up against me," Jason says with a shake of his head. He keeps talking, but Emerson has stopped listening, his brain honing in on Jason's words.

My two favorite people.
My two favorite people.

10 JASON

"GOOD JOB CLASS, HIT THE LOCKERS," Jason yells, lips sealing around the end of his whistle as he gives a quick blow to catch the attention of the stragglers out at the edge of the field. He waits until every student is back and accounted for, well past the class dismissal bell, before departing the field. A quick glance at his watch shows he's got ten minutes until his next class. Not enough time to bother heading back to his office, or enough time to sneak over to Emerson's class and see how he's doing.

He saw him this morning when they drove to work together, and he's going to see him later, but Jason misses him already. It's weird because Jason's pretty sure he's never even wanted to talk to any of his girlfriends as much as he wants to talk to Emerson. Hell, even with Theo he can go a full work day without talking to him when he has to.

Something about Emerson is different, and Jason isn't too fussed about why. At first he thought it was wanting him to settle in but they're nearing the end of October now and he can't really use that excuse. The truth is he just likes Emerson.

Pulling his phone out of his pocket, he swipes open the screen, ignoring the thirty-seven new messages in the family group chat in favor of opening his last text stream with Emerson. Smile already pulling across his face, he types out a message.

Jason
are you busy?

i have a question

The response comes within seconds, almost as if Emerson had his phone in hand. Almost as if he was waiting for Jason. There's no way he was, but it makes Jason's smile widen all the same.

Emerson
What kind of question?

Jason
if someone wanted to start reading Tolkien where should they start

Emerson
That depends on the person and the time commitment. Are they looking for the full experience? The most accepted answer is to follow the publication order which would put The Hobbit first. Obviously The Lord of the Rings follows. Tell them to not read those out of order. Ever. There's a lot of lesser known published books too like The Similiarian or the Children of Hurin that come after.

By the time he's gotten to the end of the message, Jason's smiling wider than he has since, well, since he saw Emerson this morning on the drive to work. Emerson texts the way he talks, albeit a little bolder sometimes, and it's damn endearing. Not wanting to waste a minute of his time he's quick to reply.

Jason
that was a lot of titles

lets just say this person is not a reader and has no idea what they're doing

He could tell Emerson this is about him. There's no reason not to. Except that Jason kind of wants to surprise him. For the last week, he's been putting up with Jason rambling about football at lunch, listening in earnest while Jason spews player stats and works through plays. And even though he doesn't understand or care about football, he never asks Jason to stop talking. It makes Jason want to do the same in turn. He's never been a big reader, but ever since he overheard Emerson telling his students that audiobooks are reading, he's been thinking about picking one up for his runs. If he just so happens to want to learn more about Emerson's special interest so he gets to infodump, well, that's just him being a good friend.

His phone dings alerting him to a new message from Emerson.

Emerson
Anyone can be a reader. Is it one of your players? I could get them a spreadsheet with relevant Tolkien facts including publication order. Maybe a reading log too.

Jason
you have a Tolkien spreadsheet?

Emerson
Well, no, but I can make one.

He's so earnest Jason can hardly stand it, and he intends to tell him as much. Not enough people tell Emerson how smart and funny and handsome he is. If they won't, then Jason will. It's what Emerson deserves, and there's no rule against complimenting friends. He compliments Theo and his brothers. This is no different.

Jason
you are adorable

It takes a few seconds longer than usual, but when it does, it's so very Emerson.

Emerson
I think we should explore the possibility that you have questionable taste.

"What's got you smiling like that, Coach?"

Jason looks up at Matty's familiar voice to see him and Vicente, who prefers to go by his last name Sanchez, sharing matching shit-eating grins.

"None of your business," Jason grumbles, pocketing his phone. "Don't you two have somewhere to be? Mr. Caldwell's class is on the other side of campus."

"Caldwell," Sanchez snarks. "*Pinche pendejo.*"

"Language," Jason reminds him even though he echoes the sentiment. Caldwell's been a pain in the ass lately, likely because of homecoming on the horizon. Jason has lost count of how many times he's wanted to use equally colorful language, in both English and Spanish, to tell Caldwell off.

Unfortunately, he can't, and his position demands he not let his players do it either, even if it's deserved.

"Sorry, Coach," they echo.

"Go on and get out of here before I have to walk you to class so you're not late. Don't give Caldwell a reason to single you out. I know both of you will make me and this team proud."

Matty's usual smile falters before he shoves his hands in his pockets. "Yes, Coach."

Jason waits until they're across the field to pull his phone back out to read the second half of Emerson's text.

Emerson
You might be the first person in the world to think Tolkien spreadsheets were cute.

Jason
I told you, you're cute and for the record I have impeccable taste

case in point, pineapple on pizza

Emerson
Absolutely not. The only acceptable topping for pizza is cheese.

Jason
agree to disagree

Emerson
We can agree you are wrong.

The warning bell rings, leaving Jason feeling much like one of his students as he keeps his eyes glued on his screen while walking towards the gym, unable to to stop texting Emerson until the very last second.

Jason
feisty Emmy coming out

I like it

speaking of pizza, im hungry

Emerson
You're always hungry. Did you eat breakfast?

Jason
yes but that was hours ago

you still coming to my office for lunch

Emerson
I come every day. Except for Friday, obviously.

Jason
lucky me

you know the kids would love if you came

especially Arlo

Emerson
Maybe one day. I think one jock is enough for me at lunch time.

The late bell rings, and Jason knows he's got to put his damn phone away or risk making a hypocrite of himself in front of his kids, many of whom he has to remind daily that they don't need to be glued to their phones. Even as he sees familiar faces watching him, he can't stop himself from sending one final text.

Jason
ill see you at lunch

Smiling to himself, he pockets his phone. Not even the good natured teasing from his seniors who catch him is enough to dim his good mood.

THE SECOND EMERSON steps into his office, Jason's spidey senses go off. There's a tightness to the clench of his jaw and a hunch in his shoulders, but the frantic way he spins his fidget ring is the final kicker.

"What's wrong?" Jason asks.

Emerson breathes deeply, exhaling a heavy sigh. He doesn't answer immediately, moving further into the office so he can shut the door behind him, the sounds of schoolyard activity that usually filter in through the open gym doors quieting.

Were it anyone else Jason might push but he's learned better, understands the way Emerson's brain processes questions and stress. Rather than push for answers he's desperate for, he busies himself with getting them set up. He grabs a Dr. Pepper and a green apple Gatorade from the fridge, depositing them on the edge of his desk along with everything else he's got in his fridge: sliced jicama with tajin, fruit salad and baby carrots. He has no intention of eating the latter, unsure what possessed him to even buy them or put them in his fridge. The only good carrot is the kind in *albondigas*.

"So," he starts, unwrapping his sandwich. "My kids were giving me hell today."

At Emerson's raised eyebrow, he continues.

"They thought I had a girlfriend," he explains before taking a huge bite. He can't help chuckling to himself as he chews, recalling the absolute chaos that had been his third period. None of his damn seniors would do anything except try and find out who he'd been texting the entire time.

Emerson unpacks his own lunch, eyes on Jason as he withdraws his peanut butter sandwich. "Do you?"

"Have a girlfriend?" Jason chokes. "Hell no. You'd know if I did. I talk to you more than anyone. Besides they were just needling me because they caught me texting at the start of class. Which, by the way, was not a girl. I was texting you."

Emerson's eyes widen, the pale green nearly translucent under the shitty lighting in Jason's office.

"What exactly made them think it was a girl?" Emerson asks. He takes a bit of his sandwich, fixing Jason with an unblinking stare.

Not long after they met, Emerson mentioned how stressful he found eye contact with most people, never sure how much to use. He said he tended to avoid it while talking but had been told he used too much when listening. Jason assured him that however much he looked or didn't look at him was fine, and he meant it. Secretly though, he loves it when Emerson does the intense stare thing while he talks, the undivided attention lighting up the middle child part of his brain that loves to be sure someone is paying attention to him.

"You know how they are," Jason shrugs, thinking about the way they'd tried to turn dodgeball into twenty questions. He knows a lot of people hate teenagers, but he loves their unfiltered curiosity and thirst to find themselves. "They said I was smiling at my phone like a lovesick teenager. Nosy little shit heads."

"But you were just texting me?"

"Obviously," Jason confirms, grabbing a piece of watermelon out of the fruit salad. "Did I ever tell you about the time when I was four and Charlie told me if I swallowed a watermelon seed it would grow in my belly—sprout vines and everything?"

Emerson takes a bite of his sandwich before shaking his head.

"I always believed Charlie, even when Andrew told me not to. Anyway, we were eating watermelon, and it was full of seeds we were supposed to spit out onto a napkin, and Charlie looked me dead in the eye and told me to be careful not to swallow one, or it would grow in my stomach and eventually kill me."

"That's illogical and also scientifically impossible," Emerson points out, curling his legs beneath him in the office chair.

"I know that now," Jason laughs, "but I was a kid. Anyway, I accidentally swallowed one despite my best intentions not to and cried all night. I couldn't eat watermelon for years."

"I think I'm glad I didn't have siblings," Emerson muses. "Although Landon was bad enough."

Jason clenches his jaw so hard his teeth grind. Emerson's cousin is the biggest piece of shit he's ever heard of, and Jason sincerely hopes he never has the misfortune of meeting him. Despite the way Emerson has tried to play off the unkind words from Landon, it's clear they left a lasting impression.

With a heavy sigh, Emerson sets his half-eaten sandwich on top of its tupperware before laying it on Jason's desk.

"I talked to Mr. Caldwell on the way here."

"What did he want?" Jason asks, trying to keep the bitterness from his tone. He's downplayed how horrible he thinks he is, if only because as the head English teacher, Emerson is forced to interact with him far more than Jason, and he never wants to influence Emerson's opinion or add to his stress.

"He wants me to take his place chaperoning the homecoming dance." Emerson pulls his knees to his chest in a way that should not be possible given his height, but then Emerson is lanky and lean, his body able to contort itself into positions that Jason's much thicker body could never. "I suppose want isn't the right word. He told me he'd taken the liberty of putting me down to chaperone in his place."

"Tell him no," Jason grumbles. "Or better yet, to fuck off."

"I would never," Emerson gapes. "Besides, I don't think saying no is an option."

"I'll talk to him."

"No, it's—*no*." Emerson twines his arms around his legs until he's made a little ball of himself, chin resting on his knees and his eyes on the edge of the desk.

"You don't have to do anything you're not comfortable with, Emmy."

As he hoped, the nickname does the trick. Emerson turns his face in Jason's direction, cheek resting on his knees. "You're chaperoning."

"I am," Jason confirms. He told Emerson as much weeks ago, casually suggesting he come too, but Emerson had shut him down swiftly with an uncharacteristic bite, and Jason hasn't mentioned it again. He's not sure why the idea of going to a school dance upset him so much, but he suspects he's about to find out.

"They're pretty loud, but you've got your ear defenders, and you can step outside as often as you need."

"It's not that. Or it is I guess, but that's not the—ugh." Emerson turns his face into his knees, tapping his fingers against his leg.

Watching Emerson be uncomfortable makes Jason feel like there's a rock lodged in his throat. He wishes he could take away everything that ever made him upset, wishes he could fix it all.

"I don't have anything to wear," Emerson blurts.

Of all the things Jason expects to hear, that isn't it.

"You can wear anything," Jason tries.

Emerson lifts his face from his knees to look at Jason. "What are you wearing?"

"A suit," Jason answers.

Emerson sighs so heavily Jason feels it in his gut.

"To be fully transparent, this is the same suit I've worn to the last three homecoming dances. It's not new or anything."

Despite this clarifying information, Emerson doesn't relax.

"You would look handsome in a suit. My aunt always dressed me up for church in these itchy, stiff ones that made me feel like I was choking. I used to sneak to the bathroom and try to take it off, but I'd get in trouble. It didn't matter that I told her I hated them. Then at holidays, she always dressed me and Landon in matching suits for family photos for the holiday cards even though the ones with me in them never made it on the card because I always took the suit jacket off or undid the buttons, and they said I ruined the photos."

A flare of white hot anger pierces Jason. He's never hated anyone, but he hates Emerson's family. He can't fathom how anyone could make a child feel unloved or unwanted, especially someone as precious and special as Emerson. The desire to protect Emerson now, to show him what it's like to have people who care about you and appreciate you, is staggering.

It makes Jason think of his own parents. He hasn't talked to them this week, and he makes a mental note to call them later and see if he can finagle a way to get Emerson invited to a family dinner, or maybe Thanksgiving. Well, if Emerson wants. He'll have to ask him first, but now isn't the right time. Jason's family would love Emerson, he knows it. The fact that his own family so easily disregarded his needs makes Jason feel upset and helpless so he focuses on the now, on something tangible he can fix.

"You know you don't have to wear a suit," Jason points out, not wanting to dwell on his thoughts to the point of ignoring Emerson. "There's no official dress code or anything."

"Yes, I do," Emerson protests. "Or at least, something nice but dress shirts are a sensory nightmare. That stiff cotton doesn't move and when I'm uncomfortable, I get snappish. And then I'll snap at you, and you'll hate me."

Oh. *Oh.*

"Emmy."

"I've never been to a school dance, ever. No one invited me, why would they?"

Jason's natural inclination is to interrupt and try to fix, but there's no fixing what's already happened, so he bites his tongue and waits, sensing Emerson's need to get this out.

"Then you came along with your smile and your kind words, and you did what no one in my life had done—you invited me. You didn't tell me I couldn't handle it before I tried, or try to get me to not go because you didn't wanna deal with it. But I panicked and snapped at you, and I've been too embarrassed to bring it up since. Now Mr. Caldwell wants me to take his place as chaperone, and I'm going to be out of sorts and cranky and you're going to see—see the real me."

Leaning so far forward he nearly falls out of his chair, Jason rests his hand on the arms of Emerson's chair. "I want you to listen to me. I'm not going to run away if you get overstimulated or snap at me. I've got three brothers, one of whom is an absolute chaos gremlin. Literally nothing you do can scare me off. I don't want you to tone it down or mask, do you understand?"

"People say that but they don't mean it," Emerson whispers, the force of what he's holding in palpable.

Jason was lucky to grow up in a family where he was loved, every second of every day. He cannot begin to imagine anything else. While he might not be able to relate to Emerson's trauma he can feel it, has seen his brothers and his students suffer, understands exactly what it means to love someone who questions if they were meant for this world.

"I mean the words I say," Jason promises, sliding his hands down the arms of the chair. Beneath the hem of his brown trousers, Emerson's got on a pair of socks with swords on them, and Jason reaches out before he can think twice about it, giving his ankles a gentle squeeze. "I like you, Emmy. You and me, we're solid. Nothing's gonna change that."

Emerson's eyes are focused on where Jason's hands are wrapped around his ankles. He doesn't ask if he should move them. Jason has touched him enough to know it's welcome. Maybe not all friends touch as much as they do, but it works for them. Jason can never resist touching him when he's near: a reassuring shoulder squeeze, a quick hug, or a long one when he has the chance. The touch always makes Emerson's tension ease, and it makes Jason feel so good, he's given up wondering if it's unusual. It occurs to him that most friends wouldn't be holding their friend's ankles, but that's because Emerson wouldn't let them.

Sure, Emerson has gotten a little friendlier with some of the other staff, especially Mabel, but no one else is allowed to touch. Only Jason is afforded that privilege. Which is maybe because Emerson knows him, always indulging Jason's tactile nature. Emerson really is such a good friend. One of the best, ever.

"The way I see it, we have two options," Jason tells him. "If you don't want to chaperone, then let me talk to Mr. Caldwell, or even Mabel. We can figure it out. But if you want to go, well I hear there's this really awesome P.E. teacher, who is also chaperoning. Word on the street is that he knows some really embarrassing dances, and he likes to have fun."

"I can't dance."

"You can stand in the corner and laugh at me," Jason offers. He smooths his thumb over the arch of Emerson's ankle, all but on his knees now in his desperation to make Emerson's smile return. "Or I could teach you to dance. Not to brag, but I've been told I'm a great teacher."

"Why do you make it sound so easy," Emerson asks.

"I'm either that impressive or that stubborn," Jason grins. "You don't have to decide this second but—"

"I'd like to go." Emerson's chest expands with the force of his breath, which he holds for a few seconds before letting it out. "With you. As uh, chaperones. As friends."

Friends. He knows they are, but hearing Emerson say it

without hesitation, given his history, makes Jason's heart swell with affection.

All but throwing himself back into his chair, Jason tips backwards to grab his phone off the far edge of his desk. "Only one thing left to do."

"What?" Emerson asks, uncurling himself in curiosity. His legs drop to the floor and his shoulders straighten while he watches Jason.

"Call Andrew."

"Your big brother?"

"Uh-huh," Jason confirms, already calling. It rings twice, Emerson's confused *why* mumbled at the same time Andrew answers the phone.

"What's wrong?" Andrew asks.

"Why do you always assume something is wrong when I call you?" Jason questions, switching the phone to speaker so Emerson can hear as well.

"Maybe because that's usually when you or Alec call me."

"Nothing is wrong," Jason assures him. "But I do need something. Or we do."

"*We*," Andrew echoes. "Am I on speaker phone?"

"Yup," Jason confirms. "Me and Emerson are making homecoming plans and—"

"Emerson, your teacher friend?" Andrew interrupts. "The one you told me about before."

The weight of Emerson's gaze is heavy, but Jason merely shrugs, not at all embarrassed about being caught talking about Emerson.

'*All good things,*' he mouths silently.

It's clear Emerson is curious, but he resists asking questions, eyes darting between Jason and the phone in his hand. Were this either of his other brothers, he'd be pestered to death with questions, but because this is Andrew, the easy acceptance comes without a struggle.

"What do you guys need?" The question is accompanied by the loud clicking of his keyboard. How Andrew can hold a conversation and work on complicated stats at the same time is beyond Jason, but it's not the first time he's done it, so Jason shouldn't still be surprised by Andrew's multitasking capabilities.

"Emerson needs a suit for homecoming," Jason explains.

"I assume off the rack is not what you're going for."

"You'd assume correctly," Jason confirms. "We need something tailored to his sensory needs. Stylish but very comfortable."

Emerson's face scrunches up, and he shakes his head.

"I see what's happening here. You need me to get you guys in with Denise," Andrew muses, the loud tap tap of his keyboard suddenly stopping.

"Not me, I've still got that suit from a few years ago. But Emerson needs something." He turns his attention to Emerson. "Denise is Andrew's tailor. Well, she does a lot of custom work too, like Charlie's suits when he has a gallery opening for example. But mostly just for Andrew, he's very...particular about his clothing."

"Some of us don't like the feeling of seams," Andrew grumbles. "Nor do we want to look like we're walking around in something we slept in."

"He means Charlie," Jason tells Emerson in a mock whisper.

Andrew's thoughtful hum filters through the phone. "Is Emerson looking for something off the rack that needs to be tailored or something custom?"

"I think custom would be the best bet for comfort," Jason answers easily.

"I can't afford a custom suit," Emerson hisses.

If Andrew heard Emerson's outburst he says nothing, far too tactful. "She's not taking on any new clients, but I might be able to pull a few strings. When do you need it?"

"Homecoming is uh—" he pauses, assessing the best way to break this to someone with Andrew's desire to plan far, far ahead for everything. "Next weekend."

"Are you serious?" Andrew whistles long and low, grumbling to himself for a minute before he finally speaks. "Just so we're clear, you want me to get you in with one of the most sought after tailors in the area to get your friend a custom suit, which you need ready in nine days?"

"Yup," Jason confirms, ignoring the way Emerson is gaping at him. "That's a very accurate read on the situation. Well done, Andrew."

There's a long pause before Andrew replies, "I'll see what I can do."

"I knew you'd come through for me," Jason crows. "Best big brother in the whole world."

"I said I'll try," Andrew reminds him. "It took weeks the last time I needed to get Charlie a new custom suit for that gallery opening in Santa Monica last year. But—Denise likes me. I might be able to get her to do me a very huge favor. Let me handle this. I'll text you when I figure out the details."

"You're the best, Andrew."

"Yeah, yeah, you all love me and can't live without me," Andrew sighs with the air of someone long suffering. Then again he's been putting up with all three of his younger brothers' bullshit for years so maybe he is. "I'll talk to you later, Jason. Also ignore everything Charlie put in the group chat. I did not—well, it's not true, that's all you need to know," Andrew says in a rush, hanging up the phone before Jason can ask what the fuck he's talking about.

"What just happened?" Emerson blinks.

"When it comes to Charlie and Andrew, I've learned sometimes it's better not to ask," Jason explains, unable to resist sneaking a peak at the group chat which is up to over one hundred messages. A peak at the clock affirms he has no time to figure out what the fuck is going on. He swipes open his notes app, scrolling until he finds his Emerson list—one that's grown quite a bit since he started it—adding never been to a school dance (make sure he has fun!) before shutting off his phone, laying it face down on his desk to return his attention to more important matters—Emerson and his lunch.

JASON LEANS against the wall of the coffee shop, sipping at his iced white mocha and staring down the street. Andrew told them to meet him here at two, and while it's only five minutes after, that's as out of character for him as it would be for Emerson to be late.

Luckily he's got something sweet and cold to sustain him. They'd screwed up Emerson's chai latte, something Emerson had refused to tell them. Jason found out they'd added espresso after watching Emerson grimace several times in the span of five minutes. Refusing to let Emerson ingest something he hated, he'd taken the drink back in and politely asked them to fix it, which with the afternoon rush seems to be taking forever. Jason offered to wait for it himself, but Emerson said he'd rather not meet Andrew alone and sent Jason to wait outside where he's been the last few minutes.

He takes another sip of his mocha, wishing he'd gotten that scone he was ogling when he catches sight of Andrew's cherry red Mazda sailing down the road. It slows in front of the tailor's a few store fronts down, pulling up against the curb. Andrew hops out, pushing his hair off his face and waving to Jason before plunking a few quarters in the meter.

"You're late," Jason yells, "you're never—" but the rest of his words cut off when the passenger door opens and out steps a carbon copy of Andrew, if Andrew was dressed by a toddler—his neon green crocs, purple linen trousers and garish floral shirt a stark contrast to Andrew's pale pink and tan ensemble. "Why the hell are you here, Charlie?"

"Is that any way to greet your favorite big brother?" Charlie asks, pushing his shades up into his hair.

Andrew steps in front of Charlie. "Pretty sure I'm his favorite big brother after what I agreed to in order to get this done."

That makes Jason frown. After their phone call in his office yesterday, he'd merely texted it was done along with an address and time. Jason didn't realize it'd been difficult for him.

"What did you do in order to get Denise to see him anyway?" Charlie asks, crossing his arms. "I've been trying for a year, and she still won't even see me. The only reason she makes my suits is because she can fit them to your body."

"We don't need to talk about it," Andrew says with a dismissive wave of his hand. "Where is this Emerson, by the way?"

"He's probably not real," Charlie interjects. The problem with these two is they never let him get a damn word in. "Remember when he was five and told us his best friend was a mermaid?"

"To be fair, he did watch The Little Mermaid a lot," Andrew points out. "I think he had a crush on Ariel."

"No I didn't," Jason lies, unsure how he can always feel like a little kid around them.

"My money is still on Emerson being fake," Charlie continues, like Jason didn't say anything. "I bet our baby here just needed a new suit because he split his old one with his thick thighs and—"

"Emerson isn't imaginary," Jason all but yells, having the wherewithal to blush when a family walking by them stares. He can't believe he's got to deal with both of them. Just Andrew was fine. Andrew is predictable and easy, at least alone. With Charlie, he's feistier, and then there's Charlie himself, who is a wildcard. Jason has no idea if his sometimes charming, other times brusque, personality will be off putting to Emerson.

"You don't both need to stay you know," Jason points out.

"See, imaginary," Charlie says. "He's trying to get rid of us."

"Of course he's real," Jason gapes.

"Who's real?" Emerson asks.

Jason spins to find Emerson at his back, delicate fingers curled around his freshly made drink. He lifts it, taking a slow sip. Judging by the happy taps of his fingers against the side of his cup it must be correct this time.

"You," Jason answers quietly, unsure why he can't take his eyes off the droplet of chai latte stuck on the corner of Emerson's mouth.

"Jason Matias King."

"What?" Jason asks, startling at the use of his full name.

He turns around to find both of his brothers watching him with matched expressions, as if they practiced it in a mirror.

"This explains everything," Andrew utters.

"It really does," Charlie replies.

"Explains what?" Jason tries.

"He's a redhead," Charlie and Andrew answer at the same time. Already Jason's headache is coming on. He wasn't prepared for both of them.

Beside him, Emerson reaches for his hair, taking a step closer to Jason, making him reel with a surge of protectiveness.

"Don't be a dick and talk about people like they're not here, dude." Jason levels a look at his brothers.

"My apologies," Charlie says with a smile. "I was rendered temporarily speechless by your friend's beauty."

Emerson chokes on his tea. Jason chokes on his own tongue. What the fuck is Charlie doing? He's always been an outrageous flirt, but he should know not to do that with Emerson. Sure Emerson is gay and single, but he would never date someone like Charlie. His brother is great—talented and loyal but also way too much for Emerson. He needs someone calmer, more gentle. Someone who will appreciate him. Plus Charlie doesn't want a relationship. He could never make Emerson happy.

Not that Jason spends a lot of time thinking about people dating Emerson. He did once, and it left him feeling vaguely confused and with heartburn.

"You didn't mention how pretty he is, baby brother." Charlie smirks, stepping forward and holding out his hand towards Emerson. "Charlie King, pleasure to meet you."

"Emerson," he replies, reaching his own hand out as well. He lets Charlie shake it, and that familiar burn in Jason's gut intensifies. Maybe he needs an antacid.

"I'm Andrew." His brother steps forward, holding his hand out next. "It's always lovely to meet a friend of Jason's. He never lets us meet any of them."

"Except Theo," Charlie points out.

"Theo is really nice," Emerson says.

"You've met Theo?" Andrew questions.

"Yeah, he and Alec came over to Jason's for pizza night last week."

Immediately, Andrew and Charlie turn towards each other seemingly having some kind of silent conversation. Jason gulps down his mocha, desperate for more sugar and caffeine to deal with whatever is happening.

"If you'll excuse me," Charlie mutters, turning to walk down the street.

"Where is he going?" Jason asks.

"Presumably calling Alec to find out why he didn't know about pizza night," Andrew answers, as if it were obvious. "Come on, let's head inside. I need to apologize to Denise for being late. Fucking Charlie wouldn't pick a shirt."

Turning to Emerson, Jason offers a smile. Emerson tries to return one, but it looks a bit more like a grimace.

"It'll be fine, I won't leave. Unless you want me to."

"No." Emerson shakes his head. "Don't leave, please."

"You're stuck with me, Emmy," Jason loops an arm around Emerson's shoulders, walking him towards the tailor's. When they reach the door, Andrew holds it open, his gaze lingering on where Jason has Emerson pulled close to his side.

"What?" Jason asks, feeling like a defensive teenager.

"I didn't say anything," Andrew says.

"Your face said something."

"I'll make sure and have a private meeting with my face later to discuss the issue," Andrew deadpans.

Jason groans. Charlie's louder than life personality so often takes center stage, it's easy to forget what a spitfire Andrew can be. Then again, it's easy to forget a lot about Andrew who often fades into the background when Charlie is around.

"You know—" Jason starts, cutting himself off when Denise comes into the front sitting area. He's only met her a few times from when she did his suit a few years ago, but she looks exactly as he remembers. She's dressed impeccably as always, her dress shirt rolled to her elbows and a delicate gold chain hanging around her thick neck. Her gray hair is trimmed short on the top and buzzed on the sides, and there's a stern air about her that softens when she catches sight of Andrew.

"There you are, Doll." Denise walks right to Andrew, smiling when he bends down to kiss her cheek. "You're never late."

"Sorry about that," Andrew sighs, shoving his hands into his pockets. "Charlie's fault."

"Where is that trouble-making shadow of yours anyway?" Denise scoffs.

"Outside making a call, he'll be in shortly."

Denise hums before turning to face Jason and Emerson. "You must be my special appointment. Emerson, right?"

"Yes. Thank you for seeing me on short notice," Emerson says, fidgeting with the cardboard sleeve on his drink. "I hope it's not any trouble."

"Oh, he's handsome and sweet," Denise grins, giving Jason more indigestion. Maybe he had too much salsa on his eggs this morning. "Why don't you come with me in the back and we'll get you all set. No trouble at all, sweetheart."

"Don't worry, she's great with people like us," Andrew offers, clearly sensing Emerson's unease.

Emerson's confusion is evident. "Gays?"

"I'm ace actually," Andrew offers, surprising Jason. He's not remotely in the closet, but he's also painfully private with people he doesn't know. "I meant neurodivergent. Just let her know what you need."

The smallest flicker of relief passes across Emerson's face, and Jason wants to hug Andrew. He doesn't, if only because Andrew is incredibly selective with who touches him and when.

"I'll take care of him, don't worry. You two stay out here, make yourself comfortable. And if Charlie comes, tell him not to touch *anything*."

"Why do I feel like there's a story there?" Jason asks Andrew, all the while keeping his eyes glued to Emerson's receding back as he's led into a private room.

"There's always a story with Charlie, but I'm more interested in what's going on with you and Emerson."

"What do you mean?"

"What do I mean," Andrew scoffs. "You looked like you wanted to crush your drink when Charlie flirted with him."

"I did not," Jason objects. "Besides, he shouldn't flirt with Emerson."

"Why?"

"Because," Jason grumbles, slumping back into the sofa cushion. The couch is definitely more decorative than comfortable, especially for someone of Jason's size. He half feels like he might break it, hunching his shoulders in and staring at his mocha.

"You never cared when Charlie used to flirt with Theo."

"Why would I care if Charlie flirted with Theo?" Jason asks.

Andrew's face takes on a pinched expression. "*Jason.*"

"Your face is using its outside voice again."

"I can't help it," Andrew sighs, scrubbing a hand over his face. "I told myself I wouldn't interfere, but it's killing me."

"You are kind of a know-it-all, but we love you anyway."

Andrew flips him off, but the corners of his mouth turn up in a small smile. "Look, just think about it."

"About what?"

"About Emerson," Andrew says gently.

"I think about Emerson all the time," Jason points out.

"I bet you do," Andrew mutters, glancing towards the door. "Charlie would be better at this, but the asshole isn't here."

"Better at what?" Jason asks. "You're being weird, even for you."

"Have you considered that maybe you like Emerson?"

"Of course I like Emerson, he's the best," Jason says, sloshing a bit of his mocha on his sweats. "What are you implying?"

"I wasn't implying anything. I was flat out saying it," Andrew sighs. "Though apparently not explicitly enough."

The bell above the door jingles as Charlie saunters into the room, making his way directly to Andrew and infringing on his personal space despite there being plenty of room for him to sit on the other chair. "What are we talking about?"

"Emerson," Andrew answers.

"Nothing," Jason replies at the same time.

"Oh, are we talking about Jason's massive fucking crush on Emerson? He is really pretty."

"Stop calling him pretty," Jason snaps, the first half of his sentence taking twice as long to register. "Wait, what?"

"Your crush," Charlie says, ignoring the way Andrew thumps him on the backside of the head.

"We talked about tact, Charlie."

"Fuck, tact. Jason is our brother, and I can't sit around watching him make puppy eyes without saying something. Unless he doesn't want to ask Emerson on a date, at which point I'd be happy to do the honors. Maybe he'd let me wine and dine him in that new suit he's getting and—"

"Don't you dare ask him out," Jason growls.

Rather than look put out by his tone Charlie merely grins. "Why, because you want to? Because you've had a thing for redheads since you were a kid? Or is it because you look at Emerson like you simultaneously want to wrap him a hug and talk about feelings while also devouring him?"

"Charlie," Andrew whispers, tone warning and leaving Jason reeling. Does he really look at Emerson like that?

"I'm just being honest," Charlie tells Andrew. "Besides I'm not going to ask him out, he's too—sweet for me."

"Emerson is perfect," Jason frowns. "You would be so lucky."

"Do you see this," Charlie says to Andrew before he returns his attention to Jason. "Listen, you should ask him out, before someone else does."

That burning in Jason's chest intensifies, and it occurs to him that it is, quite possibly, not heartburn. He thinks about Emerson and his little resting grumpy face. Emerson and his endless Lord of the Rings facts. Emerson and his toothy smile when Jason offers him a Dr. Pepper every day. Emerson and his beautiful red hair and kissable full lips. Emerson and his peanut butter sandwiches and quiet laugh. Emerson and his beautiful, brave heart.

Emmy. *His* Emmy.

"Oh shit," Jason whispers, the sudden clarity staggering. "I have a crush on Emerson."

11 EMERSON

EMERSON FOLLOWS Denise into the back, hardly paying attention to his surroundings, his own mind processing. Jason warned him the twins could be a little intense, and they were but not in the way Emerson expected. Charlie was a little much, though nice enough. He'd liked Andrew though, with his steady demeanor. He reminded Emerson a bit of Jason, albeit a lot less smiley and open. He had the same calm countenance as Jason though.

Thinking about the twins, it's impossible not to compare them to Jason. They were both friendly enough, and definitely handsome, although in a much different way. They had the same black hair as Jason, but where Jason's short hair is always a little messy and wind tousled like he was just playing outside, Andrew's is perfectly styled, not a hair out of place. Charlie's got thick waves that look purposely styled in a way that he wants to look messy but is too perfect to actually be so. The twins are tall too, maybe two inches taller than Emerson but not nearly as tall as Jason.

Despite those variances, their relation is clear in the shape of their big brown eyes and the slant of their noses, but the differences are bigger than the similarities. Where Jason is thick, Andrew and Charlie are both lean and lanky. Where Jason's face is more square, the twins have a sharpness to their features. They're attractive, undeniably so, yet neither of them can hold a candle to Jason.

Not that Emerson should be thinking about how handsome Jason is with his big smile, big body and even bigger heart. With a resigned sigh, Emerson knows there's no point stopping his own train of thought. He's got a crush on Jason. Although that word hardly feels appropriate. A crush is something small, unsubstantiated. By definition, it's a brief and intense infatuation. Nothing about what he feels for Jason is brief and infatuation implies a shallowness which couldn't be further from the truth.

What he feels for Jason is *more.* He likes the way Jason fills the silence with words that are easy to listen to, often not expecting Emerson to join into the conversation but always including him. Then there are the times where Jason manages not to talk because he's listening, letting Emerson ramble about one of his students or a book he read. Sometimes it's in person and other times in massive walls of text messages that he always responds to as if he's actually interested.

Certainly, his looks are eye-catching. Jason is the kind of attractive that everyone around him takes notice of. Emerson might not pick up on a lot of things, but he can't pretend he doesn't see the way men and women alike stare. Not that Emerson can blame them. Jason's absolutely gorgeous. He's the kind of handsome that makes Emerson curl his hands around himself in bed every night when there's no one around to bear witness to his secret thoughts. The kind of handsome that makes Emerson ache with desire when he imagines all the things he'd do to Jason, or maybe if he was feeling particularly brave, things he might ask Jason to do to him. That is if he had the chance. Which he knows he won't, ever. Jason doesn't like Emerson like that because Jason isn't gay.

Thankfully his looks are easy enough to ignore, at least most of the time. Emerson's been attracted to men before. He knows what it's like to have a physical reaction to someone he has no chance with. The difficulty is, that it's not Jason's looks that have Emerson's heart beating faster and his thoughts dwelling on how warm and safe Jason is in every way.

Jason is Emerson's favorite person in the entire world. He's the person he wants to see even when he doesn't want to be around anyone. Jason is everything good in the world, and Emerson is maybe a little bit in love with him.

"Emerson?"

Startled, Emerson looks up to find Denise watching him.

"Sorry, were you talking?" he asks, waiting for her annoyance. People always get annoyed when he zones out.

"I was just asking what the occasion is. Andrew only mentioned needing it by Saturday, not what it was for."

"Homecoming," Emerson answers. "Me and Jason are going together."

"You two make a very sweet couple." Denise's expression softens. "Did you want to match his suit?"

"Couple," Emerson croaks. "No, we're not—no. He's not...he doesn't...we're going together. As chaperones. Non-romantic chaperones because Jason is straight, and we're just friends you see."

"Sure thing, doll face." She doesn't press or prod, but her eyes never leave Emerson's face, making him squirm. "You look so much like her."

"Like who?"

"Your mother," Denise answers. "Beth."

Goosebumps spring up across both of Emerson's arms, and it's all he can do not to collapse against the wall.

"You knew my mom?"

"Sure did. I was a senior when she was a freshman. You can imagine I wasn't too popular back then. I didn't fit into what a girl was supposed to look like, especially in high school. I've always been butch and loved menswear. Your mom though, she was an angel. Always sat with me at lunch even when no one else would. The second you walked into the store I knew. You look exactly like her."

Giving in to the weakness, he slumps against the wall, the words hardly processing. He'd known it was possible to meet people who knew his mom coming back to her hometown, but so far he'd not had much luck. Mabel was the only person who had worked at the school when his mom was there and she didn't remember his mom. He knows because he asked.

"I was sorry to hear about her passing," Denise says, guiding Emerson over to a small seating area. "I never saw her again after she graduated. Last I heard, she got pregnant and moved to the east coast somewhere."

"Pennsylvania," Emerson offers. He spins his ring while trying to ignore the tears he feels pooling at the corners of his eyes. His aunt and uncle never talked about his mom after she died. Sometimes, it felt as if they thought they could will away Emerson's grief by pretending she never existed at all. He wondered sometimes if his aunt even missed her sister, or if having to raise Emerson was just a reminder of the sibling she would've been happier to forget.

"What was she like?" Emerson asks, desperate for a memory of her that isn't his own. He was so young when she died that sometimes he's not sure if the things he remembers about her are real or simply things he wishes had been true.

"She was like sunshine," Denise answers, lowering herself into the chair opposite Emerson. "She was the kind of person who helped everyone, even when she didn't have the time or resources. She was always smiling too, made you feel like she actually wanted you around, you know?"

"Yeah," Emerson whispers, finding it easier to remember her now. She'd always made Emerson feel so loved, as if the things he liked and did and needed were okay.

His mother always smelled like roses. She had red hair and Emerson's nose and eyes. She had a loud laugh and liked dresses. These are the things he knows are true.

"I might have a photo of us somewhere in my garage. I could look for it, if you'd like," Denise offers.

The depth of desire this invokes is boundless. How desperately he wanted to see photos of his mother growing up, his own paltry few photos hidden away in his room, where his aunt and uncle couldn't shove them away in the attic like she never existed, were never enough to sustain the longing.

Lost for words, the most Emerson can manage is nod.

Denise smiles in return, and it softens her features. "I'll let Andrew know if I find it."

Emerson's heartbeat seems too fast for his body, every thud of it inside his chest uncomfortable. Sometimes he becomes aware of his own pulse in a way that makes it feel like he's on the verge of a panic attack. It's difficult to explain to other people the way he can randomly become so aware of the seams on his socks or his own heartbeat that he quite literally wishes he could take his own skin off, or maybe lay on the floor and become one with the carpet.

Closing his eyes and breathing deep, he waits. Any second Denise is going to push for more conversation, to ask questions Emerson can't answer about his mother or the suit. He's too flustered to think about what she might ask to script a response, which only makes his heart rate increase. To his surprise, all that happens is the soft background noise of classical music. When he opens his eyes, it's to find the lighting has been dimmed, somehow making him feel less exposed.

"Andrew likes it like this, thought you might too," she says in explanation. "I left a portfolio on that table in front of you if you wanna flip through and see if any of the styles catch your eye. I just remembered an important email I forgot to send, but I won't be more than fifteen minutes, if you'll excuse me."

It's not until the door to the office on her left has clicked shut that Emerson reaches for the black portfolio on the table, hefting it into his lap. His fingers draw back and forth over the spine in a rhythmic pattern until he's calmed his breathing. Several more moments pass before he opens the book to reveal an array of suits in various cuts and styles. The first few are simple, reminiscent of the stuffy, traditional ones his aunt always forced him into. He continues to flip the pages, hardly paying attention when his gaze lands on something different. His first and only thought is being picked up by Jason in this, how it might feel to have those warm, kind eyes directed his way in something like this. It's silly he knows. Jason isn't actually his date, but Emerson's never even been on a real one. Never dressed up for a guy, or even himself, and the idea of doing it makes unexpected butterflies flutter in his belly.

Sure, Jason won't be looking at him with attraction, but he still might like how Emerson looks. He's always complimenting Emerson when he wears green, or telling him he's handsome. While Emerson is sure it's just something Jason does with all his friends, it still makes him feel good. After a lifetime of having his shortcomings and flaws pointed out, Jason's freely given compliments and praise feel like the first rays of sunshine after a harsh winter.

Suddenly, it's all Emerson can do not to hide his face in his hands and scream, unable to distract himself from his thoughts of Jason. Would Jason like the color? The fit? Would he tell Emerson he looked nice? Maybe even that he looked pretty? Hearing Charlie say it had made Emerson feel squirmy and awkward. But it doesn't feel like that when Jason says it, and it's kind of embarrassing how bad he wants to find a reason for him to do so.

Emerson swallows around a rush of emotions too complicated and messy to differentiate. Longing, confusion, grief, and most of all Jason himself. Drawing his fingers over the photo he finds it impossible to pretend this isn't what he wants. He stares at it for so long Denise returns to the room, hovering near Emerson for long seconds before she finally speaks.

"Find something you like, sweetheart?"

He holds his breath, weighing his options. This is the kind of suit that will make people look at him. He won't be able to hide in the background, but he's done that for so long. Maybe it's alright now. Maybe it's safe to stop hiding. Besides, he won't be alone. Jason will be there, and that makes Emerson feel brave enough to answer honestly.

"Yes."

AN HOUR LATER, Emerson is quite certain he doesn't want to ever be measured for a suit again. Andrew was right that Denise was patient and accommodating, but Emerson quickly realized that while he's often desperate to be touched, it's only when that touch comes from Jason that it's soothing. Jason's touch is firm, grounding. He always gives Emerson's neck or shoulder a deep pressure squeeze that makes his body buzz with happy feelings. In stark contrast, Denise's touches had been light, probably in an attempt to be respectful. While appreciated, it made it feel like feathers were ghosting across his skin in the worst way possible.

By the time Emerson emerges into the front sitting room, he's all kinds of cranky. Between being touched too much and crying over his mom, he feels like someone scrubbed his insides over with sandpaper. All he wants to do is go home and burrow on his couch under his weighted blanket for a few hours with Lord of the Rings on in the background.

Bracing himself for a bunch of people staring at him, he's surprised to find the front sitting room empty aside from Jason.

"Where are your brothers?"

Jason almost drops his phone, fumbling it between his big hands as he stares at Emerson. His cheeks are flushed red, almost as if he's overheated, and Emerson wonders if he's hot.

"I uh, sent them home," Jason says, twisting his phone in his hands. "Fuckers were driving me nuts."

Relief makes Emerson's shoulders sag. "Oh good, I don't wanna be around anyone. Wait, that's rude."

Jason barks out a laugh. "It's honest, which for the record I like."

"Okay," Emerson says, relief heavy in his chest.

"Why don't I get you home," Jason offers. "Get me out of your hair too so you don't have to people."

"You're not people," Emerson blurts.

"I'm not?" Emerson shakes his head. "What exactly am I then?"

"You're...Jason."

"And Jason is excluded from people?"

"Uh-huh," Emerson confirms, seeing no point in pretending now. He's said it. It's out there. Besides it wouldn't be the boldest or most awkward thing he's ever said to Jason yet.

"Well then I'm honored," Jason grins, somehow always, managing to say the right thing. "So do you wanna get food and watch Lord of the Rings?"

"We watched it last weekend," Emerson points out. "Besides, don't you have pizza night with Theo?"

"Not this week. He and Alec went up north for the weekend to a cabin for a belated birthday celebration for Theo. Besides, I like hanging out with you."

"We could watch something else if you'd rather," Emerson offers since he knows Jason only put his favorite movie on last week for his benefit. "Something you want."

"I'm good with anything," Jason shrugs. "If you're happy, I'm happy."

The most incredible thing is, he knows Jason means it. The first time he said it, Emerson had been so certain it was one of those weird expressions or things people say but don't mean, and he needed to try and parse the true meaning for himself. But no, whatever Jason says he means. He is an open book. Honest, easy to read and for whatever reason, seemingly happy to spend time with Emerson, regardless of what they do.

"What do you want to watch, Emmy?" Jason asks.

"Lord of the Rings," Emerson mumbles, unsure why he still feels embarrassed even though Jason clearly knows. It's hard to shake that voice in his head from his family, always giving him shit for his narrow interests. Especially Landon, who'd taken any opportunity to remind him he'd never find a boyfriend who would spend every weekend watching the same movie over and over. He might not have a boyfriend, but he has a Jason, and that's even better.

"Since we did Fellowship last week, we doing Two Towers this week? I wanna see what happens with Aragorn and Gimli."

The fact that Jason—a man who barely understood Tolkien when they met—now knows the names of the movies, including in the correct order, and some of the characters, makes Emerson stupidly giddy.

"What?" Jason scrubs his large hand over the side of his jaw, highlighting the light stubble that wasn't there just the day before. "Is there something on my face?"

"No," Emerson answers, unable to believe he got caught staring. He's usually better at pretending Jason isn't the nicest thing in the entire world to look at. "Just thinking."

"You're probably hungry," Jason muses, moving into Emerson's personal space the way he always does, like he belongs there. He drapes an arm around Emerson's shoulder, the weight of it an immediate balm to Emerson's taxed nervous system. "What are you in the mood for?"

Emerson shrugs, far too low on spoons to make decisions.

"We could order takeout or—" Jason pauses, guiding Emerson towards the front door, pausing in thought as he holds it open.

"Or?"

"I've got a loaf of bread and some peanut butter at home. I could make us sandwiches."

Moving without consciously deciding to do so, Emerson wraps his arms around Jason, relieved when the embrace is returned without fanfare or question. They stand there in the doorway, stuck halfway between the quiet of the tailor and the bustling activity out on the street.

The rise and fall of Jason's chest steadies him, as does the large hand that smooths up and down his back. As always, Jason intuitively senses that words would be too much and doesn't question the impromptu hug or the fact that Emerson, who always waits for Jason to touch first, was the one to initiate this one. All he does is hold Emerson close. He might not have much experience with hugs, but he's certain Jason's are the best in the entire world, his entire body surrounding Emerson.

When Emerson pulls back from the embrace, his mind is calm in ways it rarely is, his filter apparently gone because what he blurts next is, "Did I ever tell you that Aragorn is descended from Elros Tar-Minyatur making him the last descendant of Anárion?"

The smile that spreads across Jason's face is wide, his obvious pleasure at Emerson's unprompted infodumping as soothing to Emerson as the hug had been, albeit in a different way.

"You did not. Why don't we head to the truck and you can tell me more."

Emerson smiles, a real smile that he feels all the way in his gut. "Okay, Jason."

"WHAT ARE YOU WEARING?"

"You like it?" Jason grins, defying all odds and somehow managing to make the monstrosity of an outfit he's got on attractive. It's actually an anomaly Emerson might mull over later when he's not standing on the sidewalk with half the people at the bus stop staring at them. "I'm confused," Emerson answers, unable to stop staring. There's so much neon and all of it is very tight in ways that remind Emerson he's very gay and very, very much attracted to Jason. Maybe not usually in spandex, but then again, he's developing a Pavlovian response to Jason in gray sweats and his team hoodies, also something he wasn't objectively attracted to before. So it's quite possible he's just turned on by anything Jason wears.

The outfit is objectively kind of hideous, but Jason's thighs are so thick that the lime green spandex stretches tight, highlighting where the very short pink running shorts he's wearing over the leggings have bunched up. The shirt is equally bright, though more of a highlighter yellow. It's hard to focus on the color when the sleeves have been cut off revealing Jason's massive biceps and highlighting all that corded muscle in his forearms dusted with dark hair. The shirt also appears to be just short enough that if he lifted his arms, it might show off his stomach, and it's all Emerson can do not to turn around and run back to his apartment to hide in bed all day. He resists, if only because calling in with an incurable case of horniness for your fellow teacher is probably not an approved use of sick pay.

"It's homecoming week." Jason's tone is cheerful, as if this explains why everything he's wearing is so tight and bright. "Didn't you see the email?"

"I don't remember," he answers, tearing his eyes away from Jason's neon green thighs. He's far too embarrassed to admit his brain is currently not functioning enough to remember what was in his work email recently. There was definitely something about homecoming, but he'd been very frazzled about chaperoning. Then the business with getting a suit and the subsequent weekend, hanging out with Jason all night Saturday which had somehow led to them hanging out again Sunday. Jason reviewed game tapes on his ipad while Emerson sat next to him on the couch grading. Jason had been wearing a pair of basketball shorts that rode up his thighs showing off the dark hair there, and now he's thinking about Jason's hairy thighs again and has lost the vein of the conversation entirely. Something about spirit week he thinks.

"They did spirit week at your old high school, right?" Jason asks. "I loved it when I was still in school."

While Emerson is very happy that Jason had such an incredible time in high school, his own memories are fraught, and a lot of them he's blocked out, some intentionally and others not. He has a vague memory of the lead up to homecoming, all the cheerleaders and sports teams wearing their uniforms daily. Which incidentally led to an increase of taunting from Landon and his teammates. The excess of school spirit and inability to avoid jocks meant Emerson hid in the library, racking up detention slips in order to avoid being in class. He definitely doesn't remember any of his teachers partaking so enthusiastically though. Then again, none of his teachers looked like Jason either.

"Wait, was I supposed to dress up?" Emerson wonders, panicking, his blood running cold. Did he miss an email? Or worse, was there some kind of expectation that teachers partake in spirit week, and he was just supposed to know without being told? He looks down at his brown pants and short-sleeve green button up. He looks like a tree, and

Jason looks like a wet dream out of an eighties workout video.

"It's optional, don't worry," Jason assures him, clearly reading Emerson's mood. He tips sideways, the loose neckline of his shirt fluttering open to reveal a chest dusted in the same dark hair as Jason's thighs and forearms.

Maybe he should take that sick day after all.

"You getting in?" Jason asks.

Emerson hums, passing his bag to Jason before willing his pathetic heart and overactive imagination to calm down as he climbs into the truck. Just because Jason was extra tactile over the weekend, even for him, doesn't mean Emerson can start daydreaming about being held all the time. And sure, those daydreams sprung from reality because he'd fallen asleep halfway through the movie on Saturday, waking up cradled in Jason's arms. But Jason was just a good friend who didn't push Emerson off even when he fell asleep in inappropriate places, like his straight friend's arms.

His crush on Jason is getting entirely out of hand, which is dangerous, not because Jason would hate him. No, Jason is too damn nice for that, but because Emerson already has more than he ever dreamed, and he's not stupid enough to want more.

Not even in his wildest fantasies did he ever imagine when he moved to Southern California that he might not just survive, but thrive. Sure the days are long and often overstimulating, but they're satisfying in a way that makes it bearable. He also loves being a teacher. Somehow despite his own horrible high school experience, he still loves teenagers because they lack a filter and are brutally honest, which makes it easier for him to navigate intentions. He's also in the position of power, making him feel a hell of a lot safer. Imagining that his very straight new friend—best friend, favorite person in the entire world if he's being honest—might wake up one day and decide he has feelings for Emerson is just fanciful and outlandish.

If Emerson isn't careful, he's going to do something very stupid and fall in love with Jason.

"Emmy?"

Emerson exhales a heavy breath, turning to face Jason and oh, what beautiful torture that is. Jason's got that concerned look on his face, his attention honed in on Emerson like he cares because he does.

"Yeah?" Emerson whispers, unsure why Jason's gaze feels heavier today. Maybe it's his imagination. Maybe he's already got one foot over the cliff, ready to fall whether he wants to or not and is seeing what he wants to see. He's always had good pattern recognition, been good at noticing what other people didn't. But at the same time, the disconnect between understanding the more nuanced meanings in what he notices is sometimes lost on him. This feels like one of those times.

It feels like he's missing something, only Emerson has no idea what.

"You ready?"

Nodding, Emerson buckles his seatbelt. "Are you gonna dress up every day or—" but the rest of his sentence cuts off when Jason's engine rumbles to life and the speakers blare. It's not music that blasts through in surround sound but an audiobook. One Emerson knows by heart.

"Shit, sorry," Jason mumbles, jabbing the radio off with an uncharacteristic amount of awkwardness. "You texted you'd be a few minutes, so I shut my engine off and forgot I was listening to that."

"Jason."

"It's so loud too," Jason continues, his cheeks absolutely beet red. It occurs to Emerson that aside from last weekend at the tailor, he's never seen Jason blush, and certainly not like this. "I had it loud because the windows were down. I like some fresh air in the mornings."

"Jason."

Jason inhales, pressing on the gas pedal with a bit too much force, so Emerson is jerked backward, and both of their seat belts lock up. Jason curses under his breath, his cheeks red as a tomato now as he mumbles to himself and merges into the flow of traffic.

Utterly confused, Emerson also feels like he might cry because he very strongly suspects he knows why Jason might have been listening to this particular audiobook. He stares at the road, too emotional to look at Jason.

For a few long seconds, neither of them say a word, then Jason is rambling again.

"There was no student. I only let you think that because I was kind of embarrassed. I heard you that first day when I dropped your books off, telling your kids audiobooks were reading. Only no one had, well, no one had ever told me that. I've never been very good at reading. Theo had to tutor me all through high school so I could stay on the team. I'm not smart like Andrew, and I wasn't an art prodigy like Charlie. I was decent enough at football to be on varsity though, at least in high school, but my grades were shitty. Especially in English. Mr. Caldwell fucking hated me, and he hated that Theo helped me pass, and he's kind of the reason I just hated reading."

Jason is barely taking in a breath, his eyes never leaving the road and his hands gripping the steering wheel so tightly his knuckles go white.

"I know it's stupid because I'm a grown man, and a

teacher myself now, but sometimes I still hear him in my head telling me, maybe I'm not that smart, you know? But then you were there, day one, telling your kids that all books counted as reading. I knew objectively, but it was amazing hearing you tell them what I wish I could've heard when I was their age."

Jason's hands shift on the steering wheel as he breathes, and Emerson wishes he were better with words, with feelings. He hates that anyone ever made Jason feel dumb, or that he might be embarrassed about listening to an audiobook for whatever reason. Most of the time, Emerson isn't the biggest fan of people, but he really hates anyone who has ever hurt Jason.

"There's also the way you talk about books, Emmy. I thought—" Jason pauses, filling his cheeks with air and holding it like a chipmunk before blowing it out. "I wanted to see if maybe I could experience a book the way you do. I know I'm not a reader, and I won't ever be, but I thought maybe I could try this one and we could...we could talk about it."

It is quite possibly the kindest thing anyone has ever done for Emerson. Not sending him to therapy or classes to learn to be flexible or like other people. Not hoping he might magically have a different brain. But rather, finding a way to bridge the gap to understand Emerson's special interest.

"Jason," Emerson whispers, unsure how his heart can feel so small yet so big.

"I wanted to share it with you because it makes you so happy."

Right there. Explicit confirmation. Jason is listening to Lord of the Rings because of Emerson. *For* Emerson.

"Jason," he tries again.

"Fucking traffic, it's only a Monday," Jason mutters nervously. Emerson has never seen him nervous before.

"Jason." He uses his teacher voice, something he's never done on anyone above the age of eighteen, but it works because Jason turns to him and there, beneath the flushed cheeks and the labored breathing, is the hint of a smile from the Jason he knows and loves.

Loves.

He should probably feel more panic about that thought. He's never loved anyone besides his mother and loving her sometimes feels like a dream. Rather than upend Emerson's life, this realization makes all the loose puzzle pieces in his brain slot into place. He loves Jason.

"Sorry, Emmy," Jason sighs, tapping his hands on the steering wheel. "It's been a weird morning. Not because of you, but you know."

Emerson does not know. He has no idea what Jason is talking about, but Jason's smiling, and that makes everything feel right in the world, or at least in Emerson's world.

"Did you eat breakfast, Jason?"

Jason laughs then shakes his head. "I uh, no."

"Skipping breakfast can cause mood swings and impaired concentration," Emerson points out, popping open the glove compartment and digging out a protein bar he rips open before passing to Jason.

"Thanks," Jason mumbles, taking half the bar in one bite. He returns his eyes to the road, merging into the turn lane now that they're directly in front of the school.

"For the record, I think you're very smart, Jason. Anyone who ever made you feel differently deserves, well—I won't say what they deserve."

Jason swallows, sparing a glance at Emerson before his

attention returns to the hot mess of cars all trying to get into the school parking lot.

"Thanks, Emmy."

"And Jason."

"Yeah?"

"Thank you," Emerson whispers, sliding his hand further across the console to rest on Jason's leg. He has no idea what the hell he's doing, but he gives it a squeeze the same way Jason does when he's upset. His bravery is rewarded by Jason's shuddering exhale and blinding smile.

"Emmy," Jason starts, pausing to mutter under his breath when someone cuts him off before he turns into the parking lot. He's quiet until he's parked, turning the engine off and focusing his attention on Emerson. "There's uh, one other thing that I think I should tell you. It's uh, well, the thing is—"

"Isn't that one of your players?" Emerson interrupts, distracted by the hulking figure standing at the front of the truck staring.

"Yeah," Jason frowns, his expression pinched. "What's he doing?"

"You should check on him."

"Yeah," Jason agrees, grabbing his cooler bag and exiting the truck. Emerson has no idea if he's supposed to wait or leave them be, but before he can try and guess, Jason hurries around to his side of the truck, same as he does every morning, opening the door and offering him a hand down. At this point, Emerson is used to getting in and out of the truck and doesn't really need the help anymore. But when he'd pointed that out to Jason, he'd mumbled something unintelligible so Emerson hasn't brought it up since. Besides, it's not like he's ever going to complain about Jason touching him, or paying attention to him, or spending a few extra seconds with him.

Before he can make an escape, the kid in question has moved towards them still staring but hovering an awkward two feet away. Emerson recognizes him now as Jason's star player, the one always smiling. Except he isn't smiling now. He rocks back and forth from foot to foot, his usual confidence and swagger nowhere to be found. He's dressed in a similar get up to Jason, almost as if the entire football team planned it, but where Jason wears it with confidence, Matty appears to be shrinking in on himself.

"Morning, Matty," Jason says.

"Morning, Coach," Matty mumbles, scrubbing a hand through his hair. He looks terrible, his face all red, almost like he's been crying.

It's clear Jason has come to a similar conclusion because the worry rippling off him is palpable. "Matty?"

"So uh, funny story, Coach." Matty tugs on the strings of his backpack. "I might get banned from the homecoming game."

Jason goes very still. "What?"

"Banned from the game," Matty repeats again in a rush. He looks like he might be sick and while Emerson feels very sorry for him, he also takes a step back, vaguely uncomfortable. "Well I think the word Mr. Caldwell used on Friday was academic freeze."

"Mr. Caldwell," Jason echoes in a tone that Emerson has never heard him use before. "Why?"

"I have a book report, Coach. And uh, I tried to do it, but with practice and my job and helping my mom around the house I was tired. You know I'm not so good with English class, the words get all jumbled, and when I'm tired it's hard to focus. It was due last week, so I begged Mr.

Caldwell for an extension, but he told me Friday if it wasn't on his desk by the end of today I wasn't playing in the game." Matty's twisting his hands now, looking like he might be sick. "I spent all weekend trying, Coach. I swear I did."

"Matty," Jason tries, softening his tone.

"The words just get so messed up going from my brain to the paper, and the book was confusing and—" Matty takes a very deep breath, "I'm not going to have it for him, Coach. I'm so fucking sorry. I let you down. I let the team down. I understand if you want to kick me off."

"No one is kicking anyone off any teams," Jason says firmly, tugging Matty into a hug. Matty falls against him, his shoulders shaking like maybe he's crying. The first bell rings, students around them starting to head to class, but none of them move. Not even Emerson. When Matty pulls back, his eyes are red rimmed, and he scrubs his hands over his face looking so very young.

"I'm so sorry, Coach."

"We'll figure this out, Matty."

"I can help," Emerson blurts.

Matty turns his red rimmed eyes on Emerson. "Mr. Miller?"

A plan takes shape, one he's certain he can execute if Jason will agree.

"I've got time after class today. I'm sure if your coach will excuse you from practice we can get your book report done in a few hours."

"You don't even know what book it is," Matty protests.

"I've read all the books," Emerson tells him, confident he's read anything Mr. Caldwell might have assigned. "I can help you."

Matty frowns. "I can't miss practice."

"You can and you will," Jason challenges. "I don't want to see you anywhere near that field today. You're going to meet Em—Mr. Miller after class and work on that report until it's done, then you're going to walk it to Mr. Caldwell with a smile because you're going to be able to play in the game this Friday."

Matty sighs. "What if I can't?"

Looking at Matty, it's hard not to think about Jason, about what he'd just confessed in the truck on the way here. Was this him over a decade ago? It could have been if he hadn't had a best friend like Theo tutoring him. Emerson makes his mind up; he will not let Matty fail, not over this book report or anything else. He won't let any of the kids fail. Not if he can help it, which he can.

He's not some awkward kid anymore, struggling to know his needs or being bullied, and he isn't going to let some stick in the mud teacher with antiquated, judgmental ideas about how kids should learn make anyone else's life miserable.

"You can and you will," Emerson asserts, surprised by the confidence in his tone. "There's not a single book being used in the English curriculum for any grade this year I haven't read. I have absolutely no doubt we can get your report done today. You will play in that game this weekend, Matty."

To his immense surprise, Matty throws himself forward, wrapping Emerson in a hug that has him tumbling back.

"Easy, Matty."

"Sorry, Coach," Matty laughs, pulling back. "Sorry, Mr. Miller, I'm just—thank you."

The two-minute warning bell rings, and Matty laughs, the heavy air around him lifting like the sun peeking out through the clouds after a storm. It makes Emerson feel good, reminds him exactly what it is that he loves about teaching, about his life in Santa Leon. It's not just the literal sun that's always out around here, it's the people too, that make life here feel warm and bright.

"Get to class before you're late," Jason grins. "We don't need you getting detention today."

"Yes, Coach," Matty says, stumbling over his feet in his haste to move. "I'll see you later, Mr. Miller!"

He's gone before Emerson can reply, sprinting across the quad with all the grace and speed of a star footballer.

"That was damn nice of you, Emmy. You didn't have to do that, but I'm really fucking grateful you did."

"I know how much football means to you."

"Yeah, sure the game means a lot, but it's the kids. Kids like Matty who never felt confident until they stepped on a field. You're giving him a shot to prove to Mr. Caldwell, but mostly to himself, that he can do other things, too. You're exactly the kind of teacher these kids deserve."

Pride wells up in Emerson, making him feel ten feet tall. There'd been so much doubt when he'd chosen this career. So many people along the way, some well-intentioned and some not, questioning if he'd be able to handle it. At times, his own self-doubt had been the loudest critic of all. Now here he is, proving all of them wrong. Proving himself wrong.

When Jason slips an arm around his shoulder, pulling him close, it's the easiest thing in the world to lean into the embrace.

"Ready to kick today's ass, Emmy?"

"I'm ready," Emerson smiles, meaning every word.

12 JASON

"AFTERNOON, COACH," Eddie's smile is clipped tight, his hair in disarray and the buttons on his shirt done up wrong. "Sorry I'm late. The twins are in their *I don't like clothing phase* so getting them to put something on to get them to my parent's house was—interesting. It took me almost half an hour to get them to put underwear on."

"Alec went through that," Jason laughs, recalling the times one of his parents or his *abuela* would scoop Alec up in a blanket to get him out of the front yard naked. "It was hilarious."

"It's hilarious when it's someone else's kids and not yours," Eddie groans. "Archer ended up wearing his Halloween costume, mask and all, and Sawyer went in his bathing suit with a tutu."

"At least it's clothing," Jason grins. "Or clothing adjacent. Is Sawyer still wearing tutus with everything?"

Eddie nods, shoving his hands in his pockets. "My parents think it's a phase he'll outgrow. Which is possible. I mean he's four, so he might, but I don't like the way people talk about him like he's not there because they don't expect to see a little boy in firetruck boots and a pink tutu. Pisses me the fuck off."

"Most people aren't assholes about it though, right?"

"Nah, not where we send the kids. Their preschool is great, but I worry."

Jason breathes in the salt air, lungs oddly tight. This isn't the first time he and Eddie have had a conversation like this, but it's the first since Jason's realization over the weekend, and it hits differently.

"If anyone gives you guys a problem, let me know."

"We're good, Coach." Eddie gulps down some of the coffee Jason knows to be in his travel mug. The man is addicted. "The support is appreciated though. Honestly it's too early to know what it all means for him, he's a kid. I just want him to have the freedom to be himself until he knows who that is, you know?"

Jason does know. Or he thought he did. He's thirty and only now realizing he is maybe, possibly, not as straight as he always thought. He has no idea what he is, but he's quite certain having a crush on his male coworker means that he is not straight. Although thinking that is a disservice to Emerson. He's not just Jason's coworker, he's his friend, one of the closest he's ever had, which led Jason to spiraling the entire weekend about what it all meant. He spent a few hours convinced he was just confusing friendship with affection but then he'd thought about Emerson's pretty eyes and hard-to-earn smiles leading to the thought that he wouldn't mind kissing him—something he'd never once in over two decades of friendship thought about Theo.

"Where's Matty by the way?" Eddie's eyes scan the field where the players are currently running agility drills. "I don't see him. He's not hurt, is he? Shit, we can't lose our quarterback homecoming week, we'll be screwed."

"He's not hurt," Jason assures him, struggling to focus on football when all his brain wants to do is think about Emerson.

Why him? He's had countless close male friends before. Not once has he ever wanted to touch them the way he does Emerson. He thought it was just his normal tactile nature but after this past weekend, he's realized a few things about himself—namely that he's pretty damn handsy with Emerson. The more he acknowledged this, the easier it was to admit how much he likes touching Emerson, how right it is to have him within reach. Nothing feels as good as having his arms around him, but being able to lay a hand at his back or his shoulder is a close second.

Over the weekend, when Emerson fell asleep during their movie night, his body had slumped sideways into Jason. It'd felt so natural to lift his arm and curl Emerson into him. When Emerson woke up an hour later, he'd been sleepy, confused and then blushed when he realized he was all but in Jason's lap. For the first time Jason thought, *I could lean down and kiss him.* He did not, both because kissing people without permission isn't Jason's idea of a good time, and because realizing he wanted to kiss a man for the first had been a little overwhelming. He waited until the movie ended and Emerson was safely home before laying face down on his bed and having a minor breakdown, both dogs barking at his back as if they sensed his unease and hated it as much as Jason did.

Laying there in the dark unable to sleep, he'd tried to compare how he felt for Emerson to how he felt for any of his ex-girlfriends, but that was a futile comparison. Looking back it's easy for Jason to realize he'd always been the one pursued in relationships, oftentimes ending up with women who appreciated his size and his football reputation more than his personality. Jason has always liked making people happy. At least, until their happiness came at the expense of his friendship with Theo, or wanting to use Jason as some kind of arm candy, and then he was able to recognize how little they made *him* happy.

Sure he'd liked them at first, but Jason liked almost everyone, so he's not sure that is a good litmus test. The more he thought about it the more he realized, he'd never been all that upset when the relationships ended because he'd never been attached to any of them. Did that mean he'd been acting out of subconscious heteronormativity? He didn't think so since he enjoyed the sex, but then again Jason was also just as happy to jerk off by himself as he was to get off with someone else, so he's not even sure what that means.

When not in a relationship, he'd never liked hook ups or one night stands, finding them far too impersonal. Did that make him some level of ace? He didn't think that fit either. He didn't need an emotional connection for sex, he just preferred it.

Charlie told him in no uncertain terms that he didn't need a label to like Emerson, which was all well and good, except that Emerson liked when things made sense. How would he feel if Jason confessed while not understanding his feelings at all? Would it make him uneasy? Anxious? Maybe he doesn't even return Jason's feelings. Whatever the hell those feelings are. Being gay doesn't mean he's automatically attracted to all men, or Jason.

Maybe Emerson only likes him as a friend, and this wondering and worrying is pointless. Maybe Jason's having some giant queer awakening for nothing. Not that you have to be in a relationship to be queer, but Jason wants one. At least, he thinks he does. He'd been content to not have one for years, but watching Theo and Alec dredged up a longing for companionship that didn't quite make sense until Emerson came along and filled in all the little holes in Jason's heart he hadn't even known existed.

"You alright, Jason?"

For whatever reason, Eddie rarely calls him by his first name, so the use of it drags him from the brink.

"I'm good, just uh, remembered I forgot something," Jason lies, hating himself for the deception but needing a few minutes to gather his thoughts. It's not going to do his team any good to see him anxious, especially not this week. They count on him to always be strong and steady, and he will be. He just needs to pull his shit together. "Think you can hold down practice for me?"

"You know I can," Eddie assures him, pulling his whistle out of his pocket and slipping the lanyard around his neck like he's been waiting for just this moment.

"I'll hurry."

Eddie shakes his head, clapping Jason on the back. "I got this, no worries."

Jason grins despite the turmoil coiling itself around his lungs. He knows he can count on Eddie, which is exactly why he makes such an incredible assistant coach. Not only do the kids love him, he's reliable as hell like Jason. Or at least, as reliable as Jason is when he's not having a sexuality crisis.

Halfway across the lawn, he pulls out his phone to call Theo, pocketing it just as quickly. If there's anyone in the world who would understand what he's going through it's his best friend but something stops him. He doesn't want to ask Theo to lie to Alec or keep secrets from him, not after all the shit they've been through. Neither is he in the mood for everyone to know his business, which would happen if Alec knew.

Hell, Alec would probably throw him a coming out party. Although Jason's not sure if it counts as coming out if he's just vaguely confused and still not sure if he's got heartburn or something else, because every time he thinks about Charlie flirting with Emerson his chest burns. He kind of hates himself for keeping it a secret. He's got the world's *best* friend, and not only are all of his brothers queer, they would support him. Jason is lucky as fuck because he has nothing to lose, at least not with his family. It's just that Jason has no idea what any of this means, and he would kind of rather figure it out, at least a little bit, before making any big declarations or sharing it with his entire well-meaning but nosy as shit family.

Maybe it's panic, or maybe he's being selfish. Either way, he'd like to keep a bit of this to himself for as long as he can. For reasons he can't explain, or maybe doesn't want to think about because it makes him feel even more panicky, he knows Emerson is something special—someone once in a lifetime—and he doesn't want to fuck it up.

Whatever is going on in Jason's head he needs to be damn sure he understands it before he drags Emerson into it. Either Emerson won't return his feelings and Jason needs to be emotionally fortified to handle the rejection, or Emerson does at which point Jason better be damn sure what his feelings mean because if there is one thing Jason is sure of, it's that he won't hurt Emerson.

Whatever Emerson wants, whatever he needs, Jason wants to give him.

That alone should probably be all the tip off Jason needs. Even with his exes, he'd wanted to make them happy but not like this. Trying to mesh their wants with his own life had felt like constantly having to sacrifice what he loved and wanted for them, like two magnets trying to repel. Emerson fits into Jason's life in a way that makes it hard for him to believe less than six weeks ago he didn't even know him. Now, he can't imagine his life without him.

Now, he wants to kiss him.

That second thought floats into his brain without permission, as it's been doing a lot the last forty-eight hours. Every time he questions himself, his identity or his feelings or whether he's interested in men, he thinks about Emerson and his brain says, *well, we're interested in that one.*

He has no idea if that means he's always been into men and somehow too blind to see it, or if it's just Emerson. All he knows is everything about being with Emerson makes Jason happy, maybe the happiest he's ever been, which is saying something since he's a pretty damn happy guy. And maybe, he thinks that's always been the problem. His past relationships ending always seemed inevitable because how could anyone make him happier than he already was when he had a great family, good friends and the world's best job? But then Emerson showed up, and suddenly Jason realized even a happy life could be happier.

And Emerson? He makes Jason so god damn happy his heart feels like it might burst out of his chest.

Emerson, whose voice Jason hears right now. With a bemused smile, he looks up and notices exactly where he is. Somehow, he marched himself all the way across campus and to Emerson's classroom. He's not even sorry about his subconscious journey. Maybe this isn't the alone time he planned, but being able to check on Emerson and Matty might give him some purpose. Besides, Emerson had spent lunch today in his room making notes to help Matty this afternoon. While Jason is grateful and impressed, he also missed his standing lunch date with Emerson.

The idea that he's so out of sorts and spiraling just because he hasn't seen Emerson in seven hours is something Jason is not willing to think about too deeply. He's got enough on his mind without having to acknowledge that his feelings for Emerson—for a man—go far beyond a little physical attraction.

With the door propped open, he can hear the familiar hum of Emerson's voice followed by Matty's much deeper voice.

"I don't see how that helps."

Inching closer to the open doorway, Jason quietly cracks it open to peer inside.

"The amazing thing about literature is the way it can connect us. Whether you're reading a book entirely rooted in fantasy or something based on real life, the stories evoke emotion. I want to know how this book made you feel, Matty."

"It pissed me the fuck off, Mr. Miller," Matty answers. "The entire thing was bullshit."

"It's autobiographical," Emerson offers in a neutral tone.

"That's what pisses me off," Matty grumbles. "It's bullshit that people get treated like this. The government is supposed to help, but how can it do that when all the laws and rules it's founded on are racist as fuck. Sorry, Mr. Miller. I know I'm not supposed to say fuck in front of teachers, but it pisses me the fuck off."

"And that anger isn't misplaced. When there is injustice you should feel—" but Emerson pauses, turning his head to stare at Jason. "Looks like we've got some company. Aren't you supposed to be at practice, Mr. King?"

"Oh no, pretend I'm not here," Jason tries, holding his hands up.

"You're too big to be invisible, Coach," Matty grins. "Did you miss your favorite student? You did, right?"

"You know I can't have favorites," Jason tells him, even if the words are most definitely true. Practice today wasn't the same without him, both because of his skill but also his personality. As captain, he's the rock of the team, and it's difficult to imagine next year without him. Matty is going to be one of the kids it's hard to let go of, even if Jason is excited for the future he's got ahead of him.

"Whatever you say, Coach," Matty grins.

Emerson's lips twitch like he's trying not to smile and all the jumbled, confusing pieces of Jason's heart and brain just settle. Emerson is so handsome with his dark green shirt that makes his pale eyes almost sparkle and his hair all tousled. Seeing him now, Jason can admit that yes, an entire day without him is way too long. The implications of that are more than he can cope with right now, but with Emerson in sight, it's easy to push away the scary unknowns and focus on him.

When Emerson's lips turn up at the corners to offer Jason a small, private smile, he wants to literally stomp his feet the way he used to when he played football. There's no goal in sight, but Emerson is worth more than any touchdown.

Deciding to go for broke, Jason strides into the room and sits himself at one of the chairs beside them. Or tries to anyway. The desks are too damn small for someone of Jason's stature, and though he's squeezed himself in, he's not sure he's going to get back out of the desk without it breaking.

"That doesn't look too comfortable, Coach."

"I'm good," Jason insists, refusing to admit his ass and thighs are squashed while Emerson stares at him. "How's the book report coming?"

"Shit," Matty answers at the same time Emerson says "good."

"Mr. Miller is being nice," Matty offers.

"Mr. Miller is nice," Jason agrees, always ready to sing his praises.

"I'm also honest. I don't like lying, and I wouldn't do it to make you feel better," Emerson tells him. "You've already got your intro and a few key points marked down into your notes. You just need to add your opinion."

"My opinion is the government is fucked up," Matty frowns.

"Which can be rephrased to point out how strongly the foundational injustices that are rooted in our legal systems make you feel, because they set up a system of oppression rather than dismantling it," Emerson says.

"If I say that, Mr. Caldwell will think I cheated."

"Maybe use your words, though probably with less fucks," Emerson suggests, earning him a laugh from Jason and Matty.

"You're a kick-ass teacher, Mr. Miller. I wish you'd been here when I was a freshman. I might've liked English more."

The shift in Emerson is subtle, but since Jason's playing the watch-Emerson game, it's easy to pick up on the slight straightening of his back and the flush of pink on his cheeks. He looks surprised, but also proud, and it makes Jason want to hug him so much he finds his hands curling around the edge of the desk to keep from reaching out.

Jason is so screwed. Whatever the hell he is, it's definitely not straight.

BETWEEN THE HOMECOMING preparations Jason volunteered to help oversee—something that takes over his lunch time and every spare second he's not teaching or coaching—his classes and football practice, Jason's week is going to be a shit show. He's overly committed, something he normally takes with a grain of salt but finds is making him cranky this year. Because for the first time, there's something he wants more than making everyone else happy —Emerson.

Sure he's going to see him every day because they ride together, and yeah they text sporadically during the day and as much as they can at night before Jason passes out from exhaustion, but it's not the same. They'll have to forgo their midday lunch dates, and though they've only missed one before this week, he's not sure he realized how integral to his day it'd become until he thought about not having it. It doesn't even matter if one of them is venting about work or just shooting the shit about something random because talking to Emerson, just being with him, is always the best part of Jason's day.

When Thursday rolls around, he's managed to miss lunch with Emerson the entire week in order to oversee the homecoming committee, leaving Jason in a sour mood. This mood is matched by the weather, the normal morning coastal fog never gives way to the expected sunshine and instead offers a smattering of rain. It's not heavy, full rain; it's something annoying and misty like the sky can't decide what it's doing. It's just enough that Jason would normally have to pull his kids into the gym, but with it entirely decked out for the dance tomorrow, there's nowhere to send them except study hall, leaving him with a free period.

Rapping his knuckles on the side of his desk, he looks around for something to keep himself occupied. Deciding to catch up on stuff for the upcoming homecoming game, he goes over his player stats and finalizes some of the plays for the big game, praying the rain lets up enough for the kids to enjoy it. While he works, he makes his way through his afternoon snack and his entire lunch knowing he won't be able to have his usual open door lunch with the kids because of the gym situation. By the time the bell rings signaling the official lunch break, Jason's finished his work and his food. Rather than feel accomplished or satisfied, he is more restless than ever.

He pulls his phone out, intending to text Emerson, when he realizes he can just go see him. He knows now that Emerson eats lunch in his classroom when not with Jason. Pocketing his phone, he all but runs from his office, pulling his hoodie back on as he stalks through the gym and out into the elements. The rain is still going, but there are pockets of blue skies and sunshine far on the horizon signaling its end is near.

"Take that rain," Jason grins, finding the drops that fall on his face refreshing after too many hours spent indoors. Jason is not meant to spend the entire day inside cooped up, and the walk across campus does him good, his muscles loosening and his mind clearing. Shaking water droplets from his hair, he ducks beneath the sloped roof that covers the doorway to Emerson's classroom, ready to push it open further when the sound of a raised voice stops him in his tracks.

"You have no business interfering with my students or trying to usurp my place at the school, Mr. Miller. None."

"I wasn't—"

"You were," Caldwell snaps, the grating timber of his

voice made worse by the tone he's using. "There is no way Matthew would have passed without help, which I did not provide as he had ample time to do the work of his own volition."

"Matty needs extra accommodations."

"Matthew does not have any legal accommodations on file. I would know, as I'm his teacher, not you." Jason doesn't need to see Caldwell to imagine the sneer he's probably got in place. "He should be sitting out from the game Friday on the sidelines where he belongs, reaping the consequences of his own ill organized time management and apathy. Putting sports above academics has left him bereft, and it shows."

Jason's teeth grind. How fucking dare Caldwell talk about his kid like that, a kid who works damn fucking hard at everything, academics included given his lack of supports. Worse, how dare he yell at Emerson for stepping up when so many others haven't. Jason understands personally the limitations of helping kids without legal accommodations when there's no official diagnosis, but Caldwell is a fucking dick who would probably ignore an IEP or 504 if there was no one there to force him to legally follow it.

"Afternoon, gentlemen," Jason says, his wide smile at odds with the simmering anger burning a hole in his gut when he takes a look at Caldwell's smug face and Emerson's stricken one. He's never wanted to punch anyone the way he does Caldwell, but getting fired or arrested won't save anyone from Caldwell's bigoted asshole behavior.

"Mr. King, we're having a private conversation here. I understand you seem to think you're welcome anywhere you desire but—"

"I have a lunch appointment with Emerson," Jason interrupts, striding across the room to position himself at a slight angle between Caldwell and Emerson as if he can block Caldwell's negativity with his own body. On any given day, he lets a lot slide because there's nothing he can do about how much Mr. Caldwell dislikes him or athletes, but if he thinks he can intimidate Emerson while Jason is here, he's got another thing coming.

Over Jason's dead fucking body will anyone make Emerson uncomfortable.

"I told you, we're having a private conversation." Mr. Caldwell's eyes flare with annoyance. "This doesn't concern you. You can wait outside until I'm done speaking with Mr. Miller here."

"I'm fine right where I am," Jason counters. "And for the record, anything involving my players concerns me. If you have anything to say about one of them, feel free to say it to my face, or better yet we can have a meeting with the principal if you'd prefer."

"Whatever you heard was not a conversation for your ears, Mr. King."

"And yet my ears heard perfectly. One of my players had a book report due, which was written and turned in by the assigned deadline, removing any threat of academic freeze and freeing him to play in the game this week regardless of your personal feelings."

Mr. Caldwell bristles, clearly surprised. Jason is surprised, too. Usually he lets him get away with shit because it's easier than fighting back, but something about seeing him direct his behavior at Emerson has Jason ready to do anything to get rid of him, well, barring physical violence. Putting him in his place though is something Jason's wanted to do for years, and now seems as good of a time as any.

"Your personal feelings should have no bearing on how you teach."

"I don't know what you're implying, Mr. King, but I don't like your tone."

"You don't?" Jason muses. "Damn. How...*unfortunate*."

If steam could come out of Mr. Caldwell's head, it would, his bulbous eyes protruding with agitation and his pale cheeks flushed red. He turns his gaze away from Jason and focuses it on Emerson instead. "I'll see that you don't overstep in the future, Mr. Miller."

Without waiting for a response he turns, his sneakers squeaking on the floor as he departs.

Jason waits until he's gone to turn towards Emerson, pulling him into a fierce hug which Emerson returns with more force than usual, his longer fingers fisting so tightly in the back of Jason's hoodie it feels like he might rip a hole in it. Not that Jason would care. Clothing is replaceable, Emerson is not.

"Caldwell is a fucking dick." He rubs his hands along Emerson's spine, the line of his back tense and unmoving. "I'm sorry he gave you shit just because you were helping out one of my players. I didn't mean to drag you into whatever his issue is with the athletes."

Emerson grumbles something unintelligible from where his face is smashed into Jason's shoulder.

"What was that?" Jason asks, settling his palm on Emerson's lower back to pull him that much closer, something in his brain screaming to keep him close and safe. Sure Caldwell isn't a real threat, but he made Emerson uncomfortable, and for that Jason hates him more than ever. "I couldn't quite make it out clearly. Did you say, 'Jason, I hate Caldwell, and I hope he burns in the fires of Mordor?'"

The soft rumble of Emerson's amusement reverberates against Jason's chest and eases away the tightness. More of that same tension slips away when Emerson pulls out of the embrace and smiles at Jason.

"I did not say that," Emerson huffs, "but I might have *thought* it."

"Then I'll say it out loud for the both of us," Jason grins, relishing the feeling of Emerson in his arms.

Shit, how did he not see his feelings from the beginning? Worse, how is he supposed to cope now that he has?

"You know what?" Emerson says, taking a step back from the embrace to seat himself on the edge of one of the student desks. Jason copies his position, choosing the desk closest so his knees butt up against Emerson's.

"What?" Jason asks, pressing his knees against Emerson's. He's not exactly subtle about his increasing desire to touch, but Emerson either hasn't noticed or doesn't realize what it means.

He's not sure which is more probable; the second is most likely, given Emerson's inability to read subtext, which is the world's biggest blessing and curse all wrapped in one for this current situation. He isn't calling Jason on how obvious he's being, but he won't ever because it most likely isn't obvious to him.

It occurs to Jason that if he wants to know how Emerson feels about him having feelings for him, he's going to have to explicitly ask.

"Caldwell is an asshole." Emerson sits up straight. "How dare he."

Just, maybe not right now.

"Conversation just now registering?" Jason asks, increasing the pressure of his knee against Emerson's.

"Yes," Emerson frowns, crossing his arms. "How dare he care more about his own ego than his students. What a, a—"

"Asshole? Dick face? Fucker? I'm trying to think of

some kind of elven reference for you, but I think I used all my cool points with the Mordor thing."

The corner of Emerson's lips twitch, a sharp contrast to his furrowed features. Even mad, he's adorable and Jason itches to smooth away the lines between his pale eyebrows, to kiss his delicate brow. To—

"He's horrible," Emerson groans, dragging Jason's attention back to the conversation. "Caldwell is exactly like the teachers who used to make me think I was stupid or an inconvenience. It makes me so angry that I just shut down. He said all those horrible things, and it was like my brain froze, and I couldn't talk."

Emerson's been open about his issues with going nonverbal like that, and while Jason has never experienced it, he's beginning to understand the kind of stress response it triggers in Emerson, and he's eager to help him move past it.

"He might be a shitty person and a shitty teacher but you're not. You are the kind of teacher who gives kids hope," Jason soothes, laying his hand on Emerson's knee. "You're worth a hundred Caldwells."

"I don't know about that," Emerson protests.

"I do. You're a good teacher and this school is better with you here." Verbalizing this makes a lump form in Jason's throat, especially when Emerson's jaw wobbles. Has anyone ever told him how incredible he is? How much better off the world is with him in it? Jason doesn't think so and it makes him want to do it every day for the rest of Emerson's life, to be there at his side cheering him on and reminding him how goddamn awesome he is. Just because not everyone sees it doesn't mean it's not true. "My life is better with you here."

Emerson's pale eyelashes flutter, resting against his high cheekbones. Slowly, he breathes in and out, his eye contact so intense Jason feels like Emerson is looking into his very soul.

Suddenly, Jason is imagining what might happen if he blurted everything out right now. What's the worst that could happen if he got the nerve to simply say, *you are so special to me and I think my feelings have changed.* Except that's not right. He's not sure they've changed at all. It feels like maybe they've been there since that very first day, he just didn't know what they meant.

Maybe something else. *Emmy, I don't think I'm as straight as I thought I was, and I'm pretty sure I want to kiss you.* Terrible. Jason wishes he had a football in his hands so he could throw something. What a paltry explanation that would be for the man who deserves so much more than Jason's floundering. He knows he wants to kiss Emerson, but why is saying that out loud so difficult? Jason's never been scared of saying that to a woman before.

"Did you forget to eat?" Emerson asks, poking Jason's stomach. "You're making that pinchy face."

"I ate," Jason says, unsure how to explain his pinchy face is because he has a massive not-fucking-straight-crush on him. Does this make him bisexual? The idea of kissing any of the other male teachers here makes Jason recoil, but then again he doesn't want to kiss any of the women here either. It's been a long time since he wanted to kiss anyone, now that he thinks about it. His last few failed relationships had soured him on the dating scene in order to avoid anything superficial.

Being alone was preferable to something that wasn't real. Well, Emerson is right here and he's the realest thing Jason's ever known. It's wonderful and terrifying, and Jason feels like a bumbling teenager with his first crush all over again as he rubs his sweaty palms on his knees. There's no way he's going to survive hiding this for long. Jason is terrible at keeping secrets, and worst of all, every second that goes by where he doesn't tell Emerson feels like a lie.

"Are you nervous about the game? Or maybe about the dance?" Emerson hedges, looking unsure. "I am."

Something settles in Jason. Thinking about himself is confusing and kind of annoying. Thinking about Emerson is easy. He would much prefer to focus his attention on soothing Emerson's nerves than his own hot mess of a sexuality crisis.

"Don't be, I'll be with you the entire time. Well, maybe not the entire time because we're supposed to periodically make rounds on the dance floor, and last year I had to break up something in the bathroom I wish I hadn't seen. But I'll be with you, like, ninety-eight percent of the night."

"Ninety-eight percent, huh?"

"I'm trying to be very specific," Jason grins. "However, if this is not accurate you have permission to be mad at me."

"I won't be mad at you," Emerson says with a subtle shake of his head. "I'm not—I know we're not there to have fun. We're there to supervise and—"

"Why aren't we there to have fun?" Jason interrupts.

"Well, we're the teachers," Emerson says matter of factly.

"Teachers can have fun," Jason tells him. "I plan on having a lot of fun."

"Is someone else going?" Emerson asks.

"Is someone else—*no*. I mean fun with *you*, Emmy."

The look of surprise on his face is not something Jason thinks he can ever get used to.

"I've never been to a dance, not as a student or a teacher," Emerson says, the hint of embarrassment coloring his tone. They've talked about it before, but Jason suspects their wildly different high school experiences left lasting impressions on each of them; Emerson's, unfortunately, for the worse. "I'm not sure what I'm supposed to do there. I can't imagine that it will be very fun for you just to follow me around."

Truthfully, there's nothing Jason would rather do than spend an entire night following Emerson around. Before he can say this, Emerson is speaking again.

"I don't mind taking over most of the rounds so you can enjoy yourself," Emerson offers, as if Jason would let anyone, especially Emerson, take all the responsibility. As if for Jason there is anything in the world he would rather do than be with Emerson. Regardless of his new thoughts about holding hands and kissing, he'd still pick Emerson every time. Boring teacher duties and all.

"I'll enjoy myself because you're there," Jason assures him, the huff of disbelief followed by the hint of a smile enough to soothe the caveman part of Jason itching to hide Emerson away so from now on, no one else can ever hurt his feelings again. It's just impossible for Jason to believe that there are people who got to know him their entire life, and they never realized what a goddamn treasure he is.

Staring at those wide, green eyes all Jason can think is that Emerson is his favorite person. Even if nothing ever comes of his new feelings that would be okay; if nothing ever changes between them and all he ever gets are morning commutes and shared lunches and a phone full of text messages it will be enough because Emerson is enough.

Emerson is *everything*.

Oh fucking shit, he doesn't just have a crush on a man, he might be falling in love with one.

13 EMERSON

PINCHING the bridge of his nose, Emerson takes a steadying breath before counting to ten in his head. It's almost as if something is in the air. Something like spirit week or the homecoming game or the dance. He's pretty sure that building excitement is what's gotten into the kids, who've gone from bad to worse as the day's gone on, and he can only imagine what they're going to be like on Friday.

Though he's never personally experienced any of the school spirit fervor or pre-dance excitement for himself as a bullied outcast, he tries to be lenient with his kids, but there's only so much whispering and inattentiveness he can handle. Even Arlo, who is usually one of his most respectful students, is caught texting during class. By the time third period ends, he's given two detentions for disruptive behavior, something he's never had to do.

When the lunch bell rings, Emerson's stomach is tied in knots to the point he can't even choke down his peanut butter sandwich. Not even the quiet reprieve from students helps Emerson's nerves settle because it comes with a silence that would normally be filled with Jason's rambling. He misses Jason more acutely than he thought possible.

Unable to eat and eager for a distraction, he decides to spend his lunch period grading, turning his attention to a pile of essays on his desk from his second period class. Halfway through the first one a knock at his door interrupts his focus.

"Come in," Emerson yells, expecting a student and taken by surprise when the principal walks into his room instead.

"Good afternoon, Mr. Miller. I hope I'm not interrupting."

"Not at all," Emerson replies, pushing his chair away from his desk while trying not to panic. Mrs. Hernandez is a kind, fair principal but has never once come to Emerson's classroom unannounced, and her arrival sets his nerves on edge

"I was going to send an email, but I thought perhaps in person might be better."

"Okay," Emerson says, twisting his ring. Her smile is friendly but her tone is anything but, and not even Emerson's impeccable pattern recognition and decade of studying people is good enough for him to parse what she might say.

"There's been a complaint filed about conduct."

"What did I do?" Emerson balks, dread settling in his gut. He tries to think of anything he might have done wrong but can't think of anything aside from the one time he was late because of the bus last month but that seems unlikely.

"You haven't done anything, Mr. Miller. The complaint is about Mr. King. Given the importance of the game tomorrow we're eager to expedite the process of investigating the validity of claims."

"What claims?" Emerson frowns, struggling to think of anything Jason might have done wrong.

"There are concerns that Mr. King has used his personal relationship with you in order to influence the grades for starting players on the team."

"Jason would never. He's an amazing teacher and coach," Emerson argues, shocked at his outburst.

"I'm not here to debate Mr. King's character," Mrs. Hernandez says solemnly. "I wanted to make you aware of what we'll be discussing at the mandatory meeting with HR this afternoon."

Emerson says nothing, finding it impossible to focus on what the appropriate response might be with the emotions warring inside of him: a confusing mess of fear, indignance and anger that leave him feeling like he might be sick.

"Don't worry, Mr. Miller," Mrs. Hernandez placates, "we just want to clear up a few things."

A weird haze takes over, and while Emerson knows he's replying, he's hardly aware of his own words. In fact, he's not even sure what she said, the buzz of anxiety making it hard to absorb what's going on around him. It's almost like he's outside his body, and while he knows he says something to Mrs. Hernandez and makes it through the next two hours, he's hardly sure how.

When he walks into the front office, the only people there are Mabel, sitting at her desk typing and Jason in a chair behind her with his head in his hands. Both of them look up at his arrival, their smiles feeling entirely undeserved.

All he's done is cause trouble. He has no idea why they're both looking at him like his arrival is something to be happy about. Emerson's heart lodges itself in his throat when Mabel stands up, walking around her desk to hug him. She's so small Emerson has to hunch over to return the hug, hoping she doesn't notice the wet patch of tears he leaves on the shoulder of her hot pink sweater.

"Everything is going to be fine, Mr. Miller." She pats him on the back, her smile unwavering. "You'll see."

Emerson doesn't share her confidence and can do nothing more than nod, making his way over to the row of chairs lined up behind Mabel's desk where Jason sits. There are four, and though he wants to sit directly next to Jason he can't help worrying how that will be perceived, lowering himself into the chair furthest from him.

One of the chairs squeaks loudly, then Jason's bulk is suddenly seated beside him, their shoulders pressed together and Jason's hand on his leg. Long fingers curl around his knee in a reassuring squeeze, and Emerson closes his eyes to keep from crying again.

Though he did nothing wrong, it somehow feels like his fault. He'd inserted himself into the situation. He's the one who came to Santa Leon as an outsider and changed things. He's the one who's made things difficult for Jason.

"Breathe, Emmy." Jason's voice is calm and steady, holding none of the panic Emerson currently feels. "I already talked to them before you got here. Shitty as this all is, it's straightforward too. They're going to ask you some questions and all you need to do is tell them the truth. You can do that, I know you can."

"What if—"

"No," Jason interrupts. "You're going to be fine. Whatever they ask, you're going to answer honestly because you did nothing wrong."

The reassurance makes Emerson want to sob. He's not worried about *himself*, he's worried about Jason. What if Emerson gets him fired? Jason is one of the best teachers that Emerson has ever met; exactly the kind of person who should be working with teenagers because he loves it and the kids know it.

Jason makes his students feel safe and seen the same way he does Emerson. Alongside his teaching position is his coaching job, which Jason loves just as much. There's no mistaking his passion for the game, or his dedication to his players and this school. The idea that Emerson's presence here and his subsequent actions jeopardize everything Jason loves is enough to send him spiraling. He knows the accusations are that Jason is the one who manipulated Emerson. But aside from that being as far from the truth as humanly possible, Emerson can't ignore the fact that Jason had no problems here before Emerson came.

The only reason Emerson isn't laying facedown on the floor right now is because of the injustice of it all. The audacity of someone—Mr. Caldwell, no doubt—throwing Jason's character into question because he's pissed off is overriding Emerson's nervous system, preventing it from going into full shutdown mode. Though, his anxiety is high enough he's hardly functioning at full capacity.

"Everything will be okay, Emmy," Jason whispers, affording him the kind of promise Emerson should be saying to Jason. He's the one whose career and reputation is on the line, yet all Jason seems to care about is calming Emerson.

Sometimes Emerson hates his brain. He can think of words, can imagine telling Jason he's sorry for causing trouble or maybe promising that he'll make sure the school knows Jason did *nothing* wrong, yet despite the multitude of rehearsed sentences none of those words will come out.

"Mr. Miller," Mrs. Hernandez calls, popping her head out of the conference room. "We're ready for you."

They might be ready but Emerson is not.

Walking into the conference room is like walking into war, or at least that's how his brain perceives the situation. There's an array of people ranging from the district superintendent to the principal and an unfamiliar man who he assumes is from HR, given the laptop and papers piled in front of him.

The man from human resources gives his name but Emerson has no idea what it is, the information pushed out of his brain by his rising anxiety. His eyes track everything from the way people breathe to their shifting facial expressions, hyper aware of everything except their actual words.

While Emerson knows he answers yes and no to their various questions, everything happens quickly. Before he knows it, they're calling Jason back in. He moves without hesitation, settling himself in the chair beside Emerson. Though his hands remain folded in front of him, he presses his knee against Emerson's beneath the table where no one can see, and that small bit of contact shatters Emerson's wall of cognitive dissonance.

"Thank you gentlemen for being here," Mrs. Hernandez says as if either he or Jason had a choice in the matter. "We have no desire to drag this out, especially given the upcoming homecoming events."

Emerson can't help but wonder if this process would've been quite so expedited if it didn't involve their star football coach. He's grateful, because the idea of this having been drawn out more than a day would've rendered him nearly catatonic, but he also finds their desire to not interrupt homecoming rather egregious.

"Taking in all of the facts, there is no evidence that Mr. Miller did anything outside of what the district would hope any of their teachers would do upon noticing a student struggling with their subject matter."

"Which wouldn't have happened if Matty already had the accommodations he needs," Jason interrupts.

"Your impassioned recommendations for Matthew during this process are understood, Mr. King." Mrs. Hernandez continues, "the district will see about getting him a referral for accommodations if it's something he and his mother are interested in pursuing."

Jason's smile widens, and if Emerson weren't already a little bit in love with Jason King, he would be now. While Jason could've used his meeting time to advocate for himself, he'd apparently spent it trying to get Matty accommodations.

"Do you gentlemen have any questions?"

"Are you going to be at the game tomorrow to watch us win, Mrs. Hernandez?" Jason asks.

"You know I will, Mr. King." She smiles in that way most people do at Jason, which makes Emerson kind of happy but also uncomfortable, and he's not sure why. He should be happy everything is okay, happy that their bosses saw the truth.

Beneath the table, Jason presses his knee against Emerson's, the contact the only thing that makes sense right now. Jason continues speaking, his laughter loud as he makes a joke.

Everything is going to be okay, just like Jason promised, yet the feelings in Emerson's heart seem to suggest anything else. The fear is still there, along with an ache for something he doesn't understand when he looks at Jason. He should be happy, but all he is aware of is the staggering weight of the impending adrenaline crash.

Jason turns his smile—gregarious and handsome—on Emerson, and his heart physically aches. It occurs to Emerson what the emotions in his chest might mean, and he has no idea how to put them back in the box where they belong. He's been doing just fine having feelings for Jason, and then Caldwell came along and fucked things up with his accusations and stress. In the thick of it all, Jason was here, steady and perfect as always, and Emerson's stupid heart wants more.

He's straight, Emerson reminds himself, but it does nothing to stop the swell of longing when he looks at that smile.

Jason King is everything Emerson has ever wanted, and he cannot have him.

Denise
Your suit is ready, come pick it up anytime before I close at seven.

EMERSON READS the text from Denise for the fourth time, trying to gather the spoons to leave his apartment and pick up his suit.

Though the meeting yesterday went better than he could've expected, the hours leading up to that meeting and the emotional fallout after were rough. He hadn't even been able to stomach dinner, heading straight to bed and staying there until his alarm went off this morning.

During their ride to work Jason was unusually quiet, almost as if he sensed Emerson's unease and honored it by holding back his tendency to talk about anything and everything. That quiet lasted only until they got to the parking lot and were met with half of Jason's players waiting for him. Things didn't calm down from there, and between his students' inattentive excitement over the homecoming game and Emerson's fragile nerves, the day was far too long.

The second the school day ended, Emerson rushed home to shower, put on something more comfortable and become a human turtle for a few hours. He came out of his metaphorical shell long enough to eat a couple of plain eggo waffles and text Jason good luck before Jason had to put his phone away for the game. A game which he'd invited Emerson to but he declined. The idea of being surrounded by so many people and noises after the stress of everything left Emerson mildly nauseated, especially now that he's got to worry about how everyone perceives his and Jason's friendship.

Don't worry, was what Jason told him this morning, but that is easy for people to say, not so easy to actually follow through with if you're Emerson.

Alone with his own messy thoughts, Emerson pulls up the hood on the sweatshirt then slips his legs inside so that all of his body is hidden. Given that the hoodie belongs to Jason and is therefore several sizes too big, it's easy to do. Emerson breaths easier once he's safely ensconced in Jason's hoodie, breathing in his familiar scent.

Jason let him borrow the hoodie when he was cold last week, and Emerson has pointedly avoided returning it. Today's the first time he lets himself wear it again, as if some part of him recognized once he had it on, he'll never want to take it off.

It's just a hoodie, yet the comfort it provides Emerson's deregulated nervous system is impossible to ignore. The material is soft, worn thin from wear and the massive size an intoxicating reminder of how much bigger Jason is than him. Huddled inside of it, the faintest hint of juniper clinging to the material, Emerson can admit he wishes Jason were here. He wishes Jason was going to the appointment to pick up the suit with him, wishes he'd been able to handle going to the game to see him. He wishes for a lot of things.

Sighing heavily, Emerson peeks out of his self-made hoodie cave to stare at the clock on the microwave in the kitchen, its flickering red light a haunting reminder of what Emerson is avoiding.

Objectively, he can recognize it's not a huge deal. He is fully capable of riding the bus across town to get his suit alone. It's just that last time Jason was with him, and that made everything just a little less angst inducing. Somehow, Jason makes everything a little easier, a little safer. He knows Jason can't follow him everywhere to complete the tasks he doesn't want to do because that would be selfish and weird. But after a lifetime of having to feel anxious and deregulated almost constantly, he can't be blamed for preferring something—or someone— better.

Beyond just the comfort Jason's steady presence provides, Emerson just plain likes him. More than he's ever liked anyone. Romantically, platonically, there is no contest; Jason King is his favorite person in the entire world.

Even now when he wants to be alone, he'd rather be with Jason. It's only been a few hours since Emerson saw him, yet already he misses everything about him.

Growing up, Emerson struggled to connect—to his family, to his peers, to his few short lived crushes. He felt like an alien that someone left on Earth, as if every other person on this round planet orbiting through space got some kind of instructional manual explaining how to be a person, how to have relationships and be liked and survive. Everyone that is, except him. Then Jason came along, and he didn't try to explain the instruction manual to Emerson to make him be like everyone else, he just rewrote the damn thing as if who Emerson is, is just fine. He didn't know it was possible to find someone that might be easier to be around than being alone, but now that he has, he doesn't know what to do.

Thinking about Jason makes him think about the dance tomorrow. Jason said they're going to have fun, and while Emerson trusts Jason not to lie, he also isn't sure they share the same definition of fun.

Unable to think about the homecoming dance and the task he's putting off at the same time, Emerson grudgingly acknowledges it's time to get his suit.

Through sheer force of will, he pushes himself off the couch, not bothering to change out of Jason's massively oversized hoodie and his most comfortable sweats just to take the bus across town then straight home.

The bus ride only takes twenty minutes, which is plenty long enough for Emerson to re-check the text message from Denise half a dozen times, the urge to read it again and make sure he won't walk in when he's not supposed to is nearly unbearable. He would've preferred an appointment so he knew without a doubt that he is supposed to be here, but Denise warned him she'd be busy today and the most she could do was a drop-in.

Given the massive favor she's doing Emerson, this was not something he would challenge. Not that he would've challenged it under any circumstances really. Confrontation makes him physically ill. A lot of things make Emerson feel mildly ill now that he thinks about it. Including walking into unknown social situations.

One of the reasons he thrives in his teaching job is the steady routine and schedule—the predictability of it all—which makes Emerson's nervous system feel safer. Having to do things like walk into a tailor shop where he's only been once—with Jason, not alone no less—and where he has no idea if other people will be inside or what kind of small talk Denise might engage in, makes Emerson so uncomfortable he's slightly nauseated.

Apprehension makes him hesitate, and he stands on the sidewalk for several minutes, pulling the sleeves of Jason's hoodie over his hands before finally making his way inside. The front room is empty, but before he can walk to the counter to tap the little bell with the sign that says *ring for service*, the sound of voices filters down the hallway.

"I told you, don't ruin this suit, Charles."

"My name is not Charles and you know that."

"Serves you right for what you called Andrew last week, you—oh, hello sweetheart." Denise walks out of the back, stopping mid-sentence to smile at Emerson. "I'm glad you could make it."

Though Denise is the one talking, the only person Emerson can look at is the familiar face standing next to her. The man has a suit bag slung over his shoulder and a wide smile on his face. He looks so much like Andrew it'd be easy to think it was him, except for the paint stains covering his massively oversized jeans and the garish yellow crocs on his feet.

Charlie leans his hip against the nearest piece of furniture, grinning at Emerson. "What a pleasure seeing you again, Emerson. I was sure after last time Jason was going to hide you away."

"Hide me away where?" Emerson asks, confused.

"You behave," Denise chastises, swatting Charlie on the back of the head.

"What the hell, D? I literally only said hello."

"Uh-huh," Denise hums, narrowing her eyes at Charlie. "I've got cameras everywhere mister. I'm watching you."

"Wow," Charlie grumbles. "I don't know why everyone acts like I'm going to cause trouble. I'm a fucking delight. Besides, I only ruined one suit, *once*. It's not like I planned to spill paint thinner on a custom silk suit a week before my gala opening and requested an entirely new one at midnight."

Charlie stares at Emerson, as if some kind of response might be made, but he cannot fathom what kind of response any person might have to a statement like that.

"So," Charlie says. "Not at the game with Jason?"

"No," Emerson replies, relieved at the easily answerable question

"Why? Didn't my idiot brother invite you? I know he wanted you there."

"He's very kind," Emerson says, thinking of how often Jason includes him. "He did invite me to the game tonight, but I needed to pick up my suit. That and well, the game sounded—"

"Like an archaic demonstration of popularity and heteronormativity disguised as school spirit?"

Emerson blinks, never sure what to make of the things that come out of Charlie's mouth. "I was just going to say loud."

Charlie cocks his head to the side. "That's fair."

Unsure what else to say and floundering for conversation, his eyes hone in on the friendship bracelet on Charlie's left wrist—brightly colored pony beads in various shades of pink. There's a name on there, but Emerson can't read it. When Charlie catches him staring at it, he becomes uncharacteristically tetchy, tugging the sleeve of his hoodie down to cover it.

"Nice sweatshirt," Charlie says.

Emerson looks down at his chest, a flood of white hot

heat flaring through his body. He forgot he was wearing Jason's hoodie. *In public*. In front of Jason's big brother. Something Charlie must know from the way his eyes linger on the King name embroidered on the upper right above the Santa Leon High school logo. It hadn't occurred to Emerson he might run into anyone he knew or worse anyone Jason knew.

Maybe if Emerson stays very still and says nothing, none of this will be real, and he can go back home and hide under his weighted blanket and never come out again.

"You know, it all makes so much sense," Charlie muses, still staring at Emerson in a way that makes him twist his hands together. He knows Charlie is a good guy because of things Jason has said, but it doesn't change the fact that he makes Emerson slightly uneasy. He has none of Jason's easy going personality or even Andrew's calm demeanor. He's like his paint splattered clothing—bold and unexpected—and while that's not a bad thing, it's a bit much for Emerson, who finds his unpredictable personality unnerving.

"What uh, what makes sense?" Emerson asks when it becomes clear Charlie isn't going to elaborate further.

"In high school, all the girls used to try and steal Jason's hoodies. The football team one with his name. They wanted to wear it around campus, you know?" It's clearly a rhetorical question, which is good because Emerson has no idea what to say to that. "His ex-girlfriends did it too when he became coach and his team started winning state championships. Jason's kind of a big man on campus, and in town, as I'm sure you've noticed."

"Everyone likes Jason," Emerson replies, unsure why saying it makes his insides feel like the center of a cake that isn't quite done cooking—squishy and underdone and close to being a disaster.

"Everyone *does* like Jason, because he's really fucking nice," Charlie says, laying his suit on the edge of the couch before crossing his arms. "Jason is the nicest guy in the world, and a lot of people, especially his exes, knew that. They liked it because it meant they got what they wanted. The thing about Jason is that he's always had one giant flaw —his shit taste in women."

That wiggly uncomfortable feeling in Emerson's gut magnifies, both at the reminder of Jason being straight and at the idea of him being used.

Despite what some people think, Emerson is not naive. Just because he doesn't always understand or recognize a lot of social norms doesn't mean he isn't aware they exist. He's smart enough to know that a man like Jason—handsome, built like a brick house, and kind—might get used. He just has a hard time reconciling that objective knowledge with the man he knows, a man who deserves to be treasured.

"Jason has always picked the kind of women who would wear his hoodie in public but never in private. He was as much a trophy to them as the ones he helped his teams win." Charlie pushes off the chair, inching closer to Emerson. "You, on the other hand, had no idea I would be here when you got dressed."

"I just borrowed it," Emerson blurts, bunching the overly long sleeves in his fists. He kind of feels like he's in trouble even though he's a grown man who didn't technically do anything wrong. "I uh, I'm going to give it back. I wasn't—I mean—"

"Relax, Emerson," Charlie says, grabbing his suit off the chair. "I like you. I can see why Jason does too. You know if—"

"Charlie King, get your ass out of my store," Denise says, half a smile on her face. "Stop bothering my clients."

"One day, you're going to take me on as a client too, Denise. I can feel it. I'm growing on you."

"You're growing on me like a weed. Get out of here and tell that sweetheart brother of yours I set up an appointment in December for that suit fitting."

"What December fitting? Where's Andrew going? What's he need a suit for?" Charlie rapid fires.

"You can ask him that yourself." The look she gives Charlie would make Emerson cry if it were directed at him. "Now get out of here so I can finish with Mr. Miller without you loitering around making a nuisance of yourself or worse, ruining my samples."

"Oh for fucks sake, it was one time, Denise." Charlie sighs heavily when he gets no response. "Fine, but just know that I am only leaving because I need to call Andrew and find out about this mysterious event he's going to that I don't know about and not because you're making me."

Without breaking eye contact with Denise, he slowly inches his way towards the front door.

"You can tell yourself whatever you want," Denise says, "that doesn't make it true."

"Women," Charlie grumbles, before plastering a smile on his face and turning to look at Emerson. "It was good seeing you again. Say hi to Ariel for me."

"Who's Ariel?"

"Jason, obviously," Charlie answers, as if it's obvious. He is easily one of the most chaotic people that Emerson has ever met, which is saying a lot since he spent several hours with Jason's younger brother Alec last week. Charlie makes Alec look, well, easy. "That was his nickname when he was little because he was so obsessed with the Little Mermaid. I swear he used to parade around the house wrapped in a blanket saying it was his mermaid tail. He was a cute kid. In hindsight, his thing with redheads started early."

Emerson barely resists the urge to touch his own red hair. It's too bad he's not a woman, maybe he'd have a chance with Jason.

"Great talk we had, Emerson. We should definitely do it again. Have Jason give you my number so we can get lunch."

"Okay," Emerson agrees automatically, having absolutely no intention of following through. Honestly, if that counts as a talk it's no wonder Emerson doesn't talk to very many people. That entire interaction was confusing and left him feeling like he definitely missed something he shouldn't have, though to be fair that's his default feeling talking to most people who aren't Jason or his students.

"Are you alright to do your final fitting?"

"Sure," Emerson replies, refusing to admit he'd temporarily forgotten Denise. At least it's only them now that Charlie's left the shop though.

"You don't sound excited," she says, nodding towards the back room. "Second thoughts about the suit?"

"Not exactly," Emerson hedges.

"You wanna talk about it?"

"Is this one of those trick questions where someone asks that but doesn't mean it?" Emerson questions. "Because if it is, please just tell me so I don't embarrass myself. I promise you won't hurt my feelings if you don't actually want to talk to me. Lots of people don't and—"

"Emerson," Denise interrupts, moving to stand in front of him. She's considerably shorter, but her aura makes Emerson shut up and pay attention. It's not scary, but it is commanding. "Listen, doll face, I spent a lot of years saying shit I didn't mean to get along in this world, and I don't do that anymore. In case you didn't hear me with Charlie, I have no tolerance for bullshit anymore."

"You don't like Charlie?"

"Charlie King is a good man, talented beyond belief, and also a raging pain in my ass. But I handle him because his brother is one of my favorite people on this shitty planet we call Earth, and he loves Charlie. He's not bad, but he's a lot to handle, you know?"

Emerson remains quiet, unsure if he's supposed to actually agree or not. He feels like he shouldn't, because Jason loves Charlie. But then again, Jason spends a lot of time calling Charlie a shithead, so maybe it's okay if Emerson's feelings for him are adjacent to his feelings about holidays—something you like in small doses but find overwhelming after prolonged exposure.

"But we're not talking about Charlie, or any of the King men. We're talking about you. I might have done this as a favor to Andrew, but you come to me any time you need something, you got that? Your mom was good people and so are you. I want you to feel welcome here, alright? My door is always open if you need something tailored, or just need someone to commiserate with about those King men. Dating Jason, I'm sure you'll get used to them but—"

Dating Jason. *Dating Jason.* Denise continues speaking in an even tone but Emerson's brain buzzes while his face heats, leaving him acutely aware of every inch of his own body. He can feel every wisp of hair touching his face, the uncomfortably hard lub-dub of his heart and every seam on his clothing.

"Emerson," Denise says, clearly realizing he's zoned out.

"I'm not...me and—oh no. No," Emerson croaks. "Not that I wouldn't, because I would. I mean have you seen him?

And he's nice. He's so nice, Denise. But he's not interested in me. Why would he be? He could have anyone. Besides, he's straight."

"Straight," Denise echoes, almost as if she's testing the word out. "I've never seen a straight man look at another man the way he looked at you, sweetheart."

"Jason King is straight," Emerson repeats.

If he says it twice, maybe she will understand it.

"I'm the last person who wants to make judgments about someone else's sexuality," Denise says, tone softening. "Why don't we get this suit tried on and make sure it's perfect for tomorrow?"

Emerson nods his agreement, following Denise into the back room. Even when she hands him a photograph of his mother like promised at the fitting, his fingers tracing over a face he hasn't seen in a decade, his thoughts eventually return to Jason. He can't help but wonder exactly how it is she thinks Jason looks at him? He tries to shake away the thoughts, reminding himself that it doesn't matter if he sometimes imagines things between him and Jason turning into something more. It doesn't matter that Jason's embrace is everything he's ever wanted or that he longs to be wrapped inside this very hoodie with Jason's bare skin against his own.

None of it matters, because Jason told him he's straight and Jason doesn't lie.

Jason
I'm here.

EMERSON READS the text three times before his brain allows him to reply. Once he's texted Jason to come on up he's left waiting for Jason to make it up to his apartment and knock on the door. With nothing to do while he waits, he scrutinizes every inch of his studio apartment, acutely aware that no one else has ever been in here. For all the times Jason has picked him up or dropped him off, he's never been up to Emerson's actual apartment. It wasn't from a lack of Jason trying, but any time he offered to walk him to the door it was easier for Emerson to say *no thanks* than deal with his internalized shame about his living space. The kind he's been working hard to get over, not just for Jason but for himself. Jason's easy acceptance of Emerson, of the things that bring him joy, make it easier for Emerson to accept the things he loves too.

Growing up, his room had been his sanctuary, the only place in his aunt and uncle's home that had been his. That is unless Landon wanted to come in and steal Emerson's favorite plushie or break his LEGO, both things he did regularly but denied, always claiming Emerson was being weird and lying. It was always at that point Emerson usually started crying out of frustration, which ended up negating the truth because his aunt and uncle hated strong displays of emotion. In hindsight, there was very little about Emerson they liked.

Even into adulthood, his room was still filled with comfort items which left him open to judgment from family. Over time, to avoid harsh judgments, he got used to hiding the things that brought him joy.

A lifetime of trying to mask his neurodivergent nature and personality traits to protect himself left him an adult struggling to unmask, even now that it's safe to do so.

Because that's the crux of it. Jason is safe. He's safe in ways Emerson didn't even know was possible.

Even knowing this, it's hard for Emerson not to compare his own living space with Jason's. His studio apartment doesn't look like Jason's house, and that isn't just because of the size. Jason's home is set up like, well, an adult's. There's a couch and a television and some photographs in the living room. A perfectly respectable and average kitchen. His house is sparsely decorated. There are a lot of shoes by the front door, but it's overall a fairly average home. Emerson loves Jason's house: the oversized comfortable couch, the dogs who both finally let Emerson pet them, and the fact that it's in a quiet neighborhood where Emerson can't hear everyone who lives around him. What he loves most about it though is that Jason is there. Having been to his home a few times left Emerson thinking maybe it was time he let Jason see his own home, a decision he is currently on the verge of spiraling over.

While there are a lot of things Emerson dislikes about his apartment: the noisy upstairs neighbors who stomp around like they have shoes made of cement, the fact that someone on his floor smokes on their balcony so he can never have his window open, or the way one of the kids next door knocks on his wall when they can't sleep. Thinking about it, perhaps there's a lot of things he dislikes, but it's still his. His apartment, one that his aunt and uncle can't shame for being filled with toys and books. His own apartment that no one can sneak into and rearrange his bookshelf or break his LEGO sets.

This too small, too noisy apartment is Emerson's, and he loves it in the same way he covets his treasured possessions, because it's his and no one can take it away. With that independence comes the reality that Emerson has no one who comes over. No family, no friends. No one else has been in this apartment ever since Emerson moved in, as evidenced by the half-finished puzzle on the dining room table he never eats at or the fact that his kitchen counters are covered in papers he's in the middle of grading, not appliances.

A single bookshelf sits in the corner, overfilled with books spilling onto the floor and piled in corners. In front of the books are his favorite LEGO mini figs and the top of the shelf has his model of Rivendell. He has more LEGO sets, carefully packed away with their original instructions. They're still in boxes, partially because Emerson has no shelves to display them, but also because even though he lives here alone, it's taken him a long time to feel safe bringing them out.

His kitchen is equally chaotic, and the only thing that's not work-related on his kitchen counters is a dragon shaped cookie jar he found at a thrift store before he moved here. Emerson doesn't like cookies so it's filled with Ranch Doritos, but it was the first grown-up purchase of his life—if a mythical creature-shaped crock for baked goods counts. Emerson is very attached to it despite the paint on the end of the snout being scratched and the chip in the back tail, which he hides by wedging it in the corner.

Even his couch is used, though this one is not from a thrift store. His aunt and uncle were re-doing their second living room and were going to throw it away. Even though Emerson kind of hates the ugly floral pattern, and it reminds him of his aunt. He'd paid them fifty bucks and then spent a small fortune to bring it across the country, if only because it was familiar to sit on, and he'd desperately needed everything to not be different. There's also no coffee table because Emerson doesn't use one, only a large empty spot where there used to be a sort of blanket nest Emerson uses when he's overwhelmed and needs to lay on the floor. It was there this morning, but he balled it all up and hid it under the bed when he texted Jason to come on up.

His apartment is lived in but in a kind of haphazard *I'm a first year teacher with no money* but also I *have no idea how to let myself decorate because I was never allowed to express myself* kind of way. Something he feels very aware of when the knock on the front door comes.

Steeling his nerves, Emerson walks to the door, unsure how he can want to see Jason more than anyone in the world, yet somehow feel like he's walking to his death. It's incredibly exhausting having a brain that rebels against even the things he wants when it's afraid, and he tries to remind himself that Jason isn't going to poke fun at his toys or the size of his home. Despite knowing Jason would never tease him, the anxiety rises.

Jason knocks again and Emerson breathes slowly. In for four, hold for seven, out for eight. He does it again until the worst of it passes, turning the deadbolt and readying himself to apologize for keeping Jason waiting, when every single word and thought falls from his head at the sight of Jason standing at his front door, his smile as wide and bright as actual sunshine. He's dressed in a charcoal gray suit. The cut of it hugs every single swell and curve of Jason's body, highlighting the breadth of his thick thighs, massive chest and overall impressive girth.

What really catches Emerson's attention though is the plastic box in his hand, one he's holding almost nervously with a flower inside. Not just a flower—a boutonniere.

"Wow," Jason whispers. His chest expands with a slow, deep breath. "Emmy, you look—"

"It's too much, isn't it?" Emerson blurts, suddenly

wondering why he didn't choose something subtle like Jason, whose suit is a perfectly normal, non-attention grabbing three piece suit.

In stark contrast, Emerson's suit is anything but subtle. The cut is less traditional than usual with slim lapels and pants that hit just above his bare ankles. Unlike Jason, he's not wearing a tie but rather a loose white button up with the top two buttons undone at Denise's suggestion. Most attention grabbing of all is the color, a pale green.

It occurs to Emerson that the students are going to stare. The other chaperones might talk about him. He's going to stand out. People are going to look at him. *Jason* is looking at him.

"Not too much," Jason utters softly, his eyes never leaving Emerson's face. "You look...you look amazing."

The praise is too much. People don't look at Emerson like this—like he's the only thing in the entire world that matters.

"Gives us a spin," Jason whistles.

When he holds his hand out, it occurs to Emerson that Jason is not joking or playing a prank. Because it's Jason, Emerson lifts his hand and lays his fingers in Jason's palm, unsure why his entire body gets dizzy from one single twirl.

"Damn," Jason whispers. "You look incredible."

"Denise did the suit," Emerson mumbles. His face is burning and he's acutely aware of the way he's breathing now, hyper-aware of all of his limbs and the shape of his mouth. Is he supposed to cross his arms or put them in his pocket?

"Denise is amazing but you wear it like—" Jason stops, licking his lips. He's still staring.

"Like what?" Emerson dares to ask.

"Like it was made for you." Jason clears his throat, the

faintest hint of pink spreading across his cheeks. "I uh, I brought you something."

He holds the plastic container out to Emerson. Entirely unsure what's happening, he takes the box, popping it open. Nestled inside is a sunflower boutonniere.

Emerson is certain his heart hasn't actually stopped because he would be dead, and he's definitely alive, but he can't feel his own heart beating any longer—the feeling of soft flower petals under his fingertips the only sensation his brain can focus on.

"You brought me flowers."

"Well, a boutonniere," Jason corrects, as if the technicality diminishes what it means. "It's your first dance after all. You should have a boutonniere. Can I put it on you?"

Part of Emerson worries he's hallucinating. Did Jason really bring him a boutonniere? Is that a thing straight men do with their friends?

"I don't understand," Emerson blurts, the weight of Jason's stare and Denise's words from yesterday weighing loud and heavy. Jason isn't cruel, he doesn't lie or play tricks, but nothing happening right now makes sense. "I thought you brought boutonnieres to your date."

"You do." Jason licks his lips. "I uh—shit, can I hug you first?"

"Okay," Emerson agrees, because nothing makes sense, and he could really use a Jason hug.

"Thank you."

Making sure not to crush the boutonniere, Jason pulls Emerson into his arms, enveloping his entire body in his larger one. Instinctively, Emerson's face curls into Jason's neck. The softness of his freshly shaved skin and the clean scent of his body wash send happy little buzzes of pleasure into Emerson's brain. Jason always smells so good, and the strength of his embrace settles Emerson's nerves as Jason gives him a full body squeeze. "Shit, I've missed you."

"You saw me yesterday," Emerson points out, lips accidentally grazing the side of Jason's neck.

"Barely," Jason scoffs. "Between homecoming prep and the game, I feel like I've barely seen you all week. It was horrible."

"Not seeing me is horrible?" Emerson asks, taking another deep breath, as if by doing so he can inhale Jason's scent and permanently imprint it in his olfactory system. If he could just smell Jason on demand that would be pretty great actually. He's starting to think he's addicted to Jason's musky, clean man smell.

"Of course it is," Jason answers, the deep timbre of his voice rumbling against Emerson's chest from where they're still pressed tightly together. "Emmy, you're my favorite person."

"But...Theo," Emerson protests.

"No buts," Jason counters. "Theo will always be my best friend but you're—you're *you*, Emmy."

The way he says it makes him sound special, important even; as if Emerson being himself is something extraordinary, and not someone to be tolerated or accommodated.

Pulling out of the hug, he lifts his gaze to Jason's and what he sees there doesn't help him make sense of anything. Jason is looking at him, like—well, perhaps the way Denise suggested, and it makes Emerson shudder.

"Jason."

"Emmy." Jason lifts both hands to Emerson's face, cradling it in his large palms. "You are so fucking special. I think I'm doing this backwards. No, I know I'm doing it backwards. I feel like I'm sixteen again."

Jason laughs, something warm and soft and so full of emotion Emerson feels it in his chest, even if he doesn't understand what it means.

"Doing what backwards?" Emerson asks, afraid to move in case Jason stops touching him.

Growing up, there were times Emerson wasn't sure he was real. Sure, he knew he was technically—flesh and bone don't lie—yet his own experiences left him feeling sidelined and wayward like he wasn't a character in his own story. The way Jason is looking at him right now, his touch grounding and his eyes adoring, Emerson feels like the main character in his own life for the first time.

Emerson feels achingly, vulnerably real.

"I need to ask you something, and tell you something. Except I'm not sure which one is supposed to come first."

"You're making me nervous," Emerson admits.

"I'm sorry," Jason says, tipping his head down to rest it against Emerson's. His dark lashes rest on his cheekbones as he breathes in slow and deep. Jason's eyes are closed but Emerson can't look away. "Fuck. I'm fucking this up. I had a plan."

"A plan," Emerson echoes, still not sure what's happening but delighting in the way Jason appears to be trying to swallow Emerson's body up with his own.

"Yes. I made a plan. A how-to-get-the-guy plan. I was going to do this right and—and, shit."

"Jason."

"Yeah, Emmy?"

"That doesn't sound very straight."

Jason huffs out a laugh, rubbing his forehead against Emerson's like a cat trying to imprint. He breathes Emerson in, fluttering his eyes open so that his big, dark eyes are so close to Emerson's with their noses touching.

"Emmy, I have a secret."

Emerson breathes him in, so in love with this giant, confusing man it hurts. "It won't be a secret if you tell me."

"That's okay," Jason whispers, his lips so close they're almost pressed against Emerson's. "I don't want any secrets. Not from you."

Holding his breath Emerson waits, the soft exhale of Jason's breath against his lips and the brush of a thumb over his cheek rendering him speechless.

"Emmy, I don't think I'm straight."

14 JASON

JASON HOLDS HIS BREATH, waiting for a reaction but none comes. Emerson is almost frozen in place, his eyes unblinking as he stares at Jason with those big, wide eyes of his. They're such a pale green they're damn near translucent, the color magnified by the green of his suit.

Sucking in a deep breath, Jason does his best not to ramble, trying to give Emerson a moment to process but it's so hard not to talk. His mind is reeling with thoughts, about his confession, about how pretty Emerson looks and, most especially, about how desperate he is to kiss a man.

Well, one man in particular.

"Emmy, do you need to text instead?"

Emerson shakes his head from side to side, a stray bit of hair falling into his eyes.

"Should I stop touching you?"

Emerson shakes his head again, using his free hand to curl it tightly into Jason's suit so he doesn't move. The desperation in the touch soothes something deep in Jason. He might not have any idea what the fuck he's doing right now, but Emerson isn't shutting him out. He still has a chance.

"Tell me what you need. I'll do anything. Do you want me to get another last minute chaperone so you can process? Or should I just go back to the truck so you can have a few minutes alone? Or maybe—"

"Say it again," Emerson demands before snapping his mouth shut, unable to believe he just said that. Jason wants to kiss him all the more for not holding back with him.

"I don't think I'm straight," Jason repeats, smoothing his thumb over the arch of Emerson's cheekbone a second time, trying to ground himself with the touch. "Well, not *think*. I know."

"How do you know?" Emerson asks, barely breathing.

"I met someone. A guy—the most incredible guy. He's smart and kind, and he knows all tons of niche information about the most random things, so talking to him is always fun. He's just...amazing. He also wears a suit like it's nobody's business."

For all the hours Jason spent thinking about this moment, whether Emerson's reaction would be positive or negative, a non-reaction hadn't occurred to him.

"Emmy?"

Emerson takes a deep breath, fingers tightening in Jason's suit to the point of discomfort.

"Just so we're clear, this guy. Is he, um—"

"You," Jason finishes, realizing he was maybe not quite clear enough. "It's you, Emmy. I haven't been able to stop thinking about you since the day we met, and I didn't realize what it meant until very recently, but I know now, and I'm... I'm still not sure what I am. Bisexual maybe. Or Pan. Probably Bi but I'm not sure. I just know it's not other people, it's you. It's just you."

"What's so special about me?" Emerson asks in that way of his when he's trying to puzzle something out that he doesn't understand.

"Everything," Jason answers, letting the tips of his fingers skim Emerson's hair. It's as soft as always, and the itch to sink his fingers into it, to pull Emerson against his body and keep him there is so damn strong. If they didn't need to leave for the dance very soon he might try it.

"I don't know about that," Emerson mumbles.

"I do," Jason counters, because while there is so much about his own sexuality he is still wildly uncertain about, his feelings for Emerson are crystal clear. "I see you, Emmy. I see your bravery and intelligence and kindness, and I like it all. You are so fucking special, and I like you. I like you so damn much it should scare me, but all I feel is excitement. Liking you feels like the moment right before a game when there's nothing but possibility and hope."

There's a brief moment where Jason worries that maybe he's been too honest, too upfront and too quick. His ex-girlfriends used to complain he was intense, and clingy, but he's never understood it. If you like someone, aren't you supposed to want to tell them? To spend all your time with them? He can't imagine anything better than being allowed to be with Emerson all the time.

"Did you just compare me to football?" Emerson questions with the slightest quirk to his head.

"Uh, yes?"

"I don't know how I feel about that," Emerson says so seriously Jason worries he's fucked up. Then Emerson's lips curl up on each side in one of his rare, face splitting smiles. In this moment, Jason knows Emerson isn't like football, he's better. He's the best thing in the entire fucking world.

"I like football," Jason says, unable to stop his own face

from breaking out into a self-satisfied grin. He can't help it. He's just so goddamn happy right now. "And you. I like you very much. As a friend and also romantically. In case I didn't make that clear before."

"I did pick up on that," Emerson says, dragging his bottom lip between his teeth. "I—uh, me too."

"You like football, too?" Jason teases.

"Absolutely not," Emerson deadpans. "But I could try, for you."

"I don't want you to change for me, Emmy. I like you exactly like you are."

"I like you too," Emerson whispers. "More than I've ever liked anyone. Ever. I don't even like most people, and I definitely don't like anyone the way I like you. I want to be around you even when I want to be alone. It's absolutely terrifying, Jason."

"Hopefully not all scary," Jason says, giving in to his urges to touch and soothe by letting his hand slide around the back of Emerson's head. The reaction is instantaneous as Emerson presses into the touch ever so slightly, all the encouragement Jason needs to let his fingers sink into Emerson's gorgeous red hair.

"I'm not sure," Emerson answers, in that totally honest way of his. "It's not bad but it's...confusing."

"Should I stop?"

"Absolutely do not stop touching me," Emerson says, his hold on Jason's suit damn near punishing now. "You started this."

"I did," Jason says, pretty sure he might never stop smiling again.

"We have to go to the dance, Jason. We're going to be late. We can't be late, we'll get in trouble. And the school, oh my god, we just had a meeting with HR. What if they think we were lying and—"

"Breathe," Jason soothes. "Two teachers dating isn't against the rules as long as there isn't a power imbalance which, since we're in different departments there isn't. I checked this morning by the way, just to be sure. We'll have to disclose things to HR if this goes somewhere, and I really hope it does, but we can take it one step at a time."

Emerson's frown deepens, but all Jason can think is *cute*. So fucking cute. He loves Emerson's adorable frown. Not that he wants Emerson to worry because he's absolutely certain they won't get in trouble for dating, but he's grown rather fond of Emerson's resting frown and the way his lips—the top one just a little thinner than the bottom—turn down by default.

He wants to nibble them, wants to draw his tongue across those lips. First though, he needs to ask Emerson a very important question.

"I forgot to ask you something," Jason says, letting his thumb stroke over the shell of Emerson's ear. Even that is cute. He's not sure he's ever found anyone as attractive as he does Emerson, the sight of all his pale skin and long limbs, the line of his exposed throat and the tousle of red hair. He's absolutely fucking gorgeous, and Jason might not have any idea how to please another man sexually, but fuck, he wants to learn.

"Is it about football?" Emerson asks.

"No," Jason snorts. "Not this time. I uh, that is, Emerson Miller, will you go to the homecoming dance with me?"

"I am going to the dance with you," Emerson says.

If possible Jason's smile widens. "I mean as a date."

"Oh, no."

All the air in Jason's lungs escapes in a single puff of rejection, but he does his best to hide the sharp sting of pain from his expression. If Emerson only wants to be friends then Jason will learn how to handle that. He will do anything to keep Emerson in his life, be whatever he needs. If he only wants a friend, then that's what Jason will be.

Hell, Jason will be the best goddamn friend Emerson ever had. He will—

"You can take me out tomorrow, though."

"Wait, what?" Apparently it's his turn to be confused. "But you said no."

"Yeah, because we're chaperoning. We can't be on a date. It's work. But," Emerson pauses, "tomorrow?"

"Tomorrow," Jason repeats, heart inflating like a hot air balloon. Is Emerson saying yes? Is Emerson going to go on a date with him? Holy shit, is Jason going to have his first date with a man?

"You can take me on a date tomorrow," Emerson repeats. "If you want."

"I want. I really fucking want," Jason affirms, lowering his forehead to Emerson's. "Please."

"You don't have to beg, you know," Emerson points out, but he's smiling again and Jason feels like he won the lottery. He's pretty sure he would do anything to keep this beautiful man smiling like this.

"Alright," Jason whispers.

"You're still smiling," Emerson says, the sweetest hint of a smile softening his features.

"Pretty sure I'm going to do it all night. Sorry."

"I like your smile," Emerson admits, cheeks flushing pink. "You're...very handsome."

"You think I'm handsome?" Jason asks, preening. He spent all week trying to get a read on Emerson, to figure out if he ever caught Emerson checking him out, but either he didn't or Jason was even more oblivious than his brothers accused him of.

"You have a mirror," Emerson huffs. "You're very handsome. And big. And tall. And thick. And handsome. Wait, I said that already."

"Full permission to talk about how big and handsome you think I am any time."

"Do you like it?" Emerson asks, head tilting to the side and eyes roaming over Jason.

"I like it when you say it." Jason knows he's puffing out his chest, but he can't stop. Emerson likes that he's big and thick. Emerson thinks he's handsome. Jason kind of wants to roll around in the praise. "So you like that I'm big, huh?"

"I do," Emerson confirms, voice a little quiet and breathy, almost as if he can't believe he's saying it out loud. The hand fisted in Jason's suit jacket loosens so that those long delicate fingers of his skim up Jason's chest until his hand rests there, tapping against the left pec. His eyes lift slowly, so earnest and full of trust. "I like how it feels when you hold me. It's nice. Safe."

Safe. That one word is Jason's undoing. He's been called a lot of things in his life. Sexy. Handsome. Huge. Built like a brick house. Fun. But that right there? Being safe for Emerson? That's the best goddamn thing anyone has ever called him.

"Was that wrong?" Emerson asks quietly.

"Nothing about you is wrong, Emmy." Jason breathes him in, pressing his lips to the top of Emerson's head. "You are perfect."

"No, I—"

"Perfect," Jason interrupts, refusing to let him argue about this.

"You're stubborn."

"Uh-huh," Jason says, rubbing his cheek into the top of Emerson's head. "Your hair is soft."

"You like my hair," Emerson says, managing to make it sound like both a statement and a question.

"I like every single thing about you, Emerson Miller."

"You don't know everything about me."

"*Yet.*" Jason pulls back, smoothing down the hair he just mussed up. The *yet* is very important. Emerson doesn't know it, but Jason is going to date the fuck out of this perfect man. "Can I put on your boutonniere, Emmy?"

"Oh," Emerson says, looking down at his other hand like maybe he forgot what he was holding. He lifts the small sunflower to Jason who takes it, careful not to crush the petals. He unhooks the back, careful not to poke Emerson as he slips it into the suit material. "There."

"You sound very confident for someone who only just realized he wasn't straight. Wait, when did you realize?"

"Uh, at the tailor's last weekend, when you know—" Jason breaks off, waving one of his hands around in what he hopes is a meaningful gesture. Judging by Emerson's slightly confused expression, it's not.

"I have no idea."

"*WhenCharlieflirtedwithyou,*" Jason gets out in a rush.

The reaction is delayed, the slow dawning of realization spreading across Emerson's face. "You were jealous?"

It's easy to see he was in hindsight, which is strange because Jason has never been jealous. People used to flirt with his girlfriends and he'd shrug it off. Even when he got cheated on, the most he felt was a sting of rejection that had passed when he realized he didn't actually even like her enough to be mad beyond the betrayal of it.

Like everything else involving Emerson, things feel different. The idea of anyone else being with him sours

Jason's insides. He wants Emerson to be *his*. Which is likely a very queer thing to think about a man. It definitely puts Jason somewhere on the bisexual scale, but he's more concerned with getting the guy first and worrying about the label later.

Operation: get-a-boyfriend is in full swing.

First things first—homecoming dance. It might not be a date, but Jason's going to be damn sure Emerson has a good time. Second, he's going to take Emerson on the world's best first date. Jason's got it all planned out, spent all week researching other date options in case Emerson said yes, and he knows exactly where he wants to take him. Dating might not be exactly like football, but Jason understands how to be patient, how to wait for the right time to take your shot. He's got the plan, now all he needs to do is find a way to make the play.

"I HAVE A LOT OF QUESTIONS."

Jason can't hide his smile even if he wanted to, which he doesn't. "I expected that."

"But we don't have time for them all," Emerson sighs, staring out the window as Jason turns into the school parking lot, surprised at how full it already is. Then again, he and Emerson took a little longer at Emerson's place than planned with Jason's impromptu confession.

"How about you write them down," Jason suggests. "You can make a list."

"A list," Emerson says, sitting up a little straighter.

"Yeah, make a list of all your questions, or things you wanna talk about, and we can do that after the dance. Or on our date." Jason's smile widens until his cheeks hurt. He can't believe he gets to go on a date with Emerson. How did he get so lucky?

Emerson wastes no time in pulling out his phone, the familiar scrunch of his face as he types away at it making Jason's chest clench. It's strange to think about how different it is to his past experiences. It feels like he should be focusing more on the whole, *Emerson is a man*, thing but in his heart there's just an Emerson-shaped space. His gender doesn't really matter. Does that make Jason pansexual? Or is that still bi? He feels like he should just know, but he doesn't.

All he knows for certain is that he's never felt like this about anyone. None of his exes made his insides feel like they were full of butterflies, which makes him feel a little guilty. He hopes he wasn't a shitty boyfriend. He's pretty sure he wasn't. There just had never been a spark, even with the ones he had fun with. Hell, sitting this close to Emerson has Jason's entire body keyed up, the two feet between them might as well be the Grand Canyon. If Emerson wasn't so fixated on his list, Jason would reach out to take his hand, wanting to touch him so badly. He resists by keeping both hands on the steering wheel as he backs his truck into a spot in the back of the parking lot, hoping to give them a few minutes to talk in the car.

No sooner has he shut his engine off then he realizes this is not going to work. At least a dozen of his players are all horsing around in the middle of the parking lot, their attention clearly on Jason as they take turns shoving each other and walking towards them. If Jason had been paying attention to his surroundings and not daydreaming about Emerson's delicate fingers, he might've noticed where he was parking, but instead he's put them right in the center of future chaos.

"Ah, shit," Jason grumbles.

"What?" Emerson asks, attention shifting from his phone to Jason. "What's wrong?"

"Nothing I can't handle," Jason assures him, nodding out the front window.

Emerson's body goes stiff. "Do you want me to stay in the truck? Or uh, I don't know, hide?"

"Why would you hide?" Jason frowns.

"Because they're going to see us come together, and they might make assumptions."

"I'm not worried about that," Jason says, unbuckling his seatbelt. "We come to work together every day, besides I would never want to hide you. I was just hoping for a few more minutes alone with you. That and I know them. They're going to be rowdy as fuck."

Proving his point, Matty and Sanchez jump on each other at the same time, ending up in a haphazard dog pile on the asphalt in front of his truck.

"Looks like chaperoning duties start now," Jason laughs, giving Emerson's knee a squeeze before getting out of the truck. "What the hell are you guys doing?"

"Hey Coach," Matty yells from the ground, looking nonplussed about being buried beneath five other guys who joined the pile. "Did you bring a date or—*oh*, you brought Mr. Miller."

On cue every player turns to look behind him. Standing at the front of Jason's truck is Emerson, smoothing down his hair and smiling despite the obvious tension in his body.

"Damn, Mr. Miller, you clean up nice. You too, Coach King," Matty adds, followed by a round of cat calls and cheers from several other players. Unsure if they're whistling at him or Emerson, Jason moves around the front of his truck, trying to subtly but effectively block

Emerson. "Do I need to remind you all to be on your best behavior?"

"No, Coach," enough voices echo that Jason doesn't feel the need to repeat himself.

A hand touches his lower back and Jason turns, unable to stop the smile that spreads across his face. "Yeah?"

"I'm gonna head inside and check in with Mabel to see if she needs an extra set of hands with the photo booth. I know Mrs. Montalvo said she was going to come early to help, but she's not the most prompt. Mabel might need me."

"Sounds good," Jason tells him, unsure if Emerson actually feels the need to help or needs an excuse to get away from the commotion of over a dozen rowdy football players. Either way, he's unwilling to put him on the spot in front of the students by asking. "I'll wrangle these guys and see you inside in a little bit."

Emerson nods, making a hasty retreat that Jason watches with calculating eyes. It's not until he turns back to his kids that he realizes he wasn't the only one staring.

Matty, expectedly, is the first to break the silence.

"Coach King, is Mr. Miller your date?"

"No," Jason answers, because as Emerson so decidedly pointed out, this is not a date.

"Do you wish he was?" Sanchez asks, the nosy fucker.

"He totally does, did you see the way he was staring," Taylor, one of his other seniors, interjects. "He's been watching Mr. Miller for weeks."

"I thought this was a homecoming dance, not a gossip session," Jason snorts, arching one eyebrow at them. He doesn't like to give his players too much shit, especially since he knows they're kidding, but he doesn't want them to say or do anything that could make Emerson uncomfortable. Besides, he barely knows what this thing between them is;

he's not sure he's ready for it to be the topic of school gossip before they'd have a chance to figure it out themselves.

"But you make it so much fun, Coach. The way you always make heart eyes at him like you're in an anime and—"

Jason might not have his coach whistle with him, but he doesn't need that to get their attention. Placing two fingers between his lips, he whistles loudly, earning him some laughter and grumbles but also their undivided and quiet attention. He scrubs a hand over his jaw, struggling not to let his embarrassment show. How the hell did they all clock his feelings before he did?

"Off the ground and inside boys," Jason instructs, as eager to get the subject changed as he is to get them inside the dance. For safety, he tells himself, and not so he can see Emerson again. He watches them all stand, smoothing down their suits and poking at each other silently. "Where did you guys leave your dates anyway?"

"No dates this year, Coach," Matty answers, slinging his arm around Arlo's shoulder. Arlo looks like he has no idea how he got there, and Jason would laugh if it weren't sort of adorable. "Team bonding. We're manifesting state champions this year."

When Jason asked Matty to make Arlo feel part of the team, he hadn't realized how seriously he and the other guys would take it, but he's damn proud of them. He also suspects the lack of dates might be part of that commitment since he knows Arlo didn't ask anyone and turned down the three girls who asked him, but he wisely doesn't mention that.

"Damn right we are," Jason grins, crossing his arms. "You boys taking us all the way to state?"

"Yes, Coach!" they all exclaim at the same time.

Jason stands just that little bit taller. He'd been nervous at the start of the year with some of his big players gone, but these kids have shown him the kind of commitment and dedication that reminds Jason exactly why he loves coaching and teaching. They've also had a stellar start to the season and Jason won't be surprised if they do make it all the way to state. Nothing is a sure thing in football, but Jason's not going to jinx them with statistics and realism tonight. Tonight, his boys deserve to have fun. They kicked ass at their game last night, and they deserve this, all of them.

"Then I expect to see you all behaving like champions tonight. Party hard but safe," he says, making sure to lock eyes with each of them individually. He doesn't expect any trouble, at least not from his guys, but he still wants to be sure they set a good example for the other students. Especially the younger ones, like Arlo and the other freshman who are experiencing their first homecoming and might be tempted to cave in to peer pressure to fit in.

"Yes, Coach," Matty says, followed by him elbowing Sanchez who copies. Once they've said it, the rest of the players follow suit.

"Good, then let's get inside and have fun."

The guys nod, moving towards the gym. All except Arlo who lingers towards the back of the group. Jason slows his steps until they're a good twenty feet behind the group.

"Excited?" he asks Arlo.

"I guess." Arlo tenses. "I don't dance."

"To be fair, most of the kids just stand around and stare at each other," Jason laughs thinking of last year's dance where no one had actually danced for the first hour, all of them too nervous to be the first one. Things had only gotten moving when Jason had gotten Matty and a few of last year's seniors to join him in a very awkward rendition of "Drop It Low." Once the kids started laughing at Jason's exaggeratedly bad dance moves, they'd let loose.

With a shrug, Arlo moves forward. He's quiet, rubbing his hands on his suit jacket which he tugs at. "It's too big. Used to be my brothers."

"Jesus or Carlos?"

"Uh, Jesus. But I think it was Alejandro's before that."

"Still looks sharp," Jason tells him, stopping him in place with a hand to the shoulder. Arlo turns on his heels and Jason nods at his tie. "Mind if I fix that for you?"

"I guess." Arlo stands very still while Jason undoes the knot, carefully retying so it no longer looks like a toddler did it. With his brothers all working long hours and his mom's arthritic hands, Arlo probably tied it himself, and while there's no shame in that, Jason suspects he might feel a little more confident with it fixed.

"Did you really bring Mr. Miller?" Arlo asks once Jason has finished.

"We came together," Jason answers vaguely, aware it's kind of an evasive answer but equally aware of his position. His personal life isn't technically the students' business, but as their teacher and coach he spends more time with some of these kids than their own parents. He understands their curiosity, and with some of them—perhaps Arlo if Jason's suspicions are correct—he understands it might be more. There are other queer teachers on campus, but none of them are dating, and none of them are Arlo's football coach or favorite teacher.

Given the recent fiasco with Mr. Caldwell, it might be safer to lie, but Jason won't do that. Not only because Emerson deserves more but because Jason does too. He's only just now realizing who he is and while he might not be ready to take out an advert in the local paper to announce it, he doesn't want to hide either.

"He's not like other teachers," Arlo says, fidgeting with the end of the tie which he's untucked from his suit jacket.

"No, he's not," Jason agrees.

"I like him," Arlo says, the weight of what that means not lost on Jason. This is a kid who rarely likes anyone, who wants nothing more than to stand out, while also trying to hide in the shadows.

It occurs to Jason that liking Emerson, dating him, could be a lot bigger than merely admitting he isn't straight. He's not sure what it will mean, but looking at one of his kids watching him, waiting to see if Jason is brave enough to be himself so maybe one day he can be too, he knows he's willing to find out.

"I like him too, Arlo."

The exhale he lets out is so deep Jason feels it in his bones. He doesn't say anything else, but he doesn't need to. Sometimes words aren't fucking enough for the big feelings that get trapped inside.

"*Listo para la fiesta?*" Jason asks, switching to Spanish. He wishes his fluency was as good as Alec's but his *abuela* had been adamant her only son and grandkids not speak Spanish after the struggles she had immigrating. She was desperate for her family to adapt and acclimate to America, and in the process, they'd missed out on the richness of her culture. Growing up, he never heard Spanish spoken at home and rarely ever heard his *abuela* speak it. It wasn't until Alec was in middle school and her health declined that she allowed the comfort of her native tongue to come out and by then Jason had already moved away for college. By the time he moved back home his *abuela* had died and he'd lost his chance to learn it from her.

He's been practicing on his own though, eager to find a part of something he never had and to connect with those of his students whose primary language at home isn't English.

"*No sé,*" Arlo answers. "*¿Crees que Matty va a bailar?*"

"*Probablemente.*" Jason offers what he hopes is an encouraging smile, pretty sure he knows where this line of questioning is going. "*Podrías preguntarle.*"

Arlo stops dead in his tracks, and for a moment, Jason worries he's misread the situation.

"*Solo si quieres,*" Jason adds.

"*Yo no bailo,*" Arlo replies, before switching to English with a heavy sigh. "Also it's going to be full of people. I don't think I like people, Coach."

Arlo looks a little like he might be sick, like he did before their first game when he puked in the trash can from nerves.

"There will indeed be a shit ton of people, but if you get overwhelmed just find Mr. Miller, alright?" Jason gives Arlo's shoulder a squeeze as they stop in front of the gym, blaring music and flashing strobe lights filtering through the open door. "You got this."

Arlo nods, sparing one final look at Jason before heading off towards the rest of his team who, much to Jason's delight, have congregated outside the doors apparently waiting for Arlo. When Matty tugs him into the crowd, his frown briefly slips, an almost bashful smile on his face as he stares at Matty. It makes Jason want to find Emerson, so he wastes no time, making sure to touch base with Amy, one of the other teachers on check-in duty, before making his way into the gym.

Though it's nearly empty inside with most of the students either out on the lawn waiting to come in or still on their way—the gym is a sight to behold. Between the various teacher and student volunteers, the gym looks like a party store threw up. Streamers hang from all the doorways, clusters of balloons strung up in some kind of fancy balloon arch for a backdrop beneath the basketball hoop, all thanks to their art teacher Trey, and the refreshment tables that line the far wall are covered in various snacks and drinks donated from parents or bought from student funds.

All in all, the gym is barely recognizable from what Jason is used to, and it sets the tone for the night. He waves to various students and teachers in search of Emerson, but he's nowhere to be found. Eventually, he makes his way around the edge of the gym towards the photo booth, hoping Mabel has seen him.

"There's the best dressed woman at Homecoming," Jason grins.

Mabel waves a hand in Jason's general direction, but her cheeks darken beneath her shock of pink blush which matches her all pink pantsuit. "Don't think you can flatter me to get what you want, Mr. King."

"Who says I want something?" Jason gasps, holding his hand to his chest in mock outrage. "Maybe I wanted to just come see my favorite lady."

"Uh-huh, then why did you prowl around the edge of the gym for the last ten minutes like a lost puppy looking for something?" She directs her gaze at Jason. "Or maybe you were looking for someone. A very handsome someone in a snazzy green suit."

"I have no idea what you're talking about," Jason mumbles, unsure why the fuck everyone seems to know things he only just realized. Is he that obvious? He didn't think he was.

Mabel's smile softens as she lays her wrinkled hand over Jason's. She leans in close, her voice barely above a whisper and hard to hear over the blaring music. "He looks very fetching."

"Doesn't he?" he whispers, unsure how to put into words what a relief it is to say it to someone else. Shit, Mabel really is his favorite person at this school besides Emerson.

Mabel nods, fussing with Jason's perfectly straight tie. "I remember when you came to these dances as a student. Always surrounded by friends, always laughing. You made sure everyone else had fun all night."

"That's the point of a dance," Jason points out, not entirely sure where she's going with this. "Besides, you know I love to have a good time."

"I know you do, but more importantly you like everyone else to have a good time. Always taking care of your players and students, of the other teachers. You're a good boy, Jason," Mabel says, the slightest crack in her voice. "A good man. It does an old woman good to see you happy, to know you won't be lonely when I'm gone"

"Don't go talking about leaving and make me cry," Jason warns her. "As far as I'm concerned, you're going to be here forever."

"Pretty sure not even your level of stubbornness can make that happen," Mabel says with a keen eye. "I'm proud of you, kid."

She squeezes Jason's hand, her skin so thin and soft; Jason has the most irrational urge to cry. It reminds him of holding his *abuela's* hand for the last time, a tangible reminder of just how many years he's known Mabel and through all those, what a steady presence she's been, first in his high school life and now his adult one.

"Have you uh, you seen, uh," but Jason can't seem to get the words out around the lump in his throat.

"Mr. Miller went to get something from his classroom," Mabel offers. "Such a polite man. That first day I'd had the great idea to try and get you two to be friends, but it looks like you accomplished that all on your own."

"He's pretty great," Jason agrees, scrubbing a hand over his face. Thinking about Emerson is giving him the kind of feelings that are inconvenient for such a public place.

"There he is now," Mabel says, lifting her hand and waving him over.

Jason turns in time to see Emerson return the gesture with an endearingly awkward half-wave before hurrying across the gym. It's filled up enough he has to weave through teenagers, his cheeks flushed pink when he stops beside Jason.

"Did you run?" Jason asks, adjusting Emerson's slightly crooked boutonniere.

"Uh-huh," Emerson says, tapping the ear defenders he was definitely not wearing before. "I forgot these."

Jason frowns. "I should've reminded you about how loud it was going to be."

"It's alright, I forgot them in my classroom yesterday," Emerson says, again tapping the side of them. It's clear he put them on in a hurry because his hair is sticking up in all kinds of wonky directions, somehow charming in the way everything about Emerson is. "I thought it was bad luck when I left them, but maybe it was actually good luck."

Try as he might, Jason can't do more than stare at the picture Emerson makes in his stylish suit in sharp juxtaposition to his mussed up hair and his ear defenders with the Lord of the Rings stickers on them. It's so very Emerson in a way that fills him with a sharp burst of affection. Emerson is so without preamble, so matter of factly himself even when Jason knows he worries if that's the version of him other people want, and Jason likes him all the more for it.

"What?" Emerson asks, patting his head. "Should I take them off? They don't match, but it was loud and—"

"Don't take them off," Jason tells him, gently pushing his hand away. "You need them, you wear them. You look very handsome, Emmy."

"You always say that," Emerson protests, but the pink flush that rises on his cheeks lets Jason know the effect his words have. It's reassuring to see that perhaps he's not the only one drowning in feelings he has no idea what to do with.

"If I do, it's only because it's always true," Jason says, all but forgetting they're not alone until Mabel clears her throat loudly.

"Why don't you two boys get in the photo booth?"

"I thought it was for students," Emerson says.

"It is." Mabel grabs one of the prop crowns and sets it on Jason's head, passing Emerson a plastic sword. "I have to make sure this old lady brain of mine remembers what to do. You two get inside and help me now."

"Can't argue with Mabel," Jason grins, looping his arm around Emerson's shoulder and leading him through the doorway of the inflatable photo booth.

Though they're not entirely concealed, between the small doorway and Jason's overall girth, Emerson is entirely hidden in the corner. Something he clearly recognizes from the way his body sags on his exhale once they're inside.

"You alright?" Jason asks, skimming his fingers over the back of Emerson's neck.

Emerson nods. "It's a lot but I'll survive."

"Maybe we can aim a little higher than surviving," Jason

says, wrapping his hand around the back of Emerson's neck and giving it a gentle squeeze.

All the tension leaves Emerson's body with a single touch, his shoulders slumping and his eyes falling shut. The sight of him so relaxed because of Jason is almost more than he can bear. Emerson is never fake, he doesn't know how to be, but it's clear that most people get a masked version of him. A version Emerson has crafted for control and safety. It's still Emerson, but it's the version he feels safe showing others.

Knowing that he gets the unmasked version, the one Emerson keeps hidden away, makes Jason want to kick his feet, laugh, cry and hold on to Emerson and never fucking let him go. It's hard to believe that he's lucky enough to see the stripped down version of Emerson, to be trusted with all his joy and fear because Emerson knows that Jason can handle it, can handle him. That trust is one of the greatest gifts Jason's ever been given, and he sure as hell isn't going to fumble it.

"Have I mentioned how much I like you?" Jason asks.

"Not in the last thirty-six minutes," Emerson says seriously as if he's actually been counting. Then his lips crack into an honest to god smile and he laughs, the sound music to Jason's ears.

Emerson should always be happy, should always know how fucking special he is. If Jason thinks too hard about Emerson's past, especially his family, it makes his mood turn bitter, which is the last thing he wants tonight. Instead he focuses on right now and the way happiness lights Emerson up. He's always beautiful, but happiness looks damn good on him.

Clearly no one else appreciates Emerson the way he

deserves, meaning it's up to Jason to do it now, vocally and consistently, for as long as Emerson will let him.

"I'm neglecting my duties then," Jason replies.

"Which duty is that exactly?" Emerson asks, those green eyes of his so wide and guileless. With his face angled towards Jason and his piercing eye contact, it'd be easy to mistake the question for flirting, but Jason knows it's not. It's a genuine question, because he doesn't understand what they are. Truthfully, neither does Jason, but he wants to, as much for himself as for Emerson.

"I'm not sure exactly, but if you can be a little patient with me, maybe we can figure it out together." His fingers curl around the back of Emerson's neck. Jason wants to understand this all, to find the labels that Emerson craves, but he doesn't have the answers yet. All he knows is that these feelings he's got for Emerson are unlike anything he's felt before, and maybe it's because he's a man or maybe it's just because he's Emerson.

"I—" Emerson starts, cut off by Mabel yelling from outside the photo booth, reminding them both exactly where they are right now.

"Smile boys."

"What uh, what are we supposed to do?" Emerson asks.

"Smile," Jason tells him, tugging Emerson as close as humanly possible, arm around his shoulders so he's tucked completely into Jason's side. He might not be able to do more than this, but having him pressed so close soothes something in Jason that itches to claim and discover. He might not have a label, but he sure as hell knows what he wants, and it's Emerson.

The flash is bright, the timer on the screen counting down to signal the next photo. Jason moves quickly, positioning himself behind Emerson so his chin rests on his head, arms looped all the way around him in one of the awkward prom poses his kids do. It's absolutely ridiculous really and makes Jason feel seventeen.

When the camera flashes, the countdown goes again.

"How many are there?" Emerson asks.

"Four," Jason answers, because this is the same company the school rented from last year and he already knows the photo is going to print out on a shiny 4 x 6 when they're done, with one photo in each corner. Photos of him and Emerson on their not-a-first-date. It makes Jason smile as he stares at Emerson, so caught up in appreciating his pretty face that he doesn't pay attention to the timer or the third photo snapping.

"Oops," Jason laughs, trying to imagine what the hell kind of expression he was making for that.

"Last one," Mabel reminds them from outside.

Jason's nerves rise as the time counts down. He wasn't even this nervous before his first kiss when he was fifteen with Rebecca Andrews behind the bleachers. She'd tasted like bubblegum and smelled like sunshine and the kiss was horrible. Even still, it'd been special in the way first kisses could be and Jason wants that for Emerson, wants him to have something special to remember no matter what happens.

"Emmy."

Emerson tips his head back to look up at Jason, a question in his eyes.

"Can I kiss you?"

"Oh," Emerson's mouth falls open, his tongue darting out to swipe over his bottom lip. "Yes."

Without hesitation Jason's hand settles on the side of Emerson's face, marveling at how his palm covers so much of it. He doesn't spend too long though, eager to get a taste of Emerson. Angling his head down he presses his lips to Emerson's. His reaction is instantaneous, a shudder wracks his body while his fingers curl around Jason's wrist.

Emerson's lips are chapped, a hint of mint toothpaste in his breath as he exhales into Jason's mouth. It's surreal to be standing here, surrounded by lights and noises but only able to focus on the man in his arms. The kiss is chaste, and all too brief, but it rocks Jason to his core. A man, he is kissing a man and he likes it. He likes it a whole fucking lot.

There's a bright flash from the photobooth camera as it takes their final picture; a reminder that their time here is limited but also that there will now be photo evidence of Jason's sexual awakening.

Using every ounce of self control he possesses, Jason pulls out of the kiss. Immediately he regrets it, wanting to mold himself around Emerson once more, to chase the taste of mint on his breath and deepen the kiss. Lowering his forehead to Emerson's, he presses one more quick kiss to his lips.

"Hey."

Emerson's eyes flutter open, and the flush of pleasure that spreads across his face makes Jason wish he could take Emerson home right now. He has no idea what he'd do with him, has no idea how to make another man feel good, but fuck, he wants to try.

"Was that okay?" Jason asks, pulling back enough he can get a good look at Emerson. His cheeks are flushed and the slow rise and fall of his chest is mesmerizing.

"Yes," Emerson whispers.

"It was my first time kissing a man," Jason says, and though Emerson already knows this, it's exciting to say it out loud.

"That was my first kiss ever," Emerson offers, pulling his bottom lip between his teeth.

"Did you like it?" Jason asks.

"I think I like everything when it's with you, Jason."

Uncaring who is outside waiting for a turn, Jason pulls Emerson into a hug. His arms slip around Jason's back, the sunflower boutonniere slightly crushed between their bodies as they each hold on much tighter than is strictly necessary. Emerson's hair tickles his nose as he buries his face in it, breathing him in.

He didn't need a kiss to accept he liked men, but it sure as hell showed him one thing: whatever his feelings are for Emerson, they're big. Bigger than anything he's felt before, and he's going to need to figure out what that means.

15 EMERSON

JASON KISSED HIM.

Star football coach. Teacher of the year three years running. Big man on campus. Most popular guy at Santa Leon High. Also, nicest guy ever *and* the most handsome. *That* Jason King kissed him. The same man who keeps Dr. Pepper and Ranch Doritos in his office in case Emerson ever runs out. The guy who knows Emerson's favorite foods and texts with him when words are too hard after a long day.

Of all the things Emerson has imagined in his life, this might be the greatest. Except Jason isn't anything like one of his daydreams, he's not a dream at all. Jason is so very real and also looking at Emerson like he's something fucking special, and no one has ever looked at him like this.

For as long as he's known he had a crush on Jason, it's felt like an objective fact. Something true, but not something Emerson had any plans to try and change. There are lots of things Emerson likes and some he doesn't, and all of those are simply fixed things. Like the way Emerson likes Eggo waffles or peanut sandwiches or Lord of the Rings.

Liking Jason simply was. He was never going to do anything about it because Jason was straight. Or so he thought before tonight.

Now Jason is here looking at Emerson like he maybe wants to kiss him again, holding him so close Emerson can feel every line of Jason's massive body, and suddenly having feelings for Jason doesn't feel the same as the way he likes waffles or soft blankets. It's different—more.

So much of Emerson's life has been spent studying other people or himself, fascinated and confused in equal measure by the complexities of being a human. Along with that fascination has always come a frustration that he cannot understand his own emotions as easily as he can understand characters in a book. He's tried speech therapy, occupational therapy, even talk therapy. He's carried a laminated feelings chart in his wallet, and on more than one occasion, cried because he was so frustrated by not understanding how he felt.

Right now, this feeling bubbling up in his chest, is the most clear and solid thing he's ever experienced; it's happiness.

Jason King makes him happy.

"Boys," Mabel calls, "there's a line."

"Yeah, boys," someone much younger and decidedly male says.

"Sanchez," Jason laughs, dropping his hand. Before he steps away, he kisses Emerson's lips once more in a brief but pleasant kiss that makes Emerson's insides tingle with delight. If he'd realized just how nice kissing was maybe he'd have tried it earlier, though in hindsight that would've involved letting other people touch him or get into his personal space and so far, despite many surface level crushes, he's never ever wanted to cross that line with anyone but Jason.

"What'cha doing in there, Coach?" another voice adds. Emerson knows this one. It's Matty.

"None of your business," Jason answers, slipping out of the photo booth first. He takes off his plastic crown, depositing it on Matty's head. "If you must be so nosy, Mr. Miller and I were helping Mabel test the photo booth."

"Is that all, Coach?" Matty asks.

It's only then that Emerson notices the photo booth photo in Matty's hand. A sinking feeling floods his gut. He can hear Landon all over again. *Why would you go to homecoming? Isn't that for people who have friends? Of course you're not going to prom, weirdo, who would go with you? Bet you're gay, aren't you? Mom and Dad will never let you bring anyone home, that is if anyone ever actually wanted to date you.*

He'd been horrible and cruel, and the only saving grace was that he'd been so busy with sports and his own friends, he'd mostly ignored Emerson unless he was very bored or in a bad mood.

Emerson spent a few hours tutoring Matty this week. He knows he's a good kid and not at all like his cousin, but his own knee jerk reaction to being in front of a large group of high school athletes is hard to ignore. Especially with all of them standing there staring, one of them holding a photograph that he knows could out Jason. Emerson feels like he might be sick. He's not even sure he's breathing. His lungs are expanding but it doesn't feel like air is actually coming in.

In Emerson's short twenty-six years of life, he quickly learned that the things he loves needed to be protected. Sometimes hidden away. Part of this was born from a discomfort with being perceived, along with a hefty amount of fear of ridicule—usually from his own family. He's always minimized or hid his intense interest in things, worried about losing it or having it taken away.

He wants to hide Jason away right now. Wants to pull him back into that bubble of happiness they created in the photo booth where the perceptions of students and coworkers didn't matter. To a place where only happy memories exist. The kind his mom might have had here. Denise said his mom liked to dance, which meant she probably came to homecoming here, just like Emerson.

"Matthew Albert Smith," Jason intones in the kind of teacher voice Emerson rarely hears him use.

Matty straightens up like he's been struck by lightning while the other players howl with laughter, shoving each other and making a lot of *ohs* and *ahs* that have Emerson clenching his jaw.

"Damn, Coach," Matty whistles, "didn't have to do me so dirty."

"Yes, he did," Arlo hisses. "You're making Mr. Miller uncomfortable."

"No, I'm not," Matty protests with that same smile he always wears, a smile that drops when he looks at Emerson. Clearly his attempt to smile is not working because Matty's expression falls. "Shit, I'm sorry, Mr. Miller. I was just teasing. Honest. It's good to see Coach King happy. Besides, you're our good luck charm."

"I don't think that's true," Emerson protests, but no one seems to be listening to him.

"Mr. Miller is the best," Arlo says, snatching the photo from Matty and closing the few steps between them to pass it back to Jason who tucks it into his suit pocket. Arlo's jaw is tight, head held high as he stalks back to the group.

Emerson waits, afraid Arlo might be ostracized or yelled at, but all that happens is Matty swinging his arm around Arlo's shoulder and ruffling his hair.

"Hell yeah, he's the best." Matty's smile returns. "Mr. Miller won us homecoming."

"Then why were you teasing him?" Arlo challenges, and Emerson smiles for real, unsure he's ever seen Arlo really stand up for anything like this. He's not sure why he, of all people, might be the catalyst, but knowing how much Arlo holds back, it makes Emerson proud to see him speak up.

"I wasn't teasing Mr. Miller, I was teasing Coach. He blushes like a—"

Arlo slaps his hand over Matty's mouth, almost immediately yanking it back with a frown. "You licked me."

"Serves you right," Matty laughs.

"I don't know why I like you," Arlo grumbles, crossing his arms.

"I knew you liked me, Rosales. Come on, let's take a photo."

"You and me?" Arlo squeaks.

"Yeah, why not?" Matty reaches for Arlo's arm, pulling him into the photo booth.

"Let's go," one of the other players says, half of them shoving each other to try and squeeze into the small photo booth along with Matty and Arlo.

"Think you can handle this, Mabel?" Jason asks.

Mabel scoffs. "I've been handling teenage boys longer than you've been alive, Jason."

"Of course you have," Jason grins in that easy way of his that makes it seem like everything is normal. It's a wonder he can manage it because Emerson's entire life feels like it's teetering on the edge. Somehow it never occurred to Emerson how different it would feel, probably because it never occurred to him he had a chance with Jason. He might have wished a few times, but that wasn't the same as believing it could happen, or thinking of the possibilities.

There are possibilities now, and Emerson's brain is going in a million directions. What if Jason likes Emerson enough to realize he's not straight, but not in a relationship kind of way? What if he kisses Emerson again and realizes how woefully inexperienced Emerson is in all things relationship and wants someone who knows more to figure things out with? Even as he thinks it, nausea churns in his gut. He doesn't like the idea of Jason with anyone else. When he thought Jason was straight, he'd been fine with it, but now he's not, and Emerson doesn't understand why, just knows he feels mildly ill.

"Emmy, did you hear what I said?"

The use of his special nickname from Jason drags Emerson out of his mental spiral, but can't change that he wasn't listening. He shakes his head, frowning.

"Follow me," Jason says, lifting a hand like he's going to reach for Emerson's and then dropping it. Is that because he changed his mind or because they're chaperoning and it might be inappropriate? He supposes kissing at the dance was probably inappropriate, but no one saw them. Well, unless you count the photo from the photo booth that Matty had.

This is so complicated. Emerson hates complicated things. Why can't it be as simple as he likes Jason and Jason likes him and no one else matters?

With a bitten off sigh, Emerson follows Jason, not entirely sure where they're going until Jason leads him around the snack table and back towards his office. He trails after him, watching the students dance and wondering again if his mom ever went to homecoming.

Jason pulls a key out of his pocket, unlocking the door and flipping the light on while waiting for Emerson to step inside before shutting the door. The noises from the gym are still loud, but dulled here, and some of the tightness in his chest unwinds because this is familiar. Just him and Jason in their spot. The place where they share lunch and talk. A place where the rest of the world doesn't matter. More of that tension bleeds away when Jason closes the distance between them and pulls Emerson into a crushing hug, the deep pressure exactly what his deregulated nervous system needs.

Attempting to shove his face into Jason's neck, he's frustrated to find his ear defenders making it uncomfortable. Yanking them off, he drops them to the floor, immediately burying his face in the crook of Jason's neck. With his ear against his shoulder and his lips half-pressed to the hollow of Jason's throat, he breathes a little easier, focusing on Jason's familiar scent and the warmth of his body.

There's a fleeting thought that maybe this isn't what he's supposed to do after his first kiss, but this is what he needs and Jason won't mind. Jason never minds. Jason understands him, in ways no one ever has. Jason innately knew Emerson was overwhelmed and overstimulated and on the verge of a shutdown and brought him here—somewhere private.

The truth of the situation hits Emerson in full force. Jason likes Emerson, not just when he's happy or easy, but always. He likes him even when he's on the edge of breakdown, nearly ripping the back of Jason's suit jacket because he can't pretend he doesn't want to be closer. If Emerson could, he'd crawl inside of Jason's suit and stay there, crawl under his very skin. Everything about Jason is warm and bright, and Emerson basks in him like a man starved of sunlight.

With Jason, he doesn't need to mask, and the relief that comes with this acknowledgment has Emerson's chest aching. He doesn't want to let Jason go. Not now, not ever. He wants Jason. He wants to kiss him again, wants to go on a first date and hopefully a second and third. He wants to open himself up to all the vulnerabilities he's spent a lifetime avoiding, and it terrifies him. There's very little in his life he's ever wanted and certainly nothing as desperately as he wants Jason. This big, beautiful man isn't just Emerson's crush, he's his best friend, and somehow that makes Emerson want to cry.

Everything is going to be different now that they've kissed, and maybe it'll be a good difference, but it's still a change. But this—being held by Jason—is familiar and safe in a way very little in Emerson's life ever has been.

Suddenly liking Jason feels as fragile as spun glass and Emerson holds on all the tighter. He can't lose Jason. *He can't.*

"I'm right here," Jason whispers, as if he can read Emerson's unease. "I'm not letting go, Emmy. Not until you tell me to."

"What if I never want to let go?" Emerson whispers, the words half-garbled against Jason's neck. Saying them spikes his anxiety. He can't believe he admitted that out loud. He's too intense. He's too clingy. This is part of why he never wanted to date. Well, that and the part where he doesn't really like people very much. But mostly, it's because he knows himself and his tendency to hyperfocus, and he knows he's going to be too much.

Except Jason surprises him, as always, by somehow managing to find the right thing to say.

"That might make eating and taking a piss kind of hard, but I'd be up for the challenge."

Against the odds, Emerson laughs. Somehow, Emerson suspects that if he sincerely asked, Jason might actually try, giving him the funniest mental image while also soothing the part of Emerson that is so used to being too much for everyone.

"Be worth it," Emerson mumbles.

"Hell yeah it would," Jason agrees, those gloriously massive hands of his stroking up and down Emerson's back. "Have I mentioned I like holding you? And kissing you. The kissing was fantastic. A-fucking-plus."

"You're ridiculous," Emerson mumbles. "I bet I was horrible."

"Not possible," Jason counters so quickly it's obvious he means it. "But for the record, I'm very down to practice. Like right now, for example. If someone very handsome who happened to be in this room with me wanted to kiss me, I would be very amiable."

"I taught you that word last week," Emerson says.

"Amiable is a great word," Jason laughs.

More proof that Jason is one of a kind. So often, people get annoyed when Emerson infodumps about synonyms and random words he learned while reading, but not Jason. He always listens as if what Emerson has to say is the most interesting thing in the world. And he remembers too, often bringing them up later as if to say, *see, I was paying attention.*

The last of his unease fades, as it usually does in Jason's presence. Emerson pulls his face out of Jason's neck, blinking away unshed tears to look up at Jason. His smile widens when he catches sight of Emerson's face, wrinkles forming in the corner of his eyes from the depth of his happiness, and it shoots a damn arrow right through Emerson's heart.

"What do you say, Emmy?" His hands find purchase at Emerson's lower back, anchoring in place. "Can I kiss you again?"

Those beautiful brown eyes of his are open and earnest, so full of affection that there's only one answer it could be; there is only one answer it will ever be where Jason is involved.

"Yes." Emerson whispers.

Jason angles his head down, one hand slipping around the back of Emerson's neck. Not to control the kiss but just to touch, as if he, too, can't get enough. When his lips touch Emerson's, it's all Emerson can do not to whimper, the touch so unlike those he's experienced before. He should be used to being close to Jason, used to his freely given hugs and shoulder squeezes, but he isn't at all. Every touch from Jason feels like the first, and Emerson doesn't think he will ever get used to how good it feels to be touched and held. And now, kissed.

And oh, Jason is a good kisser, the gentle slide of lips enough to have Emerson's toes curling. It's not until Jason pulls back that Emerson realizes he's tapping his fingers on his palms—a happy stim he can't seem to control. He tries to shove his hands into his pockets, so used to trying to hide, but Jason merely reaches for his hand and kisses each of his fingers from pinky to thumb before doing the same on the other hand.

"Do you remember what I told you?" Jason's hand settles on the side of his face again. "I don't want you to hide. Not from me, or anyone. You are exactly who you're supposed to be, Emmy."

"Sorry," Emerson lets out a shuddery exhale. "I'm getting used to this...used to...being me. Just Emerson."

"For what it's worth, I like just Emerson."

"You'd be the first," he whispers, hating how much his family's opinions of him still impact him even now that they're thousands of miles away. Learning to unmask is hard. Learning to trust that someone being nice to him isn't a joke or a tool to get him comfortable and then try to change him is hard. Being a person is just hard.

"Then everyone else are fucking idiots."

"It's statistically improbable that everyone else has been wrong," Emerson points out, as much for the sake of being realistic as the insecurities clamoring at the edges of his brain.

"You know what else is statistically improbable?" Jason crowds closer, his hand sliding around to cup the back of Emerson's neck. Those thick fingers of his hold on, not tight enough to hurt but enough that Emerson relaxes under the grip.

"Hmm?" Emerson hums, finding it difficult to form full words with Jason looking at him so intensely. It has his insides squirming, but not in the painfully discomfortable way he's used to when other people make eye contact with him. This is different, makes him want things he's not sure he's ever wanted with another person. He's daydreamed about sex, touched himself plenty of times, but the idea of actually having sex with someone is just not something he spent time imagining. He's imagining it now, in ways that make his suit feel a little too tight.

"A one point safety." Emerson waits for an explanation, relieved when Jason curls his fingers in his hair and continues, "It's a play when one team scores a touchdown, but the opposing team manages to get the ball off a turnover and runs it back into the end zone for a tackle. It's improbable. So much so, it's only happened three times in college football and never in the NFL, but that doesn't mean it can't."

The irony of spending his formative years being tormented by his cousin and Landon's fellow football players, who constantly reminded him how awkward, unpopular and unliked he was, only to find a man who loves the sport like he needs it to breathe, yet somehow also thinks Emerson is equally special, makes him want to laugh. He settles for smiling, something he does a lot now.

"Are you comparing me to football again?"

"I mean, yeah." Jason grins, entirely unabashed. "Football is fucking great. Like you. Shit, I know we're supposed to get back out to the dance, but I wish I could just stay in here with you. Talk to you, kiss you."

"You can kiss me," Emerson blurts, blushing at how eager he sounds.

"Yeah?" Jason's tongue darks out to lick over the swell of his bottom lip, his smile turning sweet. It draws Emerson's attention to the dimple in his chin and the sharp line of his jaw. Jason really is handsome.

Suddenly all Emerson can think about is what it might be like if Jason were naked. With him. If they were both naked. What might it be like to feel another man against him—to feel Jason. Jason's got a lot of hair, he's got it on his chest and thighs. Emerson kind of wants to rub against it like a cat which is maybe weird, but also sounds like sensory heaven. Would Jason like that? He's used to sex with women. Women who probably aren't inexperienced.

"What's going on in that pretty head of yours?"

"Huh?" Emerson blinks, shivering when Jason's hand settles on top of his head. The weight of it is oddly soothing.

"I said what's going on in that pretty head of yours? You look a million miles away."

"I was thinking about you naked."

It's only when Jason chokes on his own spit, pink splotches blossoming on his cheeks, that it occurs to Emerson maybe he wasn't supposed to answer that question quite so honestly.

"Sorry."

"Don't ever apologize for being honest," Jason says, the faintest quiver to his voice. "Or uh, thinking about me naked. Full permission to think about me however you like whenever you like. Just uh, shit."

"What?"

Jason clears his throat, reaching down to adjust his pants. "That's gonna make chaperoning difficult."

"Are you hard?" Emerson asks, eyes drawn down to the noticeable bulge in Jason's very well tailored suit.

Jason blows out a breath, laughing softly. "Yes."

"Because I'm thinking about you naked?" Emerson presses, needing to be sure.

"I mean that," Jason confirms, still blushing, "and you just existing."

Pleasure spreads through Emerson, swift and all encompassing. Never in his life has his mere existence been something someone else was so happy about, and his fingers do their happy taps at Jason's words. It would be so easy to overthink it, to try and analyze unspoken subtext the way he has to with most people. Except Jason isn't like most people. When Jason says something, he means it. The sense of safety this affords Emerson is immeasurable. There's no second guessing or worrying. What you see is what you get with Jason King, and he sure likes what he sees.

"I should probably get back out there," Jason says, making no move to leave. "I really want to kiss you again."

"I thought you needed to leave."

"I do," Jason says, scrubbing a hand over his freshly shaved jaw. The skin is so smooth that Emerson can't help but wonder how it might feel to lick it. "I also need to kiss you."

"Need or want?" Emerson asks, unsure when his heart started beating so fast.

"Both," Jason answers, maneuvering Emerson until his back is pressed to the door. The music from outside is so loud it vibrates against his back, a stark contrast to the steady presence Jason makes against his front. "What are you doing to me, Emmy?"

"I don't think I'm doing anything," Emerson answers.

Jason's laugh is small, the sound muffled when he presses his lips to Emerson's in a kiss so sensual and slow that Emerson understands exactly what kind of problem Jason had with his suit a moment ago. He always assumed when he read about people getting aroused from just a kiss that it was an exaggeration, that it might take more stimulation to get him going since it takes him so long to get out of his own head to even jerk off. Yet with a single kiss from Jason, he's half-hard in his suit and imagining what it might be like to touch another man's cock for the first time.

Maybe all those books he read had something right after all because he's pretty sure he could die happy kissing Jason. Being driven to distraction by thoughts of sex is another thing he was certain was a literary exaggeration; yet crushed between the door and Jason's body, there is no exaggeration in thinking this is the most incredible thing he's ever felt.

"Can I?" Jason starts, pulling out of the kiss with flushed cheeks and well-kissed lips.

"What?"

"Pick you up?" Jason asks, inching both hands towards Emerson's ass.

Emerson nods, and despite the permission, he's still surprised when Jason effortlessly lifts him from the ground, his legs wrapping around Jason's waist to keep himself steady. He knew Jason was strong, but knowing something and experiencing it for himself are very different things. They also cause different reactions in his body. Knowing Jason has muscles is something that's nice for Emerson to look at, but feeling the way those muscles can move him around, holding him steady and guiding him wherever Jason wants, makes Emerson so hard it's physically uncomfortable.

"This would feel better in less restrictive clothing."

"Yes, it would," Jason agrees, kissing Emerson's jaw and down the side of his neck. "You're so sexy."

"Are you talking to me?" Emerson asks because while he's the only one Jason is kissing, that is not a word that's ever been used to describe him. He's tall with gangly arms and excessively long legs that make his pants always too short and his hair is so red it could stop traffic. He's got delicate wrists, and his skin is pale enough it might as well be see-through. He's also, despite his height, half Jason's size because there is not an ounce of muscle on his noodle-limbed body. Sexy is absolutely not a word that anyone has ever used to describe Emerson.

"Who else would I be talking to?" Jason asks, with that easy smile of his.

"Well no one, I suppose," Emerson answers, looping his arms around Jason's neck since he has no idea where else to put them. He kind of wants to touch Jason's chest but he's not sure if he's allowed and asking is harder than it should be.

"I can't stop kissing you," Jason murmurs against his lips.

"That's perfectly alright with me," Emerson answers, surprised he can form words with Jason's body so close and his lips on his.

The next kiss is deeper, Jason's mouth firm against his own. It brings a whimper to Emerson's lips, and at the first sound of it Jason's hold tightens, the tip of his tongue slipping into Emerson's mouth. He's seen people do this in movies, read enough books to assume that most people must enjoy it, yet none of the references prepare him for how good the extra stimulation feels.

Jason's tongue is probing, warm and wet, and it deepens the taste of him. It's a sensory delight, and try as he might, Emerson can't stop the wanton moan of desire that Jason pulls from him.

"Fuck," Jason curses.

"Sorry."

"No, do it again," Jason groans, fingers digging into Emerson's ass. "It's so hot."

Part of Emerson wants to protest. First sexy, now hot. Surely Jason's confused. Then again, Emerson doesn't exactly want to argue with Jason's delusions when they make him feel desired in a way he never expected to feel with another man. If Jason thinks he's those things, who is Emerson to argue?

"Emmy." Jason's voice is low and gravely, the pitch of it fueling Emerson's arousal. "Oh, Emmy."

Emerson's breath shutters in his chest as the deep bass of music from the dance pulses at his back. After a lifetime of loneliness, and years spent devoid of physical contact, Emerson's walls shatter, leaving him stripped raw and starved for affection. It's absolutely terrifying, and if Jason weren't holding him up, he's pretty sure he'd be on the floor.

"Jason," he whimpers.

"Yeah?" Jason asks, resting his forehead against Emerson's. His chest labors under his ragged breathing, his face flushed and his smile radiant. "How are you?"

It's such a Jason question. Always checking in, always worried, because he cares about Emerson. If only the answer were an easy one to give. He's not okay. He's somehow better and worse all at once. How can Emerson possibly explain how jarring it feels to experience this depth of attraction and arousal for the first time? It's not like he's ignorant about sex or averse to it. He's just spent so long shoving those desires away, along with anything else that might require human intimacy because it felt too out of reach. With one single confession and a few kisses, Jason opened the box, and there may be no putting the lid on it again.

"Are you overthinking?" Jason asks.

Emerson ponders the question. "Just regular thinking, I think."

"Your regular thinking is most people's overthinking," Jason says in that soft, affectionate way of his that makes Emerson feel like everything is alright. "Which, for the record, before you overthink that too, is something I'm very into. I love that sexy brain of yours."

"I don't think brains can be sexy," Emerson muses.

Jason grins. "Everything about you can be sexy, Mr. Miller."

"Except that," Emerson frowns. "Don't call me that. My students call me that."

"Got it," Jason laughs, unbothered and easygoing as always. "No sexy teacher time."

"Just...Jason and Emmy time."

Jason stops laughing, the intensity of his gaze staggering. "Say it again."

"Uh, which—oh." Emerson's heart thuds harder, faster. As if it knows every beat right now is for the beautiful man holding him. "Jason and Emmy."

Jason's body trembles, and when he kisses Emerson this time, there's nothing slow or sweet about it. Jason shifts his hold so that all of Emerson's weight is braced in one hand. Emerson hardly has time to marvel at Jason's impressive strength before the hand he freed is at Emerson's cheek, smoothing down the side of his face and lower until it curls loosely around his throat while he plunges his tongue into Emerson's mouth and all but devours him. Jason's kiss is demanding, eager, and Emerson feels utterly owned by the way Jason claims his mouth, the sensation as unexpectedly arousing as it is safe.

Eager for anything Jason will give him, he tips his head back against the door, exposing the line of his throat as he tightens his legs around Jason's waist. It's heady and thrilling, and Emerson feels bold making his desires clear.

"Fuck," Jason curses, mouth attaching itself to the hollow of Emerson's throat.

A moan erupts, and Emerson's face burns when he realizes that guttural needy sound came from him. He had no idea having someone suck on his neck would make every inch of his body, from his head to his toes and most definitely his cock, light up with pleasure. Clearly emboldened by the sound, Jason mouths at his throat, leaving Emerson seeing stars.

How do normal people function with this level of arousal? Emerson is losing his mind, all rational thought and propriety fleeing. He's pretty sure there's a solid reason not to come in his suit, both because of the dry cleaning bill and the whole chaperone thing, yet somehow his desire to touch and be touched overrules it all. He's never felt this desperate in his entire life, and he's pretty sure he might die if Jason stops touching him.

"No dying, Emmy."

"I didn't mean to say that out loud," Emerson groans, embarrassed, turned on and very close to rutting against Jason like a teenager.

"It's adorable," Jason huffs, his amusement somehow as arousing as the kisses he continues to pepper along Emerson's throat.

Emerson is very overwhelmed, and while it's not bad, his brain is close to short circuiting. He doesn't understand how he's supposed to feel so much—arousal, affection, desire—and still function.

"I've never liked anyone the way I like you," Jason whispers, ruining Emerson further. He kisses his way up the side of Emerson's neck. "My Emmy."

My Emmy. Two little words uttered with such casual certainty that tears prickle at the corners of Emerson's eyes. He squeezes Jason tightly, trapping his face against Emerson's throat. He's never belonged anywhere, never belonged to anyone. Until now.

"Please don't let me go," Emerson whispers, unsure if he means right now or ever.

"I've got you," Jason promises. "I—"

A solid knock at the door has both of them stilling.

Jason's eyes widen while Emerson automatically assumes the worst.

"Are we in trouble?"

"No." Jason shakes his head, some of his dark hair that's been slicked back falling loose across his forehead. "We're the teachers. Although, we probably should be out there, but we're not going to get in trouble for taking a few minutes to uh—you know."

"Sorry," Emerson starts, but Jason silences him with a chaste kiss.

"Nope, no sorry." Jason kisses him, looking physically pained when he has to pull back. "Besides I'm the one who dragged you in here. If anyone is at fault it's me, and—"

"Mr. King," someone yells loudly, knocking again with slightly more urgency. It's definitely a male voice but with the music blaring and his relative lack of familiarity with the majority of the staff here he has no idea who.

"Ugh," Jason groans, the slope of his handsome features turning down in a frown. Clearly he knows who is waiting on the other side of the door.

"Remember we didn't do anything wrong," Jason says, straightening Emerson's boutonniere then kissing his cheek. "It's no one's business what we're doing in here. You're not going to apologize, right?"

"I can try not to," Emerson shrugs. Between his family's conditioning and his brain's propensity to assume he's in trouble at all times from making an inadvertent social faux paus, apologizing comes second nature to him.

"Let me handle this then," Jason offers, smoothing back a stray lock of Emerson's hair. It pops back up, and Jason grins, trying to smooth it down a second time but the hair refuses to cooperate. Emerson knows it's pointless because he tried all day, and while he could've used gel like Jason, the sensory ick of having crunchy hair was not something he was willing to suffer. He doesn't point this out to Jason though, wanting any bit of physical contact he can have.

"Ready?"

"Not really," Emerson answers.

"Me either," Jason sighs, squatting down to retrieve Emerson's abandoned ear defenders from the floor. He carefully slides them back on Emerson's head, the lingering feeling of Jason's fingers skimming through Emerson's hair fading when Jason turns his attention to his office door. His hand turns the knob, pushing the door open and returning them to the real world with a harsh clatter of pounding music and flashing lights.

16 JASON

IRRITATION PRICKLES AT JASON. He knows they're here to chaperone. He knows someone needing him is part of what he signed up for. It's just that when he volunteered, he hadn't realized his feelings for Emerson were more than platonic or that Emerson would end up at homecoming with him. Picking Emerson up had been the most glorious torture, the sight of him in his stylish green suit enough to convince Jason that he is definitely not straight and that he wanted to kiss Emerson, possibly more than he'd ever wanted to kiss anyone in his entire life.

Knowing Emerson's lack of experience in the way of romance and intimacy, he'd done his best to be both upfront about his feelings while taking things slow and being a gentleman. But fuck it all if Emerson's trusting gaze and pretty eyes hadn't made Jason feel like a horny, lovesick teenager. Then Emerson had gone and uttered three words that had irrevocably changed something in him—Jason and Emmy. Their names spoken together like that, as if the two of them were a pair. Aside from Theo, he'd never wanted to be a pair with anyone. Sure, he'd had girlfriends, but most of them had lost interest when they realized Jason wasn't going to ditch football or Theo for them.

For years, it's been a non-issue. He'd tried to date but never felt a real spark with anyone, nor had he ever met someone who'd wanted to join their life with his without changing the most important parts to Jason, such as his relationship with Theo and football. After his last girlfriend cheated on him, he figured maybe he should lay off relationships entirely because he clearly wasn't going to find the right girl. Then came Emerson, with his adorable resting frowny face and his endless opinions on everything, from books to the shape toast should be cut into, making Jason feel *things*. Emerson, who gets along with his best friend in a way no one else ever has. Emerson, who exchanged emails with his older brother to trade book recs and made Alec laugh with a deadpan joke about hobbits that Jason still doesn't understand. Emerson, who doesn't even like football but delights in sharing in Jason's stories about games and practice.

Emerson Miller, the man who makes Jason want things he's never wanted with anyone. Despite all their differences, Emerson has situated himself in Jason's life in ways that make it impossible for him to remember what it'd been like before he came along. How is Jason supposed to go back out to the dance now? How is he even supposed to function now that he's kissed a man, knows what that man tastes like, and what kinds of sounds he makes when he's aroused?

"I'm still waiting."

The groan Jason lets out is loud. This cannot be happening.

"Caldwell," Jason yells, flinging the door open while plastering on the fakest smile possible. "What are you doing here? Didn't you make Emerson chaperone in your place?"

"That's not really any of your concern, Mr. King."

Irritation makes Jason grit his teeth. Caldwell is such an ass.

"Well, to what do I owe this unexpected...visit?"

Caldwell's entire face twitches. "You aren't controlling your players."

"What are they doing?" Jason asks, immediately switching into teacher mode.

"They're being rambunctious," Caldwell says, spitting with the force of it as if their exuberance has offended him. "Control them."

"I'm sure they're just having fun," Jason offers, relaxing now that he knows it's nothing major. "We won last night you know and—"

"I don't care if your players win the Super Bowl—"

"That's the NFL, not high school," Jason points out.

Caldwell appears deeply annoyed at being corrected. "I do not care, Mr. King. The point stands. You should be out there ensuring—"

"Ensuring what?" Jason asks when he stops speaking.

"Ensuring your players don't do something improper," Caldwell finishes, words directed to Jason even as his gaze focuses behind him. Jason doesn't need to turn around to know exactly what, or more accurately who, he's staring at. "Mr. Miller, I'm surprised to find you here. Given recent transgressions I assumed you'd take this more seriously."

"I wasn't—"

"Regardless," Caldwell interrupts, not even letting Emerson finish. "I'm sure you'll return to the dance and ensure you set a good example for the students. Perhaps being new here you don't quite understand the implications of all your actions. If you gentlemen will excuse me, I have a job to do. I expect you'll both do yours as well."

With that he departs, leaving Jason staring at his back and Emerson groaning behind him.

"Recent transgressions," Emerson repeats, his offense palpable. "I don't have any! They already finished the investigation and Mrs. Hernandez agreed we did nothing wrong. Was getting me to chaperone just some kind of power play? I don't understand, Jason. I didn't do anything."

"I know, Emmy." Jason moves to pull him into a hug. Emerson is stiff, agitation rolling off him in waves, but Jason just squeezes him tightly the way he knows Emerson likes. "Don't take it personally. Caldwell is a cranky son of a bitch. We don't give headspace to people like him."

"When you say '*we*', I know you don't mean me," Emerson replies, sagging in Jason's hold. "My brain gives headspace to everyone. I'll probably go over this conversation in my head for the next ten years."

"I could give you something else to think about for the next ten years," Jason suggests, offering Emerson a wide smile when he pulls out of the hug.

"Are you flirting?" Emerson asks. "Or trying to distract me? I can't tell."

"Both," Jason laughs, his annoyance with Caldwell fading now that he's once again alone with Emerson. He meant what he said. He's pissed at Caldwell, but given the choice between thinking about him or Emerson, it's no contest. Jason will pick Emerson every time.

"We can't," Emerson protests, though it pleases Jason to note the disappointment in his tone. "You heard Caldwell. We have a job to do."

"We do," Jason agrees. As much as he wants to stay hidden away with Emerson, he also knows he's the best man for the job to reel in his kids' excitement without trampling their spirits. "But uh, before we go out there I need to ask you one thing."

"What is it?" Emerson questions.

"It's a good question, I hope," Jason stalls, wishing the door were shut so he could hold Emerson the way he wants.

He's never hesitated to touch Emerson before, but something about Caldwell's accusatory tone and stare has Jason's hackles on edge. He doesn't want to do anything that might draw more attention to Emerson when he's clearly already anxious.

"Alright," Emerson replies.

"Will you come home with me?" Jason asks, unsure which of them is more surprised by the question—Emerson or him. He knows he should be playing it cool, but he doesn't think he knows how to be subtle or casual. Emerson's expression remains unchanged, the slight downturn of his lips making it impossible to read his feelings from his facial expression. If Jason didn't know him so well, he would almost think Emerson isn't interested. What gives him away is the way he twists the ring on his finger.

Unable to hold himself back, Jason reaches out to squeeze Emerson's wrist. "Just so you know, it doesn't have to mean anything."

"You don't want it to mean anything?" Emerson says, voice so low Jason can barely hear the words over the music from the gym.

Jason's heart falls to the floor. Shit. That was not what he meant at all, and clearly he needs to be even more direct.

"Everything with you means something because it's you. I only meant that we don't have to do anything, not even kiss more, if you don't want to. Although, I really hope you want to because kissing you was maybe the best thing that's ever happened to me. But I don't want you to feel pressured because I want to do it right, treat you right, you know because you've never done any of this before."

"So you only want me to come over and maybe kiss because I'm inexperienced?"

In hindsight, perhaps there's more than one reason Jason couldn't keep a girlfriend beyond lack of sparks. Jason could almost laugh at how embarrassingly bad he's fucking this all up if the scrunch of Emerson's confused brow isn't making him want to cry.

Time to go for broke.

"I want you to come over so I don't have to say goodbye to you," Jason tells him, laying every single one of his cards on the table. "Once we go out there, I'm going to spend hours watching you from across the room, unable to hold you or touch you the way I desperately want. There's no way I can just drop you off at home after this when all I want to do is hold you and kiss you. Or do anything with you. Everything's better when you're around, Emerson. Everything."

Emerson's jaw trembles. "Jason."

"Please come home with me, Emmy."

"I—don't know what I'm doing."

"Me either," Jason admits, taking one step closer. Trying to stay away from Emerson is like ignoring a gravitational pull. "I've never felt like this about anyone, Emmy. I'm in uncharted fucking territory here. I like you more than I've ever liked anyone, and you know, you're also a man which was a bit of a shock, let me tell you."

"What if it's too much?"

"We can talk about that and all the other questions you wrote down on your phone later. If you don't want to come home with me tonight, nothing has to change. I still want to take you on that date. I still want to be your friend. I—"

"I want to," Emerson admits, twisting his fingers so tightly it looks painfully. "But I'm scared."

Jason's exhale is a tenuous thing as he closes the space between them. One step for Emerson, the other for himself, lowering his forehead to rest it against Emerson's. "We can be scared together then."

"You don't get scared," Emerson whispers.

"I'm scared of this," Jason admits, wrapping his arm around Emerson's back. With the darkened lights and the position of Jason's office, it's unlikely anyone can see them and if they do, it's a risk he's willing to take for Emerson.

"Because I'm a guy?"

"No, because you're my Emmy." Jason breathes him in, surprised to find he is the one trembling. Jason and Emmy. *Jason and Emmy*. He's never wanted anyone the way he wants this beautiful man, and he suddenly understands a little bit of what Theo must've experienced, the kind of longing and desperation he must've felt that drove him to keep his burgeoning relationship with Jason's younger brother a secret. Jason had been so angry and so hurt, not understanding how Theo could do what he'd done. He understands now because he knows, without a shadow of doubt, that he would do anything to keep Emerson.

Theo hadn't betrayed Jason's friendship. He'd fallen in love.

"I don't want to fuck this up," Jason whispers, holding Emerson just that little bit tighter. "I don't want to hurt you. I don't want to lose you."

"You're scared of losing me," Emerson croaks as if it's the most ludicrous thing he's ever heard. "But you're—you. You're amazing. You are the best person I've ever known. I'm the one scared of losing you. I'm difficult and inexperienced and —"

Jason silences him with one final kiss, knowing they need to get back out to the dance but unable to leave this room until Emerson is more settled. If not completely, at least in where he stands with Jason.

"Whatever this is, we're in it together. We're a team. Team means family, whatever happens. Win or lose. You on my team, Emmy?"

Emerson offers a shaky exhale before nodding. "I'm on your team, Jason."

"DO you need anything from your apartment?" Jason asks, feeling as nervous as a teenager on his first date.

They'd stayed so late to ensure all the students left safely and to begin some of the clean up, that the parking lot is entirely empty, leaving no one but Jason and Emerson standing underneath the too bright parking lot light.

"I don't have a toothbrush or pajamas."

"I've got a whole pack of extra toothbrushes from Costco under my sink," Jason tells him. "And uh, you could wear mine. Well, I don't wear pajamas. I usually just sleep in sweats and a t-shirt unless it's too hot then I only sleep in my boxers."

Emerson's gaze is locked on his, unblinking. "You don't mind if I wear your pajamas?"

"No," Jason croaks, clearing his throat. Mind doesn't begin to cover it. He's never considered himself some kind of stereotypically possessive man, but the idea of seeing Emerson's lanky, lithe body in *his* clothing does it for Jason.

Ever since he offered Emerson his hoodie when he was cold and had watched the way it dwarfed him, he's been driven to distraction wanting to see it on him again. Jason knows he's a big guy, it's impossible to forget, but something about seeing proof of how much bigger than Emerson he is, makes him want to scream. Or maybe get Emerson in his bed and never let him out.

For over a year, Jason's been happily acquainted with his right hand without complaint, yet one kiss from Emerson and he's pretty sure he might die if Emerson doesn't touch him. Not that he's going to force him, or push for anything. He meant what he said before. Even if they do nothing tonight but cuddle, Jason will be over the fucking moon. He's never wanted to be around someone the way he does Emerson.

"Are you sure? You look kind of stressed?"

"I'm trying not to get hard thinking about you in my clothes or in my bed," Jason admits, because Emerson likes honesty, and he's not sure he's a good enough liar to pretend.

"You—oh." Emerson licks his lips. "I thought—Charlie mentioned girls used to steal your stuff. I thought you wouldn't like it. I've been meaning to give you your hoodie back."

"Charlie's got a big fucking mouth," Jason grumbles. "Also, don't you dare give it back."

"Why?" Emerson asks, because of course he does.

In all things, Emerson wants the truth, uncomplicated and without preamble, and it's what he's going to get. Whatever happens with Emerson, it won't fail because of communication, Jason will make sure of it.

"Because seeing you in that hoodie after you borrowed it at school a few weeks ago made me realize how much I like seeing you in my clothing." Jason closes the small space between them, reaching for Emerson the way he's been aching to do for hours. "I want to take you home and see you in my bed, in my clothes. I want you to smell like me."

"I read a book like that once," Emerson says, making Jason laugh.

"Was it a werewolf book? Pretty sure Andrew reads those. Then again, he reads a lot. I'm scared of his Kindle history."

Emerson shakes his head, his voice going very high pitched. "Fairies."

"Fairies, huh. Were you reading fairy porn, Emmy?"

"It's not porn," Emerson balks. "It's romance with um, well, sex."

"I'm just teasing," Jason whispers, letting his fingers glide into Emerson's beautiful, soft hair. In response, he tips his head back, throat exposed and eyes turning up to meet Jason's. He trusts Jason, to touch, to be gentle, and Jason wants to scream with how good it feels. He's not even doing more than playing with Emerson's hair, and it's so damn perfect.

"Do you mean it?" Emerson asks.

"Oh, Emmy. I mean everything I say."

Emerson surges up, closing the distance between them in an unexpected kiss. It's too forceful, his teeth scraping Jason's lips and his hands scrambling at Jason's suit, but the fact that Emerson—his sweet, never initiates physical contact Emerson—kissed *him* first makes this one of the best fucking kisses of Jason's life.

When Emerson pulls back, his eyes are wide like he can't believe what he just did. He touches his mouth, delicate fingers skimming over his equally delicate mouth. He really is beautiful.

"Ready to go home?" Jason asks, only realizing his slip up once the words are out of his mouth.

Part of him wants to correct himself but the truth is, he didn't misspeak. Emerson's been to his house enough now, albeit under different circumstances, that Jason wants it to feel like his home. He wants Emerson to feel welcome there, and safe.

"I'm ready," Emerson nods, "but um, there's just one thing I need from my apartment. I can't sleep without it but—"

"But what?" Jason prompts when Emerson trails off abruptly.

"I don't want you to think it's stupid."

"Nothing about you is stupid. I've told you that."

"*It'saplush,*" Emerson gets out in a jumbled rush. Before Jason can really comprehend what he's said, Emerson continues. "My mom got it for me when I was a kid and it's all I have left."

"Emmy."

"It's my favorite. It's a stuffed shark because I was obsessed with them when I was a kid, even though I'd never seen one in person. I had so many books, and I watched all the documentaries about them, so when I turned five my mom got me Sharky. After she died, and my aunt and uncle took me in, well, they didn't want our stuff. They said it was pointless to spend money moving our things when they had a house that was furnished so they just...got rid of it all. My bed, my favorite blanket, all my toys. They said they'd buy me new ones, but I didn't want new. I snuck it in my backpack because it fit in there for the plane ride. But Landon always stole it, so I had to hide him a lot, and then when I got older, he called me a baby for still having it. Maybe I shouldn't get it. That's probably not the kind of thing you bring to stay over with a man the first time, is it?"

A deep awareness of what it must have taken for

Emerson to admit that hits Jason, and he pulls Emerson into a tight hug, needing to hold him close. Emerson melts into the embrace.

"Emmy," Jason holds him close. "Do you want to go get your plush?"

When Emerson speaks, his words ghost across the side of Jason's neck where he's tucked his face. "Yes, please."

Twenty-five minutes later, they're pulling into Jason's driveway. Jason's hand is on Emerson's knee while Emerson's hands are curled protectively around his plush shark. Whether for comfort or from anxiety, Jason's not sure.

"We're here," Jason tells him, giving his knee a gentle squeeze.

"Right." Emerson undoes his seatbelt, holding Sharky close. Before he can get out of the truck, Jason's all but flung himself out of his side and raced around to get the door, opening it up and offering his hand. Emerson's lips twitch at the corner. "That was fast."

"I'm a fast man," Jason grins, chest fluttering when Emerson's fingers make contact with his own. Their hands stay connected when Jason shuts the truck door, and locks it and on the walk to the front door. "Fair warning, the dogs are gonna wake up and be noisy shits, but I can put them in the garage if it's too much."

"I thought they usually slept in the bed with you," Emerson says.

"They do. Sort of. Stella likes her dog bed in the corner and gets in bed when she wakes up. Freddie is a clingy little shit and sleeps on my legs or sometimes my head. But if that's too much you can tell me."

"We can try it out," Emerson offers, which is probably about as bold as he's likely to get. Jason will take it.

"You ready to be attacked by Stella?" Jason laughs,

turning the lock in the door. As if they've been waiting on the other side, no sooner is he turning the doorknob then Stella barks loudly, followed by Freddie yapping. "I'm home, kids."

Careful not to let Stella slip out the open door, Jason lets go of Emerson's hands so he can hold her collar, leading her backwards to make room for Emerson to come inside. He drops to his knees so she can crowd into his personal space, licking and barking like she hasn't seen Jason in a year.

"Did you miss Daddy?" Jason laughs, giving her a kiss on the top of head along with a few firm fur pets before turning to look for Freddie, who usually fights his way to Jason for attention when he's been gone longer than normal. To his surprise, Freddie isn't wailing beside them but over with Emerson who is also down on his knees. Freddie butts his head into Emerson's chest as Emerson pets him, murmuring something too low to be heard that has Freddie's paws doing their happy pitter patter.

Tucked under one arm is Sharky, under the other is Freddie. If Jason hadn't already suspected he was falling hard for Emerson, the sight of his massive, scared-of-his-own-shadow pittie rescue being happily babied by him would be all it took. As it is, Jason is pretty sure he falls just a little bit more, and his heart definitely grows, its current size not nearly big enough for all the love he wants to give Emerson.

"What?" Emerson asks when he catches Jason staring.

It would be so easy to say nothing. All too easy to pretend he's not falling hard and fast for Emerson. It would be the easiest thing in the world to play it cool, so he doesn't get himself hurt. Luckily for Jason, he's never once taken the easy way out and he doesn't plan to start now.

"I like you here."

"In the entryway?" Emerson asks, grinning like he knows he's said something funny, and he's proud of himself.

"Well sure, you look handsome everywhere." Jason crawls towards Emerson on his knees, feeling a bit ridiculous but wanting to be closer. Stella follows suit, clearly unsure why Jason is practically crawling, barking when she mistakes it for some kind of game. Only Jason isn't playing, not about this. "I meant here in my home, with my dogs. You look like you belong."

"Jason."

"I like you with me," Jason continues, physically unable to stop. "Wherever I am is where I want you. I know that's probably a little too fast, so you don't need to feel pressured to say anything back but—"

Emerson tackles him, and while Jason might have six inches and a hundred pounds on Emerson what he lacks in size he makes up for in speed. The tackle sends Jason crashing to the floor with a lap full of Emerson followed by two dogs, who take that as a permission to try and pile on too. His head thunks against the hardwood floor, which smarts, and he groans, rubbing the back of his head.

"Sorry," Emerson mumbles above him, hair falling into his eyes and his beloved plush crushed between their chests. "Oh my god, I'm sorry."

"It's okay," Jason assures him, unable to hold back his smile despite the slight twinge in his head. "By the way, full permission to tackle me any time, in any room. Bonus points if it happens on a bed sometime."

"You would let me tackle you in bed?" Emerson asks.

Jason has to physically move Freddie's giant head so he can see Emerson. "In case it wasn't clear before, you can do anything you want to me."

"Anything is really vague, Jason."

"Yeah, it is," Jason acknowledges, rubbing Freddie's belly so he doesn't get jealous. "Full disclosure, I don't exactly know what I like with another man, but I'd like to find out...with you, in case that also wasn't clear. We can go at whatever speed you want. Although, I think you unlocked a new kink for me tonight. I've never been on the bottom and not going to lie, I'm enjoying this very much."

"I can't tell if you're teasing or serious," Emerson admits, holding his plush tightly.

"I mean it. I like you on top of me, but I'd like you under me or beside me too. I just like you, Emmy. Whatever that looks like for you. Incidentally, we've spent a lot of time talking about what I like and I appreciate that you care but this—" he pauses, waving at the small space between their faces, "this is two people. Not just me. So what you like matters too."

"I have a list," Emerson blurts.

"A list," Jason echoes. "This like your list of questions?"

Emerson nods. "I started making a mental list after you kissed me, and I realized I was allowed to think about touching you."

If Jason were a peacock, his feathers would be spread wide. As it is, he pushes his chest up, ignoring the way Stella and Freddie paw at him in favor of focusing on the part of the conversation where the man of his dreams just admitted to making a mental list about all the ways he wants to touch Jason.

"What's at the top of your list?" Jason asks. "I know you put them in order of preference."

"How do you know that?" Emerson questions.

"Because I know you," Jason answers, delighted that Emerson is close enough for him to lift his head and kiss the shock off his face. His tongue slips into Emerson's mouth in a kiss that's more of a promise than a tease. When he finds his neck aching from the awkward position, he drops his head to the floor and grins up at Emerson's flushed face.

"I can't think when you do that."

"Should I stop?" Jason asks, running his thumb over the side of Emerson's neck.

"No," Emerson groans. "Just, can we change first? I'm tired of this suit. I want to be comfy. Then...then I'll tell you about my list."

"Can being comfy include cuddling in bed?" Jason questions, eager to get up off the cold, hard floor but not at all ready to lose the feeling of Emerson's body against his own like this.

"Yes," Emerson confirms, slowly rising off Jason. He stands, towering above him in his pretty green suit, his boutonniere now crushed and his hair in disarray. He looks rumpled, his plush clutched to his chest and his stare unblinking. Jason wants to crowd him into his bed and never let him go.

"Are you going to get up off the floor or just stare at me?" Emerson asks with a slight cock to his head.

"The view is damn good," Jason tells him, "but shit I feel thirty. This floor is hard."

"I'm sorry," Emerson apologizes.

"I told you it's fine," Jason assures him, rolling onto his hands and knees before rising. "Why don't we get changed and get the dogs settled, then we talk about that list of yours."

"If you don't like the ideas, you can tell me."

"I know," Jason says, and he does, finding that honesty is easy with Emerson. He never has to second guess himself and it feels good to be so secure in knowing whatever Emerson says he means. "Same goes for you."

Emerson opens his mouth then closes it, fingers twisting in the worn fabric of his plush shark. "What if...what I like isn't what you like?"

"Then we figure it out, together," Jason tells him, reaching for Emerson's other hand, hanging loosely at his side. "You and I are a team, remember?"

"Team," Emerson affirms.

Giving Emerson's fingers a squeeze, he takes the first step towards the bedroom, pleased when Emerson automatically falls into step beside him. The pitter patter of paws on the floor lets him know Stella and Freddie are following too, and Jason can't help but feel damn good that they all trust him.

He still might not be sure what label to use for his sexuality, might not even know exactly what to call the thing growing between him and Emerson, but the fact that it exists at all is enough for him right now. Whatever is happening between them feels right in a way none of his past relationships ever have, and Jason wants it—wants Emerson.

17 EMERSON

EMERSON STARES at himself in the mirror, trying to imagine what exactly it is that Jason sees when he looks at him. Before, when he'd thought Jason was straight, he assumed Jason's gazes were friendship. Sure, they seemed like more, but Emerson wasn't exactly in the position to know that. He's never had a best friend or a lover.

Lover. Emerson doesn't think he likes that word. It makes things sound tawdry or rooted in sex. While Emerson would very much like to have sex with Jason, in a myriad of ways, it's not what he wants the most. Or what he wants right now, if he's being honest.

He knows he's been in the bathroom a long time. First to brush and floss, then to change into the clothes Jason brought him. The sweatpants hung over his feet, and even when he cinched the waistband, they're still too big, so he settled on only wearing the t-shirt Jason brought him over his compression boxers.

Considering the shirt fits Jason, it hangs loosely on Emerson—the neck exposing his sharp collarbones. The way it drapes over his lanky body makes it look like he's not wearing anything underneath. He has no idea if this is something Jason might like. He's never looked at himself and tried to understand what other people might find attractive or not about him. While Emerson has certainly felt attraction to men, it's always been fleeting. He's never felt his heart in his gut or a simmering arousal. Probably because Emerson is very good at compartmentalizing, and he'd never actually wanted anything from the men he thought were handsome. He wants things from Jason. So many things.

"Everything alright in there?" Jason calls. It's expected really, since Emerson has been in the bathroom an exceptionally long time just to brush his teeth and change. He tried to brush his hair too, but Jason's got something called a boar bristle brush. He says it's good for his short, mixed hair.

Emerson has never even heard of it, only knows it made his hair look like he stuck his finger in a light socket.

Accepting this is as good as it's going to get, he takes one final deep breath before reaching for the doorknob. *This is only Jason*, he reminds himself. Jason isn't going to judge Emerson's hair or anything else about him. Jason is a good man. He makes Emerson feel happy and safe in ways he didn't even know were possible. Still, he's never shared a bed with anyone. He has no idea what the social etiquette is in this situation. He wishes he did.

Twisting his fingers, he steps into the bedroom, exhaling a shuddering breath at what he sees. Stella is fast asleep on her dog bed in the corner along with Freddie. Emerson is curious how Jason got him to sleep there if he usually sleeps in the bed, but it's not something he's going to worry about right now, too grateful he will get Jason all to himself for this first night.

The blankets have been turned down, and there is one

pillow on each side of the bed, Sharky sitting directly in the middle.

"Wasn't sure what side of the bed you prefer. Didn't wanna put him on the wrong one."

That little part of Emerson that always feels a little bit wrong rights itself. He takes the five steps to the bed and drags Sharky to the left, away from the side of the bed with the window. The blinds might be shut, but Emerson has never been able to sleep near windows, and the fact that Jason is letting him choose, even though it's his bed, loosens the knot in his chest. Before he can crawl into bed, Jason is behind him, those strong hands of his on Emerson's hips as Jason's mouth moves to the back of his neck.

"Sorry," he murmurs.

"Are you really?"

Those big hands slide around to his tummy. He's a little too skinny, his hip bones jutting out and his skin soft and squishy despite his lack of body fat. When Jason's hands slide under the shirt, he half expects him to change his mind about what he feels, but instead his fingers spread wide as Jason lets out a contented sigh.

"You smell amazing."

"Thank you," Emerson says, blushing when Jason laughs. The vibrations of it against his back are as unfamiliar as the lips that kiss their way up to the shell of his ear.

"I don't think I ever thought about how good another man could smell. I've been missing out, clearly." Jason kisses the side of his neck once more as the tummy touches morph into a full body hug from behind. "I'm so glad you're here, Emmy."

The air in his lungs expels in a shuddering exhale. He's always loved Jason's hugs, but this is the first one from behind like this, and despite Emerson's impressive vocabulary, none of the words he possesses come close to accurately describing how good it feels. He's just so big, strong and warm. That part of Emerson's brain that is almost always in fight or flight registers safety in the most basic way. A hug has never felt so good, and Emerson lets his weight fall back, a small sound of surprise falling from his lips when Jason scoops him off the floor and carries him to the bed.

Jason is careful when he sets him down, his soft laughter as he tries to covertly climb over Emerson instead of going all the way around endearing.

"You're too big to sneak you know."

"I know, but I'm doing it anyway," Jason grins, ending up on top of Emerson, knees bracketing his own with one hand on either side of the pillow. "Hey there, handsome."

"Hi."

"There's a man in my bed," Jason says.

"You have very good observational skills."

Jason barks out a laugh, glancing over his shoulder when Freddie startles. He silences himself by lowering his face into Emerson's neck, the soft rumble of his continued amusement making Emerson smile.

Eventually Jason stops laughing, his words slightly garbled against the side of Emerson's neck; yet somehow he understands every single one. "I like you so much."

A simple confession, though the impact it has is anything but. Emboldened by the words, Emerson feels brave enough to touch the way he's wanted to since Jason's confession. He moves slowly almost as if afraid Jason might tell him to stop, even though he knows logically he won't, letting the tips of his fingers skim against Jason's belly where his shirt hangs loose.

"Is this—"

"Good," Jason finishes.

Emerson forgets to breathe when he inches his hands beneath the shirt in earnest, unprepared for Jason's hitch in breathing. He hasn't even done anything yet, barely skimming his fingers over the bit of hair from Jason's treasure trail above his boxers, but from the sound Jason makes, it's almost like Emerson is touching him somewhere far more salacious.

"Is this okay?" Emerson asks, unsure why he feels like he's doing something naughty just from his hands under Jason's shirt.

"Very fucking okay," Jason says, the pitch of his voice shaky when he pulls his face out of Emerson's neck to hover above him. "Full permission to touch me anywhere you want."

The weight of Jason's gaze is palpable, but the idea of eye contact right now, even with Jason, makes his skin feel itchy. He focuses instead on Jason's mouth, memorizing the shape of his lips and the dip of the dimple in his chin as he smiles down at Emerson.

Through skyrocketing nerves and growing arousal he continues, gliding his hands up Jason's belly. The skin is smooth then it's not, the hair all over Jason's chest a delight beneath his fingers. He knew Jason had chest hair—has seen it peeking out of the top of his shirts—but knowing something exists and feeling it are entirely different, and Emerson can't stop touching it, stroking his hands over the swell of his pecs and biting on his bottom lip.

Eager to touch more, he rucks the shirt up, exploring Jason's chest with eager eyes and equally eager hands—pausing just to stroke the hair on his chest.

"I can take my shirt off," Jason offers.

"Please," Emerson whispers, still not able to look him in the eyes.

For a disappointingly long few seconds, Jason is out of reach, sitting back on his heels to tug his shirt off in one swift go before he's tumbling down on top of Emerson again without an ounce of insecurity. Not that he has anything to be insecure about. Jason's body is a thing of glory, his biceps as massive as his broad chest and the muscles in his body honed from years of physical activity and dedication. There's nothing hard about him though, the places that might be nothing but muscle in someone else are softened by Jason's love of Pop-Tarts and that Mexican peanut butter candy that Emerson always forgets how to pronounce.

"I like snack time," Jason grins when Emerson's hands give his middle a squeeze.

"I like your body," Emerson replies. "It's big and strong and safe."

"Yeah?" Jason balances himself on one hand so his other can stroke the hair back on Emerson's head. "Not too big and hairy for you?"

Emerson shakes his head, ready to revel in Jason's body any way he's allowed. He wants to shove his face between the swell of his large pecs, to feel the scratch of all that chest hair against his cheeks. He wants to touch this big, beautiful man everywhere. Jason said sex didn't have to be on the table tonight, but Emerson has waited twenty-six years for this and he's pretty sure dying is a real possibility if he's not allowed to finally have sex.

With a sudden burst of clarity, Emerson knows exactly what he wants, but getting the words to come out doesn't seem to happen. The question is right there, hovering at the edge of his consciousness and sitting heavy on the tip of his tongue. Yet, no matter how many ways he rephrases it in his mind the words won't come out.

"If talking is too hard, you can just do whatever it is you're thinking about," Jason suggests.

Were it anyone else, Emerson might be alarmed at his mind being read, but this is Jason who knows him, who can likely tell from the way he's tapping his fingers against his chest and opening and closing his mouth that being verbal is suddenly far too difficult.

"How about this," Jason says, reaching for one of Emerson's fidgety hands and lifting it to his mouth. He kisses each finger before bringing it to his chest. "You just do what feels good, whatever that looks like. If I don't like it, which between you and me is statistically impossible if you're the one touching me, then I promise to tell you. Can we do that?"

Can Emerson do that? Can he just touch and explore without overthinking and worrying? Can he take what he wants without needing to ask permission or fear it's too much? Can he make Jason feel as good as he makes Emerson feel just through his existence? He isn't sure, but he wants to try.

"Emmy," Jason whispers, clearly unsure what to make of Emerson's silence. "I'm not going to rush you. We can take this as slow as you want."

Emerson shakes his head vehemently from side to side. Slow is not what he wants. He might be a virgin but it's not because he's averse to sex. He's just never met anyone who felt worth being this vulnerable with, but Jason makes the rush of arousal and anxiety bearable. It's not scary, not in the way he always feared it might be.

"Alright." Jason bends down kissing his forehead, then his nose. He kisses each of his cheeks then takes his lips in a kiss so sweet that Emerson's toes curl beneath the blankets they're tucked under.

There have been countless times in Emerson's life when he is hyper-aware of his own body, usually when overstimulated. Times he suddenly feels every place the seams of his clothing are touching him or the wind is too abrupt against his skin. Times where his heart seems to beat too fast for his own body or his senses are on high alert in the worst way possible.

He's hyper-aware of his body now, except it's not painful or uncomfortable; it's intoxicating.

All Jason is doing is kissing him, and Emerson can't keep still, the cool cotton of the sheets beneath his legs a stark contrast to the heat of Jason's body. He wants to feel more, doesn't want Jason holding himself up. He wants to be crushed under Jason's bulk, wants to feel those gloriously thick thighs and strong legs against his own. Jason's only wearing loose boxers, so if he changed the position, his legs might rub against Emerson's. The idea takes hold until Emerson is driven mad with the need to touch more.

Unable to put words to the desire he takes action, wrapping his own legs around Jason in a silent plea while tugging on his hips. Thankfully Jason seems to get the message, his kisses turning into moans when their clothed cocks rub together.

"You're hard," Jason marvels, as if he can't believe it. Emerson echoes the sentiment even if he can't seem to say it. Jason's erection is firm, clearly bigger than his own and every time Jason shifts, it rubs against him in the most delicious pressure.

If Emerson were a cat, he'd roll Jason over and rub himself all over him, but he's not sure if that would be weird. Except, Jason said he could do what he wanted. He promised to tell Emerson if he didn't like something and Emerson trusts that Jason meant it.

Summoning all of his courage, Emerson gives Jason's hips a push. For a second, Jason looks like a puppy someone kicked, confused and sad. Emerson doesn't give him time to worry, pushing him until their positions are reversed, and Jason is the one on his back with Emerson seated on his lap, Jason's cock firm beneath his ass. His dark hair is in disarray, his cheeks flushed and his chest heaving and Emerson feels more powerful than he ever has in his life.

Jason is wrecked from a few kisses, his boxers damp from his arousal, his body flushed and wanting. Emerson did this.

"I want to see if I can fit your cock in my mouth. It feels really big, so I probably can't, but I want to try."

Jason's mouth falls open, the pink on his cheeks deepening to a dusty rose that highlights the warmth in honey-sweet brown eyes. "Uh, yes. Definitely yes."

"I have a gag reflex and no idea what I'm doing," Emerson warns, not wanting him to get his hopes up. "But I won't throw up on your dick, I promise."

Jason laughs, and Emerson's chest warms because he knows Jason's laughter isn't directed at him. Jason laughs when he's happy, which is often, but knowing he's happy right now, half-dressed with Emerson still feels good.

"I'm pretty sure whatever you do to my dick, I'll thank you. Unless you bite it, that might hurt."

"I don't want to bite your cock," Emerson frowns. "Do people do that?"

"I had an ex-girlfriend that—you know what, we don't need to talk about that," Jason says with a shake of his head. "Just do what feels good."

He's glad Jason cut that off. Emerson isn't sure if it's

jealousy that one comment sparked or something else. All he knows is he doesn't want to think about the people who have touched Jason before, or he's going to compare himself to them. He wants to focus on them right now, just him and Jason, in Jason's bed. Together.

"I want to make you feel good," Emerson blurts, surprised at how easy the words come.

"My sweet Emmy."

"Say it again," Emerson begs.

"Emmy."

"Not that," Emerson whispers. "The other part."

"You mean the part where I called you mine?" Jason hand skims over his thighs, rubbing circles just beside his knee. "You want to be mine, Emmy?"

Emerson is quite certain he's never wanted anything more in his entire life than to belong to Jason. Which is saying a lot because Emerson has spent a lot of time over the years wishing for things he couldn't have.

"I'm probably going too fast." Emerson focuses on the callous on Jason's thumb and how it feels against his skin. "This is breaking the rules a bit, isn't it? We haven't even had our first date yet, and now we're going to have sex, and I'm asking for too much and—"

"Breathe, Emmy." Jason's voice is deep and even when he speaks, his thumb continues its ministrations. "For what it's worth, there are no rules in dating. Maybe more like a playbook."

"Isn't that the same thing?"

"Nope." Jason pops the *p* while bringing his other hand up to grip Emerson's hip. "A well-crafted playbook is crucial in football. It's full of offensive and defensive plays, along with formations and strategies."

"I don't think I understand what that has to do with sex."

"Nothing I guess, but everything too." Jason squeezes his hip. "The playbook offers structure and strategy to win games, but sometimes—sometimes you have to say fuck the playbook and just make the play."

"You're comparing me to football again, aren't you," Emerson says, unsure when that became endearing.

"What can I say, I'm a simple man. I know what I like." Jason's thumb hooks under Emerson's shirt and then below his waistband, a touch as teasing as it is grounding. "What I like is you, Emmy. Consider this me making my play."

Jason clears his throat, his handsome face becoming even more handsome with the breadth of the smile that spreads across it.

"Emerson Miller, I am a very not straight man—probably bisexual if you want to be specific, which I know you do—and I want you. I want you in whatever way I can have you. So if you ask if you can be mine, I'm going to tell you yes, because I'm over here wanting the same damn thing. Ask me, Emmy, please."

Heart in his throat, Emerson utters the five scariest words of his life. "Jason, can I be yours?"

"Yes, a million times, yes." Jason surges up, kissing Emerson with all the gusto and finesse that Emerson lacks. "Fuck, you're perfect."

"Think that's you," Emerson utters, kiss drunk and stupidly happy.

Impossibly, Jason's smile widens, his dimple on full display.

"I think I should have tried this gay thing sooner. Wait until I tell Theo. Ten out of ten."

"You're ridiculous," Emerson laughs.

"Did I make you laugh? I made you laugh!" Jason actually pumps his fist in the air, looking more like one of the teenagers on his team than a thirty year old man. Maybe that's what Emerson likes about him so much. He's never afraid to be excited or share his joy. He doesn't care about being superficial, only being real. "Hell yeah. My first gay kiss, my first boyfriend, and now I made you laugh. This is the best day of my life."

"Boyfriend," Emerson croaks.

Jason stills, hand hovering in midair. He drops it to the back of Emerson's neck, smoothing his fingers back and forth. "Um, yes? I thought that was kind of what the '*be mine*' thing meant. That's what it meant right?"

"I've never had a boyfriend," Emerson whispers, unsure if he wants to smile or cry or hide.

"Me either," Jason says, curling the fingers around his neck and offering one of those firm, reassuring touches that Emerson likes so much. "We can figure it out together though. I bet we're going to be fucking awesome at being boyfriends."

As always, Jason's conviction is unshakable, and it soothes the part of Emerson that needs to know what to expect. Whatever happens, good or bad, he knows Jason isn't going anywhere.

If Jason King were a book boyfriend, he'd almost think he was too perfect. Except Jason isn't a character in one of Emerson's fictional stories. He doesn't have to fall asleep with the words of his favorite novels in his head, imagining what life might be like if he were better at being a person or if he had someone who cared about him. This is real life, and it's better than anything off the pages of one of his books. *Jason* is better because he's real.

Emerson desperately wants to feel that realness. He

wants to feel every inch of Jason's perfectly imperfect body, to feel his dips and hollows, the muscle and softness. He wants to hear the rich timber of Jason's voice, to know what another man—what his *boyfriend*—looks like when he comes.

For the first time in Emerson's life, he wants to try something messy, emotionally and physically. He wants to taste Jason's release, wants to sleep in a bed that's not his own, in the arms of the one person who feels more like home than anyplace in his entire life ever has.

Emerson wants to love Jason King. Emerson *does* love Jason King. That, certainly, is too soon to say. So he says something wildly different instead.

"Can I still suck your cock, please?"

Emerson holds his breath, heart thundering against his ribcage. For a dizzying second, he feels like maybe he might pass out, and he really wishes that his brain understood that fight or flight is meant for actual near death experiences and not asking if you can suck your first dick.

"I think that's the most polite proposition ever directed my way."

"Is that a yes then?" Emerson prompts, seeking a more explicit answer despite Jason's earlier consent.

"It's a yes." Jason's eyes crinkle, his hands roaming over Emerson's side. "Everything is a yes with you. Today, tomorrow—yes."

"Remember, I'm going to be bad at this." Emerson scoots down Jason's body and settles in the space between the spread of his legs. "I'll learn though."

"Whatever you do, I'm going to like," Jason assures him. "I'm uh, embarrassingly close to coming already. Just fair warning."

"But I haven't done anything yet."

"I know," Jason huffs. "I don't think I've been this turned on since I was a teenager, sneaking extra boxes of tissues and lotion into my room so my parents wouldn't know what I was doing. Except this is better because it's not my right hand, it's you. Sorry, I'm talking too much, aren't I?"

"I like that you talk a lot," Emerson admits, skimming his fingers over Jason's stomach. It quivers under his touch, and he curls his fingers under the waistband, heart in his throat when Jason lifts his ass so Emerson can tug them down. It requires a bit of maneuvering to get them all the way off, but when he does, there is very little oxygen left in his lungs and all the blood in his body has gone south, south, south.

If Jason in nothing but his boxers was a sight, then Jason completely naked is his every fantasy come to life. The treasure trail he saw a peek of above Jason's boxers is on full display now, the path leading down, growing thicker and darker. Emerson's eyes trail lower until they settle on where Jason's cock is nestled in a thick patch of dark hair, its girth as impressive as the rest of Jason.

Eager to touch, he lets his hands wrap around it, marveling at how thick it is and how little of it he can cover with one hand. Jason makes a strangled moan when Emerson strokes up, the hold loose and exploratory as he focuses on the sensory delight of Jason's erection in his palm.

Touching another man's dick is very different from his own; Jason's is thicker, with the foreskin at the end that exposes the slit with every downward stroke.

Curious, Emerson bends down, letting his tongue dart out to lap at the precome that's collected there. Jason lets out a low string of expletives that Emerson is ninety-nine percent sure are in Spanish and also likely meant to be favorable, if the way Jason's big body quivers is any indication.

Delighted by the feeling beneath his fingers, and the way Jason falls apart, he wonders what will happen when he actually puts his mouth on it. Bending himself in half, he means to swallow Jason's cock—or at the very least the tip of it—but almost immediately gets distracted by his body hair. The dark curls surrounding his dick are so different from the wavy hair on Jason's head or the soft fuzz on his chest. Without even consciously making the choice, Emerson's hand relaxes its hold on Jason in favor of letting his fingers drag through the hair around the thick base.

Wondering if it might feel the same against his cheek, Emerson lays himself flat on the mattress, long legs hanging off the end of the bed so that he can rub his cheek against it. The position is definitely awkward but oddly satisfying, since the base of Jason's cock butts up against his mouth and other cheek, flooding his olfactory senses with the thick scent of Jason's arousal. This close the scent is stronger and sharper, but not at all unpleasant, and Emerson breathes in a shuddery breath, his own dick achingly hard in his boxers.

The softness of Jason's skin is a contrast to the coarse hair around the base of his erection, and Emerson lets himself explore, hand trailing up and down in lazy strokes as he mouths against the side and watches a bit more precome dribble down, glistening over the thick vein that runs along the underside of his cock.

It's not until Jason makes an inhuman sound halfway between a grunt and a whimper that it occurs to Emerson he's probably not doing a very good job. He hasn't actually done more than stroke and lick, and he kind of even forgot he was supposed to be making Jason come, more interested in the sensory experience of touching another man, especially one with a lot more body hair.

"Sorry," Emerson huffs, wiping away the spit that's dripped down the side of his chin on the back of his arm.

"I'm not sorry, that was great," Jason grunts

"You liked it? I wasn't sure if, well—it's not weird?" Emerson presses, wanting the truth even while he dreads it if the answer isn't the one he wants. He rises onto his hands and knees, eyeing Jason's cock with a fortifiable mix of desire and apprehension, unsure how exactly he's supposed to fit it in his mouth.

"There is nothing weird about you, but shit—watching you just touch me like that. No one has ever touched my body the way you did just now. It took every ounce of self control I have not to come watching those pretty hands and mouth of yours."

"You really liked it?"

"Are you pressing for praise? Because I'm more than happy to give it," Jason smirks, rising onto his elbows. There's a light sheen of sweat on his face, and his cheeks are flushed. "You give the best dick fondles ever. Ten out of ten."

"You gave being gay a ten out of ten too. You're not very discerning."

"You're using very large words right now and expecting me to reply to them while you're in my bed, wearing my clothes, looking sexy as hell."

"Was that a question or a statement?"

"I don't know," Jason laughs, throwing his arm over his face. "I'm just trying not to embarrass myself by coming like a teenager all over your hands or face."

"It would be very flattering if you did that," Emerson

says, shocked at his own boldness. "Also, I uh, would not mind if you came on my face."

Jason groans loudly. "Emmy, you're going to kill me."

"Death by sex sounds like a satisfying way to go."

"I can see the headline now: local high school teacher and football coach Jason King—who spent the first thirty years of his life thinking he was straight—had his bisexual awakening due to the new teacher at school. Sources close to Mr. King tell us he liked gay sex so much that he came too hard and—" Jason makes a croaking noise, falling back on the bed.

It is so entirely ridiculous that Emerson laughs, harder and deeper than he's laughed since he was a child. He falls on his side, turning his head to muffle the sound in the mattress when one of the dogs barks. Jason says something that quiets them down, and before Emerson knows what's happening, Jason's big hands are under his armpits hefting him up the bed until they're sharing one pillow and laughing quietly.

"I didn't know sex could be fun," Emerson whispers.

"Me either," Jason says, nudging his nose into Emerson's face. "I knew it'd be good though, with you."

"Does it count as sex if neither of us have come though?" Emerson asks, squinting down between their bodies. Jason's still gloriously naked, but Emerson's boxers are damp in the front from his arousal and Jason's shirt, while comfortable, is getting in the way of him being able to rub more of his body against Jason's.

"Sex can be whatever we want, but if you're open to both of us coming, preferably soon, I would be very on board with that."

"Can I be naked, too?"

"Can you—fuck, yes." Jason's hands fly down to Emerson's shirt, all but yanking it off him, quickly followed by his boxers. "Naked Emmy time, please and thank you."

Emerson laughs again, unsure if he's ever felt so happy in his entire life. He knows the answer when Jason hefts Emerson on top of him, their bodies pressed together from the tips of Emerson's toes to their chests. Every bit of the contact is glorious, the firmness of Jason's leaking dick so different to the softness at his belly.

"Oh," Emerson gasps, eyes nearly rolling in the back of his head when Jason holds onto Emerson's hips and moves him up and down to rut their bare cocks together. "*Oh.*"

"Theo told me about this. He said it felt good." Jason continues to move him, dragging their erections together with every roll of his hips and pulling on Emerson's. "He was right."

"I like frottage," Emerson whines.

"Me too," Jason grits, fingers curling around Emerson's hips in the most gloriously possessive hold. Everything in Emerson's brain short circuits, the glide of skin on skin and cock on cock along with Jason's labored breathing is all it takes for his inexperience to show. When he comes, it's with a bitten off cry he tries to silence in Jason's neck. Through it all, Jason murmurs soft words of praise while stroking up and down Emerson's back in a way that makes him want to stay glued to Jason and never move. Something that very well might happen if he doesn't move and all the come dries on him. There's also the part where Jason hasn't come yet.

Determined to make Jason feel at least half as good as Jason made him feel, he pulls away, moving only enough to get his hands on Jason again. Emerson gives him a few strokes, watching the way Jason's thick thighs tremble before getting a jolt of confidence that he doesn't expect, slinking his way down Jason's body and engulfing as much of his cock as he can. It's not very much because Emerson's mouth is not at all big enough to accommodate Jason's girth in circumference or length, but he gets a good two inches down, which he's really proud of.

Three things rapidly become apparent. One, Emerson's gag reflex is a little more sensitive than he thought. Two, despite discovery number one, he likes the feel of Jason in his mouth, hot, heavy and thick with a salty tang. Three, and this one is the most pressing, Jason wasn't kidding when he said he was close.

"Emmy—" he gets out, fingers curling in Emerson's hair to give him a warning tug.

Unsure if he wants to try and swallow or pull back, he ends somewhere in the awkward middle, swallowing down a rather large mouthful of Jason's release while the rest of it lands on his cheeks and chin.

"Holy shit," Jason groans, petting the side of Emerson's face. "That was the single hottest thing that's ever happened to me."

Again, Emerson questions Jason's judgment, but there seems little point in voicing that out loud when it always seems to work in Emerson's favor. That and the fact that Jason looks entirely blissed out while his come drips off Emerson's face leads him to believe he wasn't entirely horrible at it.

"I would definitely do that again," Emerson muses. "Though I wouldn't mind some water. I think come makes me thirsty."

"Give me thirty seconds to regain feeling in my legs and I'll get you water." Jason offers two thumbs up along with a self-satisfied grin that makes Emerson feel as good as the shared orgasm had.

True to his word, Jason departs just half a minute later,

dropping a kiss on the top of Emerson's head before he climbs out of bed. He heads to the bathroom, leaving the door cracked just enough that the light from the bathroom filters into the bedroom. While he listens to the sound of running water, he tries to focus, but his brain is a scattered mess of things like *you sucked a cock,* to *Jason smells good,* to *you're not a virgin anymore.* At least he doesn't think so. The parameters surrounding someone losing their virginity always sounded incredibly vague to Emerson, who never understood how you could lose something that was technically not real.

When the bed dips signaling Jason's return, he turns to find Jason wearing a new pair of boxers and nothing else, unless you count his smile. In his hand is a glass of water and a damp washcloth which he brings to Emerson's face first, wiping it over his sticky chin before passing him the water. Emerson gulps it down with a thirst he's rarely experienced. To Emerson's surprise and pleasure, once he's finished Jason continues to clean him. The cloth is delightfully warm against his skin and the fact that Jason took the time to warm the water before bringing it to clean him off makes him want to hide under the pillow. Unable to look Jason in the eyes, he squeezes his shut instead. One of the stories his mom liked to tell him was about the time he'd wanted a waffle after bedtime and snuck into the kitchen, certain if his eyes were shut and he couldn't see her that she couldn't see him. This feels adjacent to that. Jason is still here, he knows he is from the hand settled on his thigh to the gentle way he draws the warm washcloth over Emerson's belly. It's just that somehow it feels safer if he can't see him.

"Do you want your phone?"

"No," Emerson whispers, feeling a bit ridiculous. He

wishes he could explain why talking is okay, but only if he's not looking at Jason.

In the beginning, Emerson had been sure once Jason saw him deregulated or overwhelmed, had to deal with the parts of his autism that weren't useful or quirky, he might grow weary of them, of him. But somehow, Jason makes Emerson feel as accepted now as he does when Emerson's able to function more like everyone else. Amazing as that is, it makes him want to hide even more. Sure it's only Jason, and yes he's safe, but being perceived after that kind of vulnerability makes his skin crawl, and Emerson squeezes his eyes shut. Somehow the simple act of not making any eye contact is what allows him to keep up the conversation.

"Is it okay if I keep talking?" Jason moves the washcloth lower, lifting Emerson's cock to clean around the base and up to the tip. There is nothing remotely sexual about the touch, yet it's as affecting as the orgasm, maybe even more so, albeit in a different way. "You can push me out of the bed if the answer is no. That's what my brothers used to do when we were kids. Well Charlie anyway, antagonistic asshole."

"M'not gonna push you out of the bed," Emerson mumbles.

"Well that's a relief. I mean you could if you needed to, but the ground is cold, and my ass might be big but that would hurt." Jason continues to wipe Emerson clean even though he's certain he must be done by now. "I liked what we did. A lot. Not just because of the orgasm, which was good. Did I mention it was ten out of ten?"

The hint of a smile plays at Emerson's lips, some of his anxiety fading with every swipe of the warmth cloth against his clammy skin. "You did."

"Good because you know that was outstanding. We

definitely are very good at sex. If there were awards, I would give them to us."

Part of Emerson wants to point out that ninety-nine percent of that is likely because Jason has more experience than him, but he doesn't, because Jason's other hand has started giving him some kind of one-handed deep pressure massage, making thinking difficult. Not a minute later, Jason drops the washcloth and uses both hands, digging into the tight muscles of Emerson's shoulders.

"I didn't know sex came with massages," Emerson murmurs, pretty close to drooling. Jason has magic hands, that's the only explanation for all the tingles of pleasure in his body right now. Nothing has ever felt this good, ever, which is saying something since he just had another man's cock against his own.

"I aim to please," Jason says, the sound of his delight evident in the pitch of his voice. "Only the best for you. Orgasm, clean up, *and* a massage. It's the boyfriend package."

Warmth floods Emerson's chest, white hot and blinding, and before he knows what he's doing, he's rolled over so he can shove his face into the pillow.

"That was a very not subtle plea for a back massage, which I will happily oblige."

"I wasn't—" Emerson starts intending to correct Jason. His brain has other plans however, all coherent thoughts leaving his body when Jason's strong hands dig into the tight muscles in his upper back. "You hunch over your desk and books too much, Emmy. I'll need to work these muscles out for you more, maybe daily."

"Nngghh," Emerson grunts.

Jason straddles his thighs, swiping his hands up and down Emerson's back alternating between massaging the muscles and soothing strokes that have Emerson boneless and melting into the mattress.

A single kiss is pressed to his spine. "Mine."

Another kiss to his shoulder. "My Emmy."

One to the other side. "My boyfriend."

A trail of kisses up his spine until Jason stops, lips hovering where Jason's hand often rests. "My beautiful, perfect Emerson."

When the tears fall, they're not sad or broken, just a release—a tight unfurling of the emptiness that's sat inside of him for so long. With every tender kiss and stroke of big hands, Jason strips away more than fatigue from his muscles.

Emerson's last thought before sleep claims him is that maybe this is what it feels like to be loved.

18 JASON

"EMMY?"

Jason leans forward, pausing the massage to stare at Emerson. He's had his eyes shut for a while in what Jason assumed was a means to regulate, but now his jaw is slack, and his left hand is curled under his chin while tiny little puffs of air come out. It occurs to him that Emerson fell asleep.

Seeing Emerson all cozy in his bed rewires Jason's brain, a million little things clicking into place. This right here is where Emerson belongs, in his bed, in his home. Along with this realization comes a host of insecurities about whether he's falling too fast and panic about why he *isn't* panicking over not realizing he isn't straight until now, when he is thirty. It's the kind of self-doubt and unease only one person can help soothe.

Jason rolls out of bed, drawing the covers over Emerson's naked form. Not entirely satisfied, he makes a trip to the hall closet to retrieve an extra soft blanket, returning to his bedroom to drape it over Emerson's slumbering form. He stays for a few seconds to appreciate how beautiful

Emerson looks even in the dark before tiptoeing from the room to find his phone, left on the charger in the living room.

A quick glance at the lock screen lets him know it's past midnight. Theo is going to be asleep. He calls anyway. While the phone rings, Jason paces, unable to get the mental image of Emerson kneeling between his legs out of his head.

"Hello," Theo slurs, definitely half-asleep.

"Who the fuck is calling in the middle of the night?" Alec grouches, sounding distinctly put out at being woken up.

"It's Jason," Theo answers.

"What's wrong?" Alec asks, sounding very alert.

"Nothing is wrong," Jason answers, even though the question was directed at Theo. "I just wanted to talk."

"Nothing is wrong," Theo relays to Alec. "He wanted to talk to me."

"In the middle of the night? Codependent fuckers," Alec grumbles. From the sound of it, he's kicking at the blankets. He never has handled being woken up well, and Jason would feel more guilty if he didn't desperately need to talk to his best friend. Besides, Theo was his first, and tonight definitely calls for utilizing best friend privileges.

"Go to sleep, Alexander," Theo whispers. The phone temporarily goes on mute, and Jason is grateful he doesn't have to hear what is likely Theo kissing his baby brother. A minute later the phone unmutes. "Okay I went into the living room. What's up? Couldn't sleep after a wild night chaperoning. Did you—"

"I had gay sex," Jason blurts.

The line goes very quiet. Too quiet for Jason's liking.

"Say something, Theo."

"I'm trying to figure out if I'm supposed to pretend to be surprised."

"Of course you are," Jason gapes.

"Right," Theo says, in that gentle tone of his. "I am so completely shocked about this. How is Emerson?"

"How do you know it was Emerson?" Jason asks.

"I don't think I'm a good enough actor for this," Theo laughs. "Listen uh, you were kind of—possessive over him, you know?"

"No, I don't know," Jason replies, unsure how to handle this. He thought Theo would be surprised. Why isn't Theo surprised?

"You touched him a lot and stared too and you—Jason, you cuddled him all night."

"He likes being touched," Jason grumbles.

"Which is fine, it's not bad, but you never even touched your ex-girlfriends that much. Incidentally, that brings me to my second point. You've never invited any of your exes over for pizza night with me. Ever."

"Well, uh—" Jason stops, thinking it over. Is Theo right? It hadn't been an active choice, but they'd all always been jealous of his closeness with Theo no matter how often he told them he wasn't in love with him. Though he'd never told Theo, it'd been a big reason more than one of his past relationships ended. The moment a girlfriend asked him to pick between her and his best friend, it was no competition. Jason had plenty of room in his heart for all the people he loved, but if someone demanded he pick, it was always going to be Theo.

"Jason, I mean this in the nicest way possible," Theo says in that same tone he uses when he's telling Alec something he thinks he might over react to. "You have never seemed—straight."

"Excuse me?"

Theo sighs. "It's not a bad thing, but any time I brought it up you shut me down saying you could be a passionate ally so I was never going to push but—"

"You knew I was bisexual," Jason blurts. The second he says it a smile spreads across his face despite the absurdity of his current conversation. This is the first time he's said it out loud, and he likes the way it sounds. He likes the way it feels.

"I mean, I didn't know what label to give it because you never wanted to talk about it, and you didn't seem interested in taking home any of the men you'd ogle."

"I didn't ogle men." At Theo's snort, Jason concedes. "Fine, maybe I did, but I was checking them out for you. I was a good wingman."

"The best wingman," Theo agrees. "The best friend. And also...not a very straight thing to do. You used to bet me which one of us could get more phone numbers."

"Oh my god, Theo. I'm bisexual."

"Welcome to the team."

"I had gay sex," Jason hisses, because even though he's in the dark living room and Emerson and the dogs are asleep, he feels like he should be whispering.

"Sex is sex," Theo laughs. "But uh, how was it?"

"Fucking fantastic. I should've had gay sex sooner. You were right by the way, frottage is amazing. What else should we try? Wait, don't answer that because anything you tell me I'm going to know you do with Alec, and I don't want to know that. In fact, don't ever give me any gay sex tips."

"No gay sex tips, got it," Theo replies, sounding like he's trying not to laugh. "But Jason?"

"Yeah?"

"I'm really proud of you. I'd hug you if I could." All of

Jason's unease melts at those two sentences. He really loves his best friend. He knew he'd make everything better.

"I like him, Theo." Jason breathes in deeply, rubbing his hand over his jaw while pacing back and forth in front of the fireplace. "I like him so much. *Shit.*"

"I know, Jason." Theo's voice is warm, familiar, and though Jason never had a doubt that his best friend would support him, his easy acceptance provides the exact comfort Jason needed. "I'm happy for you."

Jason stares down the darkened hallway, as if only now realizing he's in the living room alone when he could be in bed cuddling his boyfriend. His naked, sleepy, perfect boyfriend. What the fuck is he doing?

"Theo, I have to go."

"Sure." Theo yawns loudly, the sound crackling through the phone. "You'll call me later?"

"Yeah, of course. I love you."

"Love you too, Jason."

With that Jason clicks off his phone, dropping it at the charging station before hurrying back to the bedroom. Even in the dim light, Emerson's shock of red hair stands out like a beacon against his cream sheets—nothing but his cute nose and mess of hair visibly peeking out from the blankets. This time he's not alone though because apparently while Jason was in the living room, Freddie snuck into the bed, curled up not in Jason's spot but rather next to Emerson's back which further cements his earlier thoughts. This right here is exactly where Emerson belongs, and Jason is going to do whatever it takes to keep him.

Careful not to disturb Emerson or Freddie, he slowly lifts the blankets to slip inside. Emerson grunts quietly, mouth falling open to let out a bit of drool. It's quite possibly the most adorable thing Jason has ever seen, and he's not sure what to make of that feeling since most of the time with his exes, he felt mildly annoyed when they wanted to sleep over. Though that likely was because they always wanted to kick his dogs out of the bedroom, which made Jason want to kick them out instead.

As with all other aspects of his life, Emerson fits—as if he was always meant to be here.

In his sleep, Emerson shifts, and Jason takes the opportunity to pull Emerson's leg over his hip while slipping his arm around Emerson's middle to pull him as close to his own body as possible. The warmth of Emerson's smooth, bare skin against his own and the soft puffs of air against his neck lull Jason into a relaxed state. Breathing in Emerson's scent, Jason drops another kiss to the top of Emerson's head before closing his eyes.

SOMETHING very wiggly and warm wakes Jason up and it is not, much to his disappointment, a sexy naked redhead but rather a one-hundred pound dog with horrible morning breath. This alone is enough to make Jason frown, his displeasure turning into a full on groan when Stella howls at the same time that Freddie licks his mouth in a silent but wet morning greeting.

"Seriously you guys." Jason wipes away the drool, trying to guess what time it is. Judging by the light peeking through his window it's still pretty early, though not too early for his babies to make their displeasure at not having food and attention known. The one downside to having an early morning routine during the school year is that his dogs do not understand what a weekend is, and sleeping in is never an option.

In true, part-husky fashion Stella starts some combination of bark-howling that feels very much like *where is my breakfast, Dad.* Squinting over Emerson to see the clock, Jason sees why.

"My bad, it's a whole four minutes past when you usually eat. Did you die?"

Stella howls again as if to say yes, while Freddie flops in between Jason and Emerson, using Emerson's head as a chair so he can try and crawl on Jason's chest.

"Yes, yes, you missed me. You were so far away, weren't you, you giant baby." Freddie chuffs and Jason can't even be bothered because Freddie might be a giant baby, but he's Jason's giant baby. "Let's maybe not use Emerson's head as a chair though, huh?"

"M'fine," Emerson mumbles, but judging from the muffled words, his face is either shoved into the pillow or under Freddie and neither seem comfortable.

"That's it, no assaulting the boyfriend. We want him to come back, Freddie. A lot. You be a good boy, huh?"

Any fear Jason had that waking up to the chaos that is his two dogs might be too much is assuaged when Emerson's head pops up from beneath his blanket cocoon. His hair is even more wild than usual, pillow lines on his face, along with a very confused expression like he's not entirely sure why he's awake. He doesn't complain though, just pats Freddie.

"You're always a good boy, aren't you?"

Freddie's tail wags so hard at the praise it whacks Emerson in the neck.

"Freddie," Jason tries, but Freddie is already turning around clearly realizing there's a new human willing to baby him. "Careful, Emmy, he's gonna try to keep you forever now."

"That doesn't sound so bad." Emerson's little frown is still in place, but Jason can tell from the relaxed tone of his voice that he's happy, especially when he closes his eyes to rest his forehead against Freddie's while petting him. "I always wanted dogs growing up, but my aunt and uncle said no. I love dogs."

They can be yours, Jason almost blurts, unsure if it's considered love bombing to all but ask your new boyfriend —who you haven't technically even gone on one date with yet—to move in. He wants to do anything to make sure Emerson knows he's wanted, to spend as much time as possible with this perfect person who likes his dogs, his family and makes him laugh and smile, makes him so fucking happy he can't stop smiling.

"What?" Emerson asks.

Jason has the decency to blush at being caught staring.

"You're just beautiful, I—"

Stella howls loudly.

"I think someone else needs you," Emerson points out.

He doesn't look annoyed or put out, merely watches Jason, while continuing to pet Freddie.

"I'm going to leave this bed, but only because Stella will be unbearable if she doesn't eat in the next few minutes." He turns to look at Stella, who doesn't look at all abashed by the commotion she's making. He turns his attention back to Emerson, delighted to notice the blankets have been pushed aside by Freddie, revealing Emerson's upper body. Jason has never wanted to put something in his mouth more than Emerson's pretty pale nipples, or the flat of his belly or the cock hidden under the sheets that Jason barely got to look at last night. Enough of a peek, at least, that he knows it's slimmer and smaller than his own and nestled in dark red hair that

Jason would do anything, *anything* to get his hands and mouth on again.

"You're staring," Emerson points out.

"I know," Jason groans, wishing he had more than his boxers on. Then again, nothing he owns could hide how hard he is right now. "When I come back from feeding these little menaces, I'm going to have my wicked way with you."

"I don't know if that was supposed to be a promise or a threat," Emerson says, the end of his nose crinkling in clear confusion.

"A promise," Jason clarifies, leaning over Freddie to kiss Emerson's nose. Since he's already there, he kisses his mouth too, greedily swallowing down the soft little sigh of contentment Emerson makes. If he fit, he would crawl into Emerson's lap and rub off on him like they did last night, might even come in his boxers from how turned on he is already. That is, if Freddie didn't literally jump up between them demanding kisses of his own and letting out a pitiful howl of jealousy.

"He's so adorable," Emerson says, kissing the top of Freddie's head.

Jason wants to cry, though whether from sexual frustration or cuteness he's not sure. Maybe both. When Emerson flops back on the bed and stretches, kicking the blanket down far enough to expose his sharp hip bones and the trail of red curls, Jason nearly growls. He's never hated training his dogs to eat on a schedule to help with his morning routine more than he does at this moment, when the only thing he wants to eat is his boyfriend.

Suddenly, he can't stop thinking about a conversation he had with his brothers and Theo last year about Alec's protein shakes tasting like ass. His curiosity about how Emerson might taste, along with his eagerness to explore both his newfound sexuality and his boyfriend, has to wait though. At least, until he can feed the two noisy bosses of the house.

"Come on then," Jason says, clapping his hands and all but leaping from the bed. "Breakfast."

Not wanting to waste a second, Jason skips coffee and goes straight for the dog food, filling both their bowls then refreshing their water. He also adds a few treats to Stella's puzzle feeder and leaves two new rawhide bones in front of the fireplace, not above bribing his babies to get some alone time with Emerson.

Quickening his steps, Jason hurries down the hallway and back into the bedroom, shutting the door as quietly as possible. When he turns to face the bed, it's to find Emerson's long arms and legs outstretched across the bed, his face shoved in the pillow and his bedhead standing every which way. Emerson opens his eyes to stare at him, and something possessive and desperate flares in Jason.

Emerson is in his bed, naked, beautiful and so trusting. That's his boyfriend. Jason essentially vaults into the bed, the mattress bouncing as he climbs over Emerson and kicks the blankets off, eager to get his eyes on all of Emerson's gorgeous skin. His cock is half-hard, laying against his slim thigh and Jason reaches for it, little shivers of pleasure at how easily it fits in his own large hand. He gives it a cursory stroke and groans at the way it feels to have another man's dick hardening in his palm.

"So you were serious before," Emerson gasps.

"I mean everything I say," Jason reminds him, nuzzling into Emerson's neck and mouthing at his throat. "Can I have my way with you? I want to see what you like. I want to learn how to make you feel good."

"Yes," Emerson shudders, spreading his legs wide. "Oh."

He's fully hard now, still smaller than Jason, the perfect size for Jason to jerk off. He gives it a few more lazy strokes, staring between their bodies as he watches the way Emerson's cock—flushed such a pretty pink and leaking—looks every time it peeks through his fist.

"I wanna do everything with you," Jason confesses, more turned on than he thought possible from staring at a dick that isn't his own. If he had any doubts about his own sexuality, the desperation he feels to get his mouth on Emerson's ass and dick would clear it up. He is absolutely, one-thousand percent bisexual. "I want to taste you, everywhere. I want to blow you and rim you and then one day, when you're ready, maybe fuck you. If you'd like that. I know not all gay men like penetration so if you don't, that's okay. There's something called intercrural that would be fun and—"

"Jason," Emerson groans, his delicate fingers curling tightly in Jason's hair.

Jason lets Emerson pull his head back, tearing his eyes away from Emerson's pretty cock to look at his equally pretty face. "Yeah, Emmy?"

"If you keep talking about those things, I'm going to come."

"I want you to come," Jason says.

"Well, me too," Emerson huffs, his chest flushed pink. "But um, I want—can I—Why is this hard to say out loud?"

"Anything, Emmy."

Emerson squeezes his eyes shut. "Please fuck me."

Jason nearly nuts in his boxers. "Are you sure?"

"I've never been more sure of anything in my life. I've touched myself. I have a toy. Trust me, I like it. I want to know if it feels the same with someone real. I want—I want you, Jason. I want you inside of me when I come. Please."

He says it as if he needs to beg, as if Jason wouldn't cut open his own heart and give it to Emerson if he asked. It's absolutely terrifying, not because Jason has never fucked a man before, but because he's never fucked someone he loves. The realization should maybe feel scarier, or more confusing, but just like when he accepted his bisexuality, it just feels right. There's no panic, no questioning, just the knowledge that yes, this is who Jason is, who he's always been.

"Is that okay?" Emerson asks, peeking at Jason through one cracked eye.

Jason surges up to kiss him, pinning Emerson to the bed. "The most okay thing ever."

"Do you have, um—"

"Yes," Jason finishes, flinging an arm out to the bedside table and digging out the lube he bought.

"Have you uh, you know."

"I've never fucked a man," Jason offers, "or had anal."

"So it's a first for both of us," Emerson says.

"You're my first in so many ways, Emmy." Jason kisses him again, drunk on the soft sighs Emerson makes. He could kiss Emerson forever, but there's something very hard poking into his hip, and he wants to give Emerson everything he wants.

"Be gentle please," Emerson murmurs.

"Always gentle with you," Jason whispers, peppering kisses across his jaw. He smooths the hair off his face, kissing both closed eyes and the center of his brow.

"Okay."

"You're in control, Emmy." Jason kisses his lips once more, a promise. "I know this is new, and that sometimes that can feel scary for you so just remember you're in charge, okay? If it hurts or you change your mind, we can stop any time."

"I'm in charge," Emerson repeats, somehow making it sound like a question. "Should I prep myself so you don't have to?"

"No," Jason answers, scooting down the bed. He had no idea that he'd ever put his history of hearing about Theo's teenage discovery of the male anatomy or one night stands exploration to practical use, but turns out growing up with a bisexual best friend with a preference for men is going to help Jason lose his gay virginity.

In hindsight, his interest in Theo's experiences, which he chalked up to them being the best of friends, maybe should've been an earlier tip-off about being less than straight. Not that Jason is going to worry about that right now, or ever really. The past is in the past, and his future is right here, trembling beneath him as eager and wanting as Jason.

"If I do something wrong, just tell me."

"I'm not exactly the paragon of sexual expertise."

"No, you didn't have this on your list?" Jason asks, kissing Emerson's hip. "Which, by the way, we never got to discuss."

"This was on the list. Top of the list," Emerson huffs, eyes open now and fixed directly on the ceiling. "You kissing me was there and touching me, sucking me. But the very top of the list—that was you and me having sex. I suppose technically, it's all sex, but I wanted you on top of me, *inside* of me. At first I didn't imagine I was allowed to think about wanting you like this, but now I can, and it's literally all I can picture. Especially now that I've seen you. You're so big, and I want to be full of you, and I know it's going to feel so good. I just want you to make me feel good. Is that selfish?"

"If it is, please be selfish," Jason tells him, kissing his way across the flat of Emerson's belly from hip to hip before nuzzling his face against Emerson's erection. A bit of precome dribbles out the tip and Jason licks it, humming to himself at the unexpected saltiness. "I feel like with enough practice, I am going to be excellent at blow jobs."

Emerson makes a choked sound, throwing his arm over his face. "If I look at you, I'm going to come."

"That's very good for my ego," Jason laughs, as horny as he is happy. He moves down, dragging his tongue from the base of Emerson's erection to the tip, circling the crown with his tongue and lapping up the come that's dripping out of the tip. "Mhmm, definitely like dicks."

"Oh my god," Emerson groans.

"Not god, only Jason."

"You—Jason!" Emerson's body shaking with laughter. He stops suddenly, peering down at Jason but just as quickly he covers his face again with his arm before mumbling, "I didn't know it would be like this."

"That it would feel good?" Jason asks with the start of a frown.

"No, that it would be...fun," Emerson whispers. "I thought—if I ever found someone I trusted enough it might be awkward because you know—I don't have experience, and I talk too much or not at all, and I can't look at you. I want to look at you, but the idea of making eye contact right now makes me feel like I might be sick. Oh, that's bad. I'm sorry, I don't mean—"

"You're okay, Emmy." Jason kisses the inside of his thigh, spreading his legs apart. "I like you when you can't stop talking and when the words won't come, and I like you when you stare at me so hard I feel like you're trying to see my soul and when you squeeze those pretty eyes of yours shut. Whatever version of you I get, it's still you, still my Emmy."

Emerson's jaw trembles, his other hand flying out in search of Jason who reaches for it. He links their fingers, bringing their joined hands to his lips.

"My Emmy."

"Yours," Emerson whispers, squeezing Jason's hand so tightly it almost hurts.

"Scared?" Jason asks.

"Terrified," Emerson admits. "I'm sorry."

"Nothing wrong with being scared. I tell my kids that all the time," Jason tells him. "Sometimes being scared just means you've got something worth losing. But you're not going to lose me, alright? We're in this together and maybe we'll be kind of horrible at it, but I'm willing to practice. A lot. I volunteer to practice the gay sex with you every day."

"It's still just sex," Emerson corrects.

"I know but it's fun to say gay sex," Jason laughs, adding a generous amount of lube to his fingers. Before he brings them down to Emerson's ass, he drops onto his stomach, needing to know once and for all what he tastes like there. "Can I?"

"Can you—oh, uh—yes."

Permission granted Jason dives in, burying his face in the spread of Emerson's legs and mouthing at his crease. He ends up needing to use both hands, making a bit of a mess of Emerson he'll clean later. For now, he focuses on spreading him apart so he can mouth at his hole—finding that, much like having his tongue on a cock, he likes it. There's something intimate about it and powerful too.

Above him, Emerson is whimpering and writhing, and

it's all because Jason's dragging his tongue over his ass. The skin is puckered, his hole tight, but the longer Jason licks and sucks the looser it gets until his tongue breaches inside —another new experience—and one that Jason is eager to repeat.

"I'm gonna come if you don't stop," Emerson warns, sounding out of breath and slightly frantic.

"If I stop, can I do it again later? Or another day?"

"Jason, you can literally do that to me any time you want. Well, not at school or other public places but any other time, you know circumstances notwithstanding. But right now please, please put your cock in me."

"Dick in ass coming up," Jason grins, inexplicably excited. He can't believe he didn't try this bisexual thing beforehand, though part of him is glad he didn't. Sharing these firsts with Emerson is special, because Emerson is special.

Everything that led him to this moment was worth it because he's got this beautiful man spread out beneath him, taking up most of his bed and a considerable part of his heart.

"I'm going to finger you now, Emmy."

Emerson squirms, spreading his legs wider and affording Jason the most glorious view. Mouth watering, it takes all of Jason's self control not to mouth at that perfect ass, or to lick his balls or suck on his dick. Shit, Jason is so very gay.

"Are you going to do more than stare?" Emerson asks.

"Yes, but I gotta say the view down here is fucking great."

Emerson mumbles something unintelligible, the words turning into a sharp moan when Jason's lubed up finger rubs against his hole. The fact that Jason's mouth was just there makes him achingly hard, and he draws his finger in the same circle his tongue just made before slipping it inside. Emerson's turned on and relaxed enough that his finger slips in easily, and it's a miracle Jason doesn't come in his boxers watching it disappear into Emerson's body.

"Fuck," Jason curses, wishing he could kiss Emerson. He settles for turning his face into Emerson's thigh, rubbing his cheek against his bare skin and pressing a kiss there while fingerfucking Emerson.

It's not long before Emerson begs for more, and Jason is happy to give, making sure to add extra lube before two of his thick fingers sink into the tight heat of Emerson's ass. One of them groans, and Jason honestly isn't sure who because he's so turned on watching the way Emerson's body takes his fingers, knowing his cock is next.

"Gay sex is amazing," Jason marvels. "Being bisexual is amazing."

"Fantastic," Emerson huffs. "I'm very happy for you, Jason."

Jason knows he means it, that despite the hitch in his breathing and the impatient way he squirms, that every word Emerson speaks is the truth. Jason meant what he said too. This is fun, because Emerson is fun, and he's quite possibly Jason's favorite person, which is new and exciting and also the single most arousing moment of his life.

"Emmy, I'm so hard."

"Me too," Emerson says. "I read a book once where the main character said he was so hard it almost hurt, and I thought that was hyperbole, but it's not. I don't think I've ever been this hard in my entire life."

Pride fills Jason. He's always liked making his partners feel good, taken a lot of joy in servicing them, but this is another level. Knowing that Emerson feels that good, that turned on, because of Jason, makes him want to do a goddamn endzone dance. He suspects Emerson might not enjoy that though, so he settles before adding a third finger, the tightness and heat a promise of what's to come.

"That's enough fingers, cock now," Emerson demands, his fingers tapping rapidly in what Jason recognizes as one of his happy stims.

"Fuck it's hot when you demand my dick," Jason groans, so turned on by Emerson's forwardness he nearly comes untouched. "I just need a condom. Hang on."

Emerson continues tapping his fingers on his forearms while Jason retrieves the condom, ridding himself of his boxers, tossing them to the floor before rolling the condom down his cock and adding a generous amount of lube. He's definitely going to need to buy more because Jason suspects they're going to go through a lot in the future.

Once he's finished, he crawls back between Emerson's spread legs, smoothing his hands over the insides of his thighs. He wants to commit this sight to memory, utterly mesmerized by the sight of Emerson's mess of red hair spilling across his pillows, his long limbs and pale skin glowing in the early morning light that peeks through the gaps in his curtains. Emerson is the most beautiful thing he's ever seen, and it makes Jason's chest ache.

"I'm going to fuck you now, Emmy." He positions his erection at Emerson's entrance, teasing the tip against his hole in warning. "Are you ready?"

"Uh-huh," Emerson says, removing his arms from over his face. His eyes stay shut, but they're not squeezed tightly this time, his face less pinched as Jason presses inside. It's tighter than anything Jason's ever felt, and the guttural moan that echoes in the room definitely comes from him.

"Fuck, fuck, fuck."

"What you said," Emerson groans, fingers twitching in midair.

Reaching out, Jason links their hands together, bringing them down to the mattress above Emerson's head as he sinks all the way inside.

"Full," Emerson whimpers.

"Is it too much?" Jason worries, his thumbs stroking over the back of Emerson's hands. He wants to move but he waits, needing to make sure.

Emerson shakes his head from side to side. "S'good."

"Good," Jason exhales, caging Emerson in with his arms and knees. He lowers his mouth to Emerson's, greedily swallowing down his moans when Jason pulls back out slowly then rolls his hips forward. As if needing Jason even closer, Emerson wraps his legs around Jason's waist, locking his ankles at his lower back and arching.

After that Jason can barely think, barely breathe, losing himself in the pleasure of fucking into Emerson slow and deep while they kiss like they might die if they break apart. It feels like they might. If Jason could crawl inside of Emerson's body he would, desperate to be as close as fucking possible. His thrusts turn shaky as he presses their joined hands into the mattress while fucking him.

"Emmy," he whimpers.

Emerson moans louder, the sound shifting into something more like a hum. Whether he's consciously stimming or not, Jason isn't sure, but the vibrations of the sound against his tongue drive him to fucking Emerson just that little bit harder and deeper, until Emerson's shuddering beneath him and sobbing out a quiet warning seconds before he's coming between them in thick spurts that coat Jason's soft abs. He wants to devour Emerson, wants to memorize the sounds he makes and the way he tastes, unable to take his eyes off Emerson's raptured expression.

When his mouth goes slack and his eyes flutter open, Jason nearly sobs. Those pretty eyes open for him, look at him, and Jason feels fucking owned.

"Gonna—" he tries to warn but Emerson's heels dig into his back, and it's Emerson pulling him down into a kiss. It's Emerson swallowing down his sounds of pleasure as Jason shakes through his orgasm. It's Emerson kissing Jason's cheeks and his nose; it's Emerson pulling him down into an embrace as if he too, can't get close enough to Jason, as if trying to make them one person.

Tucking his face into Emerson's neck, he breathes him in, focusing on the feeling of Emerson's nails as they find their way into Jason's hair, on the legs still wrapped tightly around his back, locking him in place as if Emerson can't let him go either. That same ache in his chest intensifies, only this time Jason understands what it means. He could blame it on post-orgasmic haze or cuddling endorphins, but there's no point in trying to minimize what Jason knows to be true —he is in love with Emerson.

19 EMERSON

"WHAT DO you want to look at first?"

"Me?" Emerson asks.

Jason's smile widens, and Emerson isn't sure if he wants to kiss him or bury his face in Jason's neck to hide. Ever since they had sex this morning—twice—he's been oscillating between wanting to get his hands and mouth on Jason again, to feeling deeply overwhelmed and needing a hug or a cuddle. Sometimes both at the same time.

He's not sure if you can cuddle while having sex, but he adds it to his mental list of things to try, determined to talk to Jason about it later if he can get the words out. If not, maybe he'll text him the idea.

"Of course you," Jason replies. "I've been here plenty of times, though not too many to not still enjoy it. Every third grade class in Santa Leon does their end-of-year field trip at the aquarium and then again in seventh grade science after biology lab. Sometimes the seniors who get into Mrs. Montalvo's AP Environmental Science have a really cool behind-the-scenes field trip here."

"Did you do that?" Emerson asks.

"Oh no, I wasn't smart enough for that," Jason says with a shake of his head. "But my parents had a family membership when Alec was a toddler so me, Charlie and Andrew used to trade off taking him on weekends to give our parents a break from his never ending supply of energy. Come to think of it, I don't think I've been back here since Alec was little."

"I'm glad you brought me. I've never been to the aquarium."

"I know, you mentioned it once."

"Did I?" Emerson tries to recall that but isn't sure he remembers doing it. "When?"

"Uh, the second time we had lunch. You were eating your peanut butter sandwich when you looked at my yellow shirt and asked me if I was aware sharks were attracted to the color yellow, which for the record I was not. I'm so not wearing my favorite banana bathing suit on the beach ever again." Jason laughs, as if to assure Emerson he is not, in fact, bothered by the knowledge his banana print bathing suit will no longer see the light of day. "Anyways, then I said something about how I wasn't scared of petting sharks, and you told me you can't pet sharks, and I told you that you could at the aquarium near the pier, and that's when you told me you'd never been to an aquarium. I decided then and there I'd take you one day."

"Jason, that was almost two months ago."

"I know," Jason shrugs. "Can't say I realized it would be a date, but I'm pretty happy about the turn of events. I figured it might be a little too overstimulating in the evenings, but then when I found out about their early morning sensory hours on Sundays, I knew it would be perfect."

When Jason finishes talking, his expression is relaxed,

his smile easy, and he clearly has no idea what kind of impact his words have just had. Emerson is so used to being told he talks too much, that he interrupts with facts no one cares about or that his limited interests are the reason he had no friends. Yet here's Jason, who apparently not only remembers the specific details of a conversation from not long after they met, but also filed that information away and eventually used it to take Emerson on the world's most perfect first date. A date he went out of his way to find accommodations for.

If Emerson had better interoception, he might be able to differentiate between the storm of feelings swirling inside of him, but he doesn't. His feelings are a tangled mess of confusing, too big emotions that have him fidgeting with the sleeves of the hoodie Jason loaned him. This one still smells like Jason, and while Emerson has never stolen anything in his entire life, he might steal this.

"Was this okay?" Jason asks, looking inexplicably worried. "I didn't ask first because I wanted to surprise you, but maybe you're like Andrew and hate surprises."

"This was a good surprise," Emerson assures him, itching to reach for Jason but hesitating. While it's not crowded, it's still a public place, and Jason is only out to Emerson and thanks to his late night phone call, his best friend. "It is very thoughtful of you to remember. Thank you."

"Of course I remember." Jason's eyes crinkle at the corners, the lines there a natural extension of his ever present smile. The same smile that appears on his face when he reaches for Emerson's hand and tangles their fingers together.

Right here in the center of the Santa Leon Aquarium, Jason holds his hand. Given that it's Sensory Sunday—

something Emerson didn't even know existed before their arrival—the aquarium isn't crowded. There are only a handful of other groups here this early, and none of them are paying attention to Jason and Emerson. Still, it's thrilling to have Jason so casually reach for his hand in a public place, as if perhaps he needs to touch Emerson as much as Emerson needs to be touched. As if he isn't worried about anyone knowing they're here together.

In the grand scheme of firsts, holding hands is probably a small one, yet the feelings it invokes are anything but. It's another first Emerson gets to share with Jason and one that makes Emerson feel wanted and safe and happier than he's maybe ever been in his entire life. Unable to voice any of this out loud, he holds Jason's hand just that little bit tighter.

"Alright, Emmy?"

"Uh-huh, just...can you pick the exhibit?" Emerson asks, still reeling from the sex and the handholding and the sheer ease with which Jason makes him feel wanted. All of it is good, but Emerson's brain is working overtime to mentally compartmentalize all the new things he's experienced in the last twenty-four hours, making the prospect of any decision crippling.

"Sure," Jason answers.

Giving Emerson's hand a gentle squeeze, Jason guides him across the lobby of the aquarium. The weight of decision-making taken off his shoulders leaves Emerson free to take in their surroundings, marveling first at the massive replica of a blue whale hanging from the ceiling above them, then at the floor to ceiling tank that, according to the plaque they pass, is part of a tropical reef.

It's surprisingly easy to trail alongside Jason without the normal anxiety or tension that permeates most of his social interactions. Come to think of it, he can remember very few times he was ever so relaxed in a public place. While part of it might be because of the diminished crowds and the post-orgasm haze of pleasure, a lot of it is because being with someone he doesn't feel the need to mask with or hide from has taken off the weight of burdens he'd grown used to carrying.

For so long, Emerson resigned himself to feeling safest alone, yet Jason has shown him a different future—one where it's possible to be with someone who makes him feel seen, happy and loved. Because whether Jason means to or not, his actions are doing just that. He smiles at Emerson constantly, seeking him out with a meaningful gaze or a casual touch.

Emerson didn't even know it was possible for Jason to become more tactile, but since the dance he's hardly taken his hands off Emerson. A hand at the nape of his neck or the small of his back, fingers curled in his own or an arm slung around his shoulder. At first, Emerson thought Jason was trying to reassure him, but he's starting to suspect the touching might be as important to Jason as it is to Emerson.

Even now as they walk, holding his hand doesn't seem to be enough because he lifts it to his mouth, hiding his smile behind their joined palms as he kisses the back of Emerson's hand and points out a very large fish that he swears was alive when Alec was little. Jason's chatter continues as they make their way past a range of exhibits, including a family of seahorses and a mesmerizing room of jellyfish. Jason assures him they have time to come back and see it all, but he's got a plan he says, gleefully leading Emerson to their destination.

Secure in the knowledge Jason has a plan he will like, Emerson's mind drifts as he stares at various tanks and fish, losing his focus on the other aspects of his surroundings, like railings and walls, nearly walking into one. Jason quietly grabs Emerson's body to stop the collision, redirecting him with an arm around his shoulder as if tucking Emerson into his side might prevent future missteps.

"This way," Jason announces, guiding them towards a set of double doors. "Unless they changed the exhibit in the last few years. Probably should've checked the website this morning before we left, but I was a little distracted."

Heat spreads through Emerson's body, and he's certain his face must be bright red knowing exactly what Jason was distracted by earlier, specifically Emerson's ass and trying to figure out exactly how long he could rim Emerson before he sobbed through a second orgasm.

"Yup, still here," Jason happily announces while pushing the door open.

Cool morning air whips across Emerson's face as they step outside, the bite of cold air right off the shore beside them making him shiver. He's extra grateful for the warmth of Jason's borrowed hoodie and his body, leaning into the embrace while letting his eyes adjust to the drastic change in lighting. Once the sun stops affronting his overly sensitive eyes, he's able to take in their surroundings, eyes settling on a large sign that explains where Jason led them.

"Touch tanks," Emerson whispers, unable to stop his fingers from tapping in the air as he turns to smile at Jason. "You brought me to the touch tanks."

"I did," Jason grins, tipping his face down to kiss Emerson's forehead. No one is looking, but Emerson feels owned in the warmest, safest way possible, and his fingers stim faster knowing exactly what he's feeling right now—happy. "You've never gotten to pet a shark, so I thought why not start off big."

"They really have a shark I can pet?" Emerson asks, leaning against Jason as they walk towards the pools.

The touch tanks are far larger than Emerson would've imagined, spanning half the outside area with two separate pools each forming a half-circle visitors can stroll around and between. Whether it's because of the early hours or the frigid temperatures, only one other group is outside. Curious, Emerson watches a small girl with bright yellow ear defenders lean over the edge of the tank, both of her arms submerged while one of her parents holds on to the back of her shirt, presumably so she doesn't climb all the way in.

"They do," Jason confirms. "Though we've got to actually find it."

Eager to see it all for himself, Emerson takes the lead, stepping out of the safety of Jason's embrace to walk to the edge of the pool and lay his palms flat on the cement wall. He leans over, mesmerized by the way the small stingrays glide across the bottom of the tank barely disturbing the water. Not quite ready to touch them, he skims his own fingertips over the surface of the water watching the way it ripples.

He's not sure how long he stares, scanning the tanks and taking note of the various sting rays that circle. There are starfish clinging to the rocks in the center, and towards the edge what appears to be anemone and sea slugs clustered around the coral. It's incredible, so much like the books he's read and yet different too.

"I wonder if my mom came here."

"If she went to school here then yeah, definitely."

The idea that his mom might've sat in this same spot makes Emerson's insides squirm. It's not bad, but it's not exactly good either. It's something in the middle, as comforting as it is painful. If they'd made it out here when he was little, his mom might have brought him here, like the other parents. Well they probably couldn't have afforded it, but maybe during a field trip. His mom might even have been able to take off work to chaperone.

"You see the shark?"

"No," Emerson answers. "Maybe it's hiding."

Jason's hand settles at the back of Emerson's neck, his palm warm and the touch grounding. He doesn't press or hurry Emerson, just stands there quietly as Emerson gets lost in thought and plays with the surface of the water. Ten minutes later, Emerson's right arm is freezing from touching all five of the rays in the tank, twice, but he's yet to find the shark.

"I've gotta use the restroom," Jason says, squeezing the back of Emerson's neck once before pulling it away. "I'll be right back."

"Okay," Emerson replies, never taking his eyes off the tank. He's not sure how much time passes when the shadow of someone falls into his line of sight.

"Are you looking for Freya?" a woman asks. Emerson turns to see who spoke, finding a woman with long braids pulled back through her Santa Leon Aquarium cap. She's also got on a Santa Leon Aquarium polo and a name tag, so she definitely works here.

"I don't know who Freya is," Emerson tells her, staring at her name tag. Kaliyah is her name.

"Freya is our Epaulette shark," She answers. "You've been staring at the tanks for a while and thought you might be looking for her. Most people expect her to be bigger than she is, and with her brown coloration and dark spots, she's easy to miss hiding in her habitat, especially when she's in her favorite hiding spot. Want me to show you?"

"Please," Emerson answers, following her around the

back side of the touch tanks. She leans over, pointing to a small inlet in the clustered rocks near the edge. "She's right there, see her tail peeking out? Her spots help disguise her and repel predators. The funniest thing is, if you know what to look for she's easy to see, but she thinks if you can't see her head, you can't see her."

"She's smaller than I expected," Emerson confesses, wondering if he's tall enough to lean over the tank and reach her. He doesn't think so, and the thought makes him sad.

"She usually stays there most of the day unless it's feeding time," Kaliyah offers. "Which, lucky for you, is right now."

Lucky is a perfect word to describe how Emerson feels. Lucky to have been able to move to Santa Leon and start a life of his own making. Lucky to have found a job that, while most days takes the bulk of his spoons, makes him feel satisfied and proud. Lucky to have met Jason, to have found not only a best friend but a boyfriend. Lucky to have found someone who happily lets Emerson nerd out and watch the same movie for the upteenth time, or seeks out sensory hours at an aquarium so Emerson can live out his childhood dream of petting a shark.

So damn *lucky*.

As if the day couldn't get more perfect, right as Kaliyah lures Freya out with the promise of food, Jason returns—his presence noticeable even before he wraps himself around Emerson from behind. Jason's chest fits snug against his back, strong arms holding him tight, as Jason hunches to rest his chin on Emerson's shoulder.

"Surprise," he whispers, turning his hand over. Clutched inside his palm is a small plush seahorse, maybe five inches at most and a beautiful bright blue like the sea on the horizon.

"What's that?" Emerson asks around a sudden lump in his throat.

"A friend for Sharky," Jason answers, healing a part of Emerson he didn't break. "Can't have him getting lonely when I cuddle you at night."

Emerson's throat is too small, his heart too big, and words escape him as he curls his fingers around the plush. Not something to be ridiculed or hidden away, but a gift from someone who understands Emerson. Who celebrates all the parts of him, even the ones society deems difficult or childish or confusing. His thumb strokes over the soft plush, tracing the stitching in a soothing and rhythmic pattern.

"Seahorses are monogamous," Emerson whispers. "And very queer-coded."

"Well that's fucking awesome." Jason's breath is warm across the shell of his ear, the laughter in his voice going straight to Emerson's very gay, very-in-love heart. "I passed the gift shop on the way to the bathroom and had to get it for you. Clearly, it was the perfect one."

You're the perfect one, Emerson thinks, breathing in the scent of salt air and Jason's body wash, familiar and comforting as the truth of what he's suspected for weeks settles around him. He's in love with Jason. Not a question or a maybe, but a fact. He knows it the same way he knew the first time his mom made him an Eggo waffle when he was five years old and it became his breakfast of choice for the next two decades. He knows it the same way he knew after reading Lord Of The Rings for the first time that he would never be the same.

Maybe it's his autistic brain finding something it likes and not wanting to let go, or maybe it's his love-starved heart recognizing something special in Jason. Or maybe it's all of that wrapped into one amalgamation of attraction, affection and friendship.

Whatever it is, Emerson knows one thing for certain—Jason King is it for him.

Since the day Emerson's mom died, he's been adrift, felt like an out-of-place alien searching for somewhere he might belong. That place had never been with his family, hadn't been in middle school or high school or college. He'd hoped moving to his mom's hometown might magically provide the sense of belonging he'd always lacked, but not even Santa Leon with its picturesque views and perfect weather could fill the cracks in Emerson's fragile heart.

All these years Emerson's been looking for a home, it wasn't a place—it was a person. It was, *is,* Jason.

"Look, Emmy." Jason's cheek presses against his own. His joy at seeing the shark is palpable, infinitely more affecting because Emerson knows its excitement not for himself, but for Emerson. "There's your shark. You ready to pet it?"

Freya swims closer, her coloring all but disguising her against the sandy bottom, yet now that he knows what to look for he can't miss her. He draws two fingers over her smooth back, a smile growing on his face.

Under his hand is a shark, but in Emerson's heart, there is a King.

20 JASON

STRUMMING his fingers on the wheel, Jason tries not to let his nerves get the best of him. He's not usually one to get too anxious about things, but this feels big. It *is* big.

While he's brought girlfriends to meet his parents before, it was almost always out of a sense of obligation because they'd wanted to meet his family, to check off boxes in the next step of a relationship, and not because Jason wanted the people he loved most to love the person he's dating.

The weeks following the homecoming dance and their first date have been a whirlwind. Between alerting HR to their new relationship, followed by a subsequent meeting and paperwork to ensure no one like Caldwell can accuse them of misconduct, to his regular teaching duties and the start of playoffs, he's been run ragged. One bright spot in all of the stressful recent events is that Caldwell announced his retirement. Jason can't wait until that miserable jerkwad is gone forever. Sure, he hasn't tried any other shit since things went down with Matty, but Jason can't forgive him for the stress he caused Emerson. The day he found out Caldwell was finally going to be leaving Santa Leon High was one of the best days of his entire life.

The only downside in recent events is that he and Emerson haven't had time for a second date, though that hasn't stopped them from spending all of their admittedly scant free time together. Aside from their morning rides to school and shared lunches, Emerson occasionally comes to watch practice now, often bringing his grading outside, something that earns Jason a lot of chirping from his players. Emerson even came to his first football game last night, as did Theo and Alec, who came to the game for morale and to keep Emerson company. While Jason doesn't mind if Emerson never cares about football, the sight of his boyfriend sitting in the stands, watching him coach and wearing *his* coaching hoodie—the name *King* plastered across his chest for any and all to see—had done funny things to Jason.

Turns out, Jason has a bit of a possessive streak, at least where Emerson is concerned. Knowing that their relationship is now public, that people who saw Emerson wearing his hoodie would know what it means, had driven Jason to coach his best game of the season. After which, he'd taken Emerson home and fucked him in that same hoodie. It had been unequivocally the best sex of Jason's life.

Emerson rode his cock while wearing his hoodie, a mental image that is now permanently burned into his brain. They spent the next morning in bed, alternating between cuddling and fucking. Inevitably, it devolved into Emerson's favorite thing, which Jason has affectionately dubbed cuddlefucking. Much like their normal fucking, it involves a lot of nakedness and cocks but also a lot of cuddling, often ending with Emerson stuffed full of Jason's dick while they cuddle. It's the absolute fucking best. According to Theo, this is technically called cockwarming, but Jason likes cuddlefucking better.

So yeah, weeks have been full for football and fucking and cuddles, which is basically Jason's dream come true. Despite his busy schedule, when his parents called and pointed out he hadn't been to a family dinner since August —his dad all but begging him to come so they could have all their boys under one roof—Jason easily agreed. After he hung up the phone, he turned to Emerson and invited him along because why wouldn't he?

"Are you nervous?" Emerson questions, dragging Jason out of his thoughts and back to the present. He startles, blinking at the road while wondering when they got all the way across town.

"Me?" Jason asks, feigning what he hopes is a casual tone as he turns onto his parents' street. "What makes you ask that?"

"You're trying to play drums on the steering wheel," Emerson answers. He leans his head back on the headrest, angling his body sideways to better watch Jason. Judging by the way he frantically spins his fidget ring, he's more nervous than Jason is. "If you've changed your mind, it's okay."

"I definitely haven't changed my mind," Jason asserts, refusing to let Emerson worry about that. He takes his right hand off the steering wheel, resting it on Emerson's thigh and giving it a firm squeeze before turning his palm up in a wordless offering. He's rewarded when Emerson slips his hand into Jason's.

"If you're sure," Emerson hedges. There's no outward

reflection of his anxiety, but the way he grips Jason's hand tight enough to make his fingers go numb tells him all he needs to know.

"I'm sure, Emmy. I'm just excited and alright, maybe a little nervous, but that's not a bad thing."

Emerson's inhale is so deep Jason feels the echo of it in his chest.

"This is going to be great," Jason intones.

Emerson's expression is unreadable as they round the corner. He spent this morning showing Emerson photos of the house he grew up in, hoping he might be less anxious if he was familiar with it. Despite their preparations, Emerson tenses up when his parents' house comes into view.

As expected, his mom and dad's cars are in the driveway but Theo's and the twins' cars are noticeably absent from the front of the house. Jason's relief at being the first ones here is palpable. He hoped getting here a little early would give Emerson time to meet his parents before anyone else arrived, but there was always a chance someone else might already be here.

Jason pulls alongside the curb, removing his hand from Emerson's grip long enough to put his truck in park and shut the engine off before returning it to Emerson's lap. Immediately, Emerson reaches for his hand, linking their fingers, then holding their joined hands tightly with his other hand.

"You aren't having second thoughts, are you?" Jason questions.

"Me?" Emerson blinks, as if the question has taken him by surprise. "I'm more worried about you. In the span of two weeks, your entire life has changed and...and it's because of me." Emerson breathes in slow and deep, holding his breath for long seconds before letting it out in one shuddering exhale. "What if they blame me?"

"First of all, I'm a grown man so whatever choices I make, good or bad, I can take responsibility for. Second of all, you are a good choice, the best I ever made. Not my sexuality because that's not a choice, but you. Third, and this is important—my parents are going to love you because I do and—"

"What did you just say?" Emerson interrupts, his grip on Jason's hand tightening.

"My parents are going to love you," Jason repeats slowly.

"No, I mean, yes, you said that, but the other part. You said...you said—*Jason.*"

Jason stares at the man he loves, several things clicking into place. Perhaps he should be panicking, or backtracking. Surely it's too soon. Yet all Jason feels is a certainty that makes him inexplicably happy, the kind of happy that makes him want to pump his fists in the air or sprint across the field because loving Emerson feels like a goddamn championship win.

"I love you," Jason repeats, lifting Emerson's hand and bringing it to his lips. He kisses the back of his trembling hand, eyes never leaving Emerson's face. "You don't have to say it back, Emmy. I don't want you to feel pressured or stressed, but I'm not going to take it back or lie to you. I love you and—"

Emerson launches himself at Jason, scrambling across the bench seat and into Jason's lap. With lightning quick reflexes, Jason readjusts his seat as far back as it goes to make room for Emerson who, despite his long limbs, manages to curl himself into Jason's lap then promptly buries his face in Jason's neck. Wrapping his arms around

Emerson, Jason smooths his palms up and down the curve of Emerson's spine, breathing easier when he feels some of his boyfriend's tension begin to fade.

"I didn't mean to say that right now," Jason admits, "not because it's not true but because I'm not sure if it's too soon. But, Emmy, loving you comes as easily as breathing, and those feelings just wanted to come out."

Emerson's nose is shoved into the side of his neck, each of his short and shallow breaths warm against the hollow of his throat. It doesn't escape Jason's notice that while his unplanned confession has left Emerson reeling, he's not pulling away, but rather trying to get closer—his arms wrapping around Jason to smash them between the seat and Jason's body almost as if he's trying to make them one.

Though the angle is slightly awkward, Jason manages to press a kiss to the top of Emerson's head before stroking a hand through his soft red locks. Slowly, Jason breathes him in, his scent familiar now. Everything about Emerson is familiar now and it thrills Jason in unexpected ways.

"You're an easy man to love, Emerson Miller."

"No, I'm not," Emerson protests.

"You are to me," Jason counters, aware that one confession from him won't undo the trauma he suffered living with a family who never saw or acknowledged his worth. Thankfully, Jason's a patient man; if he's lucky, maybe Emerson will keep him around long enough to show him exactly how loveable he truly is.

"Other people would disagree," Emerson says, each word spoken slowly.

"Some other people are stupid, you know," Jason points out. "For example, not everyone likes football, and they're wrong about that, so clearly their judgement can't be trusted. You are excluded, obviously."

Emerson pulls back to frown at Jason. "Did you just compare me to football again?"

"Suppose I did," Jason smirks, delighted to be able to see Emerson's beautiful face, tear-stained and guileless and most importantly *his*. "I told you, I'm a man who knows what I love, and that's football and my boyfriend."

"I'm scared," Emerson admits.

Jason cradles Emerson's face in his hands, thumbs stroking over his cheeks and an echoing wetness at the corner of his eyes. Fuck, he is so in love with this beautiful man.

"I'm not going anywhere, Emmy. I love you. It's okay if you don't yet but—"

"Of course I love you," Emerson blurts, sounding halfway between laughing and crying. "I love you so much and I thought it was just me. I didn't think....I didn't think someone like you would ever, that you—*ugh*."

Emerson's adorable frown deepens. Jason can't resist the urge to lean forward and kiss it, knowing him well enough now to know his expressions don't always match his moods. At least, not in the way Jason's expressions might.

"You're so cute."

"You're so, *ugh*," Emerson groans, deepening the kiss and clenching his hands in Jason's short hair. "You big, ridiculous man."

Jason's smile threatens to split his face in two. "You mean the big, ridiculous man you're in love with."

Emerson huffs, his pale chinks pink with a blush. "Yes, Jason."

"You love me," Jason repeats, pretty sure he could run a marathon or lift a car from the endorphins running through his body right now. "My boyfriend loves me."

"You're very happy about this," Emerson says, fingers toying with the strings of Jason's hoodie.

"Damn right I am," Jason grins, puffing out his chest.

There's a very primal urge in Jason to scream from the top of the bleachers, "*I have a boyfriend and we're in love.*" He's not sure if that goes against school policy. Even if it's not, it would be too much attention for Emerson anyway, but Jason can daydream about it even if he won't actually do it.

Maybe he can get Emerson to wear his hoodie while he teaches one day. Or something else with Jason's name on it. Probably not, since Emerson has his own unofficial teaching uniform with his array of green shirts and sweaters that make him look so damn cute.

"I do love you," Emerson whispers, tugging on his hoodie strings in what Jason now knows is his way of asking for a kiss.

Eager to oblige, Jason tips his head, loving when Emerson is in his lap like this. There's something intimate and arousing about being the one who has to angle his face up to Emerson. Jason is not a small man by any means, but having Emerson above him in any capacity is incredibly appealing. He lets one hand slide around to cup the back of Emerson's head, pulling him down into a kiss that promises so much more than Jason can give in a truck parked in front of his parent's house.

Emerson's hands roam over Jason's chest, one of them slipping beneath his t-shirt and hoodie to palm at Jason's belly while the other slips down the neck of Jason's hoodie to stroke his chest hair. Slowly but surely Emerson's getting bolder with his touching, not quite as shy about showing Jason how much he enjoys his body. The thing about Emerson's touches is that more often than not they aren't sexual, at least not intentionally. Jason quickly found that Emerson enjoys digging his fingers into the softest part of Jason's stomach or thighs, or dragging his nails or face over Jason's body hair in some kind of uninhibited sensory exploration of Jason's body. He never minds how turned on Jason gets, but it's rarely his starting intention.

"It feels good," Emerson quietly whispered a few days ago, seemingly content to knead and stroke without an ulterior motive.

"Emmy," Jason groans, chubbing up in his sweats. "I'm gonna get hard if you keep that up."

"Oops," Emerson mumbles, quickly withdrawing his hands like he's been burned. "Sorry, I—"

"No sorry," Jason assures him, grabbing both of Emerson's hands between his own and bringing them to his mouth. "I love how you touch me, always. Just uh, probably not a good idea to meet the parents with a raging hard-on. At least not in these sweats."

"I like your sweats," Emerson declares in that deadpan way of his.

The statement sounds innocent but Jason's reaction isn't—likely because Emerson rubbed his cheek against Jason's dick in this same pair of sweats a few hours earlier while they watched a movie. In hindsight, he should have worn different pants, given that he's been popping boners like he's fifteen again lately. He's not sure how raging horniness relates to his bisexuality. It's possible his arousal is because Emerson is a man, or more likely just because it's Emerson. All he knows is, he should've worn pants that allowed for more discretion.

"I can't believe you love me." Emerson withdraws one hand from Jason's hoodie in favor of reaching for his hand, turning it over so he can link their fingers. "You really think they're going to like me?"

"My parents are going to adore you," Jason assures him. "My dad is probably going to try and hug you. He's a hugger. My mom too. Actually everyone in my family is a hugger except Andrew. The only person allowed to hug him is Charlie."

"I like hugs," Emerson replies, tone hesitant and hopeful.

"Me too."

"You give the best hugs," Emerson whispers. "I could hug you forever."

"Forever, huh? Count me in." Jason kisses the tip of his nose, then his lips before sighing with reluctance. "As much as I would love to keep you in my lap all night, if we want to meet them before my brothers show up we should probably get inside. Theo and Alec will likely be late, and Charlie will be too, unless he drives with Andrew, who is never late."

Reluctantly, Emerson extricates himself from Jason's embrace so he can climb back into his seat. Jason wastes no time hopping out of the truck and racing around to the other side to open the door before Emerson can, whose shy smile is worth rushing for every time.

"You don't always have to open my door, you know," Emerson points out.

"Course I don't have to," Jason says, holding out his hand to help Emerson down from the truck. "But I want to. There's a difference. Boyfriend privileges."

"You mean duties?"

"Nope," Jason says with a shake of his head, shutting the door and locking the truck before offering his hand to

Emerson again. "I definitely meant privileges. I get to take care of you. That is never a duty."

Emerson doesn't say anything, but he squeezes Jason's hand, leaning into his side in that way Jason recognizes as needing comfort when words fail him. He obliges by giving Emerson's hand a gentle squeeze before pulling and tucking Emerson against his side, arm draped around his shoulders to keep him as close as possible.

"I thought you hadn't uh, you know—told your parents about us yet," Emerson says as they walk towards the front door. "This might tip them off."

"I haven't told them yet," Jason confirms. "I've just been busy, and it seemed like something to tell them in person, not in the group chat, but I have no intention of hiding you, Emmy. I never will."

Whatever Emerson replies is too garbled to make out because he turns to shove his face into Jason's shoulder, wrapping his own arm around Jason's middle and holding on tightly as if afraid Jason might let go. Cold fingers sneak under his hoodie, settling on his tummy and lightly tapping the skin in nervousness. Jason barely reaches for the doorknob when it's yanked open, both of his parents standing there with wide eyes darting between Emerson and Jason.

"Jason, you're here."

"You were watching us from the window, weren't you?" Jason snorts.

"I would never spy on my grown children," his mom scoffs.

"Liar," Jason laughs.

"She wasn't watching you," his dad tells him. "I was."

"Damn, Dad, confessing up secrets like that without your lawyer present? You should know better."

"Your mother is the only lawyer I could ever need," his

dad grins, wrapping both arms around her from behind and kissing the top of her head. It makes Jason's smile widen, his own feelings for Emerson settling in his chest. If he's lucky, maybe he'll have the kind of relationship his parents have—forty years and still flirting like teenagers constantly.

"I think what your dad means to say is we noticed you brought someone," his mom interjects, those keen eyes of hers studying Emerson. "You mentioned bringing someone special but we thought, well—"

"We thought you were bringing a girl home," his dad finishes.

"I was not going to say that part out loud, *amor*."

"That's because you're more tactful than me. That's why you're the court lawyer, and I just work on legal documents in my office." He turns his gaze on Emerson, smiling friendly. "Kim is amazing. Best lawyer in Southern California. They're going to cry when she retires next year."

"You're retiring?" Jason gapes.

"I told you not to mention that yet." His mom swats his dad's arm which is still wrapped around her. "Who cares about retirement, I want to know more about your *friend*. Introduce us."

The way she says friend means she knows exactly how friendly they are. Then again, the way Jason's all but wrapped himself protectively around Emerson was likely the first giveaway.

"Mom, Dad—this is Emerson."

"Nice to meet you, Emerson," his dad says, extending a hand which Emerson awkwardly shakes.

"You too, sir."

"Oh no, no 'sir' around here. You just call me 'Art.'"

"Can I hug him?" his mom blurts, looking like the only

thing stopping her from throwing her arms around Emerson is the way his dad is still hugging her.

"Why are you asking me?" Jason laughs. "He's right here."

"Well, you're kind of holding on to him, sweetie." His mom smiles, pushing a stray curl out of her eyes. "Emerson, sweetheart, do you mind if I hug you?"

"Oh, um, sure ma'am," Emerson says, straightening himself stiff as a board.

"Ma'am," his mom laughs. "Just call me Kim. Or Mom."

"Mom," Jason groans.

"What?" his mom laughs. "You haven't brought anyone home in years. I'm not stupid. Besides, I've never seen you look so happy. Anyone who makes my boy smile like this can call me Mom. Well, if he wants. I'm sure he's got his own mother, but—"

"She's dead," Emerson offers.

Both his parents go very still, until his mom practically twitches.

"Can she hug you before she starts crying?" Jason whispers to Emerson.

Emerson nods, that permission all Kim needs before Emerson's got an arm full of Jason's mother. Despite her small stature, it's Emerson who curls into her, his shoulders hunching as he hides his face in her curls. She tightens her hold on Emerson, whispering something Jason can't make out. Whatever she's said makes Emerson's shoulders drop further. They stay like that for long seconds, and when Emerson pulls out of the hug, both their eyes are watery.

"So," his mom says, clearing his throat. "A boyfriend. Can't believe you didn't warn me."

"Sorry, I know I should've told you I was bisexual before."

"Sweetie, I've known you were bisexual since you were seventeen and couldn't take your eyes off Theo's date to prom."

"What the hell, Mom?"

"No, it was earlier than that," his dad counters. "Remember that boy Theo went to homecoming with sophomore year? Jason kept checking out his ass."

"What the fuck, Dad?" Jason groans.

"You're right," his mom nods, ignoring Jason. "I forgot about that. You've got a good memory."

"Hard to forget the first time you notice your son—"

"Oh my god! Stop it!" Jason laughs, relieved at their easy acceptance of his sexuality and also deeply embarrassed. He also really wants to talk to Theo now because he has no memory of that specific event.

"Sorry," his mom says, not sounding sorry at all. "Besides, you know we only care about our boys being happy. You don't ever have to come out to anyone you don't want to, Jason. I meant you should've warned me you were bringing home someone special. You said you were bringing a friend over. I would've made a home cooked meal instead of ordering takeout if I'd known you meant someone *special*."

"Takeout is probably for the best," his dad soothes, kissing the top of her head.

"I want to know more about this homecoming thing," Jason demands. "I don't remember—" but his words are cut short by the sound of very loud voices coming up the driveway.

"I don't understand why we had to rush," Alec sighs. "You're being so weird today."

"I'm not being weird," Theo counters.

Jason turns to greet them, his bulk temporarily shielding

Emerson from view as he watches his best friend and brother amble up the walkway. Despite Alec's grumbling, he and Theo are holding hands, and Alec's expression is light.

"What's up, asshole?" Alec grins, throwing his arms around Jason in a hug. He moves when Theo demands a turn, clapping Jason on the back before pulling him into a bear hug.

"How's it going?" Theo quietly inquires.

"Good," Jason answers, clinging to Theo for a few extra seconds. "Really good."

Theo pulls back from the hug with that familiar smile of his, and Jason's heart is so damn full having most of his favorite people in one place.

"Emerson is here," Alec loudly announces from behind them. "How come no one told me he was coming?"

Jason turns to reply, automatically slipping his arm around Emerson's shoulder to pull him close. Before Jason can get a word out, Alec's eyes widen comically, and he lets out a string of colorful expletives in both English and Spanish.

"Motherfucker," Alec curses again, having already drawn the attention of everyone in the house. "I lost the fucking bet."

"What bet?" Jason asks.

Alec doesn't answer, turning his attention to Theo. "All afternoon you reminded me about this dinner, making sure I kept on track so we weren't late. Did you know?" Alec jabs his finger in the center of Theo's chest not taking a breath or waiting for his reply. "Fuck you, you knew."

Alec huffs, crossing his arms in what is unmistakably a pout.

"Alec," Theo tries.

"Don't *'Alec'* me, asshole," Alec grumbles, turning his attention to Emerson. "Sorry, Emerson. Hi."

"Um, hello," Emerson replies, clearly unsure how to take what's happening.

"He's not mad," Jason whispers. "He's just a nosy fucker like Charlie who hates being the last to know anything."

"I'm not a nosy fucker! I—"

"Hello," Andrew says, appearing out of seemingly nowhere in the doorway. He's so damn quiet it's hard to believe he's a King sometimes.

In stark contrast, Charlie's loud voice echoes up the walkway. "Annie, you left me in the car. What were you in such a hurry—oh, what's all this then?"

At his side, Emerson tenses under the scrutiny of Jason's entire family, everyone staring at them as Charlie and Andrew work out what everyone else already knows.

"Ah, fuck," Charlie curses, draping himself over Andrew's back dramatically. "I lost the bet."

"I didn't," Andrew smirks. "Nice to see you again, Emerson."

"Hi Andrew," Emerson says, tightening his arm around Jason's waist.

"I see you boys all know Emerson," his mom says, eyeing them keenly.

"Emerson went to pizza night with Theo and Alec a few weeks ago," Charlie says. "Jason's been crushing on Emerson forever."

"The fuck, Charlie?" Jason gapes.

"Behave," Andrew hisses to Charlie.

"What?" Charlie shrugs. "He has. We can all stop pretending we don't know now."

Emerson squirms beside him, clearly uncomfortable. As if reading Emerson's unease, Andrew effectively draws everyone's attention off Emerson with one single sentence.

"Charlie's seeing someone."

"You are?" both their parents gasp.

"What the fuck?!" Alec yells, throwing his hands in the air. "Is everyone keeping secrets from me?"

"Thank you," Jason mouths to Andrew, who winks at Emerson.

"You threw me under the bus," Charlie groans, shoving Andrew like they're thirteen and not thirty-two. "Andrew has a crush on a hockey player."

Andrew's cheeks flush a deep red while he turns to shoot daggers at Charlie with his glare. "I do not have a crush. I said he was aesthetically pleasing to look at. I don't even know him."

"You know you can have crushes on people you don't know. You can even fuck them," Charlie points out.

"I don't want to fuck him," Andrew hisses. "Besides, you'll fuck anything or anyone so you're not one to talk about the parameters of a crush. Which again, I do not have."

"If you say so," Charlie shrugs, entirely unabashed by everyone listening to this conversation.

"Was no one going to tell me anything?" Alec butts in, clearly still put out.

"I wanna know about the bet," Jason interjects.

"Oh that," Charlie shrugs. "We've all had a bet going for years about when you'd finally realize you weren't straight and bring a guy home."

Jason blinks, entirely unsure how to respond to this.

"To be fair, we were not *all* part of the bet," Theo clarifies.

"Theo wasn't part of the bet because Theo would've

told you about the bet," Alec pipes up. "You two can't keep secrets from each other for shit."

Theo looks like he wants to argue then shrugs, making Jason laugh. He fucking loves his family, ridiculous antics and all.

"I think I'm going to go put on a pot of coffee," his mom announces, reaching for his dad's hand. "Help me, *amor*."

"Of course," he answers, following her out of the entry like a besotted teenager.

"You're coming with me," Alec says, grabbing Theo's hand and dragging him towards the stairs. Jason does not want to know what they're going to do, so he turns his attention on the twins who are back to quietly bickering.

"I can't believe you told them about—" Charlie stops when he realizes Jason and Emerson are watching them.

"Told us about who?" Jason prompts, dying of curiosity. To his knowledge, Charlie hasn't had a relationship in almost a decade, seemingly content to fuck his way through Southern California without care or commitment.

"No one," Charlie answers. "By the way Emerson, you're looking enchanting tonight. Green is really your color."

A now familiar feeling burns in Jason's chest that he finally recognizes as not heartburn. He frowns at Charlie. "Get your own boyfriend."

"I don't want a partner, thanks. I'm very happy being a manwhore."

"Manwhore implies women are the default. You're just a whore," Andrew supplies with a charming smile.

Charlie opens his mouth then closes it. "Shit, you're right. Fucking internalized misogyny."

"Are they always like this?" Emerson whispers.

"Afraid so," Jason replies, realizing that his brothers

were on much better behavior at the tailor's. Now that he's brought Emerson home, he's privy to their unfiltered chaos.

"Okay," Emerson nods, taking it in stride.

"If you will excuse us, me and Charlie have to discuss the terms of my winning bet."

"No we don't," Charlie tries. "I want to talk to Emerson, and—"

Whatever Andrew whispers makes Charlie change his tune. Jason really wishes he knew how Andrew controlled Charlie because he's the only one who ever has been able to.

"Never mind, me and Andrew have to talk."

With that, they disappear down the hallway, quietly whispering in that way they do like no one else exists. It's not until their voices fade into the sitting room off the kitchen that Jason fully relaxes.

"So," Jason laughs. "Are you ready to run away? They're a lot."

"They're amazing," Emerson whispers. "I like your family, Jason. Maybe not for like prolonged periods, except for Andrew, but uh, they're nice. And they obviously love you."

"They're pretty great," Jason agrees, because he loves his nosy, noisy family. "They're going to love you, you know."

"Because you do?"

"Well partly," Jason answers, turning Emerson so he's directly in front of Jason. He cups his cheeks, "but just because you're you. I told you, Emmy, you're an easy man to love."

Uncertainty shines in his eyes, but this time he doesn't argue. What he does do is rise onto tip-toes, pressing his lips to Jason in a kiss that floods Jason with pleasure. He wraps his arms around Emerson's neck, kissing him once more before pulling him into a hug.

The front door is still wide open, cool night air and the glow of the street light filtering into the warmth of the house. Jason takes it all in, the stars outside twinkling brightly while the sound of his family's playful teasing filters out from the other room.

"I'm so happy, Jason," Emerson whispers, burrowing into his chest.

Jason holds him all the tighter, everything he's ever wanted in his arms. "Me too, Emmy. Me too."

EPILOGUE
EMERSON

Jason
hey emmy

you wanna hear a funny joke

AFFECTION FILLS EMERSON chests as he reads the message. Technically, he shouldn't be checking his phone, but it's the five minutes between classes. His next one is a study hall, so he made an exception, eager to see if there were any messages from Jason. He saw him that morning, and at lunch, but Emerson misses him just the same.

Emerson
That depends. Is it about football?

He doesn't expect a reply until later, so when his phone dings immediately he grabs it off his desk, eager to read Jason's message before his students start filing into the room.

Jason
not this time ;)

but if it was I bet youd laugh

Emerson
That is statistically unlikely.

Jason
one day im going to tell a football joke you like

however today is not that day

ready?

Jason doesn't wait for Emerson's answer, shooting off the joke before he can reply.

Jason
why do hobbits laugh when they run?

Emerson
I have no idea. Why?

Jason
because the grass tickles their balls

Emerson snorts. The joke is so bad it's almost funny. Even better than the joke is that Emerson can easily picture Jason's face after sending it. He's probably so proud of himself that his face is split wide in a smile, those familiar wrinkles at the corners of his eyes deepening. Emerson can almost hear Jason's booming laughter, and it makes him smile more than the actual joke had.

Ever since they finished listening to the audiobook of *The Return of the King* last month, Jason's been making even more bad Lord of the Rings jokes than usual. It's horrible and also absolutely wonderful.

Jason
did you laugh

you laughed right?

Emerson
I laughed a little bit. I don't think hobbits are quite that short though. According to Tolkien they're around two and half to three and half feet, roughly. Plus they wear pants so the grass wouldn't touch their genitals.

Jason
its still funny

because balls

Emerson laughs this time, not because of the joke but because of Jason's response. While Emerson might not personally understand that kind humor he appreciates Jason's horrible jokes because of how much they amuse his boyfriend. He also appreciates that in between endless jokes he hears from his students and football players, Jason always peppers in nerdy jokes for Emerson's benefit.

Thinking about Jason makes Emerson's chest flutter. It's been almost eight months since their first date. Eight of the best months of Emerson's entire life. In that time, he's come to find out that home is indeed a person and his is Jason. He also moved out of his tiny apartment and into Jason's house six weeks ago, a change which has been surprisingly easy to adjust to given that by their third date they were all but living together already. Or at least Emerson was half-living with Jason, spending most weekends there and slowly acquiring spaces in Jason's home, from the reading nest Jason made for Emerson in his office to the bookshelf he built in the living room just for Emerson's books and even his LEGO. Eventually Jason pointed out paying rent on his apartment was pointless since almost all of his stuff had migrated to Jason's house already. So, breaking the lease and making it official was easy.

Waking up to Jason every morning is the best thing that's ever happened to Emerson, even if Jason is far too happy at six am, and he hums loudly while making coffee.

Jason King is the single greatest thing in Emerson's life, and the urge to text him and tell him so is staggering. Somehow, Jason never has any idea how remarkable he is, shrugging off compliments with a laugh and a smile as if it's nothing, when he is in fact *everything*.

"Mr. Miller."

Realizing he's zoned out entirely, Emerson plasters on what he hopes passes for a smile while discreetly hiding his phone in his desk drawer.

Sitting up straighter, he takes in the student standing in front of him, not at all surprised to find him there. Of all the kids who use his study hall, Arlo Rosales is the one most likely to come to him for help.

"Hey, Arlo. Did you need some help with that history report you're working on?" Emerson asks, always happy to help with any subject the students need, even when it's not his own.

Arlo shakes his head, dark hair falling into his eyes. He has his arms behind his back, and his body shakes with the force of his foot tapping.

"Everything okay?" Emerson questions.

Arlo nods, glancing at the open door before locking his gaze on Emerson.

"I have something for you," Arlo blurts, withdrawing his hand from behind his back. There, clutched in his right hand, is a long stemmed sunflower, some of the petals slightly crushed.

"Arlo, what—"

"It's not from me," Arlo hurries, as if Emerson might mistakenly accuse him of trying to give him flowers. "It's from Coach."

"Mr. King gave you a flower for me?" Emerson queries, unsure what to make of it.

Since that first boutonniere, Jason has taken to bringing Emerson bouquets of sunflowers for special occasions—his birthday, their six month anniversary, and a house full of them the day Emerson officially moved in. Having one of his players bring Emerson flowers is entirely new and unexpected, however.

"Well uh, thank you," Emerson says, taking the flower. Automatically, he lifts it to his face, unable to hide his smile behind its wide yellow petals. "Did he—" but Arlo has already retreated to his seat.

There's very little time for Emerson to try and make sense of the flower before another one comes, this time from one of Jason's junior players who Emerson knows by face but not name. Cash or Carter maybe. Emerson is woefully horrible with names for kids he doesn't teach or speak to regularly.

"Here you go, Mr. Miller," the kid grins, his crinkly-eyed smile offering no clues as to what on Earth is happening before he deposits a second sunflower on Emerson's desk then disappears from the classroom without explanation or another word.

The kid's arrival and departure, especially since he's in his football jersey, garners enough attention that Emerson has to stand up and remind them to keep it quiet for the students who are studying. By the time he's settled down their chattering, someone else is at the door. A someone that Emerson knows very well—Sanchez, one of Jason's senior players, standing in his study hall with another sunflower.

Over the next twenty minutes, six other players come and go, each of them leaving Emerson with another sunflower, a rising amount of confusion and a classroom full of gossiping students whose giggling and whispers can no longer be contained. Emerson almost gets his phone out of his desk to text Jason and ask what the heck is going on, regardless of what his students think of him for texting in class, when there's a loud knock on the door—despite it being open.

"Mr. Miller," Matty yells, leaning against the door frame. With his charming smile and good looks, all eyes move to him.

"I don't think you have a study hall this period, Matty."

"I don't?" Matty gasps, pretending to be entirely shocked. "Mr. Miller, that is brand new information."

"I highly doubt that," Emerson deadpans, earning him laughter.

"You're hilarious, Mr. Miller. Really."

Were it almost anyone else, Emerson might assume based on past experience that Matty is being sarcastic. The past few months watching Jason's practices and games, and tutoring Matty on a regular basis as part of his new 504 plan, has shown him that, much like Jason, Matty pretty much always means what he says.

Matty pushes off the door frame while simultaneously holding out his left hand, which was previously hidden behind his back. In his hand is another sunflower, though unlike Arlo and the other players, he doesn't drop it off and run. Rather he walks directly into the middle of Emerson's study hall and dramatically bows while clearing his throat like some kind of medieval herald.

"This is for you." Matty brandishes the sunflower at Emerson, clearly relishing the attention he's garnering. "From Coach."

The eyes of every student are on Emerson, well except for Arlo who is watching Matty with hunched shoulders and a blush. Emerson takes the flower, staring at it with a mix of confusion and something he doesn't quite understand but that makes him feel warm.

"Uh—" Emerson stutters, staring at the flower. "Thank you."

"You're welcome," Matty smiles, hopping into a standing position. "There's something else for you, but you're going to need to step outside to get it, Mr. Miller."

"Outside," Emerson echoes, the repetition offering no clarity to the situation.

"Yup, outside." Matty claps his hands gleefully, stepping towards the open door. "Right now. Like right now, right now."

Half the class stands, the sound of chairs scraping on linoleum paling in comparison to the students chatter as Emerson's feet guide him towards the open door. He's not even sure what he expects, but it's certainly not what he comes face to face with.

"Hi," Jason grins, standing on the lawn outside of Emerson's classroom.

Though Emerson saw him just a few hours ago, his heart clenches in familiarity as he takes in Jason's wide smile that he loves so much, his dark hair blowing in the wind since he's due for a haircut and that handsome dimple in his chin on full display. He's dressed in his usual uniform of gray sweats and his favorite coaching sweatshirt. Behind

Jason stands what must surely be half the football team who just delivered flowers to Emerson. Matty runs to join them, dragging Arlo out of the classroom by the elbow towards the group, laughing good-naturedly before he drops Arlo's arm and leaps onto Sanchez's back.

Stepping into the yard, Emerson lifts a hand to shield his eyes from the sunlight. "What's going on?"

"I need to ask you something, Emmy."

"Right now?" Emerson asks, glancing behind him, confirming his suspicions that all of the study hall students are eavesdropping.

It's not unusual for Jason to stop by during one of his study halls if he's free, but usually all that happens is Jason waving from the door or sneaking in with a snack if he thinks Emerson hasn't remembered to eat. He's never interrupted class before, which in and of itself would be enough for Emerson to hear him out, but given that it's Jason, he trusts whatever it is will be alright even if his brain is going a million different directions struggling to guess where exactly that might be.

"Yes, right now." Jason's smile widens, settling a little of Emerson's unease. Not all of it, but enough for him not to panic. If Jason is smiling, whatever is going on has to be good. "It's very important."

"Alright." Emerson takes another step closer to Jason, ignoring the erratic lub-dub of his heart while Jason turns around to take something from one of his players. When he faces Emerson this time, there's a giant poster board in his hands—haphazardly adorned in Jason's familiar chicken scratch handwriting with hearts and glitter. Emerson is pretty sure he might be hallucinating.

"Emerson Miller, will you go to prom with me?"

All around him students cheer, Jason's players shaking

his shoulders and cheering while his own students clap excitedly behind him. There was a point in high school where the idea of more than one person looking at him had caused complete shutdowns, the prospect of being perceived deeply correlated with shame and bullying. That feeling prickles at the back of his mind, never completely gone, but it is silenced by the safety Jason's love provides.

"*Jason.*"

Jason closes the distance between them, letting his poster drop to the ground. It falls onto the grass, glitter and paint shimmering in the sun and revealing another sunflower in Jason's hand; only this one is quite different from the ones he was gifted earlier. This one is made out of LEGO, and Emerson doesn't cry, but he comes close. Closer still when Jason stands directly in front of him, his presence shielding Emerson from everything. "Hey, Emmy."

"Hi."

"You look handsome."

"You said that this morning," Emerson says, tugging at his own pale green shirt. He can feel his cheeks heating, but given his propensity to turn into a tomato in direct sunlight, it's unlikely anyone will know it's an effect of Jason's words. Their time together has done nothing to diminish Jason's love of offering him praise and compliments. If anything, he gets bolder all the time. He can only imagine what Jason might be like in a few years.

"Well, it's still true. You'll be the most handsome guy at prom," Jason tells him, brushing back Emerson's hair. "I know we're chaperoning, but we both know how that went last time. I want you to be my date, Emmy."

"I've never been to prom."

"I know," Jason tells him kindly. "Trust me, I have a

plan. No hotel because you hate sleeping away from home and no fancy restaurant because you don't like those, but there will be food and dancing and uh, something I can't mention on school grounds."

Heart buoyed by lightness, Emerson can't help but smile.

"You don't have to do all that, you know."

"I know, Emmy. I told you, loving you is a privilege I won't ever take for granted. So will you make me the happiest teacher at Santa Leon and be my co-chaperone date to prom?"

"Don't make him beg, Mr. Miller, he will. He's a simp," Matty yells, earning him a few heckles from the other players.

"Behave, Matthew," Jason intones, his good mood given away by his gregarious grin.

Matty laughs along with the other players, and it's so strange for Emerson to be standing here surrounded by people who respect and like him and a boyfriend that makes him so very happy. One that brings him LEGO flowers and wants to make new memories with him and never fails to make Emerson feel seen and valued exactly as he is.

"This is for you, by the way," Jason says, lifting the LEGO sunflower. "Did you know these are harder to put together than they seem if your hands are huge? I don't think LEGO are meant for these hands."

He laughs, wiggling his long, thick fingers, and all Emerson wants to do is kiss them, remembering the way they feel holding him close, carding through his hair, or entwining in his own.

"I love your hands," Emerson whispers, wanting these words to be solely for Jason. He purposely grazes his fingers over Jason's as he takes the flower.

For a man who loves words more than anything in the world, Emerson finds himself lost for anything that might do justice to his feelings right now.

"This one won't die, Emmy. You can keep it forever."

"Like you?"

"Yeah, like me." Jason's smile is brighter than the sun—warm, beautiful and so full of love it physically hurts. He bends down, kissing Emerson's forehead to a cacophony of whistles and cheers. "Is that a yes then? Will you come with me to prom?"

These words come easy, as does loving Jason King.

"*Yes.*"

KEEP IN TOUCH

Thank you so much for reading Make the Play. Publishing my second novel means so much to me. If you enjoyed it, I would love it if you'd leave a review on your favorite bookish site or share with friends. These kinds of recommendations and reviews mean everything to indie authors!

Rainbows, love and coffee,
Lucky

If you want a bonus scene of Jason & Emerson, and to stay up to date with Lucky's writing and behind the scenes sneak peaks be sure to join her mailing list (Tinyurl.-com/LuckyHartMail).

You can also find Lucky on various social media sites.

- Follow Lucky on Amazon here.
- Follow Lucky on Instagram here.
- Follow Lucky on TikTok here.

- Find Lucky on BlueSky Social Here.
- Find Lucky on Goodreads here.
- Find Lucky on Story Graph here.

ABOUT THE AUTHOR

Lucky writes character-driven, contemporary mm romance. Her debut novel "Cross the Line" begins the “Kings of Heart” series, each featuring one of four brothers on their sometimes messy, sometimes tender paths to happily ever after. “Make the Play” continues this series, bringing us back to Santa Leon and the King family. Each book can be read as a standalone, but Lucky thinks it’s more fun to read them all in order.

Lucky is a millennial who grew up on fanfic, a lifelong West Coast resident, and a Canva Pro enthusiast. Queer and neurodivergent representation is deeply important to her as a member of both communities, and she loves exploring intersectional experiences through her fiction as a writer and a reader.

When she's not writing, her favorite things include drinking coffee, walking on the beach, staying up late to finish her latest read, and filling her house with rainbows.

ACKNOWLEDGMENTS

This book wouldn't have been possible without Vix. As an autistic author, my characters have become my special interest. Her constant encouragement and support (and letting me ramble for hours about my characters) fueled my creativity and joy. Her endless encouragement and support got me through real life struggles, writer's block and everything in between. I love you, Vix.

Thank you to my author community. You all know who you are, and I am so grateful for you. Being an indie author is incredible and fulfilling and also so much harder than I ever imagined. Having the support of other authors and seeing the way this community uplifts and supports is inspiring and impactful.

Another thank you to BootyFeathers who isn't just my artist but one of my best friends. Your love of my characters comes through in your incredible art and brings them to life, and I am so grateful for you. Thank you.

Thank you to my editing team who made this book the best version of itself it could be. You guys also cheered me on, supported me and encouraged me, and this book couldn't exist without you.

Big thank you to my Street Team for helping me share my writing and characters and of course to the ARC readers who gave these boys a chance.

And to every reader who has picked up this book and read it, who carries these characters with you and shares my words, thank you. I appreciate you.

www.ingramcontent.com/pod-product-compliance
Ingram Content Group UK Ltd.
Pitfield, Milton Keynes, MK11 3LW, UK
UKHW040811240425
5607UKWH00028B/302

9 798992 802306